Dear Reader,

It was so much fun for me to return to Cardwell Ranch. *Crime Scene at Cardwell Ranch* has been read by more than two million readers, so it was a treat to go back and find out what happened to the Justice and Cardwell families in the sequel. *Justice at Cardwell Ranch* is a story I've wanted to write for a long time.

When I was a girl, we had a cabin just down the road from where these books take place. I have such wonderful memories of the Gallatin Canyon. My brother and I had a fort out in the woods and spent hours exploring in what is now a wilderness area. I skied at Big Sky many times, and have hiked with a friend to Ousel Waterfalls, where part of this story takes place.

I hope you enjoy this return trip to the "canyon."

B.J. Daniels

www.bjdaniels.com

ABOUT THE AUTHOR

USA TODAY bestselling author B.J. Daniels wrote her first book after a career as an award-winning newspaper journalist and author of thirty-seven published short stories. That first book, *Odd Man Out,* received a four-and-a-half-star review from *RT Book Reviews* and went on to be nominated for Best Intrigue that year. Since then, she has won numerous awards, including a career achievement award for romantic suspense and many nominations and awards for best book.

Daniels lives in Montana with her husband, Parker, and two springer spaniels, Spot and Jem. When she isn't writing, she snowboards, camps, boats and plays tennis. Daniels is a member of Mystery Writers of America, Sisters in Crime, International Thriller Writers, Kiss of Death and Romance Writers of America.

To contact her, write to B.J. Daniels, P.O. Box 1173, Malta, MT 59538, or email her at bjdaniels@mtintouch.net. Check out her website, www.bjdaniels.com.

Books by B.J. Daniels

HARLEQUIN INTRIGUE

Other titles by this author available in ebook format.

USA TODAY Bestselling Author

B.J. Daniels

JUSTICE AT CARDWELL RANCH
&
CRIME SCENE AT CARDWELL RANCH

HARLEQUIN®
entertain, enrich, inspire™

ISBN-13: 978-0-373-83787-8

JUSTICE AT CARDWELL RANCH &
CRIME SCENE AT CARDWELL RANCH

Copyright © 2012 by Harlequin Books S.A.

The publisher acknowledges the copyright holder of
the individual works as follows:

JUSTICE AT CARDWELL RANCH
Copyright © 2012 by Barbara Heinlein

CRIME SCENE AT CARDWELL RANCH
Copyright © 2006 by Barbara Heinlein

Recycling programs
for this product may
not exist in your area.

www.Harlequin.com

Printed in U.S.A.

CONTENTS

This book is dedicated to my amazing husband.
He makes all this possible along with inspiring me
each and every day. Thank you, Parker.
Without your love, I couldn't do this.

JUSTICE AT CARDWELL RANCH

Prologue

Nothing moved in the darkness. At the corner of the house she stopped to catch her breath. She could hear music playing somewhere down the street. Closer, a dog barked.

As she waited in the deep shadow at the edge of the house, she measured the distance and the light she would have to pass through to reach the second window.

When she'd sneaked into the house earlier, she'd left the window unlocked. But she had no way of knowing if someone had discovered it. If so, they might not have merely relocked it—they could be waiting for her.

Fear had her heart pounding and her breath coming out in painful bursts. If she got caught— She couldn't let herself think about that.

The dog stopped barking for a moment. All she could hear was the faint music drifting on the night breeze. She fought to keep her breathing in check as she inched along the side of the house to the first window.

A light burned inside, but the drapes were closed. Still, she waited to make sure she couldn't hear anyone on the other side of the glass before she moved.

Ducking, she slipped quickly through a shaft of illumination from a streetlamp and stopped at the second bedroom window.

There, she waited for a few moments. No light burned inside the room. Still she listened before she pulled the screwdriver from her jacket pocket and began to pry up the window.

At first the old casement window didn't move and she feared she'd been right about someone discovering what she'd done and locking the window again.

When it finally gave, it did so with a pop that sounded like an explosion to her ears. She froze. No sound came from within the room. Her hands shook as she pried the window up enough that she could get her fingers under it.

Feeling as if there was no turning back now, she lifted the window enough to climb in. Heart in her throat, she drew back the curtain. She'd half expected to find someone standing on the other side lying in wait for her.

The room, painted pink, was empty except for a few pieces of mismatched furniture: a dresser, a rocking chair, a changing table and a crib.

She looked to the crib, fearing that she'd come this far only to fail. But from the faint light coming from the streetlamp, she could see the small lump beneath the tiny quilt.

Her heart beat faster at the thought that in a few minutes she would have the baby in her arms.

She heard the car coming down the street just seconds before the headlights washed over her. Halfway in the window, there was nothing she could do but hurry. She wasn't leaving here without the baby.

Chapter One

The breeze rustled through the aspens, sending golden leaves whirling around him as Jordan Cardwell walked up the hill to the cemetery. He wore a straw Western hat he'd found on a peg by the back door of the ranch house.

He hadn't worn a cowboy hat since he'd left Montana twenty years ago, but this one kept his face from burning. It was so much easier to get sunburned at this high altitude than it was in New York City.

It was hot out and yet he could feel the promise of winter hiding at the edge of the fall day. Only the memory of summer remained in the Gallatin River Canyon. Cold nightly temperatures had turned the aspens to glittering shades of gold and orange against the dark green of the pines.

Below him he could hear the rushing water of the Gallatin as the river cut a deep winding course through the canyon. Across the river, sheer granite cliffs rose up to where the sun hung in a faded blue big Montana sky.

As he walked, the scent of crushed dry leaves beneath his soles sent up the remembered smell of other autumns. He knew this land. As hard as he'd tried to escape it, this place was branded on him, this life as familiar as his own heartbeat—even after all these years.

He thought of all the winters he'd spent in this canyon listening to the ice crack on the river, feeling the bite of snow as it blew off a pine bough to sting his face, breathing in a bone-deep cold that made his head ache.

He'd done his time here, he thought as he turned his face up to the last of the day's warmth before the sun disappeared behind the cliffs. Soon the aspens would be bare, the limbs dark against a winter-washed pale frosty sky. The water in the horse troughs would begin to freeze and so would the pooling eddies along the edge of the river. The cold air in the shade of the pines was a warning of what was to come, he thought as he reached the wrought-iron cemetery gate.

The gate groaned as he shoved it open. He hesitated. What was he doing here? Nearby the breeze sighed in the tops of the towering pines, drawing his attention to the dense stand. He didn't remember them being so tall. Or so dark and thick. As he watched the boughs sway, he told himself to make this quick. He didn't want to get caught here.

Even though it was a family cemetery, he didn't feel welcome here anymore. His own fault, but still, it could get messy if anyone from his family caught him on the ranch. He didn't plan to stick around long enough to see any of them. It was best that way, he told himself as he stepped through the gate into the small cemetery.

He'd never liked graveyards. Nor did it give him any comfort to know that more than a dozen remains of their relatives were interred here. He took no satisfaction in the long lineage of the Justice family, let alone the Cardwell one, in this canyon—unlike his sister.

Dana found strength in knowing that their ancestors had been mule-headed ranchers who'd weathered everything Montana had thrown at them to stay on this ranch. They'd settled this land along a stretch of the Gallatin, a crystal clear trout stream that ran over a hundred miles from Yellowstone Park to the Missouri River.

The narrow canyon got little sunlight each day. In the winter it was an icebox of frost and snow. Getting up to feed the animals had been pure hell. He'd never understood why any of them had stayed.

But they had, he thought as he surveyed the tombstones. They'd fought this land to remain here and now they would spend eternity in soil that had given them little in return for their labors.

A gust of wind rattled through the colorful aspen leaves and moaned in the high branches of the pines. Dead foliage floated like gold coins around him, showering the weather-bleached gravestones. He was reminded why he'd never liked coming up to this wind-blown hill. He found no peace among the dead. Nor had he come here today looking for it.

He moved quickly through the gravestones until he found the one stone that was newer than the others, only six years in the ground. The name on the tombstone read Mary Justice Cardwell.

"Hello, Mother," he said removing his hat as he felt all the conflicting emotions he'd had when she was alive. All the arguments came rushing back, making him sick at the memory. He hadn't been able to change her mind and now she was gone, leaving them all behind to struggle as a family without her.

He could almost hear their last argument whispered on the wind. "There is nothing keeping you here, let alone me," he'd argued. "Why are you fighting so hard to keep this place going? Can't you see that ranching is going to kill you?"

He recalled her smile, that gentle gleam in her eyes that infuriated him. "This land is what makes me happy, son. Someday you will realize that ranching is in our blood. You can fight it, but this isn't just your home. A part of your heart is here, as well."

"Like hell," he'd said. "Sell the ranch, Mother, before it's too late. If not for yourself and the rest of us, then for Dana. She's too much like you. She will spend her life fighting to keep this place. Don't do that to her."

"She'll keep this ranch for the day when you come back to help her run it."

"That's never going to happen, Mother."

Mary Justice Cardwell had smiled that knowing smile of hers. "Only time will tell, won't it?"

Jordan turned the hat brim nervously in his fingers as he looked down at his mother's grave and searched for the words to tell her how much he hated what she'd done to him. To all of them. But to his surprise he felt tears well in his eyes, his throat constricting on a gulf of emotion he hadn't anticipated.

A gust of wind bent the pine boughs and blew down to scatter dried leaves across the landscape. His skin rippled with goose bumps as he suddenly sensed someone watching him. His head came up, his gaze going to the darkness of the pines.

She was only a few yards away. He hadn't heard the woman on horseback approach and realized she must have been there the whole time, watching him.

She sat astride a large buckskin horse. Shadows played across her face from the swaying pine boughs. The breeze lifted the long dark hair that flowed like molten obsidian over her shoulders and halfway down her back.

There was something vaguely familiar about her. But if he'd known her years before when this was home, he couldn't place her now. He'd been gone too long from Montana.

And yet a memory tugged at him. His gaze settled on her face again, the wide-set green eyes, that piercing look that seemed to cut right to his soul.

With a curse, he knew where he'd seen her before— and why she was looking at him the way she was. A shudder moved through him as if someone had just walked over *his* grave.

LIZA TURNER HAD WATCHED the man slog up the hill, his footsteps slow, his head down, as if he were going to a funeral. So she hadn't been surprised when he'd pushed open the gate to the cemetery and stepped in.

At first, after reining her horse in under the pines, she'd been mildly curious. She loved this spot, loved looking across the canyon as she rode through the groves of aspens and pines. It was always cool in the trees. She liked listening to the river flowing emerald-green below her on the hillside and taking a moment to search the granite cliffs on the other side for mountain sheep.

She hadn't expected to see anyone on her ride this morning. When she'd driven into the ranch for her usual trek, she'd seen the Cardwell Ranch pickup leaving and remembered that Hud was taking Dana into Bozeman today for her doctor's appointment. They were leaving the kids with Dana's best friend and former business partner, Hilde, at Needles and Pins, the local fabric store.

The only other person on the ranch was the aging ranch manager, Warren Fitzpatrick. Warren would be watching *Let's Make a Deal* at his cabin this time of the morning.

So Liza had been curious and a bit leery when she'd first laid eyes on the stranger in the Western straw hat. As far as she knew, no one else should have been on the ranch today. So who was this tall, broad-shouldered cowboy?

Dana had often talked about hiring some help since Warren was getting up in years and she had her hands full with a four- and five-year-old, not to mention now being pregnant with twins.

But if this man was the new hired hand, why would he be interested in the Justice-Cardwell family cemetery? She felt the skin on the back of her neck prickle. There was something about this cowboy… His face had been in shadow from the brim of his hat. When he'd stopped at one of the graves and had taken his hat off, head bowed, she still hadn't been able to see more than his profile from where she sat astride her horse.

Shifting in the saddle, she'd tried to get a better look. He must have heard the creak of leather or sensed her presence. His head came up, his gaze darting right to the spot where she sat. He looked startled at first, then confused as if he was trying to place her.

She blinked, not sure she could trust her eyes. *Jordan Cardwell?*

He looked completely different from the arrogant man in the expensive three-piece suit she'd crossed paths with six years ago. He wore jeans, a button-up shirt and work boots. He looked tanned and stronger as if he'd been doing manual labor. There was only a hint of the earlier arrogance in his expression, making him more handsome than she remembered.

She saw the exact moment when he recognized her. Bitterness burned in his dark gaze as a small resentful smile tugged at his lips.

Oh, yes, it was Jordan Cardwell all right, she thought, wondering what had made her think he was handsome just moments before or—even harder to believe, that he might have changed.

Six years ago he'd been the number one suspect in a murder as well as a suspect in an attempted murder. Liza had been the deputy who'd taken his fingerprints.

She wondered now what he was doing not only back in the canyon, but also on the ranch he and his siblings had fought so hard to take from their sister Dana.

DANA SAVAGE LAY BACK ON THE examining table, nervously picking at a fingernail. "I can't remember the last time I saw my feet," she said with a groan.

Dr. Pamela Burr laughed. "This might feel a little cold."

Dana tried not to flinch as the doctor applied clear jelly to her huge stomach. She closed her eyes and waited until she heard the heartbeats before she opened them again. "So everything is okay?"

"Your babies appear to be doing fine. Don't you want to look?"

Dana didn't look at the monitor. "You know Hud. He's determined to be surprised. Just like the last two. So I don't dare look." She shot a glance at her husband.

He stood next to her, his gaze on her, not the screen. He smiled, but she could see he was worried.

The doctor shut off the machine. "As for the spotting…"

Dana felt her heart drop as she saw the concern in Dr. Burr's expression.

"I'm going to have to insist on bed rest for these last weeks," she said. "Let's give these babies the best start we can by leaving them where they are for now." She looked to Hud.

"You can count on me," he said. "It's Dana you need to convince."

Dana sat up and laid her hands over her extended stomach. She felt the twins moving around in the cramped space. Poor babies. "Okay."

"You understand what bed rest means?" the doctor asked. "No ranch business, no getting up except to shower and use the bathroom. You're going to need help with Hank and Mary."

That was putting it mildly when you had a four- and five-year-old who were as wild as the canyon where they lived.

"I'm sure Hud—"

"You'll need more than his help." The doctor pressed a piece of paper into her hand. "These are several women you might call that I've used before."

Dana didn't like the idea of bringing in a stranger to take care of Hud and the kids, but the babies kicked and she nodded.

"Doc said I was going to have to watch you like a hawk," Hud told her on the way home. Apparently while she was getting dressed, Dr. Burr had been bending his ear, down the hall in her office. "You always try to do too much. With the kids, the ranch, me—"

"I'll be good."

He gave her a disbelieving look.

"Marshal, would you like a sworn affidavit?"

He grinned over at her. "Actually, I'm thinking about handcuffing you to the bed. I reckon it will be the only way I can keep you down for a day let alone weeks."

Dana groaned as she realized how hard it was going to be to stay in bed. "What about Hank and Mary? They won't understand why their mommy can't be up and around, let alone outside with them and their animals." Both of them had their own horses and loved to ride.

"I've already put in for a leave. Liza can handle things. Anyway, it's in between resort seasons so it's quiet."

September through the middle of November was slow around Big Sky with the summer tourists gone and ski season still at least a month away.

Dana knew October was probably a better time than any other for her husband to be off work. That wasn't the problem. "Hud, I hate to see you have to babysit me and the kids."

"It's not babysitting when it's *your* wife and kids, Dana."

"You know what I mean. There are the kids and the ranch—"

"Honey, you've been trying to do it all for too long."

She *had* been juggling a lot of balls for some time now, but Hud always helped on the weekends. Their ranch manager, Warren Fitzpatrick, was getting up in years so he had really slowed down. But Warren was a fixture around the ranch, one she couldn't afford to replace. More than anything, she loved the hands-on part of ranching so she spent as much time as she could working the land.

When she'd found out she was pregnant this time she'd been delighted, but a little worried how she was going to handle another child right now.

Then the doctor had told her she was having twins. *Twins?* Seriously?

"Are you all right?" Hud asked as he placed his hand over hers and squeezed.

She smiled and nodded. "I'm always all right when I'm with you."

He gave her hand another squeeze before he went back to driving. "I'm taking you home. Then I'll go by the shop and pick up the kids." Her friend Hilde had the kids in Big Sky. "But I'd better not find out you were up and about while I was gone."

Dana shook her head and made a cross with her finger over her heart. She lay back and closed her eyes, praying as she had since the spotting had begun that the babies she was carrying would be all right. Mary and Hank were so excited about the prospect of two little brothers or sisters. She couldn't disappoint them.

She couldn't disappoint anyone, especially her mother, she thought. While Mary Justice Cardwell had been gone six years now, she was as much a part of the ranch as the old, two-story house where Dana lived with Hud and the kids. Her mother had trusted her to keep Cardwell Ranch going. Against all odds she was doing her darnedest to keep that promise.

So why did she feel so scared, as if waiting for the other shoe to drop?

Chapter Two

Jordan watched Deputy Liza Turner ride her horse out of the pines. The past six years had been good to her. She'd been pretty back then. Now there was a confidence as if she'd grown into the woman she was supposed to become. He recalled how self-assured and efficient she'd been at her job. She was also clearly at home on the back of a horse.

The trees cast long shadows over the stark landscape. Wind whirled the dried leaves that now floated in the air like snowflakes.

"Jordan Cardwell," she said as she reined in her horse at the edge of the cemetery.

He came out through the gate, stopping to look up at her. "Deputy." She had one of those faces that was almost startling in its uniqueness. The green eyes wide, captivating and always filled with curiosity. He thought she was more interesting than he remembered. That, he realized, was probably because she was out of uniform.

She wore jeans and a red-checked Western shirt that made her dark hair appear as rich as mahogany. She narrowed those green eyes at him. Curiosity and suspicion, he thought.

"I'm surprised to see you here," she said, a soft lilt

to her voice. She had a small gap between her two front teeth, an imperfection that he found charming.

"I don't know why you'd be surprised. My sister might have inherited the ranch but I'm still family."

She smiled at that and he figured she knew all about what had happened after his mother had died—and her new will had gone missing.

"I didn't think you'd ever come back to the ranch," she said.

He chuckled. "Neither did I. But people change."

"Do they?" She was studying him in a way that said she doubted he had. He didn't need to read her expression to know she was also wondering what kind of trouble he'd brought back to the canyon with him. The horse moved under her, no doubt anxious to get going.

"Your horse seems impatient," he said. "Don't let me keep you from your ride." With a tip of his hat, he headed down the mountain to the ranch house where he'd been raised.

It seemed a lifetime ago. He could barely remember the man he'd been then. But he would be glad to get off the property before his sister and her husband returned. He planned to put off seeing them if at all possible. So much for family, he thought.

WHEN DANA OPENED HER EYES, she saw that they'd left the wide valley and were now driving through the Gallatin Canyon. The "canyon" as it was known, ran from the mouth just south of Gallatin Gateway almost to West Yellowstone, fifty miles of winding road that trailed the river in a deep cut through the mountains.

The drive along the Gallatin River had always been breathtaking, a winding strip of highway that followed the blue-ribbon trout stream up over the continental divide. This time of year the Gallatin ran crystal clear over green-tinted boulders. Pine trees grew dark and thick along its edge and against the steep mountains. Aspens, their leaves rust-reds and glittering golds, grew among the pines.

Sheer rock cliffs overlooked the highway and river, with small areas of open land, the canyon not opening up until it reached Big Sky. The canyon had been mostly cattle and dude ranches, a few summer cabins and homes—that was until Big Sky resort and the small town that followed at the foot of Lone Mountain.

Luxury houses had sprouted up all around the resort. Fortunately, some of the original cabins still remained and the majority of the canyon was national forest so it would always remain undeveloped. The "canyon" was also still its own little community, for which Dana was grateful. This was the only home she'd known and, like her stubborn ancestors, she had no intention of ever leaving it.

Both she and Hud had grown up here. They'd been in love since junior high, but hit a rocky spot some years ago thanks to her sister. Dana didn't like to think about the five years she and Hud had spent apart as they passed the lower mountain resort area and, a few miles farther, turned down the road to Cardwell Ranch.

Across the river and a half mile back up a wide valley, the Cardwell Ranch house sat against a backdrop of granite cliffs, towering dark pines and glittering aspens. The house was a big, two-story rambling affair with a wide front porch and a brick-red metal roof. Behind it stood a huge weathered barn and some outbuildings and corrals.

Dana never felt truly at home until they reached the ranch she'd fought tooth and nail to save. When Mary Justice Cardwell had been bucked off a horse and died six years ago, Dana had thought all was lost. Her mother's original will when her children were young left the ranch to all of them.

Mary hadn't realized until her children were grown that only Dana would keep the ranch. The others would sell it, take the profits and never look back until the day they regretted what they'd done. By then it would be too late. So her mother had made a new will, leaving the ranch to her. But her mother had hidden it where she hoped her daughter would find it. Fortunately, Dana had found it in time to save the ranch.

The will had put an end to her siblings' struggle to force her to sell the land and split the profits with them. Now her three siblings were paid part of the ranch's profit each quarter. Not surprisingly, she hadn't heard from any of them since the will had settled things six years before.

As Hud pulled into the ranch yard, Dana spotted a car parked in front of the old house and frowned. The car was an older model with California plates.

"You didn't already hire someone—"

"No," Hud said before she could finish. "I wouldn't do that without talking to you first. Do you think the doctor called one of the women she told you about?"

Before Dana could answer, she saw that someone was waiting out on the broad front porch. As Hud pulled in beside the car, the woman stepped from out of the shadows.

"Stacy?" She felt her heart drop. After six years

of silence and all the bad feelings from the past, what was her older sister doing here?

"SURPRISE," STACY SAID WITH a shrug and a worried smile. Like Dana, Stacy had gotten the Justice-Cardwell dark good looks, but she'd always been the cute one who capitalized on her appearance, cashing in as she traded her way up through three marriages that Dana knew of and possibly more since.

Just the sight of her sister made Dana instantly wary. She couldn't help but be mistrustful given their past.

Her sister's gaze went to Dana's stomach. "Oh, my. You're *pregnant*."

"We need to get Dana in the house," Hud said, giving his sister-in-law a nod of greeting. Stacy opened the door and let them enter before she followed them in.

Dana found herself looking around the living room, uncomfortable that her sister had been inside the house even though it had once been Stacy's home, as well.

The house was as it had been when her mother was alive. Original Western furnishings, a lot of stone and wood and a bright big airy kitchen. Dana, like her mother, chose comfort over style trends. She loved her big, homey house. It often smelled of something good bubbling on the stove, thanks to the fact that Hud loved to cook.

Dana preferred to spend her time with her children outside, teaching them to ride or watching a new foal being born or picking fresh strawberries out of the large garden she grew—just as her own mother had done with her.

As she looked at her sister, she was reminded of some of her mother's last words to her. "Families stick together. It isn't always easy. Everyone makes mistakes. Dana, you have to find forgiveness in your heart. If not for them, then for yourself."

Her mother had known then that if anything happened to her, Jordan, Stacy and Clay would fight her for the ranch. That's why she'd made the new will.

But she must also have known that the will would divide them.

"It's been a long time," Dana said, waiting, knowing her sister wanted something or she wouldn't be here.

"I know I should have kept in touch more," Stacy said. "I move around a lot." But she'd always managed to get her check each quarter as part of her inheritance from the ranch profits. Dana instantly hated the uncharitable thought. She didn't want to feel that way about her sister. But Stacy had done some things in the past that had left the two of them at odds. Like breaking Dana and Hud up eleven years ago. Dana still had trouble forgiving her sister for that.

Stacy shifted uncomfortably in the silence. "I should have let you know I was coming, huh."

"Now isn't the best time for company," Hud said. "Dana's doctor has advised her to get off her feet for the rest of her pregnancy."

"But I'm not *company*," Stacy said. "I'm family. I can help."

Hud looked to his wife. "Why don't you go. It's fine," Dana said and removed her coat.

"So you're pregnant," her sister said.

"Twins," Dana said, sinking into a chair.

Stacy nodded.

Dana realized Hud was still in his coat, waiting,

afraid to leave her alone with Stacy. "Are you going to pick up the kids?"

He gave her a questioning look.

"I thought you probably had more kids," her sister said. "The toys and stuff around."

Dana was still looking at her husband. She knew he didn't trust Stacy, hated she'd been alone in their house while they were gone and worse, he didn't want to leave the two of them alone. "Stacy and I will be fine."

Still he hesitated. He knew better than anyone what her siblings were like.

"Stacy, would you mind getting me a drink of water?" The moment her sister left the room, Dana turned to her husband. "I'll be *fine*," she said lowering her voice. "Go pick up the kids. I promise I won't move until you get back." She could tell that wasn't what had him concerned.

He glanced toward the kitchen and the sound of running water. "I won't be long."

She motioned him over and smiled as he leaned down to kiss her. At the same time, he placed a large hand on her swollen stomach. The babies moved and he smiled.

"You have your cell phone if you need me?"

Dana nodded. "The marshal's office is also on speed dial. I'll be fine. Really."

Stacy came back in with a glass full of water as Hud left. "I'm glad things have turned out good for you. Hud is so protective."

"Thank you," she said as she took the glass and studied her sister over the rim as she took a drink.

"I would have called," Stacy said, "but I wanted to surprise you."

"I'm surprised." She watched her sister move

around the room, touching one object after another, seeming nervous. Her first thought when she'd seen her sister was that she'd come here because she was in trouble.

That initial observation hadn't changed. Now though, Dana was betting it had something to do with money. It usually did with Stacy, unfortunately.

Years ago Dana had found out just how low her sister would stoop if the price was right. She had good reason not to trust her sister.

"The place hasn't changed at all," Stacy was saying now. "Except for the pile of toys in the sunroom. I heard Hud say he was going to pick up the kids?"

"Hank and Mary, five and four."

"You named your daughter after Mother, that's nice," Stacy said. "I thought you probably would." She seemed to hear what she'd said. "I want you to know I'm not upset about Mother leaving you the ranch. You know me, I would have just blown the money." She flashed a self-deprecating smile. "And you're pregnant with twins! When are you due?"

"Eight weeks." When she finally couldn't take it anymore, Dana asked, "Stacy, what are you doing here?"

"It's kind of a strange story," her sister said, looking even more nervous.

Dana braced herself. If Stacy thought it was a strange story, then it could be anything. Her sister opened her mouth to say something, but was interrupted.

From upstairs a baby began to cry.

"What is that?" Dana demanded.

"I haven't had a chance to tell you," Stacy said as she started for the stairs. "That's Ella. That's my other surprise. I have a baby."

LIZA PARKED HER PICKUP ACROSS the road from Trail's End and settled in to wait. She had a clear view of the small cabin Jordan had rented. Like a lot of Big Sky, the string of cabins were new. But it being off-season and the cabins' only view being Highway 191, she figured they weren't too pricey. She wondered how Jordan was fixed for money and if that's what had brought him back here.

Pulling out her phone, she called Hud's cell. He answered on the third ring. She could hear the kids in the background and a woman's voice. Hilde, Dana's best friend. He must be at Needles and Pins.

"How's Dana, boss?" she asked.

"Stubborn."

She laughed. "So the doctor *did* prescribe bed rest."

"Yes. Fortunately, I know you can run things just fine without me."

"Probably more smoothly without you around," she joked.

He must have heard something in her voice. "But?"

"Nothing I can't handle," she assured him. "But you might want to give Dana a heads-up."

"Dana already knows. Stacy's at the house right now."

"Stacy?"

"Who were *you* talking about?" Hud asked.

"Jordan."

She heard Hud swear under his breath.

"I saw him earlier on the ranch, actually at the family cemetery," Liza said.

"What's he doing in the canyon?"

"He didn't say, but I found out where he's staying. He's rented a cabin past Buck's T-4." Buck's T-4 was a local landmark bar and hotel. "I'm hanging out, watching to see what he's up to."

"Probably not the best way to spend taxpayers' dollars, but I appreciate it. As far as I know, he hasn't contacted Dana."

"Let me know if he does. In the meantime, I'll stick around here for a while."

"You really need to get a life, Deputy," Hud said. "Thanks. Let me know if you need help."

"So Stacy's here, too?"

"We haven't heard from any of them in six years and now two of them are in the canyon? This doesn't bode well."

That had been her thought exactly.

"I don't want them upsetting Dana," he said. "All we need is for Clay to show up next. This couldn't come at a worse time. I'm worried enough about Dana and the babies. I have a bad feeling this could have something to do with that developer who's been after Dana to sell some of the ranch."

"The timing does make you wonder," Liza said.

"I'm going back to the ranch now."

"You stick close to Dana. I'll let you know if Jordan heads for the ranch." Hanging up, Liza settled in again. She knew it could be a while. Jordan might be in for the night.

The canyon got dark quickly this time of year. With the dark that settled over it like a cloak came a drop in temperature. She could hear the river, smell the rich scent of fall. A breeze stirred the nearby pines, making the branches sway and sigh. A couple of stars popped out above the canyon walls.

The door of the cabin opened. Jordan stepped out

and headed for his rented SUV parked outside. He was dressed in a warm coat, gloves and a hat, all in a dark color. He definitely didn't look like a man going out for dinner—or even to visit his sister. He glanced around as if he thought someone might be watching him before climbing into his rental.

Liza felt her heart kick up a beat as she slunk down in the pickup seat and waited. A few moments later she heard the SUV pull out. She started the truck, and sitting up, followed at a distance.

To her relief, he didn't turn down Highway 191 in the direction of the Cardwell Ranch—and his sister's house. Instead, he headed north toward Big Sky proper, making her think she might be wrong. Maybe he was merely going out to find a place to have dinner.

He drove on past the lighted buildings that made up Meadow Village, heading west toward Mountain Village. There was little traffic this time of year. She let another vehicle get between them, all the time keeping Jordan's taillights in sight.

Just when she started speculating on where he might be headed, he turned off on the road to Ousel Falls. They passed a few commercial buildings, a small housing complex and then the road cut through the pines as it climbed toward the falls.

Liza pulled over, letting him get farther ahead. Had he spotted the tail? She waited as long as she dared before she drove on up the road. Her headlights cut a gold swath through the darkness. Dense pines lined both sides of the mountain road. There was no traffic at all up this way. She worried he had spotted her following him and was now leading her on a wild-goose chase.

She hadn't gone far when her headlights picked up

the parking lot for the falls. Jordan's rental was parked in the empty lot. She couldn't tell if he was still in the vehicle. Grabbing her baseball cap off the seat, she covered her dark hair as she drove on past.

Out of the corner of her eye she saw that the SUV was empty. Past it near the trailhead, she glimpsed the beam of a flashlight bobbing as it headed down the trail.

A few hundred yards up the road Liza found a place to pull over. She grabbed her own flashlight from under the seat, checked to make sure the batteries were still working and got out of the truck.

It was a short hike back to the trailhead. From there the path dropped to the creek before rising again as it twisted its way through the thick forest.

The trail was wide and paved and she found, once her eyes adjusted, that she didn't need to use her flashlight if she was careful. Enough starlight bled down through the pine boughs that she could see far enough ahead—and she knew the trail well.

There was no sign of Jordan, though. She'd reached the creek and bridge, quickly crossed it, and had started up the winding track when she caught a glimpse of light above her on the footpath.

She stopped to listen, afraid he might have heard her behind him. But there was only the sound of the creek and moan of the pines in the breeze. Somewhere in the distance an owl hooted. She moved again, hurrying now.

Once the pathway topped out, she should be able to see Jordan's light ahead of her, though she couldn't imagine what he was doing hiking to the falls tonight.

There was always a good chance of running into a

moose or a wolf or worse this time of year, a hungry grizzly foraging for food before hibernation.

The trail topped out. She stopped to catch her breath and listen for Jordan. Ahead she could make out the solid rock area at the base of the waterfall. A few more steps and she could feel the mist coming off the cascading water. From here, the walkway carved a crooked path up through the pines to the top of the falls.

There was no sign of any light ahead and the only thing she could hear was rushing water. Where was Jordan? She moved on, convinced he was still ahead of her. Something rustled in the trees off to her right. A limb cracked somewhere ahead in the pines.

She stopped and drew her weapon. Someone was out there.

The report of the rifle shot felt so close it made the hair stand up on her neck. The sound ricocheted off the rock cliff and reverberated through her. Liza dove to the ground. A second shot echoed through the trees.

Weapon drawn, she scrambled up the hill and almost tripped over the body Jordan Cardwell was standing over.

Chapter Three

"You have a *baby?*" Dana said, still shocked when Stacy came back downstairs carrying a pink bundle. "I'm just having a hard time imagining you as a mother."

"You think you're the only one with a maternal instinct?" Stacy sounded hurt.

"I guess I never thought you *wanted* a baby."

Stacy gave a little shrug. "People change."

Did they? Dana wondered as she studied her sister.

"Want to see her?" Stacy asked.

Dana nodded and her sister carefully transferred the bundle into her arms. Dana saw that it wasn't a blanket at all that the baby was wrapped in, but a cute pink quilt. Parting the edges, she peered in at the baby. A green-eyed knockout stared back at her.

"Isn't she *beautiful?*"

"She's breathtaking. What's her name?"

"Ella."

Dana looked up at her sister, her gaze going to Stacy's bare left-hand ring finger. "Is there a father?"

"Of course," her sister said with an embarrassed laugh. "He's in the military. We're getting married when he comes home in a few weeks."

Stacy had gone through men like tissues during a sad

movie. In the past she'd married for money. Maybe this time she had found something more important, Dana hoped, glancing down at the baby in her arms.

"Hello, Ella," she said to the baby. The bow-shaped lips turned up at the corners, the green eyes sparkling. "How old is she?"

"Six months."

As the baby began to fuss, Stacy dug in a diaper bag Dana hadn't seen at the end of the couch. She pulled out a bottle before going into the kitchen to warm it.

Dana stared at the precious baby, her heart in her throat. She couldn't imagine her sister with a baby. In the past Stacy couldn't even keep a houseplant alive.

As her sister came out of the kitchen, Dana started to hand back the baby.

"You can feed her if you want."

Dana took the bottle and watched the baby suck enthusiastically at the warm formula. "She's adorable." Her sister didn't seem to be listening though.

Stacy had walked over to the window and was looking out. "I forgot how quiet it is here." She hugged herself as a gust of wind rattled the old window. "Or how cold it is this time of year."

"Where *have* you been living?"

"Southern California," she said, turning away from the window.

"Is that where you met the father?"

Stacy nodded. "It's getting late. Ella and I should go."

"Where are you *going?*" Dana asked, alarmed, realizing that she'd been cross-examining her sister as if Stacy was one of Hud's suspects. She couldn't bear the thought of this baby being loaded into that old car outside with Stacy at the wheel.

"I planned to get a motel for the night. Kurt's got some relatives up by Great Falls. They've offered me a place to stay until he gets leave and we can find a place of our own."

Dana shook her head, still holding tight to the baby. "You're staying here. You and Ella can have Mary's room. I don't want you driving at night."

LIZA SWUNG THE BARREL OF HER gun and snapped on her flashlight, aiming both at Jordan. "Put your hands up," she ordered.

He didn't move. He stood stock-still, staring down at the body at his feet. He appeared to be in shock.

"I said put your hands up," she ordered again. He blinked and slowly raised his gaze to her, then lifted his hands. Keeping the gun trained on him, she quickly frisked him. "Where is the weapon?" She nudged him with the point of her gun barrel.

He shook his head. "*I* didn't shoot him."

Liza took a step back from him and shone the flashlight beam into the pines. The light didn't go far in the dense trees and darkness. "Who shot him?"

"I don't know."

She squatted down to check for a pulse. None. Pulling out her phone, she called for backup and the coroner. When she'd finished, she turned the beam on Jordan again. "You can start by telling me what you're doing out here."

He looked down at the body, then up at her. "You know I didn't kill him."

"How do I know that?"

True, she hadn't seen him carrying a rifle, but he could have hidden one in the woods earlier today. But how did he get rid of it so quickly? She would have heard him throw it into the trees.

"What are you doing here at the falls in the middle of the night?"

He looked away.

She began to read him his rights.

"All right," he said with a sigh. "You aren't going to believe me. I was meeting him here."

"To buy drugs?"

"No." He looked insulted. "It's a long story."

"We seem to have time." She motioned to a downed tree not far from the body but deep enough in the trees that if the killer was still out there, he wouldn't have a clear shot.

Jordan sighed as he sat down, dropping his head in his hands for a few moments. "When I was in high school my best friend hung himself. At least that's what everyone thought, anyway. I didn't believe he would do that, but there was no evidence of foul play. Actually, no one believed me when I argued there was no way Tanner would have taken his own life."

"People often say that about suicide victims."

"Yeah. Well, a few weeks ago, I got a call from…" He looked in the direction of the body, but quickly turned away. "Alex Winslow."

"Is that the victim?"

He nodded. "Alex asked if I was coming back for our twenty-year high school reunion."

"You *were?*" She couldn't help her surprise.

He gave her an are-you-kidding look. "I told him no. That's when he mentioned Tanner."

"Alex Winslow told you he was looking into Tanner's death?"

"Not in so many words. He said something like, 'Do you ever think about Tanner?' He sounded like he'd been drinking. At first I just thought it was the booze talking."

He told her about the rest of the conversation, apparently quoting Alex as best as he could remember.

"Man, it would take something to hang yourself," Alex had said. "Put that noose around your neck and stand there balancing on nothing more than a log stump. One little move… Who would do that unless they were forced to? You know, like at gunpoint or…I don't know, maybe get tricked into standing up there?"

"What are you saying?"

"Just…what if he didn't do it? What if they killed him?"

"They? Who?"

"Don't listen to me. I've had a few too many beers tonight. So, are you sure I can't talk you into coming to the reunion? Even if I told you I have a theory about Tanner's death."

"What theory?"

"Come to the reunion. Call me when you get into town and I'll tell you. Don't mention this to anyone else. Seriously. I don't want to end up like poor old Tanner."

"That could have just been the alcohol talking," Liza said when he finished.

"That's what I thought, too, until he wanted to meet at the falls after dark. Something had him running scared."

"With good reason, apparently. Alex Winslow is a former friend?"

Jordan nodded.

"You weren't just a little suspicious, meeting in the dark at a waterfall?"

"I thought he was being paranoid, but I played along."

"You didn't consider it might be dangerous?"

"No, I thought Alex was overreacting. He was like that. Or at least he had been in high school. I haven't seen him in twenty years."

"Why, if he knew something, did he wait all these years?"

Jordan shrugged. "I just know that Tanner wouldn't have killed himself. He was a smart guy. If anything he was too smart for his own good. I figured if there was even a small chance that Alex knew something…" He glanced over at her. "Apparently, Alex had reason to be paranoid. This proves that there is more to Tanner's suicide."

She heard the determination in his voice and groaned inwardly. "This proves nothing except that Alex Winslow is dead." But Jordan wasn't listening.

"Also it proves I wasn't such a fool to believe Alex really did know something about Tanner's death."

She studied Jordan for a moment. "Did he say something to you before he was shot?"

His gaze shifted away. "I can't even be sure I heard him right."

"What did he say?"

"Shelby."

"Shelby?"

He nodded. "We went to school with a girl named Shelby Durran. She and Tanner were a couple. At least until Christmas our senior year."

Hud HAD JUST RETURNED with the kids when he got the call about the shooting.

"Go," Dana said. "I'll be fine. Stacy is here. She said she'd have the kids help her make dinner for all of us."

He mugged a face and lowered his voice. "Your sister *cooking?* Now that's frightening."

"Go," his wife ordered, giving him a warning look. "We can manage without you for a while."

"Are you sure?" He took her hand and squeezed it. "You promise to stay right where you are?"

"Promise."

Still, he hesitated. He'd been shocked to walk into the house and see Dana holding a baby. For a few moments, he'd been confused as to where she'd gotten it.

"Has Stacy said anything about where she's been?" he asked, glancing toward the kitchen. He could hear the voices of his children and sister-in-law. They all sounded excited about whatever they were making for dinner.

"Southern California. She's headed for Great Falls. There's a military base located there so that makes sense since she says the baby's father is in the military."

"If Stacy can be believed," he said quietly.

Dana mugged a face at him. But telling the truth wasn't one of her sister's strong suits. It bothered him that Dana was defending her sister. He figured the baby had something to do with it. Dana was a sucker for kids.

"Stacy seems different now," she said. "I think it's the baby. It seems to have grounded her some, maybe."

"Maybe," he said doubtfully.

"Go on, you have a murder investigation to worry about instead of me."

"You sound way too happy about that."

LIZA ALREADY HAD THE CRIME scene cordoned off when Hud arrived. He waved to the deputy on guard at the falls parking lot as he got out of his patrol SUV. The coroner's van was parked next to the two police vehicles.

"The coroner just went in," the deputy told him.

He turned on his flashlight and started down the trail. Hud couldn't help thinking about his wife's siblings trying to force her to sell the family ranch. They'd been like vultures, none of them having any interest in Cardwell Ranch. All they'd wanted was the money.

Jordan had been the worst because of his New York lifestyle—and his out-of-work model wife. But Stacy and Clay had had their hands out, as well. Hud hated to think what would have happened if Dana hadn't found the new will her mother had made leaving her the ranch.

He smiled at the memory of where she'd found it. Mary Justice Cardwell had put it in her favorite old recipe book next to "Double Chocolate Brownies." The brownies had been Hud's favorite. Dana hadn't made them in all the time the two of them had been apart. When they'd gotten back together six years ago, Dana had opened the cookbook planning to surprise him with the brownies, only to be surprised herself.

Two of her siblings were back in the canyon? That had him worried even before the call from his deputy marshal that there'd been a murder. And oh, yeah, Liza had told him, Jordan Cardwell was somehow involved.

Now as he hiked into the falls, he tried to keep his temper in check. If Dana's family thought they were going to come back here and upset her—

Ahead he saw the crowd gathered at the top of the falls. He headed for the coroner.

Coroner Rupert Milligan was hugging seventy, but

you'd never know it the way he acted. Six years ago, Hud had thought the man older than God and more powerful in this county. Tall, white-haired, with a head like a buffalo, he had a gruff voice and little patience for stupidity. He'd retired as a country doctor to work as a coroner.

None of that had changed in the past six years. Just as Rupert's love for murder mysteries and forensics hadn't.

"So what do we have?" Hud asked over the roar of the falls as he joined him.

Rupert answered without even bothering to look up. "Single gunshot through the heart. Another through the lungs. High-powered rifle."

"Distance?"

"I'd say fifty yards."

"That far," he said, surprised. The killer would have needed the victim to be out in the open with no trees in the way to make such a shot. Like at the top of a waterfall. "Any idea where the shot came from?"

Rupert had been crouched beside the body. Now he finally looked up. "In case you haven't noticed, it's dark out. Once it gets daylight you can look for tracks and possibly a shell casing. And once I get the body to Bozeman for an autopsy I might be able to tell you more about the trajectory of the bullet. Offhand, I'd say the shot came from the other side of the creek, probably on the side of the mountain."

"So either it was a lucky shot or the killer had been set up and waiting," Liza said, joining them. "The killer either picked the meeting spot or was told where the victim would be."

Rupert shifted his gaze to her and frowned. Being from the old school, the coroner made no secret of the fact that he didn't hold much appreciation for women law enforcement. If he'd had his way, he would have put them all behind a desk.

Hud liked that Liza didn't seem to let him bother her. His deputy marshal's good looks could be deceiving. Small in stature, too cute for her own good and easy-going, Liza often gave criminals the idea that she was a pushover. They, however, quickly learned differently. He wondered if Jordan Cardwell thought the same thing about the deputy marshal. If so, he was in for a surprise.

"Which could mean either that the victim was expecting to meet not only Jordan Cardwell up here, but also someone he trusted," she continued. "Or—"

"Or Jordan told the killer about the meeting," Hud interjected.

Liza nodded and glanced over to the stump where Jordan was waiting. "That is always another possibility."

"One I suggest you don't forget," Hud said under his breath. "If it's all right with you, I'll take our suspect down to the office."

She nodded. "I want to wait for the crime scene techs to arrive."

Hud hadn't seen Jordan for six years. As he walked toward him, he was thinking he could have easily gone another six and not been in the least bit sorry.

"You just happen to come back to the canyon and a man dies," he said.

"Good to see you again, too, brother-in-law. I guess my invitation to the wedding must have gotten lost in the mail, huh?"

"What are you doing here, Jordan?"

"I already told your deputy marshal."

"Well, you're going to have to tell me, too. Let's get out of the woods and go to my office. You have a rifle you need to pick up before we go?"

Jordan gave him a grim, disappointed look. "No, I'm good."

THE DOOR OPENED A CRACK. "Oh, good, you're awake," Stacy said as she peered in at Dana. "I brought you some still-warm chocolate chips cookies and some milk."

"That was very thoughtful of you," Dana said, sitting up in the bed and putting her crossword puzzle aside. Earlier, before her doctor's appointment, Hud had made her a bed in the sunroom so she wouldn't have to go up the stairs—and would be where she could see most of what was going on. She patted the bed, and her sister sat down on the edge and placed the tray next to them.

"I'm just glad you let me stay and help out. It was fun baking with Hank and Mary. They are so cute. Hank looks just like a small version of Hud and Mary is the spitting image of you. Do you know..." She motioned to Dana's big belly.

"No," she said, taking a bite of cookie. "We want to be surprised. Did you find out ahead of time?"

Stacy had cautiously placed a hand on Dana's abdomen and now waited with expectation. The babies had been restless all day, kicking up a storm. She watched her sister's face light up as one of the twins gave her hand a swift kick.

Stacy laughed and pulled her hand back. "Isn't that the coolest thing ever?"

Dana nodded, studying her older sister. Stacy had changed little in appearance. She was still the pretty one. Her dark hair was chin-length, making her brown eyes the focus of her face. She'd always had that innocent look. That was probably, Dana realized with a start, why she'd been able to get away with as much as she had.

"So did you know ahead of time you were having a girl?" she asked again.

Stacy shook her head and helped herself to a cookie. "It was a surprise."

"Speaking of surprises…" She watched her sister's face. "Jordan is in town."

"Jordan?" Had Stacy known? "What is *he* doing here?"

"I thought you might know."

Stacy shook her head and looked worried. "I haven't heard from him since we were all here six years ago." She made a face. "I still feel bad about trying to force you to sell the ranch."

Dana waved that away. "It's history. The ranch is still in the family and it makes enough money that you and our brothers get to share in the profits. You know I think my lawyer did mention that he'd received notice that Jordan was divorced."

"I wonder how much of his ranch profits he has to give to Jill? That woman was such a gold digger." Stacy laughed as she realized the irony. "I should know, huh? Back then I figured if I was going to get married, I might as well get paid for it." She shook her head as if amazed by the woman she'd been. "Have you heard from Clay?"

"No." She helped herself to another cookie and sipped some of the milk. "He hasn't been cashing his checks lately. My attorney is checking into it."

"That's odd," Stacy agreed. "Well, I need to clean up the kitchen."

"Thanks so much for giving the kids their baths and getting them to bed." Mary and Hank had come in earlier to say good-night and have Dana read a book to them before bed. They'd been wearing their footie pajamas, their sweet faces scrubbed clean and shiny. They'd been excited about helping their aunt Stacy cook.

"Thank you so much for all your help," Dana said, touched by everything Stacy had done.

"I'm just glad I was here so I could." She smiled. "I didn't know how fun kids could be."

"Wait until Ella is that age. Mary loves to have tea parties and help her daddy cook."

Stacy nodded thoughtfully. "Let me know if you need anything. Knowing you, I can guess how hard it is for you to stay down like this."

Dana groaned in response. She couldn't stand the thought of another day let alone weeks like this. "Thanks for the cookies and milk. The cookies were delicious."

Stacy looked pleased as she left the room.

Chapter Four

Hud walked out with Jordan to the road, then followed him to the marshal's office. Once in the office he got his first good look at his brother-in-law. Jordan had been only two years ahead of Hud in school, three years ahead of his sister Dana. His brother-in-law had aged, but it hadn't hurt Jordan's looks. If anything the years seemed to have given him character, or at least the appearance of it.

"Why don't you have a seat and start at the beginning?" Hud said, dropping into his chair behind his desk.

"I thought Liza was handling this case?"

"*Liza?* You mean Deputy Marshal Turner?" He shouldn't have been surprised Jordan was on a first-name basis with the deputy. He, of all people, understood the charm of the Justice-Cardwell genes. Dana could wrap him around her little finger and did.

"Don't think just because she's a woman that she isn't a damned good marshal," Hud said to his brother-in-law. "She's sharp and she'll nail you to the wall if you're guilty."

"If you have so much confidence in her abilities, then why are you here?"

Hud gritted his teeth. Jordan had always been difficult. At least that hadn't changed. "Several reasons. None of which I have to explain to you. But—" He held up a hand before Jordan could speak. "I will because I want us to have an understanding." He ticked them off on his fingers. "One, I'm still the marshal here. Two, Liza has her hands full up at the site. Three, I want to know what happened on that mountain. And four, your sister is my wife. I don't want her hurt."

With a smile and a nod, Jordan ambled over to a chair and sat. "Dana doesn't have anything to worry about. Neither she nor the ranch is why I'm back in the canyon."

"Why *are* you here?" Hud asked, snapping on the recording machine.

"It doesn't have anything to do with family."

"But it does have something to do with Alex Winslow."

"Alex was a good friend from high school. I didn't kill him." Jordan sighed and looked at the ceiling for a moment.

Hud noticed that he was no longer wearing a wedding ring. He vaguely remembered Dana mentioning that she'd heard Jordan was divorced from his ex-model wife, Jill. The marriage had probably ended when Jordan didn't get the proceeds from the sale of the ranch.

"If Alex was your friend, I would think you'd be interested in helping us find his killer," Hud said. "Not to mention you're neck deep in this. Right now, you're the number one suspect."

Jordan laughed. "Does that work on most of your suspects?" He shook his head. "I came back because Alex called me. He hinted that he might know something about Tanner's suicide but it was clear he didn't want to talk about it on the phone. He said he'd share his theory with me if I came to our twenty-year high school reunion. The next time I talked to him, he sounded scared and wanted to meet at the falls. That's it."

That was a lot. Hud wasn't sure how much of it he believed. But at least he had some idea of what might have brought Jordan back to town—and it wasn't family.

"Tanner Cole committed suicide when the two of you were seniors in high school. Why would that bring you back here after all these years?"

"When your best friend commits suicide, you never stop thinking you could have done something to stop him. You need to know *why* he did it."

"Unless that person leaves a note, you never know. Tanner didn't leave a note, as I recall."

Jordan shook his head.

"Did you talk to Alex before he was shot?"

"As I told your deputy, I heard the shot, he stumbled toward me, there was another shot and he went down. All he said was the word *Shelby.* At least that's what I thought he said." Jordan shrugged. "That was it."

Hud studied him openly for a moment. "Maybe the bullets were meant for you and the killer missed."

Jordan sighed. "What are you insinuating?"

"That maybe Tanner didn't commit suicide. Weren't you the one who found his body?"

Anger fired Jordan's gaze. "He was my *best* friend. I would have taken a bullet *for* him."

"Instead, another friend of yours took the bullet tonight," Hud said. "You're telling me you came all this way, hiked into the falls in the dark, just for answers?"

"Why is that so hard for you to understand?"

"What about Alex Winslow? Don't I remember some falling-out the two of you had before you graduated?"

"It was high school. Who remembers?"

Hud nodded. "Is Stacy in the canyon for the same reason?" Stacy had been in the grade between the two of them.

"Stacy?" Jordan looked genuinely surprised. "I haven't seen or talked to her in years."

"Then you didn't know that not only is she back in the canyon, she also has a baby."

Jordan laughed. "Stacy has a *baby?* That's got to be good. Look, if that's all, I need to get some sleep."

"Once Liza allows you to, I'm sure you'll be leaving. I'd appreciate it if you didn't upset Dana before then. She's pregnant with twins and having a rough go of it."

"I'm sorry to hear that," Jordan said, sounding as if he meant it. "Don't worry, I won't be bothering my sister. Either of my sisters," he added.

"Then I guess we're done here."

A WHILE LATER, DANA HEARD HUD come in. She heard him go upstairs to check on the kids, before coming back down to her room. He smiled when he saw her still awake and came over to her side of the bed to give her a kiss.

"So everything's all right?" he asked.

"I'm the one who should be asking you that. You said there'd been a shooting?"

He nodded. "Liza's got everything under control. The crime techs are on their way from Missoula." He sounded tired.

"Stacy kept a plate of dinner for you. She made chicken, baked potatoes and corn," Dana said. "Then she and the kids baked chocolate chip cookies." She motioned to the cookies on the tray next to the bed.

Hud gave her a who-knew-she-could-cook look and took one of the cookies.

Who knew indeed? Dana couldn't believe the change in her sister. She felt horribly guilty for not trusting it. But even Stacy was capable of changing, right? Having a baby did that to a person. But Stacy?

Unfortunately, the jury was still out—given her sister's past.

"Did she mention how long she's staying?" Hud asked, not meeting her gaze.

"She was planning to leave earlier, but I asked her to stay. I'm sure she'll be leaving in the morning."

Hud nodded. She could tell he would be glad when Stacy was gone. Dana couldn't blame him. Her sister had hurt them both. But she desperately wanted to believe Stacy had changed. For Ella's sake.

Unfortunately, like her husband, Dana had a niggling feeling that Stacy wasn't being completely honest about the real reason she'd come to the ranch.

EXHAUSTED, JORDAN WENT BACK TO his cabin, locked the door and fell into bed with the intention of sleeping the rest of the day.

Unfortunately, Deputy Marshal Liza Turner had other plans for him.

"What do you want?" he said when he opened the cabin door a little after eleven o'clock that morning to find her standing outside. He leaned a hip into the door-jamb and crossed his arms as he took her in.

"What do I want? Sleep, more money, better hours, breakfast."

"I can't help you with most of that, but I could use food. I'll buy."

She smiled. "I know a place that serves breakfast all day. We can eat and talk."

"No murder talk until I've had coffee."

"Agreed."

Liza drove them to the upper mountain. The huge unpaved parking lots sat empty. None of the lifts moved on the mountain except for the gondolas that rocked gently in the breeze.

"It's like a ghost town up here," he commented as they got out of her patrol SUV.

"I like the quiet. Good place to talk. Most everything is closed still. Fortunately, there are enough locals that a few places stay open."

The café was small and nearly empty. Liza led him outside to a table under an umbrella. The sun was low to the south, but still warm enough it was comfortable outside. A waitress brought them coffee while they looked at the menu.

Jordan ordered ham and eggs, hash browns and whole wheat toast.

"I'll have the same," Liza said and handed back the menu. As soon as the waitress was out of earshot, she said, "You didn't mention last night that you and the victim were no longer friends at the end of your high school years."

"So you spoke with Hud." He looked toward the mountains where snow dusted the peaks, making them gleam blinding bright. "It was a stupid disagreement over a woman, all right? Just high school stuff."

She nodded, not buying it. "What girl?"

"I don't even remember."

Liza's look called him a liar, but she let it go. "I'm still confused why he contacted *you*. He must have had other friends locally he would have talked to."

"Obviously he must have talked to someone locally. One of them knew where he was going last night and killed him." Jordan said nothing as the waitress served their breakfasts. He picked up his fork. "Look, do we have to talk about this while we eat? I feel like I got him killed."

"You can't blame yourself, or worse, try to take the law into your own hands." She eyed him for a long moment. "Why would I suspect that's what you're planning to do?"

He chuckled. "If you talked to my brother-in-law he would have told you that I'm not that ambitious. Anyway, you're the deputy marshal. I'm sure you'll find his killer."

She took a bite of toast, chewed and swallowed before she said, "You contacted Tanner's girlfriend from his senior year in high school."

Jordan took her measure. "Why, Liza, you've been checking up on me. I contacted Shelby before I went up to the falls last night. She said she had nothing to say to me about Tanner. That was high school and so far back, she barely remembers."

"You didn't believe her?" Liza asked between bites.

Jordan laughed. "High school was Shelby's glory days. Just check out our yearbook. She is on every page either as president or queen of something. Not to mention she was dating Tanner Cole, the most popular guy in school. She was in her element. I'd bet those were the best days of her life and that nothing she has done since will ever compare."

Liza considered that for a long moment before she asked, "So you talked to Shelby before last night. Before the only word Alex got out after he was shot was her name?"

"Like I said, she and Tanner dated."

"When you talked to Shelby, did you mention Alex or where you were meeting him?"

He gave her an exasperated look. "Do you really think I'm that stupid? Alex was acting terrified. I wasn't about to say anything until I talked to him."

"And yet you called Shelby."

"Yeah. I just told her I was in the area as if I was here for the twenty-year reunion and worked Tanner into the conversation. I didn't realize then that anything I might do could put anyone in danger, including her."

"That's so noble. But I thought you didn't like her. In fact, I thought you were instrumental in breaking up her and Tanner."

He shook his head and took a bite of his breakfast. "You're determined to ruin my appetite, aren't you?"

"Is it true?"

"I couldn't stand Shelby and that bunch she ran with. But you're wrong. I had nothing to do with breaking her and Tanner up, no matter what Hud thinks, as I'm sure that's where you got your information."

Liza lifted a brow. "You weren't the one who snitched on her?"

"Wasn't me." He met her gaze. "Why keep questioning me if you aren't going to believe anything I say?"

"I don't want you involved in my investigation," she said. "That includes asking about Tanner among your old friends—and enemies."

He smiled. "What makes you think I have enemies?"

She smiled in answer as she smeared huckleberry jam on a piece of her toast.

He watched her eat for a few moments. He liked a woman who ate well and said as much.

"Does that line work on women?" she asked.

He laughed. "Every time."

They finished their breakfast in the quiet of the upper mountain. She was right about it being peaceful up here. He liked it. But once winter came, all that would change. The parking lots would be packed, all the lifts would be running as well as the gondola. The mountain would be dotted with skiers and boarders, the restaurants and resorts full. He recalled the sounds of people, the clank of machinery, the array of bright-colored skiwear like a rainbow across Lone Mountain.

Tanner had loved it when Big Sky took on its winter wonderland persona. He'd loved to ski, had started at the age of three like a lot of the kids who grew up in the shadow of Lone Mountain.

With a start, Jordan found himself looking high up on the peak, remembering one of the last days he and Tanner had skied the winter of their senior year. Tanner had always been gutsy, but that day he'd talked Alex and him into going into an out-of-bounds area.

They hadn't gone far when Tanner had gone off a cornice. The cornice had collapsed, causing a small avalanche that had almost killed him.

"Hey, man. You have a death wish?" Alex had asked Tanner when they'd skied down to find him half-buried in the snow.

Tanner had laughed it off. "Takes more than that to kill me."

"I THOUGHT YOU'D BE HAPPIER down here," Hud said as he opened the curtains in the sunroom. "You can leave the door open so you can see everything that is going on."

Dana shot him a look. Seeing everything that was going on was his not-so-subtle way of saying he wanted her to keep an eye on her sister.

They'd all gathered around her bed after breakfast. Stacy hadn't made any attempt to leave. Just the opposite, she seemed to be finding more things she wanted to do before she and Ella packed for the rest of their trip.

"Is there any chance you could stay another day or so?" Dana asked her now as Stacy picked up her breakfast tray to take to the kitchen.

Her sister stopped and looked up in surprise. Her face softened as if she was touched by Dana's offer. "I'd love to. I can cook and help with the kids. Hud has this murder investigation—"

"My deputy marshal is handling all of that," Hud interrupted, shooting Dana a what-could-you-be-thinking? look. "Plus the crime techs are down from Missoula. I am more than capable of taking care of Dana and the kids and—"

Dana had been holding Ella since finishing her breakfast. She quickly interrupted him. "Stacy, that would be great if you can. I know Hud won't mind the help and I love having you and Ella here."

Her husband sent her a withering look. She ignored it and looked instead into Ella's adorable face.

"Is Auntie Stacy going to stay, Mommy?" Mary asked excitedly.

"Yes, for a few more days. Would you like that?" Both children cheered.

"Auntie Stacy is going to show us how to make clay,"

Hank said. "You have to put it in the oven and then paint it."

Stacy shrugged when Dana looked at her. "I found a recipe on the internet. I thought they'd like that."

"That was very thoughtful," she said and shot her husband a see?-everything-is-fine look. "I know Hud will want to check in with the murder investigation, and there are animals to feed."

He tried to stare her down, but Dana had grown up with three siblings. Having to fight for what she wanted had made her a strong, determined woman.

"Fine," Hud said as he left the room. "Stacy, if you need me, Dana has my number. I have animals to feed."

"He'll check in with Liza," Dana said. "He can pretend otherwise, but he won't be able to stay away from this case."

"Are you sure it's all right if I stay?" Stacy asked. "Hud doesn't seem—"

"He's just being territorial," she said. "He can't stand the idea that anyone might think he can't take care of his family." Dana reached for her sister's hand and squeezed it. "I'm glad you and Ella are here."

LIZA FIGURED JORDAN CARDWELL had lied to her at least twice during breakfast.

"I need to know everything you can remember that led up to Tanner's death," she said when they'd finished their breakfast and the waitress had cleared away their plates and refilled their coffee cups.

The scent of pine blew down on the breeze from the mountain peaks. She breathed in the fall day and pulled out her notebook. They still had the café deck to themselves and the sun felt heavenly after so little sleep last night.

"We were seniors." Jordan shrugged. "Not much was going on."

"Who did Tanner date after his breakup with Shelby?"

"A couple of different girls."

"Who was he dating in the weeks or days before he died?" she asked.

"Brittany Cooke." The way he said it gave him away.

"You liked her?" she asked with interest.

His shrug didn't fool her.

"You used to date her?"

He laughed, meeting her gaze. "You got all that out of a shrug?"

"Who were *you* dating at the time?" she asked.

"I don't see what—"

"Humor me."

"I can't remember."

She laughed and leaned back in her chair to eye him. "You don't remember who you were dating the spring of your senior year? Give me a break."

"I wasn't dating anyone, really. It's a small community, cliques. There weren't a lot of options unless you dated someone from Bozeman. I was just anxious to graduate and get out of here."

"Shelby and Brittany were in one of these cliques?"

"Not Brittany. Brittany and Shelby got along, but she was never really one of them. But Shelby, yeah. She was the leader of the mean girls—you know the type. Too much money, too much everything."

Liza knew the type only too well. "So what happened when Brittany went out with Tanner?"

"I'm sure Shelby would deny it, but her and her group of friends closed Brittany out."

"What did Tanner think about that?"

"He thought it was funny. Believe me, that wasn't why he killed himself. Don't get me wrong, Tanner liked Shelby. He went with her a lot longer than any other girl. But once he found out she'd been trying to get pregnant to trap him, it was all over. He wasn't ready to settle down. He'd worked two jobs all through high school while getting good grades so he could do some of the things he'd always wanted to do. Both of us couldn't wait to travel."

"And get out of the canyon," Liza said.

"Tanner not as much as me. He would have come back to the family ranch. He was a cowboy."

"He wasn't from Big Sky resort money?"

"Naw, his folks have a ranch down the canyon. They do okay, just like everyone else who still ranches around here. As my sister is fond of saying, it's a lifestyle more than a paying career. Tanner *loved* that lifestyle, was happiest in a saddle and not afraid of hard work."

"He sounds like a nice, sensible young man."

"He was." Jordan looked away toward the mountains for a long moment. "He worked a lot of odd jobs throughout high school. That's how he ended up at that cabin on the mountain. He talked his folks into letting him stay there because it was closer to school. He traded watching the landowner's construction equipment for the small cabin where he lived that spring."

"He didn't want to live at home?"

Jordan grinned. "Not his senior year. His parents were strict, like all parents when you're that age. Tanner wanted to be on his own and his folks were okay with it."

"So who were the mean girls?"

"Shelby, the leader. Tessa, her closest ally. Whitney. Ashley. They were the inner circle."

"And Brittany?"

"She was always on the fringe. Last I heard Brittany had married Lee Peterson and they have a bunch of kids. I think I heard they live in Meadow Village. Shelby married Wyatt Iverson. She'd started dating him after she and Tanner broke up. Wyatt's father was a contractor who built a lot of the huge vacation homes. It was his maintenance cabin where Tanner stayed with his equipment." He stopped, a faraway look coming to his gaze. "Shelby has a yoga studio near the Gallatin River."

For a life he'd put behind him, Jordan certainly knew a lot about the players, Liza thought as she closed her notebook.

Chapter Five

Yogamotion was in a narrow complex built of log and stone, Western-style. Liza pushed open the door to find the inside brightly painted around walls of shiny mirrors.

According to the schedule she'd seen on the door, the next class wasn't for a couple of hours. A lithe young woman sat behind a large desk in a room off to the side. She was talking on a cell phone, but looked up as the door closed behind Liza.

"You should be getting the check any day. I'm sorry, but I have to go," she said into the phone and slowly snapped it shut, never taking her eyes off the deputy marshal.

"Shelby Iverson?"

As the woman got to her feet she took in Liza's attire, the boots, jeans and tan uniform shirt with the silver star on it. "I'm Shelby *Durran-Iverson*."

"Liza Turner, deputy marshal." Big Sky was small enough that Liza had seen Shelby around. The canyon resort was situated such that there were pockets of development, some pricier than others depending on where you lived.

Shelby lived in a large single-family home on the

north side of the mountain on the way to Mountain Village, while Liza lived in a condo in Meadow Village. She and Shelby didn't cross paths a lot.

"I'd like to ask you a few questions," the deputy said.

"Me?" The catch in her throat was merely for effect. Shelby Durran-Iverson had been expecting a visit from the marshal's office. Everyone within fifty miles would have heard about Alex Winslow's murder at the falls last night. Word would have spread through Big Sky like a fast-moving avalanche.

Liza had to wonder, though, why Shelby thought *she* would be questioned. "It's about the shooting last night."

"I don't know anything about it," she said.

"But you knew Alex."

"Sure. Everyone from around here knew him."

"You went to high school with him?" Liza asked, pulling her notebook and pen from her pocket.

"Do I need a lawyer?"

"You tell me. Did you shoot Alex?"

"No." Shelby sounded shocked that Liza would even suggest such a thing.

"Then I guess you don't need a lawyer. I just need to ask you a few questions so I can find the person who did shoot him."

"I still can't see how *I* can help." But she motioned Liza to a chair and took her own behind the desk again. Liza could tell that Shelby was hoping to learn more about the murder, getting more information out of her than she provided.

Settling into a chair across the desk from her, Liza studied Shelby. She was a shapely blonde who looked as if she just stepped out of a magazine ad. Her hair was pulled up in a sleek ponytail. Everything about her seemed planned for maximum effect from her makeup to her jewelry and the clothes on her back. She wore a flattering coral velvet designer sweatsuit that brought out the blue of her eyes and accentuated her well-toned body.

"I understand you used to date Tanner Cole," Liza said.

"*Tanner?* I thought you were here about Alex?"

"Did you date Alex, too?"

"No." She shook her head, the ponytail sweeping back and forth. "You're confusing me." She flashed a perfect-toothed smile, clearly a girl who'd had braces.

"I don't want to confuse you. So you dated Tanner how long?"

She frowned, still confused apparently. "Till just before Christmas of our senior year, I guess."

"But the two of you broke up?"

"I can't understand how that—"

Liza gave her one of her less-than-perfect-toothed smiles. She'd been born with a slight gap between her front teeth that her parents had found cute and she had never gotten around to changing. "Humor me. I actually know what I'm doing."

Shelby sighed, making it clear she had her doubts about that. "Fine. Yes, I dated Tanner, I don't remember when we broke up."

"Or why?"

The yoga instructor's eyes narrowed in challenge. "No."

"Here's the thing, I'm trying to understand why Tanner killed himself and why now one of his friends has been murdered."

"I'm sure there is no possible connection," Shelby

said with a mocking laugh as if now she knew Liza didn't know what she was doing.

"So Tanner didn't kill himself over you?"

"No!"

"So you weren't that serious?"

Shelby fumbled for words for a moment. "It was high school. It seemed serious at the time."

"To you. Or Tanner?"

"To both of us." She sounded defensive and realizing it, gave a small laugh. "Like I said, it was *high school*."

Liza looked down at her notebook. "Let's see, by that spring, Tanner was dating Brittany Cooke? Wasn't she a friend of yours?"

Shelby's mouth tightened. "Tanner was sowing his oats before graduation. I can assure you he wasn't serious about Brittany."

"Oh? Did she tell you that?"

"She didn't have to. She wasn't Tanner's type." Shelby straightened several things on her desk that didn't need straightening. "If that's all, I really need to get back to work."

"I forgot what you said. *Did* you date Alex?"

"No, and I'd lost track of him since high school."

"That's right, he'd moved down to Bozeman and had only recently returned to Big Sky for the class reunion?"

"I assume that's why he came back."

"You didn't talk to him?" Liza asked.

Shelby thought for a moment. More than likely she was carefully considering her next answer. If Liza had Alex's cell phone in her possession, she would know who he called right before his death—and who'd called him.

"I might have talked to him since I'm the reunion

chairwoman. I talked to a lot of people. I really can't remember."

"That's strange since you talked to Alex five times in two days, the last three of those calls just hours before he was killed."

Shelby didn't look quite so put-together. "I told you, it was about the reunion. I talked to a lot of people."

"Are you telling me he didn't ask you about Tanner's alleged suicide?" Liza said.

"*Alleged* suicide?"

"Apparently, Alex had some questions about Tanner's death."

Shelby shook her head. "I might have heard that, but I wouldn't have taken anything Alex said seriously." She leaned forward and lowered her voice even though they were the only two people there. "I heard he had some sort of breakdown." She leaned back and lifted a brow as if to say that covered it.

"Hmm. I hadn't heard that." Liza jotted down a note. "Whom did you hear this from?"

"I don't—"

"Recall. Maybe one of your friends?"

Shelby shook her head. "I really can't remember. I'm sure you can find out if there was any truth to it."

Liza smiled. "Yes, I can. What about Brittany?"

"What about her?" Shelby asked stiffly.

"Do you still see her?"

"Big Sky is a small community. You're bound to see everyone at some point," Shelby answered noncommittally. "She and her husband, Lee Peterson, own a ski shop up on the mountain. Now I really do need to get to work," she said, rising to her feet.

"Did you see Tanner the night he died?"

"No. As you are apparently aware, we had broken up. He was dating Brittany. If anyone knows why he killed himself, she would, don't you think?"

"Even though she and Tanner weren't that serious about each other?"

Shelby's jaw muscle bunched and her blue eyes fired with irritation. "If she doesn't know, then who would?"

"Good question. Maybe Alex Winslow. But then he isn't talking, is he?" Liza said as she closed her notebook and got to her feet. "One more question. Why would the last word Alex Winslow would say be your name?"

All the color washed from her face. She sat back down, leaning heavily on her desk. "I have no idea."

AFTER BREAKFAST, JORDAN WENT back to his cabin and crashed for a while. He figured Liza would be keeping an eye on him. Not that he knew what to do next. He couldn't just hang out in this cabin, that was for sure. But he'd been serious about not wanting to put anyone else in danger.

When he woke up, he realized he was hungry again. It was still early since the sun hadn't sunk behind Lone Mountain. According to his cell phone, it was a quarter past three in the afternoon.

He found a small sandwich shop in Meadow Village, ordered a turkey and cheese and took a seat by the window overlooking the golf course. Lone Mountain gleamed in the background, a sight that brought back too many memories. There'd been a time when he'd told himself he'd left here because he didn't want to be a rancher. But coming back here now, he realized a lot of his need to leave and stay gone had to do with Tanner's suicide.

When the waitress brought out his sandwich, he asked if he could get it to go. He followed her to the counter and was waiting when he heard a bell tinkle over the door and turned to see someone he recognized coming through.

With a silent curse, he put a name to the face. Tessa Ryerson. She had already spotted him and something about her expression gave him the crazy idea that she didn't just happen in here. She'd come looking for him.

Before he could react, the waitress brought out his sandwich in a brown paper bag and handed it to him. He dug out the cost of the sandwich and a generous tip and handed it to the server, before turning to Tessa.

She had stopped just a couple of feet from him, waiting while he paid. When he turned to her, he saw that she looked much like she had twenty years ago when the two of them had dated. She wore her light brown hair as she had in high school, shoulder length and wavy, no bangs. A hair band held it back from her face.

She seemed thinner, a little more gaunt in the face, than she had the last time he'd seen her. He recalled that she'd always struggled to keep her weight down. Apparently, she'd mastered the problem.

He couldn't help noticing that her ring finger was bare. Hadn't he heard that she'd gone through a bad divorce from Danny Spring? Two years ahead of them in school, the guy had been a jerk. Jordan recalled being surprised when he'd heard that she'd married him.

"Jordan," Tessa said a little too brightly. "Imagine running into you here."

"Imagine that," he said, now sure the only reason

she'd come in here, crazy or not, was to see him. So did that mean she'd followed him? Or had she just been looking for him?

"Oh, are you getting your sandwich to go?" she asked, sounding disappointed as she glanced at the bag in his hand as if just now noticing it. "I missed lunch and I hate eating alone. Would you mind staying?"

How could he say no even if he'd wanted to? Anyway, he was curious about what she wanted. "Sure, go ahead and order. I'll get us a table."

"Great."

He took a seat away from the girl working behind the counter, positioning himself so he could watch Tessa while she ordered. She dug nervously in her purse, paid for a small salad and a bottled water, then joined him at the table.

"So you came for the reunion," she said, smiling as she unscrewed the lid on her water bottle.

He smiled at that and dug his sandwich out of the bag and took a bite.

"Wow, it's been so long."

"Twenty years," he said between bites.

"I guess you heard about Danny and me." She sighed. "But I've put it behind me."

Too bad the look in her eyes said otherwise. He suspected the slightest thing could set her off if asked about her marriage. Unfortunately, he could remember how he was right after Jill had left him. He didn't want to go there again.

"So wasn't that awful about Alex?" she said. "Were you really there?"

He gave her points for getting right to what she really

wanted to talk to him about. He nodded and took another bite of his sandwich. She hadn't touched her salad.

"When I heard, I just couldn't believe it. How horrible. Do they know who shot him?" she asked when he didn't answer. "I heard it could have been a stray bullet from a hunter."

"Really?" he said. "I heard it was murder. Someone wanted to shut Alex up."

"Who told you that?" she cried.

He said nothing for a moment, letting her squirm. "The state crime lab trucks have been up at the falls since last night looking for evidence to track them to the killer. I thought you would have heard."

Tessa fiddled with her water bottle, looking worried. "Why would anyone want to kill Alex?"

He shrugged. "Probably because he'd been asking a lot of questions about Tanner's suicide. But you'd know better about that than I would."

"Me?"

"I'm sure Alex talked to you." He wasn't sure of anything except that he was rattling her. "If you know something, I'd suggest you talk to Deputy Marshal Liza Turner. Alex was murdered and there is an investigation into Tanner's death, as well. It's all going to come out."

"I don't know *anything*." She squeezed her plastic water bottle so hard it crackled loudly and water shot up and out over the table. She jumped up and grabbed for a stack of napkins.

He watched her nervously wipe up the spilled water, almost feeling guilty for upsetting her. "Then I guess you have nothing to worry about. But I wonder if Alex said the same thing."

"This is all so upsetting." She sounded close to tears.

He reached across the table and put a hand on hers. "Tessa—"

"Please, don't," she said, snatching back her hand. "I told you. I don't know anything."

He put down his sandwich to study her. Why had she come looking for him? Why was she so scared? "You and Shelby have always been thick as thieves. What don't I know about Alex's death? Or Tanner's, for that matter?"

She shook her head. "How would I know? Shelby wasn't even dating Tanner then."

"No, but she'd conned you into breaking up with Alex to go out with me. I thought you were just playing hard to get when you wanted to always double date with Brittany and Tanner. I should have known Shelby put you up to spying on him."

"I don't know what you're talking about," she said. "But I do remember you didn't mind double dating. It was Brittany you wanted to be with. Not me." She got to her feet, hitting the table and spilling some of her salad.

"Brittany," he said under his breath. "Thanks for reminding me of that prank you and your friend Shelby pulled on her." It was straight out of a Stephen King novel.

Tessa crossed her toned arms over her flat chest, her expression defiant. He'd expected her to stomp off, but she didn't. Whatever the reason that she'd wanted to see him, she hadn't got what she'd come for apparently.

That spring of their senior year was coming back to him after years of fighting to forget it. Hadn't he had a bad feeling he couldn't shake even before Alex had called him? "Did Shelby send you to find me?" He let out a laugh. "Just like in high school. What is it she wants to know, Tessa?"

"I have no idea what you mean."

He laughed. "Still doing her dirty work even after all these years."

Tessa snatched up her water bottle from the table with one hand, the untouched salad with the other. "I know what you think of me."

"I think you're too smart to keep letting Shelby run your life."

She laughed at that. "Run my life? Don't you mean *ruin* my life? She practically forced me to marry Danny Spring. It wasn't until later that I found out her husband was trying to buy some land Danny owned and thought my marriage would get it for Wyatt." She smiled. "It did."

"Then what are you doing still being friends with her?" he demanded.

"*Seriously?* Because it's much worse to be Shelby's enemy, haven't you realized that yet? My life isn't the only one she's destroyed. Clearly, you have forgotten what she's like."

"No, I don't think so. I know what she did to Tanner."

"Do you?" she challenged.

"She got pregnant to trap him into marrying her. If she hadn't miscarried, he probably would have married her for the kid's sake." Something in Tessa's expression stopped him. "She did have a miscarriage, didn't she? Or did she lie about that, as well?"

Tessa looked away for a moment.

Jordan felt his heart drop. *My life isn't the only one she's destroyed.* The thought came at him with such force, he knew it had been in the back of his mind for a long time.

"She didn't do something to that baby to get back at Tanner, did she?" he asked, voicing his fear.

"I have to go," Tessa said, glancing toward the parking lot.

He followed her gaze, seeing her fear as a white SUV cruised slowly past. He recognized Shelby Durran-Iverson behind the wheel. She sped up when she saw Tessa hurry out of the sandwich shop, barely missing her as she drove away.

Jordan stared after both of them for a moment before he wrapped up his sandwich. He'd lost his appetite. Worse, he wasn't sure what his best friend would have done if he'd found out Shelby hadn't miscarried early in the pregnancy, but waited as long as she could, then aborted his baby to hurt him.

He realized it was possible Tanner really had killed himself.

Chapter Six

The ski shop Brittany Cooke Peterson and her husband, Lee, owned on the mountain was still closed for the season.

But Liza found her at the couple's condo in Meadow Village. Brittany answered the door wearing a black-and-white polka-dot apron over a T-shirt and jeans. Her feet were bare and her dark hair in disarray. She brushed a long curly lock back from her face, leaving a dusting of flour on her cheekbone. In the background a 1960s hit played loudly. As Brittany's brown eyes widened to see the deputy sheriff at her door, Liza caught the warm, wonderful scent of freshly baked cookies.

"Don't touch that pan, it's hot," Brittany said over her shoulder after opening the door.

"Did I catch you in the middle of something?" Liza asked facetiously.

Brittany laughed. "Not at all."

"Mommy, Jake stuck his finger in the icing," called a young female voice from the back of the large two-story condo.

Brittany wiped her hands on her apron. "Come on in. We're baking iced pumpkin cookies."

Liza followed the young woman through a toy-cluttered living room and into a kitchen smelling of cinnamon and pumpkin.

Three small children balanced on chairs around a kitchen island covered in flour and dirty baking bowls and utensils. One of the children, the only boy, had icing smudged on the side of his cheek. Brittany licked her thumb pad and wiped the icing from the boy's face, took an icing-dripping spoon from one girl and snatched a half-eaten cookie from the other girl as if it was all in a day's work.

The two girls, who Liza realized were identical twins, appeared to be about five and were wearing aprons that matched their mother's. The boy had a dish towel wrapped around his neck like a bandana. He was a year or so younger than the girls.

"You'd better have a cookie," Brittany said as she finished slipping warm ones from a cookie sheet onto a cooling rack.

Liza took one of the tall stools at the counter, but declined a cookie.

"Just a little icing on them, Courtney," her mother said to the girl who had the spoon again and was dribbling thin white icing over each cookie as if making a masterpiece. The other girl watched, practically drooling as her sister slowly iced the warm cookies. "Okay, enough sugar for one day. Go get cleaned up." They jumped down and raced toward the stairs. "And don't argue!" she called after them.

With a sigh, Brittany glanced around the messy kitchen, then plopped down on a stool at the counter and took one of the cookies before turning her attention on Liza. "Sure you don't want one?" she asked between bites. "They aren't bad."

"They smell delicious, but I'm fine."

"You didn't come by for cookies," Brittany said. "This is about Alex, isn't it?" She shook her head, her expression one of sadness. "I heard it was a hunter."

"A hunter?"

"You know, someone poaching at night, a stray bullet. It had to be. No one would want to hurt Alex. He was a sweetheart. Everyone liked him."

"Not everyone," Liza said.

Brittany turned solemn. "So it *was* murder. That's the other rumor circulating this morning." She shook her head.

"Any idea who didn't think he was a sweetheart?"

"No one I can think of."

"What about Tanner Cole?"

Brittany blinked. "Even if he came back from the dead, he wouldn't have hurt Alex. They were friends."

Liza smiled. She liked the woman's sense of humor. "Do you know why Tanner killed himself?"

"No. I suppose someone told you that Tanner and I were dating at the time." Brittany chuckled as she realized whom. "Shelby. Of course."

"She did mention that if anyone knew, it would be you. Did Tanner seem depressed?"

"Far from it. He was excited about graduating. He had all these plans for what he was going to do. I think he already had his bags packed."

"He was planning to leave Big Sky?"

"Oh, yeah. He'd been saving his money for years. He wanted to backpack around Europe before college. He had a scholarship to some big college back east."

"What about you?"

"I was headed for Montana State University."

"Weren't you upset that he was leaving?"

She shook her head as she helped herself to another cookie. Upstairs, Liza could hear the kids squabbling over the water and towels. "It wasn't like that between me and Tanner. I liked him. A lot. But I knew from the get-go that it wasn't serious."

"Had it been serious between him and Shelby?"

Brittany stopped chewing for a moment. She sighed and let out a chuckle. "If you talk to Shelby it was. She was planning to marry him, apparently. She loved his parents' ranch and used to talk about when she and Tanner lived on the place, what their lives were going to be like."

"She must have been upset when he broke it off and started dating you."

Brittany laughed. "Livid. But Tanner told me he'd just gone through a scare with her. She'd apparently gotten pregnant."

"On purpose?"

"Tanner thought so. He said he'd dodged a bullet when she miscarried…" Brittany seemed to realize what she'd said. "So to speak. Anyway, he didn't trust her after that, said he didn't want anything to do with her. They broke up right before Christmas. She'd been so sure he would be putting an engagement ring under the tree for her."

"How could Shelby have thought that was going to happen?" Liza asked. "Surely she knew what Tanner was planning to do once they graduated."

"Sure, she knew, but Shelby was so used to getting what she wanted, I think she'd just convinced herself it was going to happen."

"Maybe she thought a baby would be the tipping point," Liza suggested.

"And it probably would have been. Tanner loved kids. He wanted a bunch when he settled down. If she had been pregnant, I still don't think he would have married her, but he would have stuck around to help raise his child. He was that kind of guy. But he was over Shelby. Nothing could have made him go back to her."

"Did she know that?" Liza asked.

Brittany broke a cookie in half and played in the icing for a moment. "I think she did. She really was heartbroken. She cried hysterically at the funeral. I'd never seen her like that. I actually felt sorry for her."

"But you didn't feel sorry enough not to go out with Tanner."

Brittany shrugged. "It was high school. Tanner asked me out. He was a nice guy and a lot of fun. Shelby knew it wasn't serious. She didn't blame me."

"But she did Tanner?"

Brittany smiled. "Let me put it this way. If Shelby was the kind to make voodoo dolls and stick pins in them, she would have had one with Tanner's name on it. But she moved on quick enough. Tanner was barely in the ground before she was dating Wyatt Iverson. One thing about Shelby, she seems to bounce back pretty fast."

"Wyatt Iverson of Iverson Construction?" Liza said. "Isn't that the same construction company that Tanner was working for at the time of his death?"

Brittany nodded and got up to go to the bottom of the stairs to yell up at the kids to quit fighting. When she came back she began to clean up the kitchen. "Wyatt was four years ahead of us in school, so I didn't really know him. But later that summer his father went bankrupt, shot Harris Lancaster and went to prison. Malcolm was never the same after that, I guess. He died in a boating accident. At least that's what they called it. He drowned up on Canyon Ferry. Everyone suspected he killed himself. I've gotten to know Wyatt a little since then. He never got over what happened with his father. That's one reason he's worked so hard to get the construction company going again." She looked up. "Sorry, that's probably a whole lot more than you wanted to hear."

"You like Wyatt."

Brittany smiled at that. "*Like* might be a little strong. He and Shelby are cut from the same cloth. Both go after what they want and the rest be damned." She frowned. "Why all the questions about Tanner?"

"Tanner was Alex's friend."

"And now they're both dead," Brittany said with a nod.

"With all Tanner's plans, he doesn't sound like someone who would commit suicide before graduation. Was anything else going on in his life that you knew of? Maybe with his parents, his friends?"

Brittany shook her head. "His parents are still happily married and still live on the ranch. His friends were fine—well, that is, they were until last night." She sighed. "There was the vandalism, though."

"*Vandalism?*" Liza asked.

"Tanner was staying in the cabin at the construction site in payment for watching over Malcolm Iverson's equipment. There was a party at the cabin one night. The next morning, Malcolm discovered his equipment had been vandalized. Tanner blamed himself."

"Enough to kill himself?"

"I didn't think so at the time. Wyatt didn't even blame Tanner. The party hadn't been his idea in the first place. Tanner was really responsible, but everyone showed up with beer and things must have gotten out of hand. But who knows. Maybe Tanner was taking it harder than any of us knew. Wyatt talked his father into letting Tanner stay at the cabin even after the vandalism. So I really don't think that had anything to do with Tanner's death."

"Well, thank you for the information," Liza said.

"It's kind of strange, though. I heard Jordan Cardwell was back in the canyon—and that he was at the falls when Alex was shot?"

"Why is that strange if they were friends?"

"Because he and Alex had a huge falling-out the night of the party."

Liza felt her pulse quicken. "Over what?"

"I never knew. I just remember Tanner refused to take sides. He said they'd work it out."

"Did they?"

"Not that I know of. Jordan left right after graduation and seldom came back. I'm not sure he and Alex ever spoke again."

"Could it have been over a girl?"

Brittany laughed. "Isn't it always?"

"So who would that girl have been?"

"If I had to guess, I'd say Tessa Ryerson. Shelby's BFF."

Liza laughed. "Best friend forever? Is that still true?"

Brittany nodded and crossed her fingers. "Shelby and Tessa, they're like this and always have been. I was surprised when Jordan went out with Tessa since he never could stand Shelby."

DANA HAD DOZED OFF FOR A WHILE, she realized. She woke to find Hud lying on the bed next to her. Listening, she could hear the sound of their children's voices coming from the kitchen along with that of her sister's. She placed a hand on her stomach, felt her two babies and tried to relax. Nothing seemed to be amiss and yet, when she'd awakened...

"What's wrong?" she asked, turning her head to look at her husband.

Hud was staring at the ceiling. "You're going to think I'm crazy."

"I've never thought you were anything but completely sane in all instances," she joked.

"I'm serious," he said, rolling over on his side to look at her.

She saw the worry etched in his handsome face. "What?"

"You aren't going to want to hear this."

"Hud!"

"Something's wrong," he said. "I feel it."

She sighed. "Your marshal intuition again?" She felt her eyes widen, her heartbeat kicking up a notch. "About the murder investigation?"

"It's your sister."

She groaned and, shaking her head, turned to look at the ceiling. "What are you saying?"

"Have you noticed the way she is with the baby?" he demanded, keeping his voice down even though the bedroom door was closed.

Dana hadn't noticed. Usually when her sister brought the baby in, she would hand Ella to her to hold.

"It's as if she has never changed a diaper," Hud was saying.

"She's probably nervous because you're watching her. She's new at this."

He shook his head. "She stares at Ella, I swear, as if she's never seen her before. Not just that," he rushed on. "She arrived with hardly any clothes for the baby and when she came back from buying baby food, I asked her what Ella's favorite was and she said carrots. You should have seen her trying to feed Ella carrots—"

"Stop. Do you realize how ridiculous you sound?" She'd turned to look at him again. "I repeat, what are you *saying?*"

Hud clamped his mouth shut for a moment, his eyes dark. "Okay, I'll just say it. I don't think that baby is hers. In fact, I don't even think the baby's name is Ella. That baby quilt has the name Katie stitched on it."

"Okay, you are *crazy,*" Dana said. "The quilt is probably one she picked up at a secondhand store or a friend lent it to her."

"A friend? Has she received even one phone call since she's been here?" He shook his head. "No, that's because your sister doesn't have friends. She never has."

"You don't know that she hasn't made friends the past six years."

"How could she? She moves around all the time. At least that's her story. And what does she do for money, huh?"

"She didn't go to college or learn a trade so of course she has a hard time supporting herself." Dana knew she was grasping at any explanation, but she couldn't stop herself. "One look at Stacy and you can see she doesn't have much. It's probably the best she can do right now. And you know babies can change their food likes and dislikes in an afternoon. As for diapering…"

Hud shook his head stubbornly.

"Is she helping with the kids?"

"Sure, she seems right at home with a four- and five-year-old." He sighed. "I still have a hard time trusting Stacy."

"I know. She stole five years from us, breaking us up with one of her lies so I understand why you would question everything about her now." Dana didn't want to admit that she had felt the same way around her sister. But when she saw her sister with Ella—

"Okay," Hud said. "After dinner I might check in with Liza and see how the investigation is going." He placed a large hand on her belly and waited for their twins to move as if needing reassurance.

She could see that it was hell for him having a murder investigation going on while he was home playing Candy Land and Old Maid. But she saw something else in his expression, as well. "You're going to your office to do more than check in, aren't you? You're going to investigate my sister."

"I just want to do some checking on her. Just to relieve my mind."

She knew there would be no stopping him no matter what she said. "I want to get to know my niece. After everything that has happened between us and Stacy, it wouldn't take much for us to never see her or Ella again."

"If Ella isn't her baby—"

"You're wrong. So go ahead and see what you can find out."

He bent down to kiss her before getting to his feet. "You're probably right about everything."

Dana nodded as he left the room. But she hated that she didn't feel sure about anything right now. To make matters worse she was trapped in bed, her children were out making clay with a woman who her husband thought might be a kidnapper and meanwhile, her brother Jordan was involved in a murder case.

All she needed right now was for her younger brother, Clay, to show up.

Her babies moved. She splayed her fingers over them, whispered that she loved them and did her best not to cry.

Chapter Seven

Jordan hadn't been back to the cabin long when he heard a knock at his door. He put his unfinished sandwich in the small kitchenette refrigerator, then peeked out the window. He was in no mood for company.

"You've been holding out on me," Liza said when he finally opened the door.

He'd let her knock for a while, then had given up that she wasn't going to take the hint and leave him alone. He was in no mood after his run-in with Tessa and no longer sure about Tanner's death any more than he was Alex's.

"I beg your pardon?" he said.

"Tessa Ryerson Spring. You dated her at the same time Tanner was dating Brittany."

He sighed and stepped back to let Liza in, not wanting to discuss this on the cabin stoop. "I'd forgotten I dated her."

"Uh-huh." The deputy marshal came into the small cabin and looked around. "Why did you and Alex fight over her?"

Jordan shook his head and laughed. "I don't recall."

She smiled. "Try again. It sounds as if it was quite the fight. Didn't speak to each other for years. Does that refresh your memory?" She sat down on the end of his bed and crossed her legs, leaning back on her hands, her gaze on him.

"Make yourself comfortable," he said sarcastically.

"I thought this might take a while."

He sighed and pulled out a chair from the small table that constituted the dining room. He straddled it and leaned his arms on the back as he looked at her. The woman was like a badger burrowing into a hole.

"Fine. It isn't something I like to talk about but since you're determined... Shelby talked Tessa into breaking up with Alex and going out with me so we could double date with Tanner and Brittany."

"Tessa was a spy?"

He nodded.

"But it doesn't explain why you dated Tessa. Or does it?" She grinned. "Brittany. You wanted to be close to her. Wow, what a tangled web we weave."

"Happy? When I found out what Shelby had done, I told Tessa off." He shrugged.

"Which explains why you and Alex got into a fight over her how exactly?"

"I might have called her some names. Alex took offense. When I told him how far Tessa would go to do Shelby's dirty work, he took a swing at me. I swung back. We were in high school. Stuff like that happened."

"Alex had forgotten all about it when he called to talk to you about Tanner?"

Jordan shrugged. "I assume so."

Liza got to her feet and walked around the cabin for a moment. "You all talk about high school as if it was kid stuff." She let out a chuckle. "You forget. *I* went to high school."

"That doesn't surprise me," Jordan quipped.

"Then this probably won't, either. I let mean things happen to other students. No, worse than that, sometimes I was part of those things. I ran into one of the girls who was terrorized recently. She told me that she still has scars from the way she was treated."

He said nothing, afraid she'd been that girl. Liza would have been just different enough that he suspected she hadn't been in a group like Shelby's. He'd sensed a rebellious spirit just under her surface, a fire that the girls who followed Shelby didn't have.

She suddenly turned to face him, her expression angry and defiant. "Don't tell me that what happened in high school didn't matter. It mattered to Tanner and now I believe it has something to do with Alex Winslow's death, as well. What I'm trying to understand is what *happened*."

"You and me both," he said, feeling guilty because he'd been one of the popular kids. In his teens he hadn't given much thought to those who weren't. "If it helps, I saw Tessa today." He held up a hand before she could berate him for getting involved in her investigation. "*She* sought me out. I went to get a sandwich and she came in. She either followed me or had been looking for me."

"What did she want?"

"I don't know. Maybe just information about Alex's death. I thought at first Shelby had sent her. But then Shelby drove past and Tessa got all scared and left."

"What did you tell her?"

"She asked why anyone would want Alex dead. I said it could have something to do with him asking around about Tanner's death."

The deputy sheriff let out an unladylike curse.

"I wanted to see her reaction."

"And?"

"It spooked the hell out of her. She knows something. When I was talking to her I had a thought. If Tanner *did* kill himself, it would have had to be over something big. What if Shelby didn't have a miscarriage? What if she lied about that, maybe as a test to see if Tanner loved her, who knows?"

"What are you suggesting, that she was never pregnant?"

"No, that she aborted the baby," he said. "That she did it out of meanness to get back at him. To hurt him in a way that would haunt him to his grave."

Liza said nothing for a few moments. "You think that little of Shelby?"

He met her gaze and held it. "Tessa is her best friend. She knows the truth. I also think she's scared of that truth coming out."

"Wait, even if you're right and Shelby did do something to get back at Tanner, that wouldn't be something that she'd kill Alex to keep secret."

"Couldn't it? Shelby is all about getting what she wants, whatever it takes, and Tessa and her other minions have always followed her blindly."

"You don't think they'd draw the line when it came to out-and-out murder?" Liza demanded.

"Not if they had something to do with Tanner's death. What's another body if Alex was getting too close to the truth?"

Liza nodded. "So your graduating class from Big Sky was small, right?"

Jordan reached behind him to pick up the crumpled

piece of paper he'd left on the table. "This is the list of people who RSVP'd that they would be attending the reunion this weekend," he said, handing it to her. "I marked the other two girls who ran with Shelby in high school. Ashley and Whitney."

Liza considered the wrinkled-up paper in her hand, then looked at him quizzically.

"I had to dig it out of the trash before I flew out here. I wasn't planning to attend—until Alex called. Then I was curious about who was coming."

"Let me guess," Liza said. "You're planning on going to the reunion now?"

He smiled. "Not without a date. What do you say? Come on, this way you can get to see all the players in their natural habitat."

Liza actually seemed at a loss for words for a moment. "I feel like you're asking me to the prom."

"If you're expecting a corsage, a rented limo, champagne and a fancy hotel room afterwards…" He saw her expression and stopped. "You didn't go to prom?"

"I'm not wearing a prom dress," she said, ignoring his question.

"Just don't wear your silver star or your gun," he joked, hating that he'd been right. She was one of the girls who'd been tormented by girls like Shelby and Tessa.

LIZA STOOD IN FRONT OF HER closet. She hated to admit how few dresses she owned—and what she did have were old and out of style, though hardly worn. Worse, she hated that she cared what she wore to the reunion.

She'd been a tomboy, so dresses had never really appealed to her. Add to that her profession, she'd had little need of anything besides jeans and boots.

"I don't know what I'm going to wear," she said when Dana answered the phone. "I know it doesn't matter. It's not like it's a date."

"No, going out with a suspect probably couldn't be called a date," her boss's wife agreed with a chuckle. "Come over. You're welcome to dig through my closet. I'll call Hilde. She's more girlie than either of us. She'll help."

"Thanks," Liza said, relieved. She definitely needed help.

"How is the investigation going?" Dana asked.

Liza knew Dana must be bored to tears now that she was being forced to stay in bed. "Slowly." She didn't want to admit that it brought up a lot of high school memories, ones she thought she'd left behind when she'd graduated.

"And Jordan?" Dana asked.

She didn't know how to answer that. "He's fine. Actually, I get the feeling he's changed. Don't worry," she said quickly. "If he hasn't, I'll be the first to know. He's still a suspect."

"But you don't think he killed Alex Winslow."

"No. I think he really did come back to find out what happened to his friend Tanner. It's looking like he had reason to be concerned."

Dana was silent for a moment. "Tell him to stop by, if he wants to."

"I will. I'll drop by later this afternoon for the clothing search." In the meantime, she thought, closing her closet door, she wanted to pay Tessa Ryerson Spring a visit.

DANA COULDN'T HELP THINKING of Jordan and half wishing she hadn't told Liza to have him stop by. Feeling the babies kick, she willed herself not to worry about Stacy or her brother. Instead, she put in a quick call to Hilde, who, of course, was delighted to help with Liza's clothing dilemma.

"I'll gather up some dresses and bring them over later," her best friend said. "Can I bring you anything?"

"Maybe some needlepoint from the store?" Dana suggested, cringing since the mere thought had always given her hives.

"Oh, girl, you really are bored to tears!" She laughed as she hung up.

After she'd found her mother's will and got to go back to ranching, Dana had become a silent partner in Needles and Pins, the small sewing shop she and Hilde had started in Meadow Village. She'd never been the one who sewed. That had been Hilde. But Dana had always loved working with her best friend in the shop.

She missed it sometimes. Not that she and the kids didn't often stop in to visit. Mary and Hank loved all the colorful bolts of fabric and Hilde always had some fun craft for them to do.

"Look what we made, Mommy!" Mary and Hank cried in unison now as they came running into the bedroom. They held up the clay figures, and Dana praised them for their imagination and their choice of multiple bright colors.

Behind them, Stacy stood in the doorway looking on with what appeared to be contentment. Dana had been watching her sister all day. She hated letting Hud's suspicions cloud her forgiving thoughts about Stacy. She'd missed having a sister all these years. Not that she and Stacy had been close like some sisters. There were no tea parties, doll playing or dressing up for pretend weddings.

Stacy had done all those things, but Dana had been an outside kid. She loved riding her horse, climbing trees, building forts. Two years older, Stacy had turned up her nose at most things Dana thought were fun and vice versa.

"Okay, let's clean up our mess," her sister told the kids. "I think that's your daddy who just drove up."

As they scampered out of the room, leaving a couple clay figures beside her bed to keep her company, Dana waited expectantly for Hud. She knew where he'd gone and what he'd been up to—running a check on her sister. A part of her feared what he might have discovered.

She listened. The moment he came in the house, Mary and Hank were all over him. He played with them for a moment, and, like her, praised everything they'd made before coming into the bedroom. When he closed the door, she knew the news wasn't going to be good.

LIZA COULDN'T SHAKE the feeling that Jordan was right about the two deaths being connected. While anxious to talk to Tessa Ryerson Spring, she went to the office and pulled out the Tanner Cole investigation file. There wasn't much in it since the coroner had ruled the death a suicide.

The incident had happened back up the North Fork where the victim had been staying in a cabin. His body had been found hanging from a tree limb in sight of the cabin, a rope noose around the victim's neck. There was evidence of a log stump having been dragged over under the limb of the tree. When the body was found, the stump was on its side, a good foot from the dead man's dangling boots. Cause of death was strangulation.

The victim was found by Jordan Cardwell, who'd gone looking for Tanner when he hadn't shown up for school.

Attached were a half dozen black-and-white photographs taken at the scene. She flipped through them, noticing that the tree where Tanner was found hanging was next to a fire ring. She could see that there were dozens of footprints around the scene, no doubt because the area had been used for a party. Other stumps had been dragged up around the campfire area. Numerous discarded beer cans could be seen charred black in the firepit.

As she started to put the file back, something caught her eye. The investigating officer had been Brick Savage—Hud's father.

HUD SMILED SHEEPISHLY at his wife after closing the door. She was watching him expectantly. He wished she didn't know him so well sometimes. Walking over to the bed, he bent down and, touching her cheek, kissed her. "You get more beautiful every day."

She swatted his hand playfully as he drew back. "If you think you can charm me—"

He laughed as she moved over to let him sit on the edge of the bed next to her. "Just speaking the truth." She *was* beautiful. The pregnancy had put a glow in her cheeks and her eyes. Not that she wasn't a stunner anytime. Dana had always smelled of summer, an indefinable scent that filled his heart like helium. He counted his blessings every day he woke up next to her.

"Okay, charmer, let's hear it," she said. "With you being so sweet, I'm guessing it's bad news."

He shook his head. "Am I that transparent?"

"Hud," she said impatiently.

"I didn't find out much. There wasn't much to find out. Apparently, she doesn't have credit cards or even a checking account."

"She's in the process of moving and not having credit cards is a good thing."

He sighed, seeing that she was determined to think the best. But then, that was Dana. But with her family, their history proved that he definitely had reason to be suspicious. He knew she wanted to believe that Stacy had changed. He did, too. He was just a whole lot more skeptical than Dana.

"A tiger doesn't change its spots," he said.

"Isn't it 'a zebra doesn't change its stripes' and what does that even mean?" she demanded.

"I had a look in her car last night after everyone went to bed. If she's moving to Great Falls, she sure didn't pack much." He held up his hand. "I know. She apparently doesn't have any money. But she gets the check from the ranch profits."

"You know that isn't enough to live on."

"Well, you'd think she would have had a job for the past six years."

"Stacy didn't go to college so more than likely she can't make much more than minimum wage."

He shook his head. "I could find no employment in her past."

"So she worked off the books somewhere. Or maybe the baby's father has been taking care of her and now she can't work because she has a baby to raise."

Yeah, Hud thought. That's what had Dana so desperate to believe Stacy had changed. That baby. Ella was cute as a bug's ear. No doubt about that. Just the thought of Stacy raising the child, though, terrified him.

"So that's all you found," Dana said.

He nodded. "No warrants or outstanding violations." No missing kids on Amber Alert who matched either the name Katie—or Ella's description.

"So there is nothing to worry about."

"Right." He just wished he could shake his uneasy feeling.

"And don't you go interrogating her," Dana said. "Give her the benefit of the doubt. She is in absolute awe of that baby. She couldn't be prouder of Ella. It's the first time I've seen my sister like this."

He nodded, not wanting to argue with her. He needed to keep Dana in this bed for their twins' sake. Placing a hand on her stomach, he felt their babies move. It had a calming effect on him. Just as being here with his family did.

But in the other room he could hear Stacy with the kids. Something wasn't right with her story. Call it his marshal intuition. But Stacy wasn't telling them the truth. And as much as he hated to think it, whatever she was lying about, it had something to do with that precious baby.

TESSA RYERSON SPRING didn't answer her phone so Liza drove over to the house. Getting out of the patrol SUV, she walked past the garage, noting that at least one vehicle was inside, before she rang the doorbell.

She had to ring it four times and knock hard before Tessa appeared. She'd wrapped a towel around her head and pulled a robe on, no doubt hoping Liza would think she'd been in the shower.

"I'm sorry," she said, looking more than a little flustered. "Have you been standing here long?"

Long enough. "Mind if I come in for a moment? Or you can come down to the office? Which works better for you?"

"Actually, I was just…" Tessa gave up and said, "I suppose I have a few minutes." She stepped aside to let Liza in. "I should make some coffee."

"No, thanks. Why don't we sit down for a minute." She could tell that Tessa wanted something to occupy herself. Jordan was right about one thing. Tessa was nervous and clearly afraid.

"This won't take long," Liza assured her.

The woman finally perched on the edge of the couch. Liza took a chair across from her. Like many of the residences at Big Sky, the decor was made to look like the Old West from the leather furniture to the antler lamps. The floor was hardwood, the rugs Native American, the fireplace local granite.

Tessa straightened the hem of her robe to cover whatever she was wearing beneath it, then fiddled with the sash.

"I'm here about Alex Winslow's death."

"Oh?" Her smile was tentative. "Why would you want to talk to *me?*"

"You were a friend of his in high school."

"Yes, but that was twenty years ago."

"But you talked to him recently. The calls were on his cell phone," Liza said.

Tessa's eyes widened with alarm. Her hand went to her forehead as if suddenly struck with a migraine.

Clearly she hadn't expected anyone to know about the calls.

"I'm curious what you talked about," Liza said.

After a moment the woman pulled herself together. "I'm sorry. I'm just upset. I heard he was murdered?"

"So what did you talk about?"

"The reunion. Shelby must have told him to call me. I'm in charge of the picnic on Sunday. It's going to be at the top of the gondola. Weather permitting, of course." Her smile was weak, nervous. She worked at the robe sash with her fingers, toying with the edges.

"You and Alex dated in high school."

She nodded. "For a short while."

"But you were close?"

"I'm not sure what you mean."

"I mean Alex trusted you. He would have confided in you."

"I don't know what you're asking."

"He would have told you if he had some reason to suspect that Tanner Cole didn't kill himself." The statement had the effect Liza had hoped for.

Fear shone in the woman's eyes. Her hand went to her throat. Jordan was right. She knew *something*.

"Had you ever been up to the cabin where Tanner was staying that spring before high school graduation?" Liza asked.

"I might have."

"With Alex?"

"Maybe. I really can't remember."

"Do you knit?" Liza asked.

"What?"

"I wondered if you knitted because this case started like a loose thread in a sweater. At first it was just a small problem, but once it started unraveling…" She shook her head. "Alex started it unraveling. Now it's going to come apart. No doubt about it."

Tessa managed a smile. "That's an odd simile."

"Metaphor," Liza said. "It's a metaphor for murder. Alex was just the beginning. As this unravels, more people are going to die. Because even though you believe you can keep this secret, whoever killed Alex is afraid you can't. You see how this works? You just can't trust each other anymore and when push comes to shove…"

"I'm sorry, Deputy," Tessa said, getting to her feet. "I have no idea what you're talking about and I'm running late for an appointment. She held her head in a regal manner. Liza got a glimpse of the girl Tessa had been when she and Shelby and the others had been on the pinnacle of popularity and thought nothing could bring them down. But as they all seemed fond of saying, "that was high school." This was real life.

"Think about it, Tessa. If they think you're the weak link, they'll attack you like rabid dogs." Liza rose. "I'll see myself out."

Chapter Eight

Jordan hadn't seen his father since the last time he was in Montana. They talked once in a while by phone, but they really didn't have much to say to each other.

For a long time Jordan blamed his mother for the divorce, believing she cared more about the ranch than she did her husband. There was probably some truth in that. But the divorce wasn't all her fault. She hadn't driven his father away. Angus Cardwell was more than capable of doing that himself.

He found his father at Angus's favorite watering hole, the Corral, down the canyon from Big Sky. Angus had been one handsome cowboy in his day. It was easy to see even now why Mary Justice had fallen in love with him.

Unfortunately, Jordan's mother had loved ranching and her husband had loved bars and booze. The two hadn't mixed well. Angus had taken the healthy settlement Mary had offered him and had left amicably enough. He'd made the money last by working an odd job here and there, including cash he and his brother made playing in a Country-Western band.

Most of the time, though, Angus could be found on a

bar stool—just as he was now. And most of the time his brother Harlan would be with him—just as he was now.

"Well, look what the cat dragged in," Angus said as Jordan made his way down the bar toward them. Like all out-of-the-way Montana bars, everyone had looked up to see who'd come through the door. Angus and Harlan were no exceptions.

"Hey, Bob," his father called to the owner as he slid off his stool to shake Jordan's hand and pound him on the back. "You remember my eldest."

Bob nodded, said hello and dropped a bar napkin in front of an empty stool next to Angus. Uncle Harlan nodded his hello and Angus patted the stool next to him and said, "What would you like to drink, son?"

Jordan wasn't in the mood for a drink, but he knew better than to say so. Angus took it personally when anyone wouldn't drink with him—especially his son. "I'll take a beer. Whatever's on tap."

Bob poured him a cold one and set it on the napkin, taking the money out of the twenty Angus had beside his own beer.

"What are you doing in Montana?" Uncle Harlan asked.

"I was just asking myself that same thing," Jordan said and took a sip of his beer. He could feel his father's gaze on him. News traveled fast in the canyon. Angus and Harlan would have heard about the shooting night before last.

He braced himself for their questions. To his surprise, that wasn't the first thing his father wanted to know.

"Been to see your sister yet?" Angus asked.

"Not yet. I wasn't sure Dana would want to see me."

"You know better than that." He took a drink of his beer. "That is, unless you're going to try to hit her up for money. No one will want to see you in that case."

Jordan shook his head. "I'm not here looking for money."

"In that case," his father said with a laugh, "you can buy the next round."

Two beers later Jordan asked his father if he remembered when Tanner Cole died.

Angus nodded solemnly. "He hung himself up by that construction site. I remember he was staying up there because there'd been some vandalism."

"There'd been some before Tanner moved into the cabin?" Jordan asked in surprise.

Angus nodded. "Couldn't prove who did it, but Malcolm Iverson was pretty sure it was his competitor, Harris Lancaster, trying to put him out of business. So he hired the kid to keep an eye on things."

Jordan hadn't known about the earlier vandalism or that Iverson had suspected Harris Lancaster.

"Malcolm probably couldn't have survived financially the way things were going even if his equipment hadn't been vandalized a second time," Uncle Harlan said. "Your friend must have taken it hard, though, since everyone blamed it for forcing Iverson into bankruptcy. Apparently, he'd let his equipment insurance lapse."

"How did I never hear this?" Jordan said.

"You were a senior in high school," his father said with a laugh. "You had your nose up some girl's skirt. You were lucky you even graduated."

"Tanner never said anything about this," he said more to himself than to his father and uncle.

Angus tipped his beer up, took a swallow, then turned his gaze on his son. "You can't blame yourself. Malcolm had no business hiring a kid to watch over his equipment. I'm just sorry you had to be the one to find your friend like that."

Jordan nodded, remembering the day he'd gone up to the construction site looking for Tanner. He'd been worried about him since it wasn't like Tanner to miss school.

He'd never forget parking and walking up the road to find the front door of the cabin open. He'd called Tanner's name and gotten no answer and yet, his friend's pickup had been sitting next to the cabin.

One glance and he'd seen that it was empty. He'd heard the creaking sound and at first thought it was a tree limb scraping against another limb.

It wasn't until he turned toward the fire pit where the party had been held the night of the vandalism that he saw the shadow. A breeze had stirred the pines, making the shadow flicker over the dead campfire. He'd called Tanner's name again, then with a sinking feeling he'd followed the creaking sound until he saw what was casting the long shadow over the fire ring.

He would never forget the sight of his best friend hanging from the tree limb.

Jordan took a drink of his beer, cleared his throat and said, "I never believed that Tanner killed himself. I knew he blamed himself for the vandalism because of the party up there that night, but now with Alex murdered... I have to find out what really happened."

"If I were you, I'd stay out of it," Angus said, looking worried. "Two of your friends are dead. Whatever's going on, you might be next."

LIZA HAD TO ADMIT IT. She was having fun. She and Dana had hit it off from the first time they'd met and Hilde was a whole lot of fun.

"Oh, you have to try this one," Hilde said as she pulled a black-and-white polka-dot dress from the huge pile she'd brought. "It's one of my favorites."

They'd been laughing and joking as Liza tried on one dress after another. Hilde had kidded Dana after exploring her closet and deeming it probably worse than Liza's.

"You cowgirls," Hilde said. "Jeans, jeans, jeans. Don't you ever just want to show off your legs?"

"No," Liza and Dana had said in unison.

The polka-dot dress was cute and it fit Liza perfectly. "Do you think it's *too* cute? Maybe it's not dressy enough," Liza asked.

"Come on, this is Montana, no one dresses up," Dana said.

Hilde rolled her eyes. "Sweetie, this is Big Sky and all the women will be dressed to the nines. The men will be wearing jeans, boots and Western sports jackets, but for these women, this is a chance to pull out all those expensive clothes, bags and high heels they're just dying to show off."

"Then I'm wearing this," Liza said, studying her reflection in the mirror. She loved the black-and-white polka-dot dress. "This is as dressy as this cowgirl is going to get."

Dana laughed. "Good for you."

As Liza changed back into her jeans, boots and uniform shirt, Dana said, "So have you seen my brother?"

She shook her head. "Not since earlier. I haven't had a chance to talk to him, either."

"He is still a suspect, right?" Hilde asked, sounding worried.

Liza realized that her two friends were worried about her being taken in by Jordan. She had to smile, warmed by their concern.

"I hope I don't have to remind you that he was best friends with both Tanner and Alex and now they're both dead," Hilde said. "I grew up around Jordan. He always had a temper." She shot a look at Dana, who nodded, though with obvious regret.

"People change," Liza said, instantly regretting coming to Jordan's defense. She saw Hilde and Dana exchange a look. *"What?"*

"It's Stacy. I think *she's* changed," Dana said.

"You *hope* she's changed," Hilde corrected.

"Hud told me he was doing some checking into her past," Liza said. "I assume he didn't find anything."

"That's just it, he found nothing and that has him even more worried," Dana said. "Him and his marshal intuition."

Liza laughed. "Don't be joking around about our intuition." She'd been a green deputy six years ago, but Hud had taken her under his wing after seeing what he called an instinct for the job. Now he trusted her to handle this investigation and that meant everything to her.

The three women visited for a while longer, then Liza said she had to get moving. "The cocktail party and dinner is tonight. I've studied up on the players. Jordan had a list of those attending. Surprisingly, or maybe not, all eight of the Big Sky senior graduates will be up at Mountain Village tonight. Everyone but Alex and Tanner, that is." It was a small class twenty years ago. Although they attended high school down in Bozeman, they wanted their own reunion up here. Only in the past few years had Big Sky gotten its own high school.

"Just be careful," Dana said. "I know a few of those women." She pretended to shudder. "They're vicious."

"I don't think they're that bad," Hilde said. "I work out at Yogamotion. They're nice to me."

This time Dana and Liza exchanged a look. Hilde was petite, blonde and lithe. She would fit right in.

Dana reached for Liza's hand and squeezed it. "Just don't forget that one of them could be a killer."

JORDAN HAD SPENT THE REST of the afternoon writing down everything he could remember about his senior year of high school, especially what might pertain to Tanner and Alex.

The trip down memory lane had exhausted him. When he glanced at his watch, he'd been shocked to see how late it was. He quickly showered and changed and drove over to pick up his date.

What surprised him was the frisson of excitement he felt as he rang Liza's bell. He realized with a start that he hadn't been on a real date in years. Since his divorce he'd stayed clear of women.

When he'd left the canyon, he'd shed the cowboy side of him like an old snakeskin. He'd wanted bright lights and big city. He'd wanted sophistication. He'd kicked the Montana ranch dust off his boots and hadn't looked back.

That was how he'd ended up married to Jill. He'd been flattered that a model would even give him a second look. She'd been thrilled that he came from Montana ranch stock, saying she was bored with New York City–type men.

What he hadn't realized was that Jill thought he had money. She'd thought the ranch was the size of Ted Turner's apparently and couldn't wait to get her hands on the funds it would bring in once it sold.

He'd gotten caught up in trying to make her happy, even though she'd quit modeling the moment they were married and spent her days spending more money than he could make on Wall Street.

Now he could admit that he had become obsessed with keeping her. Although he hadn't acknowledged it to himself back then, he'd known that if he ran out of money, Jill would run out on him.

And she had—just as Dana had predicted. He hadn't wanted to hear it six years ago. Hell, he didn't like to think about it even now. The truth hurt. He'd fought back, of course, driving an even wider wedge between himself and his younger sister.

When Dana had discovered their mother's new will in that damned cookbook at the ranch house, Jill had realized there would be no ranch sale, no gold at the end of the rainbow, and she'd split. In truth, she'd already had some New York male model lined up long before that.

It had been some hard knocks, but he felt as if they had maybe knocked some sense into him. He saw things clearer than he had before. Mary Justice Cardwell had tried to instill values in her children. He'd rejected most of them, but they were still at his core, he thought as he rang Liza Turner's doorbell again.

When the door opened, he was taken completely off guard by the woman standing there. Liza took his breath away. She was wearing a black-and-white polka-dot dress that accentuated curves he'd had no idea were beneath her uniform. Her beautiful long curly hair had been pulled up, wisps of curls framing her face and she smelled heavenly.

"Wow, you look killer," he said when he caught his breath.

"So to speak," she said, sounding embarrassed as she quickly stuffed her gun into her purse. "My feet already hurt in these shoes."

He smiled at her. "You can kick them off the minute we hit the dance floor."

"Dance floor?" she asked, cocking an eyebrow.

"Didn't I mention I do one hell of a two-step?"

She took him in, her gaze pausing on his cowboy boots.

"Dana had a box of my clothes dropped off at the cabin," he said, feeling sheepish. It was so like Dana to be thoughtful. He'd found the boots as well as a couple of dress Western shirts and a Western-cut sports coat. He'd been surprised when everything still fit.

"You are a man of many surprises," she said, sounding almost as if she meant it.

He laughed. "You haven't seen anything yet." As he walked her to his rental SUV, he breathed in her scent, thinking he couldn't wait to get this woman in his arms on the dance floor.

DANA SUCKED ON HER BLEEDING finger. Needlepoint wasn't for her, she decided after jabbing herself another time. She surveyed her stitches and cringed. As Stacy came into the bedroom, she tossed the needlepoint aside, glad for an interruption.

Earlier, Mary and Hank had come in and colored

with her before their naps. She missed holding them on her lap, missed even more riding horses with them around the corral. All these beautiful fall days felt wasted lying in bed. But Hud had promised to take both kids out tomorrow.

As Stacy came over to the side of her bed, Dana saw that her sister had the cookbook open to their mother's double chocolate brownies.

"Is it all right if I make these?" Stacy asked.

They were Hud's favorite. That's why Mary Justice Cardwell had tucked her new will in her old, worn and faded cookbook next to the recipe. She'd wanted Dana not only to have the ranch—but the man she loved beside her.

"Sure. Hud would like that," Dana said, disappointed she couldn't even do something as simple as bake a pan of brownies for her husband.

"Mother used to make them for Dad, remember? Do you ever see him?"

"On occasion. Usually a holiday. He and Uncle Harlan keep pretty busy with their band." And their drinking, but she didn't say that.

Stacy nodded. "I might see them while I'm here. Maybe tomorrow if you don't mind me leaving for a little while in the morning?"

"Stacy, you don't need to ask. Of course you can go. Hud will be here."

"I suppose I know where I'll find Dad. Would you mind keeping Ella? I won't go until I put her down for her morning nap. I don't want to take her to a bar."

"I would be happy to watch her. You can bring her in here for her nap. She'll be fine while you're gone."

Stacy smiled, tears in her eyes, and gave Dana an

impulsive though awkward hug. "I've missed you so much."

"I've missed you, too."

Her sister drew back, looking embarrassed, grabbed the cookbook and left. In the other room, Hud was playing fort with the kids. She could see a corner of the couch and chairs pulled into the middle of the room and covered with spare blankets.

Hud caught her eye. He smiled and shrugged as if to say, maybe she was right about her sister. Dana sure hoped so.

LIZA BRACED HERSELF AS JORDAN ushered her into the lodge at Mountain Village for the Friday-night dinner and dance. Tomorrow there would be a tour of Big Sky and a free afternoon, with the final picnic Sunday.

A room had been prepared for the reunion party that impressed her more than she wanted to admit. A DJ played music under a starry decor of silver and white. The lights had been turned low, forming pockets of darkness. Candles flickered at white-clothed tables arranged in a circle around the small shining dance floor.

A few couples were dancing. Most were visiting, either standing next to the bar or already seated at the cocktail tables.

"Hilde was right," Liza whispered. "I *am* underdressed." The women were dressed in fancy gowns and expensive accessories. The men wore jeans and boots and Western sports jackets, looking much like Jordan.

"You look beautiful, the prettiest woman here," Jordan said, putting his arm around her protectively.

She grinned over at him. "You really can be charming when you want to, Mr. Cardwell."

"Don't tell Hud," he said. "I've spent years cultivating his bad opinion of me. I'd hate to ruin it with just one night with you." He put his hand on her waist. "Let's dance." He drew her out on the dance floor and pulled her close. She began to move to the slow song, too aware of her dance partner and his warm hand on her back.

Jordan *was* full of surprises. He was light on his feet, more athletic than she'd thought and a wonderful dancer. He held her close, the two of them moving as one, and she lost herself in the music and him as she rested her cheek against his shoulder. He smelled wonderful and she felt safe and protected in his arms. The latter surprised her.

The night took on a magical feel and for the length of several Country-Western songs, she forgot why she and Jordan were here. She also forgot that he was a murder suspect.

When the song ended, she found herself looking at him as if seeing him for the first time. He appeared completely at home in his Western clothes. They suited him and she told him so.

He smiled at that. "I thought I'd dusted the cowboy dirt off me when I left here. My mother used to say this land and life were a part of me that I could never shed." He quickly changed the subject as if he hadn't meant to tell her those things. "Looks like everyone is here except for Tessa, Alex and Tanner. That's the nice thing about having a small graduating class. They're fairly easy to keep track of. Shall we get a drink?"

They'd done just that by the end of the next song when Shelby took the stage. She gave a short speech, updating anyone who didn't know about the members of the class, announced who had come the farthest, who had changed the most, who had the most kids.

"I thought we should have a few minutes of silence for Alex," she said at the end. "Since he can't be with us tonight."

Liza spotted Tessa, who'd apparently just arrived. There was chatter about the murder around the tables, then everyone grew silent. It seemed to stretch on too long. Liza found herself looking around the room at the graduates.

She quickly picked out the main players Jordan had told her about. Shelby and her husband, contractor Wyatt Iverson; Tessa, who'd come alone; Whitney Fraser and husband and local business owner, Von; and Ashley Henderson and husband, Paul, had all congregated to one area of the room. Ashley and her husband and Whitney and hers appeared to be cut from the same cloth as Shelby and Wyatt. Brittany Peterson and husband, Lee, were visiting at a table of former students who were no longer Big Sky residents.

As Liza took them all in, she knew that what she was really looking for was a killer.

Wyatt Iverson was as handsome and put-together as his wife, Shelby. Liza waited until he went to the bar alone before she joined him.

"Wyatt Iverson? I don't think we've met. I'm Liza Turner—"

"Deputy marshal in charge of the Alex Winslow case," he said with a wide smile. "I know. I checked. I wanted to make sure someone capable was on the case. I heard great things about you."

"Thank you." She recalled a rumor going around that Wyatt was considering getting into national politics.

Right now he served on a variety of boards as well as on the local commission. Wyatt was handsome and a smooth talker, a born politician and clearly a man with a driving ambition. He'd brought his father's business back from bankruptcy and made a name for himself, not to mention a whole lot of money apparently.

Shelby joined them, taking her husband's arm and announcing that dinner was being served in the dining room. "Everyone bring your drinks and follow me!" Ashley and Whitney fell into line and trailed after Shelby, just as Tessa did, but according to Jordan they'd been doing that for years.

To no one's surprise, Shelby had distributed place cards around a long table. Liza was surprised to see that she and Jordan were near the center, with Tessa and Brittany and her husband, Lee, at one end and Shelby's inner circle at the other.

She noticed that Tessa seemed surprised—and upset—when she found herself at the far end of the table. Clearly Tessa had done something Shelby hadn't liked. Either that or Shelby was sending her friend a message. If Shelby had anything to do with Alex's murder and Tessa knew about it, Liza feared that Tessa might get more than banished at the reunion dinner table. Whatever had Shelby upset with her could get Tessa killed just as it had Alex.

Chapter Nine

Jordan could have wrung Shelby's neck even before dinner was served. They'd all just sat down when Shelby insisted everyone go around the table and introduce their dates and spouses before dinner was served.

When it came Jordan's turn, he squeezed Liza's hand and said, "This is my date, Liza Turner."

"Oh, come on, Jordan," Shelby said. "Liza Turner is our local deputy marshal and the woman in charge of investigating Alex's murder." She smiled as she said it, but Jordan couldn't miss the hard glint in her eyes. "So, Deputy, tell us how the case is going."

"It's under investigation, that's all I can tell you," Liza said.

Shelby pretended to pout, making Jordan grit his teeth. "Oh, we were hoping as Alex's friends we could get inside information."

Jordan just bet she was. Fortunately, the staff served dinner and the conversations turned to other things.

"How have you been?" Brittany asked him. She was still as strikingly beautiful as she'd been in high school, but now there was a contentment about her.

"Good. You look happy," he said, glad for her.

"My life is as crazy as ever with three small ones

running around and…" She grinned. "Another one on the way. Surprise!"

"Congratulations," Jordan said, meaning it. She didn't seem in the least bit upset to be seated away from Shelby and her other classmates. Unlike Tessa, who hadn't said a word or hardly looked up since sitting down.

Everyone offered their congratulations to Brittany, including Shelby, who seemed to have her ears trained on their end of the table.

"How many does this make now?" she asked.

"Four, Shelby," Brittany said, smiling although Jordan could tell Shelby irritated her as much as she did him.

Shelby pretended shock. "I think you get the award for most children and also our Look Who's Pregnant! Award."

Jordan glanced over at Liza. He knew she was taking all of this in. Like him, he was sure she'd noticed the way Tessa had been acting since they'd sat down. Also, Tessa had been hitting the booze hard every time she could get the cocktail waitress's attention.

Jordan couldn't have been happier when dessert was finally served. Shelby had been running the dinner as if it was a board meeting. He noticed that, like Tessa, Shelby had been throwing down drinks. Just the sound of her voice irritated him. He was reminded why he hadn't wanted to come to his reunion.

"Jordan, what was the name of your wife, the one who was the model?" Shelby asked loudly from the other end of the table.

He didn't want to talk about his marriage or his divorce. But he knew Shelby wasn't going to let it go.

"Jill Ames. She was my *only* wife, Shelby," he said and felt Liza's calming hand on his thigh.

"Jill Ames is *gorgeous.* What were you thinking letting her get away?" Shelby said and laughed. She gave Liza a sympathetic look. "Jill Ames would be a hard act to follow."

"Shelby, you might want to back off on the drinks," Brittany said, throwing down her napkin as she shoved to her feet. "Your claws are coming out." She shot Jordan and Liza an apologetic look and excused herself before heading for the ladies' room. Shelby glared after her for a moment, then followed her.

LIZA WAITED UNTIL SHELBY disappeared down the hallway before she, too, excused herself. She was within ten feet of the ladies' room door when she heard their raised voices. She slowed, checked to make sure there was no one behind her, before she stepped to the door and eased it open a few inches. She could see the two reflected in the bathroom mirrors, but neither could see her.

"How dare you try to embarrass me," Shelby screeched into Brittany's face.

"Embarrass *you?* Seriously, Shelby?" Brittany started to turn away from her.

Shelby grabbed her arm. "Don't you turn your back on me."

"Touch me again and I'll deck you," Brittany said as she jerked free of the woman's hold. "I don't do yoga every day like you, but I do haul around three kids so I'm betting I'm a lot stronger and tougher than you are. I'm also not afraid of you anymore."

"Well, you should be."

"Are you threatening me?" Brittany demanded as

she advanced on her. "This isn't high school, Shelby. Your reign is over." She turned and went into a stall.

Shelby stood as if frozen on the spot, her face white with fury as Liza stepped into the ladies' room. Seeing the deputy marshal, Shelby quickly spun around and twisted the handle on the faucet, hiding her face as she washed her hands.

Liza went into the first stall. She heard Brittany flush, exit the next stall and go to the washbasin. Through the sound of running water, she heard Shelby hiss something.

"Whatever, Shelby." Brittany left, but a moment later someone else came in.

"Aren't you talking to me? What's going on?" Tessa whined, sounding like a child. "Are you mad at me? I don't understand. I haven't done *anything.*"

She was sure Shelby was probably trying to signal that they weren't alone, but Tessa was clearly upset and apparently not paying attention.

"I told you I wouldn't say anything. You know you can trust me. So why are you—"

"Tessa, this really isn't the place," Shelby snapped.

"But all evening you've—"

Liza had no choice but to flush. As she opened the stall door, both Tessa and Shelby glanced in her direction. "Ladies," she said as she moved to the sinks and turned on the water.

"I could use some fresh air," Shelby said. "Come outside with me for a minute." She smiled as she took Tessa's arm and practically dragged her out of the bathroom.

Liza washed her hands, dried them and then stepped out. She could see Shelby and Tessa on the large deck in what was obviously a heated discussion. She watched them for a moment, wishing she could hear their conversation, but having no way to do that went back to the table and Jordan.

"Everything okay?" he asked quietly.

She smiled at him. "Great."

"I love your dress," Brittany said.

Liza laughed. "That's right. You like polka dots. I remember your apron." Liza liked Brittany. She could see why Jordan had had a crush on her in high school. Probably still did.

With dinner over, everyone began to wander away from the table and back into the first room where the music was again playing.

Liza pulled Jordan aside and told him what she'd overheard.

"So basically you just wanted to let me know I was right about Tessa," Jordan said, grinning.

"Apparently, you can be right once in a while, yes." She smiled back at him, realizing he was flirting with her again and she didn't mind it.

A few moments later Shelby came back in from the deck. She put her game face on again and breezed by them, already dancing to the music before she reached the dance floor. But she didn't fool Liza. Shelby was trying hard to hide whatever was really going on with her and Tessa.

"I'm going to talk to Tessa," Liza said. "Save me a dance."

As JORDAN LEFT THE DINING ROOM and joined the others, he spotted Shelby talking to her other two cohorts. Ashley and Whitney could have been sisters. They were both brunettes, both shapely, both pretty—at least from a distance. He knew his perception of them had been poisoned a long time ago.

He liked to think all of them had changed, himself included. But he could tell by the way Ashley and Whitney were listening to Shelby that they still followed her as blindly as they had in high school. It made him sad. Brittany had grown up, made a life for herself and seen through Shelby. But apparently Brittany was the only one who'd made the break from Shelby's control.

"Jordan, do you have a minute?"

He turned to find Paul Henderson, Ashley's husband. Paul had been two years ahead of them in school. "Sure," he said as Paul motioned to the empty lobby of the lodge.

"I hope I'm not speaking out of school here," Paul said. "But there's a rumor going around that Alex was asking about Tanner before he was…killed. I figured if you really were with him at the falls, then he must have talked to you."

"We didn't get a chance to talk," Jordan said, wondering if Paul had any information or if he was just fishing.

"Oh." He looked crestfallen.

"*You* talked to him?"

Paul nodded and met Jordan's gaze. "I wasn't sure if I should tell the deputy marshal."

"What did Alex tell you?"

He hesitated for a moment, then said, "Alex asked me if I remembered the party Tanner had that night at the cabin, the night the equipment was vandalized."

Jordan nodded. He vaguely remembered the party. He'd drunk too much and, after his fight with Tessa, had left early with some girl from Bozeman who he couldn't even remember. "Were you there?"

"No. I was grounded from the past weekend. He was asking if I knew where Shelby was that night."

"Shelby?"

"He wanted to know if Ashley had been with her."

"And was she?"

"That's just it. I told Alex that I thought she was because she called a little after two in the morning. She'd been drinking. We argued and I hung up. The next day when I asked her where she'd been the night before, she swore she didn't go to the party. But Alex said something about some photos from the party that night that proved not only were Ashley and Whitney there, but Shelby and Tessa were, too."

"Why was he interested in photos of the party?" Jordan asked.

Paul shrugged. "That's just it. I can't imagine what some photographs of a high school kegger twenty years ago could have to do with anything. That's why I haven't said anything to the deputy marshal."

"Did you ask Ashley about them?"

"She still swears she wasn't at the party that night, but…" He looked away for a moment. "I'd like to see those photos. Alex seemed to think there was something in them that could explain why Tanner is dead."

"I'll mention it to the deputy marshal," Jordan said. "She might want to talk to you."

Paul looked relieved. "I didn't know if I should say anything, but I'm glad I did. Okay, back to the party, huh?" He didn't look as if he was enjoying the reunion any more than Jordan had enjoyed dinner.

The only thing that kept Jordan from calling it quits was the thought of another dance with Liza.

TESSA STOOD AT THE DECK railing, her back to the lodge. She looked cold and miserable and from the redness around her eyes, she'd been crying.

Liza joined her at the railing. "Shelby's trying to bring you back under control, you know."

Tessa glanced over at her and let out a laugh. "I'd pretend I didn't know what you were talking about, but what would be the use?"

"Talk to me, Tessa. Tell me what Shelby is so terrified I'll find out?"

Tessa hugged herself and looked away. A breeze whispered in the nearby pines. Earlier it had been warm. Now though, the air had cooled. It carried the promise of winter. Closer, Liza could hear the muted music from inside the lodge. The party was resuming. She was betting that Shelby wouldn't leave Tessa out here long. If Liza didn't get the truth out of her quickly—

A door opened behind them. "Tessa?" Whitney called from the open doorway. "Shelby needs your help with the awards."

"I'll be right there," she said over her shoulder and started to turn toward the lodge.

"Tessa," Liza said, feeling her chance slipping through her fingers. She was genuinely afraid for Tessa. For some reason, the woman had been cut from the herd. Liza feared for the woman's life.

"Let me think about things. Maybe I'll stop by your office Monday."

Liza nodded. The one thing she'd learned was when to back off. "I can help you."

Tessa laughed at that and looked toward the lodge. "I'm not sure anyone can help me," she said and pushed off the railing to go back inside.

Liza bit down on her frustration. Tessa needed her best friend's approval. But surely she was tired of playing Shelby's game.

Telling herself this night hadn't been a total waste, Liza waited for a few moments before going back inside. The moment she saw Jordan, she thought, no, this night had definitely not been a waste.

He stood silhouetted in the doorway, reminding her that she'd come with the most handsome man at the party. Suspect or not, Jordan Cardwell was a pretty good date, she thought as he drew her into his arms and out on the dance floor.

Out of the corner of her eye she saw that Shelby had Tessa in the corner. Liza meet Tessa's gaze for a moment before the woman shoved away from Shelby and dragged Wyatt Iverson out on the floor to dance with her.

"You might want to talk to Paul Henderson," Jordan said, as they were leaving the reunion party a few dances later. "Apparently, Alex asked him about the party at the cabin that night. Alex thought there were photographs taken at the party that might have something to do with Tanner's death."

"Photographs?" Liza asked. She'd settled into the SUV's passenger seat, still feeling the warmth of being in Jordan's arms on the dance floor. She'd had fun even though she hated to admit it since she was supposed to be finding a murderer.

"Paul wasn't at Tanner's kegger, but he seems to think Ashley might have gone and lied about it."

"And how does all of this lead to Alex's death?" she asked, wanting to hear Jordan's take on it.

"Tanner was staying in a cabin up on the mountain to keep an eye on Iverson Construction equipment," he said as he drove. "He throws a party, the equipment gets vandalized, he gets in trouble. Malcolm Iverson, who is on the edge of bankruptcy, believes his competitor Harris Lancaster is behind the vandalism in an attempt to take over his business. Malcolm goes gunning for him, shoots Harris accidentally and goes to prison for a couple of years. When he gets out, he drowns in a boating accident." He looked over at her. "These things have to be connected and if there really are photographs from Tanner's party, then maybe they tie it all together—and explain why Tanner is dead."

"Tanner sounds like such a sensible kid," Liza said. "Why would he throw a party at the cabin with the construction equipment nearby?"

"He swore he didn't. People just started showing up. So he went with it. But after the equipment was vandalized, he felt horrible about it." He shrugged as he drove down the mountain. "I know he blamed himself."

"Was Tanner drinking a lot that night?"

Jordan sighed. "I don't know. I got drunk and left with some girl."

"So if these photographs exist, then they might not just show who was there and with whom, the photographer might have captured the vandalism on film."

"That's what I was thinking, and if Ashley's father, Harris Lancaster, was behind it, he would have good reason not to want the photographs to surface and so would Ashley."

Liza thought of the suicide scene photos in Tanner's

file, the campfire ringed with rocks, the charred beer cans, all the tracks at the scene. "If Harris was questioned about the vandalism, there should be something down at the office in the file."

"Both Malcolm Iverson and Harris Lancaster are the kind of men who would have taken the law into their own hands," Jordan said. "And so are their sons. I doubt either of them reported anything."

"I think I should talk to Harris Lancaster," Liza said.

"Let me go along. Just to make sure you're safe. Truth is, Lancaster is the kind of man who won't take a female deputy seriously. No offense."

"Oh, none taken," she said sarcastically. "But you've done enough, thanks. So what do you have planned tomorrow?"

He'd grinned over at her. "Worried about me?"

"Tell me I don't have any reason to be."

"Look, I'm touched but—"

"It isn't personal, so save it," she said quickly. "I have one murder on my hands, maybe two. I don't need you adding another one for me to solve."

"Don't worry, Deputy. I have no intention of getting myself killed. I'll watch my back. You do the same."

She nodded. "I'm driving up to West Yellowstone to see Brick Savage. He was the investigating marshal on Tanner's death."

"I need to go see my sister. But maybe I'll see you later tomorrow? How about dinner?"

She shook her head. "I don't think that's a good idea."

"I get it. You're afraid that over dinner I might charm you into thinking I'm harmless, if you weren't careful."

"You aren't that charming and you're far from harmless."

He grinned at that. "I'm going to take that as a compliment."

"I was sure you would."

As he drove toward her condo, he said, "Seriously, watch your back tomorrow."

WHEN THEY REACHED LIZA'S CONDO, Jordan insisted on walking her to her door.

"This really isn't necessary," she said, shaking her head at him as she dug for her key. He saw the glint of her weapon in her purse along with her badge. For a while on the dance floor, he'd forgotten she was a deputy marshal. She was merely a beautiful woman in his arms.

"A gentleman always walks his date to the door."

"This isn't a date."

"Because I'm a suspect?"

She looked up from searching in her purse for her key. He'd noticed that she'd suddenly become ill at ease when he'd driven up in front of her condo. Now she froze as he moved closer until they were a breath apart.

"Do you really think I'm dangerous?" he asked.

Her laugh sounded nervous. "Absolutely."

"Well, date or not, I had fun with you," he whispered and kissed her gently. She still hadn't moved when he drew back to look into her beautiful green eyes.

He knew he should leave it at one quick kiss, turn and walk away, but there was something so alluring about her that he gripped her waist and pulled her to him. This time he kissed her like he'd wanted to since the day he'd seen her sitting astride her horse, watching him from the darkness of the trees. There'd been something mysterious and sensual about her even when he'd realized who she was.

Now she melted into him, her hands going to his shoulders, her lips parting, a soft moan escaping from deep within her.

He felt his own desire spark and catch flame. It had been so long since he'd felt like this, if he ever had before. Liza was slight in stature, but had curves in all the right places. There was something solid and real about her. He couldn't help thinking how different she was from his ex, Jill. Jill ate like a bird. If she'd consumed even a portion of the food Liza'd had tonight at the dinner, she'd be anxious to get inside the condo and throw it all up. He'd gotten so sick of her constant dieting and complaining about the way she looked.

Liza was so different from any woman he'd ever known. She knew who she was and what she wanted. She looked perfect as she was, felt perfect. He wanted to sweep her into his arms, take her inside and make love to her until daylight.

AT THE SOUND OF A VEHICLE coming up the street, Liza pushed back from the kiss as if coming up for air. She was breathing hard, her heart pounding, desire making her blood run hot.

As a white SUV slowly drove past, she saw the woman behind the wheel and swore.

"Shelby," she said, mentally kicking herself for not only letting this happen but also wanting it to.

Jordan turned to watch the vehicle disappear down the street. "Sorry."

It was bad enough that a lot of people didn't think a woman could do this job. She'd only made it worse by letting someone like Shelby see her kissing Jordan Cardwell.

"I should never have gone to the reunion dinner with you," she said.

"You were working."

"That kiss wasn't work."

"No," he said and grinned at her.

"Go home," she said.

He raised both hands and took a step back. "You want to pick me up at the cabins or should I meet you tomorrow to—"

"I already told you. I can handle this without your help."

He stopped. "Liza, I'm not giving up until Alex's killer is caught."

"It's too dangerous."

He studied her for a moment. "Too dangerous for who?" he asked, stepping to her again. He cupped the side of her face with one of his large hands. She was surprised to feel the calluses. Taking his hand, she held it to the light.

"I thought you worked on Wall Street?" she asked, hating the suspicion she heard in her voice. Worse, that Jordan had heard it.

"I used to. I quit. I've been working construction for a few years now."

"Do you even live in New York City?"

He shook his head. "Why are you getting so upset?"

"Because I've run background checks on everyone involved in this case—except *you*."

"Because you know I didn't kill Alex."

"Do I?" She glared at him, although it was herself she was angry with.

He held up his hands again. "I'm sorry if one little kiss—"

"It wasn't one little kiss," she snapped and closed her eyes as she realized what she'd said. The kiss had shaken her. Worse, it had sparked a desire in her for this man, of all men.

"Run your background check. Do whatever it is you have to do," he said as he took a step away. "I have nothing to hide. But know this. That wasn't just some little kiss for me, either. If I had my way, I'd have you inside that condo and I'd be taking off your clothes right now. Good night, Deputy Marshal. I had a nice time. You make a nice date."

With that, he turned and walked to his vehicle while she stood trembling on the condo stoop thinking about what he'd said. Imagining the two of them tearing at each other's clothing. She knew that if he had taken her inside, they would have never made it to the bedroom.

As he drove away, she stood breathing in the cold night air, trying to still the aching need inside her. She'd always prided herself on her strength and determination. Nothing had kept her from realizing her goal to get where she was now. That had meant not letting a man either slow her down or stop her dead in her pursuit.

She wasn't going to let Jordan Cardwell ruin not just her reputation, but her credibility as a deputy marshal. The realization that she wanted him as much as he wanted her shocked her. No man had ever interested her enough for the problem to come up before. She reminded herself that Jordan was a suspect.

After a moment she dug into her purse until she found her key. With shaking fingers, she unlocked the door and stepped inside.

Even before she turned on the light, she knew something was terribly wrong. Someone had ransacked her condo.

She stood staring at the mess, trying to make sense of it. Why would someone do this? Her heart began to pound. This felt as if it was a warning.

Or had someone been looking for something and not finding it, just decided to tear the place up? Were they looking for the photographs Alex had been asking about?

Either way, she felt as if she'd gotten the message. Unfortunately, she'd never been good at heeding these kinds of warnings.

If anything, she was more determined than ever to solve this case and get Jordan Cardwell off her suspect list.

Chapter Ten

Saturday morning after cleaning up her condo, Liza drove up the canyon. It was one of those amazing Montana fall days. The sky was robin's-egg blue and not a cloud was in sight. The deciduous trees along the river glowed in bright blinding golds and deep reds next to the dark green of the pines.

At the heart of it all was the Gallatin River, running clear and beautiful, as it wound through the canyon and rocks. Harris Lancaster lived in a large modern home that looked as if it had been picked up in some big city and accidentally dropped here by the river.

His wife answered the door and pointed Liza toward a building a ways from the house. She followed a graveled path to the door and knocked.

Harris was a big burly brisk man with a loud deep voice and piercing gray eyes. Liza tried to imagine him in the very feminine furnishings of the house she'd glimpsed before his wife had closed the door.

His office looked like him, large and messy. The space was taken up by everything from dirty outdoor clothing and piles of papers and building plans to equipment parts and an old couch that Liza suspected he probably slept on more often than not. Given the pristine look of the house and Malcolm's wife, Liza doubted he was allowed to set foot inside it.

He cleared off an old wooden chair, motioned her into it and took a seat behind his cluttered desk. "So what's this about?" The office smelled of cigar smoke.

"I want to talk to you about Tanner Cole," Liza said.

"Who?"

"He worked for Malcolm Iverson twenty years ago when he was in high school."

He laughed. "*Seriously?* I can't remember who works for me right now, why would I remember who worked for Malcolm?"

"Tanner committed suicide twenty years ago after Malcolm Iverson's construction equipment was vandalized. It was just days before Malcolm shot you and went to prison."

He shook his head. "I try not to think about any of that."

"Tanner was in the same class as your daughter Ashley. He lived in a cabin near the construction site. Malcolm held Tanner responsible, but ultimately, he believed you were behind the vandalism that forced him into bankruptcy."

He scoffed at that. "Malcolm didn't know anything about running a business. He spent too much time in the bar. But I had nothing to do with vandalizing his equipment. He was just looking for someone to blame. Anyway, I heard the vandalism was kid stuff. You know, sugar in the gas tanks, broken and missing motor parts. Pure mischief. That's what happens when you get a bunch of drunk kids together."

"Or it was made to look like kids did it," she noted, but Harris Lancaster didn't seem to be listening.

"I do remember something about that Tanner boy now that you mention it. Ashley was real upset. We all were," he added. "Tanner's family has a ranch on the way to West Yellowstone. Too bad, but I don't see what any of that has to do with me."

"You benefited by Malcolm going broke."

He shrugged. "Maybe, at the time. But there was plenty of work to go around. His son and I are competitors, but we aren't shooting each other and we're both doing quite well."

He had a point. Maybe his problems with Malcolm and vice versa had nothing to do with Tanner's death. Maybe it had been guilt. Or maybe there were some photographs somewhere that told a different story.

JORDAN PULLED UP OUT IN FRONT of the house where he'd been raised. He sat for a moment just looking at the large two-story house. The other day when he'd come into town, he'd driven in from the other side of the ranch to make sure no one was at home before he'd come down to borrow a hat.

At least that had been his excuse. He'd wanted to wander around the house without anyone watching him. He knew his sister would think he was casing the joint, looking for valuables he could pawn or sell on eBay.

He and Dana had always butted heads, although he wished that wasn't the case. He'd always respected her. She worked harder than anyone he knew and made the rest of them feel like slackers.

Even after the good luck he'd had after Jill had left, he still felt like he could never measure up to Dana. Now as he opened his car door and climbed out, he half expected Dana to meet him on the porch. Possibly with a shotgun in her hands. Then he remembered that Hud had said she was pregnant with twins and having a hard time.

At the door, he knocked. It felt strange to knock at a door he'd run in and out of for years.

To his surprise, Stacy opened the door. He'd thought she was just passing through. But then again that would explain the beater car with the California plates he now saw parked off to the side. He hadn't even noticed it he'd been so busy looking at the house.

"Stacy," he said, unable to hide his surprise.

"Jordan?" She put a lot into that one word.

"It's all right. I didn't come by to cause trouble. I just wanted to see my sister. Sisters," he corrected. "And my niece and nephew."

"Nieces," she said and stepped back to let him come in.

"That's right. Hud said you have a baby?"

"Don't sound so surprised." Stacy studied him for a moment. "I'll see if Dana is up to having company."

"I'm not company. I'm *family*."

She lifted an eyebrow as if to say, "Since when?"

As if *she* should talk, he thought as she headed for the downstairs sunroom that had been their parents' bedroom, then their mother's and now apparently Dana's.

"Where are the kids?" he called after Stacy.

She shot him a warning look. "Down for their naps."

"Sorry," he whispered. He stood in the doorway, afraid to step in and feeling badly that it had come to this.

Stacy returned a moment later. She didn't look happy. "Dana isn't supposed to be upset."

"Thanks for the warning," he said and stepped across the living room to the doorway Stacy had just come from.

He stopped the moment he saw Dana. She looked beautiful, propped up against an array of pillows. Their gazes locked and he stepped the rest of the way into the room, closing the door behind him.

"Hey, sis," he said.

"Jordan." She began to cry.

With a lump in his throat at her reaction, he closed the distance and bent down to hug her awkwardly. "Are you all right?" he asked, pulling back to look at her. "You look...beautiful."

"I thought you were going to say...big," she said laughing and crying as she wiped at her eyes. "It's the hormones," she said, pointing at her tears. "I cry over everything."

"That explains it. For a minute there I thought you might have missed me," he said as he pulled up the chair next to the bed.

She stopped drying her tears to meet his gaze. "You seem...different."

He smiled. "Oh, I'm still that stubborn, temperamental brother you remember. But maybe some of the hard edges have gotten knocked off."

Dana nodded. "Maybe that's it. Hud told me why you were in town."

"I didn't think you wanted to see me or I would have come by sooner."

"You're my older brother."

"Exactly," he only half joked.

The bedroom door opened. Stacy stuck her head in.

"I think I'll run that errand I told you about yesterday. The kids are still down. Should I move Ella?"

"No, I'll have Jordan bring her in before he leaves."

Stacy looked to her brother as if she wasn't sure that was a good idea.

"I haven't dropped a baby all day," he said.

"And Hud should be back any minute," Dana said to reassure her sister.

Stacy mugged a face at him and closed the door. He listened to her leave. But it wasn't until they both couldn't hear her old beater car engine any longer before they spoke.

"I did a lot of soul searching after everything that happened," he said. "I'm sorry."

"Me, too."

"I went up to the cemetery and saw Mom the first day I got here. I borrowed a hat. Nothing else," he added quickly.

"Jordan, this ranch is your home, too."

"I know, sis," he said, putting a hand on her arm. "Mom always thought I'd come back and want to help you ranch."

Dana chuckled at that. "She said Stacy and Clay were gone, but you…well, she said there was ranching in your blood."

"Yeah. So tell me what's going on with you."

She placed her hands over her huge stomach. "I'm on bed rest with these two for the last weeks. I'm going insane."

He laughed. "I can imagine. And Stacy is…?"

"She's been great. Mary and Hank adore her."

"Mary and Hank. I can't wait to meet them."

"You should come back for dinner tonight," Dana said.

He shook his head. "Not sure that's a good idea given the way your husband feels about me, not to mention everything else going on right now."

"I wish you would. At least once before you leave," Dana said, tearing up again.

"You and your hormones." He got up and hugged her again. Straightening to leave, he asked, "So where's this baby I'm supposed to bring you before I leave?"

At the sound of the front door opening, Dana said, "Sounds like Hud's home. You'll have to come back to meet Ella."

"I'll try. You take care of yourself and your babies." As he opened the door, he came face-to-face with his brother-in-law again. "I was just leaving and no, I didn't upset her."

Hud looked past him to Dana. "What is she crying about then?"

"It's just the hormones," Dana said.

Jordan shrugged. "Just the hormones."

As he left, he found himself looking toward the barn, remembering his childhood here. Amazing how the place looked so different from the way he remembered it the last time he was here. Had he really tried to force his sister into selling it, lock, stock and barrel?

He felt a wave of shame as he walked to his rental SUV and climbed inside.

"WHERE'S STACY?" HUD ASKED as he stuck his head in the bedroom door later.

Dana saw that he had Ella on one shoulder. She realized she'd fallen asleep after Jordan had left and had awakened a few moments ago when she'd heard the baby cry.

"She said she wanted to go see Angus," Dana said groggily as she pulled herself up a little in the bed. "She said she wouldn't be gone long." Glancing at the clock beside her bed, she was shocked to see what time it was. "She hasn't come back?"

Hud shook his head. "I just changed Ella. I was going to heat some formula for her." He sounded worried.

Past him, Dana could see that it was dark outside. She felt a flutter of apprehension. "Stacy should have been back by now. Here, I'll take the baby. Call my father. Maybe they got to visiting and she just lost track of time."

"The kids and I are making dinner." Hud handed her Ella. "They ordered beanie wienies."

"Sounds great." She could smell the bacon and onions sizzling in the skillet. But her gaze was on the baby in her arms. Ella smiled up at her and she felt her heart do a somersault. Stacy was just running late. She probably didn't remember how quickly it got dark this time of year in the canyon.

A few minutes later, Hud came into the bedroom. "I called your father. He hasn't seen Stacy."

She felt her heart drop, but hid her fear as the kids came running in excitedly chanting "beanie wienies."

Hud set up Mary and Hank's small table in the bedroom so they could all eat dinner with her. The beanie wienies were wonderful. They finished the meal off with some of the brownies Aunt Stacy had made.

"Is Auntie Stacy going to live with us?" Mary asked.

"No, she's just visiting," Dana told her daughter. There was still no sign of Stacy. No call. Dana found herself listening, praying for the sound of her old car coming up the road. But there was only silence. "I'm not sure how long your aunt can stay."

Hank looked over at Ella who was drooling and laughing as she tried to roll over on the other side of the bed. "She can't leave without her baby," he said. "Can she?"

She shot Hud a look. Could Stacy leave without her baby?

"I'm going to call Hilde and see if she can come over while I go look for Stacy," Hud said. "I called Liza but she's in West Yellowstone. Apparently, she went up there to talk to my father about the case she's working."

Dana nodded, seeing her own worry reflected in his face.

"I'll call you if I hear anything." Big Sky was relatively small. Stacy couldn't have gone far. Unless she'd changed her mind about seeing their father and gone into Bozeman for some reason. But she'd said she would be back before Ella woke up from her nap. What if something had happened to her sister?

Trying to rein in her fear, Dana told the kids to get a game for them all to play.

"Ella can't play, Mommy," Mary cried. "She'll eat the game pieces."

"No, Ella will just watch," she told her daughter as she fought the dread that Stacy hadn't changed at all.

In that case Dana hated to think what that might mean. That Stacy wouldn't be back? Or worse, she'd left her baby. If it was her baby.

Chapter Eleven

Jordan felt at loose ends after leaving his sister's. On impulse he drove as far as he could up the road to the construction site where he'd found Tanner that horrible morning twenty years before.

The road was now paved and led up to a massive home. He could tell from the looks of it that the owner wasn't around and probably didn't come up but for a few weeks in the winter and summer.

The house had been built on a cleared area high on the mountain where the construction equipment had been parked twenty years ago. The small log cabin where Tanner had lived was gone. So was the campfire ring. Nothing looked as it had except for the tree where he'd found Tanner hanging that spring day.

There was also no sign that this was the spot where his best friend had taken his life. No log stumps. No rope mark on the large old pine limb. Nothing left of the tragedy even on the breeze that moaned in the high boughs. Jordan doubted the place's owners knew about the death that had occurred within yards of their vacation home.

He felt a sadness overwhelm him. "Why, Tanner? Why the hell did you do it?" he demanded as he looked up at the large limb where he'd found him. "Or did you?" He feared they would never know as he looked again at the dried-pine-needle-covered ground. Did he really think he was going to find answers up here?

Too antsy to go back to his cabin, he drove up the canyon. When he saw his father's truck parked outside the Corral, he swung in. He found his father and uncle sitting on their usual stools at the bar.

"Son? I thought you would have left by now," Angus Cardwell said. "Bob, get my son a beer."

Jordan noticed there were a few men at the end of the bar and several families at the tables in the dining area eating.

Angus slapped his son on the back as Jordan slid onto a stool next to him. The bar smelled of burgers and beer. Not a bad combination, he thought, figuring he understood why his old man had such an infatuation with bars.

"What have you been up to?" Uncle Harlan asked him.

"My twenty-year class reunion," he said, figuring that would suffice.

"You actually went to it?" his father said with a laugh.

"I went with the deputy marshal."

Both older men hooted. "That's my son," Angus said proudly.

Jordan had known that would be his father's reaction. It was why he'd said it. He was just glad Liza hadn't been around to hear it.

The draft beer was cold and went down easy. Heck, he might have a burger while he was at it. He settled in, listening to the watering hole banter, a television over the bar droning in the background.

"Your deputy figured out who killed that man at the falls?" his uncle asked him.

"Not yet, but she will," he said with confidence.

His father smiled over at him and gave him a wink. "That what's really keeping you in the canyon, ain't it?"

Jordan smiled and ordered burgers for the three of them.

Later when he drove back to Big Sky and stopped by the Marshal's Office, he was disappointed to learn that Liza hadn't returned from West Yellowstone. He thought about what his father had said about his reasons for staying around. If he was being honest with himself, Liza definitely played into it.

LIZA FOUND BRICK SAVAGE sitting on the deck of his Hebgen Lake home. She'd heard stories about him and, after he'd ignored her knocks at his front door, braced herself as she approached his deck.

"Mr. Savage?"

He looked up, his gaze like a piercing arrow as he took in her uniform first, then studied her face before saying, "Yes?"

"I'm Deputy Marshal Liza Turner out of the Big Sky office. I'd like a moment of your time."

"You have any identification?" His voice was gravelly but plenty strong.

She pulled her ID and climbed a couple of steps so he could see it.

He nodded, amusement in his gaze. "Deputy Marshal. Times really have changed. I heard my son left you in charge of the murder case."

"That's correct."

"Well, come on up here then," Brick said and pushed himself up out of his chair. He was a big man, but she could see that he used to be a lot bigger in his younger days. There was a no-nonsense aura about him along with his reputation that made her a little nervous being in his company.

He shoved a chair toward her as she reached the deck and waited for her to sit before he pulled up a weather-grayed log stump and settled himself on it.

"I hate to take your chair," she said, wondering about a man who had only one chair on his deck. Apparently he didn't expect or get much company. Did that mean he didn't see much of Hud and family?

"So?" Brick said as if his time was valuable and she was wasting it.

"I want to ask you about Tanner Cole's death. He was a senior—"

"I know who he was. Found hanging from a tree up on the side of the mountain overlooking Big Sky twenty-odd years ago," Brick said. "What do you want to know?"

"Was it a suicide?"

He leveled his gaze at her. "Wasn't it ruled one?"

"At the time. Is it possible Tanner had help?"

"It's always possible. Was there any sign of a struggle like scratches or bruises? Not according to the coroner's report but if you did your homework, you'd already know that. As for footprints, there were a lot of them. He'd had a beer bash, kegger, whatever your generation calls it. He'd had that within a few days so there were all kinds of tracks at the scene."

She knew all this and wondered if she'd wasted her

time driving all the way up here. Past him she could see the deep green of the lake, feel a cold breeze coming off the water. Clouds had already gathered over Lion's Head Mountain, one of the more recognizable ones seen from his deck. Add to that the sun had already gone down. As it was, it would be dark before she got back to Big Sky.

"I can tell you this, he used his own rope," Brick said.

She nodded. "What about Jordan Cardwell?"

"What about him?"

"You found him at the scene. Is there any chance—"

"He didn't kill his friend, if that's what you're asking."

"You're that sure?" she said, hearing the relief in her voice and suspecting he did, too. She'd started to like Jordan, suspect or not. She knew it was a bad idea on so many levels, but there was something about him...

"What did you really come up here to ask me?" Brick demanded.

"I guess what I want is your gut reaction."

"My gut reaction isn't worth squat. Do I think he killed himself?" The former marshal shrugged. "Strangulation takes a while. Gives a man a lot of time to reconsider and change his mind, but with all his body weight on the rope, it's impossible to get your fingers under the rope and relieve the pressure."

She looked at him in surprise. "Are you telling me he—"

"Changed his mind and clawed at the rope?" He nodded.

"Why wasn't that in the coroner's report?"

"It's not uncommon. But also not something a family member ever wants to know about. I would imagine Rupert wanted to spare them any more pain."

Liza shook her head. "But couldn't it also mean that Tanner Cole never meant to hang himself? That someone else put that rope around his neck?"

"And he didn't fight until that person kicked the log out?" Brick asked. "Remember, there were no defensive wounds or marks on his body."

"Maybe he thought it was a joke."

The elderly former marshal studied her for a moment. "What would make you let someone put a noose around your neck, joking or otherwise?"

That was the question, wasn't it?

"You think he killed himself," she said.

He shrugged. "Prove me wrong."

HUD SPENT A GOOD TWO HOURS canvassing the area for his sister-in-law before he put out the APB on her vehicle. He checked with the main towing services first, though, telling himself her car could have broken down. All kinds of things could have happened to detain her—and maybe even keep her from calling.

But after those two hours he knew in his gut that wasn't the case. Stacy had split.

At the office he did something he'd hoped he wouldn't have to do. He began checking again for kidnappings of children matching Ella's description and realized he needed to narrow his search. Since Stacy was driving a car with California plates...

He realized he should have run her plates first. Feeling only a little guilty for having taken down her license number when he'd first become suspicious of her, he brought up his first surprise.

The car had been registered in La Jolla, California—but not to Stacy by any of her former married names or her maiden name of Cardwell.

The car was registered to Clay Cardwell—her brother.

He picked up the phone and called the family lawyer who was handling the dispersing of ranch profits to Dana's siblings.

"Rick, I hate to bother you, but I need to get a phone number and address for Dana's brother Clay. I understand he's living in La Jolla, California."

Rick cleared his voice. "Actually I was going to contact Dana, but hesitated when I heard she's on bed rest at the ranch pregnant with the twins."

News traveled fast, Hud thought. "What's up?" he asked, afraid he wasn't going to like it.

"Clay. He hasn't been cashing his checks. It's been going on for about six months. I just assumed he might be holding them for some reason. But the last one came back saying there was no one by that name and no forwarding address."

Hud swore under his breath. Six months. The same age as Ella. Although he couldn't imagine what the two things could have in common or why Clay hadn't cashed his checks or how it was that his older sister was driving a car registered to him.

"I think we need to find him," Hud said. "I'd just as soon Dana didn't know anything about this. Believe me, she has her hands full right now. One more thing, though. Stacy. Did she give you a new address to send her checks?"

"No. She's moved around so much, I wait until I hear from her and usually send them general delivery."

"Well, could you do me a favor? If you hear from her, call me."

"I thought she was here in the canyon."

"She was, but right now she's missing and she left a small…package at the house."

It was dark by the time Liza drove past the Fir Ridge cemetery, climbed up over the Continental Divide and entered Gallatin Canyon.

This time of year there was little traffic along the two-lane road as it snaked through pines and over mountains along the edge of the river.

She kept thinking about what Brick Savage had told her. More to the point, the feeling she'd had when she'd left him. He'd challenged her to prove Tanner Cole had been murdered. No doubt because he knew it would be near impossible.

And yet if she was right and Alex's murder had something to do with Tanner's death, then the killer had shown his hand.

Pulling out her phone, she tried Hud's cell. In a lot of spots in the canyon there was no mobile phone service. To her surprise it began to ring.

"Marshal Savage," he snapped.

"Sorry, did I catch you at a bad time?" she asked through the hands-free speaker, wondering if he was in the middle of something with the kids.

"Liza. Good. I'm glad you called. Did you get my message?"

She hadn't. Fear gripped her. Surely there hadn't been another murder. Her thoughts instantly raced to Jordan and she felt her heart fall at the thought that he might—

"It's Stacy," he said. "She left the house earlier. No one has seen her since. She hasn't called. I've looked all over Big Sky. She left the baby at the house."

"What?" It took her a moment to pull back from the thought of another murder. To pull back from the fear and dread that had had her thinking something had happened to Jordan. "Stacy wouldn't leave her baby, would she?"

"Knowing Stacy, I have a bad feeling the baby isn't even hers."

Liza was too shocked to speak for a moment. "You think she...stole it?"

"Something is wrong. I've suspected it from the get-go. Dana was hoping I was just being suspicious because it's my nature, but I'd been worried that something like this would happen. I didn't want Dana getting attached to that baby, but you know Dana, and Ella is adorable, if that is even her name."

"Oh, boss, I'm so sorry."

"So you spoke to my father?" Hud asked.

"He was the investigating officer at Tanner Cole's suicide."

"What did he tell you?"

"That it was Tanner's rope."

Hud let out a humorless laugh. "That sounds like Brick. Have you met him before?"

"Never had the honor. He must have been a treat as a father."

"You could say that." He sighed. "Look, Hilde's at the house. I'm going to make another circle through the area to look for Stacy before I go home."

"I'm about twenty minutes out. Do you want me to stop by?"

"If you don't mind. I know you're busy with this murder case…"

"No problem. I'll see you soon." She snapped the phone shut, shocked by what he'd told her. She was so deep in thought that she hadn't noticed the lights of another vehicle coming up behind her.

She glanced in the mirror. One of the headlights was out on the approaching car. That struck her about the same time as she realized the driver was coming up too fast.

She'd been going the speed limit. By now the driver of the vehicle behind her would have been able to see the light bar on the top of her SUV. Only a fool would come racing up on a Marshal's Department patrol car— let alone pass it.

And yet as she watched, the driver of what appeared to be an old pickup swerved around her and roared up beside her.

Liza hit her lights and siren, thinking the driver must be drunk. She glanced over, saw only a dark figure behind the wheel wearing a black ski mask. Her heart jumped, but she didn't have time to react before the driver swerved into her. She heard the crunch of metal, felt the patrol SUV veer toward the ditch and the pines and beyond that, the river.

She slammed on the brakes, but was traveling too fast to avoid the truck crashing into her again. The force made the vehicle rock wildly as she fought to keep control. The tires screamed on the pavement as the SUV began to fishtail.

Liza felt the right side of the vehicle dip into the soft shoulder of the highway, pulling the SUV off the road. She couldn't hold it and felt her tires leave the pavement. A stand of trees blurred past and then there was nothing but darkness as she plunged over the edge of the road toward the dark green of the river.

Chapter Twelve

Hud was headed home when he heard the 911 call for an ambulance come over his radio. His heart began to race as he heard that the vehicle in the river was a Montana marshal's patrol SUV.

He threw on his siren and lights and took off up the canyon toward West Yellowstone. As he raced toward the accident, he called home, glad when Hilde answered the phone.

"Tell Dana I'm running a little late," he said to Hilde. "Don't act like anything is wrong." He heard Dana already asking what was going on. Hilde related the running a little late part.

"We're just fine," Hilde said.

"It sounds like there's been an accident up the canyon," he told her. "It's Liza. I don't know anything except that her car is in the river. I don't know how long I'm going to be."

"Don't worry about us."

"Is it my sister?" Dana demanded in the background.

"I heard that. Tell her I haven't found Stacy. I'll call when I have news. I just don't want Dana upset."

"Got it. I'll tell her."

He disconnected and increased his speed. Liza was

like family. How the hell did she end up in the river? She was a great driver.

As he came around a bend in the windy road, he saw her patrol SUV among the boulders in the Gallatin River. Some bypassers had stopped. Several of the men had flashlights and one of them had waded out to the patrol vehicle.

Hud parked, leaving his lights on to warn any oncoming traffic, then grabbing his own flashlight, jumped out and ran toward the river. As he dropped over the edge of the road to it, he recognized the man who was standing on the boulder beside Liza's wrecked vehicle.

"Jordan?" he called.

"Liza's conscious," he called back. "An ambulance is on the way. I'm staying with her until it gets here."

Hud would have liked to have gone to her as well, but he heard the sound of the ambulance siren and climbed back up the road to help with traffic control.

All the time, though, he found himself wondering how Jordan just happened to be on the scene.

"WHAT'S HAPPENED?" DANA demanded the moment Hilde hung up. "Don't," she said before Hilde could open her mouth. "You're a terrible liar and we both know it. Tell me."

"He hasn't found your sister."

She nodded. "But something else has happened."

"There's been an accident up the canyon. He needed to run up there."

Dana waited. "There's more."

"You're the one who should have gone into law enforcement, the interrogation part," Hilde said as she came and sat down on the edge of the bed. On the other side of Dana, baby Ella slept, looking like an angel. Hilde glanced at the baby, then took Dana's hand as if she knew it was only a matter of time before her friend got the truth out of her. "Hud didn't know anything about the accident except that Liza is somehow involved."

"Oh, no." Her heart dropped.

"Now don't get upset and have these babies because Hud will never forgive me," Hilde said quickly.

Dana shook her head. "I'm okay. But I want to know the minute you hear something. Are you sure you can stay?"

"Of course."

"You didn't have a date?"

Hilde laughed. "If only there were more Hudson Savages around. All of the men I meet, well…they're so not the kind of men I want to spend time with, even for the time it takes to have dinner."

"I *am* lucky." Dana looked over at Ella. "What if Hud is right and Ella isn't Stacy's baby?"

"Where would she have gotten Ella? You can't just get a baby off eBay."

"She could have *kidnapped* Ella. You know Stacy."

"I'm sure Hud checked for any kidnapped babies six months old with dimples, blond hair and green eyes," Hilde argued.

"Yes, green eyes. You might have noticed that all the Justices have dark brown eyes and dark hair, including Stacy."

"Maybe the father has green eyes and Stacy carries a green-eyed gene. You don't know that Ella isn't Stacy's."

"No," Dana admitted, but like Hud, she'd had a bad

feeling since the moment Stacy had arrived. "I think Stacy only came here because she's in trouble and it has something to do with that poor little baby."

"You think that's why she left Ella with you?"

Dana fingered the quilt edge where someone had stitched the name Katie. "I wish I knew."

JORDAN WOKE WITH A CRICK in his neck. He stared down at the green hospital scrubs he was wearing for a moment, confused where he was. It came back to him with a start. Last night his clothes had been soaking wet from his swim in the river. He'd been shivering uncontrollably, but had refused to leave the hospital until he knew Liza was going to be all right.

That's how he'd ended up in scrubs, he recalled now as he sat up in the chair beside Liza's bed and smiled at the woman propped up staring at him now.

"What are you still doing here?" she asked, smiling.

"I *was* sleeping." He stood up, stretched, then looked to see what she was having for breakfast. "You haven't eaten much," he said as he took a piece of toast from the nearly untouched tray.

"I'm not very hungry."

He was famished and realized he hadn't eaten since yesterday at noon. "How are your ribs?" he asked as he devoured the piece of toast.

"They're just bruised and only hurt when I breathe."

"Yep, but you're breathing. Be thankful for that."

Liza nodded and he saw that her left wrist was also wrapped. Apparently, it was just badly sprained, not broken. His big worry, though, had been that she'd suffered internal injuries.

Apparently not, though, since all she had was a bandage on her right temple, a bruised cheek and a scrape on her left cheek. She'd been lucky.

"So what did the doctor say?" he asked.

"That I'm going to live."

"Good."

She looked almost shy. "Thank you for last night."

He shrugged. "It's wasn't anything. I just swam a raging river in October in Montana and clung onto a slippery boulder to be with you." He grinned. "I'm just glad you're all right." He'd been forced to leave the room last night while Hud had talked to her, but he'd overheard enough to more than concern him.

"You said last night that someone forced you off the road?" he asked now. "Do you remember anything about the vehicle?"

She narrowed her gaze at him and sighed. "Even if I knew who did it, I wouldn't tell you. I don't want to see you get killed."

He grinned. "Nice that you care—"

"I told you, I don't have time to find your killer, too."

"Why would anyone want to kill me? On second thought, scratch that. Other than my brother-in-law, why would anyone want me dead?"

"Hud doesn't want you dead."

"He just doesn't want me near my sister."

"Can you blame him?"

"No," he said with a sigh. "That's what makes it worse. I would be the same way if someone had treated my wife the way I've treated my sister." He looked away.

"Do you mean that?"

He grinned. "Do you question everything I tell you?"

"Yes."

He laughed and shook his head. "I've been more

honest with you than I have with anyone in a very long time. Hud doesn't want me near you, either." He met her gaze and saw something warm flash in her eyes.

"I talked to the investigating officer in Tanner's death yesterday before the accident," she said, clearly changing the subject. "He cleared you as a suspect, at least in Tanner's death."

"Did Brick Savage tell you what I did the day I found Tanner?"

"I would assume you were upset since it was your best friend."

"I broke down and bawled like a baby until Hud's old man kicked me in the behind and told me to act like a man. He said I was making myself look guilty as hell." He chuckled. "I took a swing at him and he decked me. Knocked me on my butt, but I got control of myself after that and he didn't arrest me for assaulting an officer of the law so I guess I respect him for that."

Liza shook her head. "Men. You are such a strange breed. I think it would have been stranger if you hadn't reacted the way you had."

He shrugged. "Tanner left a hole in my life. I've never had a closer friend since. Sometimes I swear I can hear his voice, especially when I do something stupid."

She smiled. "So he's still with you a lot."

"Yeah. You do know that when I say I hear him, I don't really *hear* him, right?"

"I get it."

"I didn't want you to think I hear voices. It's bad enough you still see me as a suspect."

She nodded slowly. "I meant what I said about wanting you to be safe. You need to keep a low profile."

"How can I do that when I have a reunion picnic to go to this afternoon?"

"You aren't seriously planning to go?"

"What? You don't think I can get another date?" he joked.

"What do I have to do to make you realize how dangerous this is?"

His expression sobered. "All I have to do is look at your face and think about where I found you last night."

"You could be next," she said quietly. "What time is the picnic?"

"The doctor isn't going to let you—"

"What time?" she demanded.

"One."

"I'll be there."

He grinned. "Good, I won't have to find another date." He wanted to argue that she needed to stay in bed. He couldn't stand the thought that she was now a target. Last night when he'd seen her car in the river— Just the thought made it hard for him to breathe even now.

He barely remembered throwing on the rental car's brakes, diving out and half falling down the bank to the river. All he could think about was getting to her. The moment he'd hit the icy water of the Gallatin, he'd almost been swept away. He'd had to swim to get to her, then climb onto a large slick boulder to reach the driver's-side door.

At first he'd thought she was dead. There was blood from the cut on her temple.

Impulsively, he reached for her hand now. It felt warm and soft and wonderfully alive. He squeezed her hand gently, then let it go.

"Unless you need a ride, I guess I'll see you at one on the mountain then," he said and turned to leave.

"Liza isn't going anywhere, especially with you," Hud snapped as he stepped into the hospital room. "I'll speak to *you* in the hall," he said to Jordan.

Liza shot him a questioning look. Jordan shrugged. He had no idea why his brother-in-law was angry with him but he was about to find out.

"Later," he said to Liza and stepped out in the hall to join Hud.

The marshal had blood in his eye by the time Jordan stepped out into the hall. "What were you doing at the accident last night? Were you following Liza?"

He held up his hands. "One question at a time. I had tried to call her. I knew she'd gone up to West Yellowstone to talk to your father. I got tired of waiting for her to return and drove up the canyon. I was worried about her."

"Worried about her?" Hud sighed. "And you just happened to find her?"

"The other driver who stopped can verify it."

"Did you pass another vehicle coming from the direction of the accident?"

"Several. A white van. A semi. An old red pickup."

"The red pickup. Did you happen to notice the driver?"

He shook his head. "I just glanced at the vehicles. I wasn't paying a lot of attention since I was looking for Liza's patrol SUV. You think the truck ran her off the road."

Hud didn't look happy to hear that Jordan knew about that. He ignored the statement and asked, "Where is Liza going to meet you later?"

"At the reunion picnic up on the mountain."

"Well, she's not going anywhere." Hud started to turn away, but swung back around and put a finger in Jordan's face. "I want you to stay away from her. I'm not sure what your game is—"

"There's *no* game. No angle. Liza is investigating Alex Winslow's murder. I've been helping her because I know the players and I think it is somehow tied in with Tanner's death."

"That better be all there is to it," Hud said and started to turn away again.

"What if that isn't all it is?" Jordan demanded, then could have kicked himself.

Hud turned slowly back to him. "Like I said, stay away from Liza." With that, he turned and pushed into his deputy's room.

"Tell me you weren't out in the hall threatening the man who saved me last night," Jordan heard Liza say, but didn't catch Hud's reply, which was just as well.

He collected his clothes at the nurse's station, changed and headed for the canyon and Big Sky. Now more than ever he wanted to get to the bottom of this. Someone had tried to kill Liza. He didn't doubt they would try again.

But what were they so afraid she was going to find out? He suddenly recalled something he'd overheard Hud say to his deputy marshal last night at the hospital. Something about her condo being ransacked. Someone thought she had something. The alleged photographs?

LIZA COCKED HER HEAD at her boss as he came around the end of her bed. "Well?" she asked.

He gave her a sheepish look. "You don't know Jordan like I do. He's…he's…"

"He's changed."

Hud shook his head. "I really doubt that he's changed any more than his sister Stacy."

"Talk about painting them all with the same brush," she said.

"Look, I don't want you getting involved with him."

Liza grinned. "I'm sorry, I must have misheard you. You weren't telling me who I can get involved with, were you, boss?"

"Damn it, Liza. You know how I feel about you."

She nodded. "I'm the most stubborn deputy you've ever had. I often take things in my own hands without any thought to my safety. I'm impulsive, emotional and driven and I'm too smart for my own good. Does that about cover it?"

"You're the best law officer I've ever worked with," Hud said seriously. "And a friend. And like a real sister to my wife. I just don't want to see you get hurt."

She smiled. "I can also take care of myself. And," she said before he could interrupt, "I can get involved with anyone I want."

He looked at his boots before looking at her again. "You're right."

"That's what I thought. Did you bring the information I asked for?" she asked, pointing to the manila envelope in his hand and no longer wanting to discuss Jordan.

Truthfully she didn't know how she felt about him—waking up to see him sleeping beside her hospital bed or being in his arms the other night on the dance floor.

"I brought it," Hud said with a sigh. "But I don't

think you should be worrying about any of this right now. How are you feeling?"

"Fine," Liza said, reaching for the manila envelope and quickly opening it.

"There are Alex's phone calls over the past month as well as where he went after arriving at Big Sky."

Liza was busy leafing through it, more determined than ever to find out who'd killed him—and who'd tried to do the same to her the night before.

"Alex was in the middle of a contentious divorce?" she asked, looking up in surprise from the information he'd brought her. "He had a *wife?*" When she'd notified next of kin, she'd called his brother as per the card in his wallet.

"Her name is Crystal."

"A classmate?"

Hud nodded. "But not from Big Sky. She lived down in Bozeman."

"What was holding up the divorce?" Liza asked.

He shook his head and had to take a step back from the bed as Liza swung her legs over the side and stood up. *"What are you doing?"*

"I'm getting up. I told you, I'm fine. Just a little knock on the head and a few cuts and bruises and a sprained wrist, but it's my left wrist, so I'm fine. All I need is a vehicle."

He shook his head. "I can't allow—"

"You can't stop me. Someone tried to *kill* me. This has become personal. Not only that, you need to stay close to home," she said as she rummaged in the closet for her clothes. "No sign of Stacy yet?" He shook his head. "What about the baby?"

"The lab's running a DNA test. We should be able

to tell if the baby is Stacy's by comparing Ella's DNA to Dana's. Liza, you're really not up to—"

"Could you see about my clothes?" she asked, realizing they weren't anywhere in the room. Her clothes had been wet and the nurses had probably taken them to dry them. "Stubborn, remember? One of the reasons I'm such a good law officer, your words not mine." She smiled widely although it hurt her face.

He studied her for a moment. "Clothes, right. Then get you a vehicle," he said, clearly giving up on trying to keep another woman in bed.

DANA WATCHED HILDE TRYING to change Ella's diaper until she couldn't take it anymore. "Give me that baby."

Hilde laughed. "You make it look so easy," she said, handing Ella to her.

Ella giggled and squirmed as Dana made short work of getting her into a diaper and a sleeper. Hud had come in so late, Hilde had stayed overnight and gotten someone to work for her this morning. He'd promised to be back soon.

"I'm just so glad Liza is all right," she said as she handed Ella back to Hilde. Through the open bedroom door she could see Mary and Hank playing with a plastic toy ranch set. She could hear them discussing whether or not they should buy more cows.

"Me, too," Hilde said. "Fortunately, Liza is strong."

"Hud's worried now that she and Jordan might be getting involved."

Hilde arched an eyebrow. "Really?"

"I have to admit when Jordan stopped by, he did seem different. But then again I said Stacy had changed, so what do I know? I can't believe we haven't heard anything from her. What if she never comes back?" Dana hadn't let herself think about that at first, but as the hours passed... "Did she leave anything else besides Ella and the baby's things?"

"I can check. She was staying in the room I slept in last night, right?"

"I would imagine Hud already checked it, but would you look? That should tell us if she was planning to leave the baby all along or if something happened and she can't get back."

Hilde jiggled Ella in her arms. "Watch her for a moment and I'll go take a look." She put the baby down next to Dana on the bed. Ella immediately got up on her hands and knees and rocked back and forth.

"She is going to be crawling in no time," Dana said with a smile. Stacy was going to miss it. But then maybe Stacy had missed most of Ella's firsts because this wasn't her baby.

Hilde returned a few minutes later.

"You found something," Dana said, excited and worried at the same time.

"You said she didn't have much, right?" Hilde asked. "Well, she left a small duffel on the other side of the bed. Not much in it. A couple of T-shirts, underwear, socks. I searched through it." She shook her head. "Then I noticed a jean jacket hanging on the back of the chair by the window. It's not yours, is it?"

"That's the one Stacy was wearing when she arrived."

"I found this in the pocket."

Dana let out a surprised groan as Hilde, using two fingers, pulled out a small caliber handgun.

ALEX WINSLOW'S WIFE, CRYSTAL, lived up on the hill overlooking Bozeman on what some called Snob Knob. In the old days it had been called Beer Can Hill because that was where the kids used to go to drink and make out.

The house was pretty much what Liza had expected. It was huge. A contentious divorce usually meant one of three things. That the couple was fighting over the kids, the pets or the money. Since Alex and Crystal apparently had no children or pets, Liza guessed it was the money.

She parked the rental SUV Hud'd had delivered to the hospital and walked up to the massive front door. As she rang the bell, she could hear music playing inside. She rang the bell a second time before the door was opened by a petite dark-haired woman with wide blue eyes and a quizzical smile.

"Yes?" she asked.

Liza had forgotten her bandages, the eye that was turning black or that all the blood hadn't completely come out of her uniform shirt.

She'd felt there wasn't time to go all the way back to Big Sky to change. Her fear was that if she didn't solve this case soon, someone else was going to die.

"Crystal Winslow? I'm Deputy Marshal Liza Turner. I need to ask you a few questions in regard to your husband's death."

"*Estranged* husband," Crystal Winslow said, but opened the door wider. "I doubt I can be of help, but you're welcome to come in. Can I get you something?" She took in Liza's face again.

"Just answers."

Crystal led her into the formal living room. It had

a great view of the city and valley beyond. In the distance, the Spanish Peaks gleamed from the last snowfall high in the mountains.

"How long have you and Alex been estranged?"

"I don't see what that has to do—"

"Your *estranged* husband is dead. I believe whoever murdered him tried to do the same to me last night. I need to know why."

"Well, it has nothing to do with me." She sniffed, then said, "A month."

"Why?"

For a moment Crystal looked confused. "Why did I kick him out and demand a divorce? You work out of Big Sky, right? I would suggest you ask Shelby."

"Shelby Durran-Iverson?"

She nodded, and for the first time Liza saw true pain in the woman's expression—and fury. "I knew he was cheating. A woman can tell. But *Shelby?* I remember her from high school. People used to say she was the type who would eat her young."

"That could explain why she doesn't have any children," Liza said. She still felt a little light-headed and knew this probably wasn't the best time to be interviewing anyone.

"Did Alex admit he was seeing Shelby?"

Crystal gave her an are-you-serious? look. "He swore up and down that his talking to her wasn't an affair, that he was trying to get her to tell the truth, something involving Tanner Cole."

"You remember Tanner?"

"He hung himself our senior year. I didn't really know him. He was a cowboy. I didn't date cowboys. No offense."

Liza wondered why that should offend her. Did she look that much like a cowgirl?

"I think your husband might have been telling you the truth. I believe he was looking into Tanner's death."

"Why would he do that?"

"I was hoping you could tell me since I suspect that's what got him killed."

"You don't know for sure that he wasn't having an affair with Shelby though, right?"

"No, I don't. But Alex mentioned to other people that he felt something was wrong about Tanner's suicide, as well. He didn't say anything to you?"

"No."

"Do you or your husband own any weapons?"

Crystal looked appalled. "You mean like a Saturday night special?"

"Or hunting rifles."

"No, I wouldn't have a gun in my house. My father was killed in a hunting accident. We have a state-of-the-art security system. We didn't need *guns*."

Liza nodded, knowing what that would get Crystal if someone broke into the house. She could be dead before the police arrived. "Alex didn't have weapons, either?"

"No. I still can't believe this was why Alex was spending time with Shelby."

"Did she ever call here?"

Crystal mugged a face. "Shelby said it was just to talk to Alex about Big Sky's reunion plans. They wanted their own. Ours wasn't good enough for them."

Liza could see that Crystal Winslow had been weighted down with that chip on her shoulder for some time.

"But I overheard one of his conversations," she said

smugly. "Shelby was demanding something back, apparently something she'd given him. He saw me and said he didn't know what she was talking about. After he hung up, he said Shelby was looking for some photographs from their senior year. He said she was probably using them for something she was doing for the reunion."

"You didn't believe him?"

"I could hear Shelby screeching from where I was standing. She was livid about whatever it really was."

"Did he send her some photos from high school?"

"I told you, that was just a story he came up with. He had some photographs from high school. I kept the ones of me and gave him the rest."

"Where are those photos now?"

"I threw them out with Alex. I assume he took them to his apartment," she said.

"Do you have a key?"

"He left one with me, but I've never used it." She got up and walked out of the room, returning a moment later with a shiny new key and a piece of notepaper. "Here's the address."

Liza took it. "Was that the only Big Sky friend who contacted Alex?"

"Right after that was when Alex started driving up to Big Sky and I threw him out."

"What made you suspect he was seeing Shelby?" Liza asked.

For a moment, Crystal looked confused. "I told you—"

"Right, that a woman knows. But how did you know it was *Shelby?*"

"After Tanner broke up with her in high school, she

made a play for Alex. He was dating Tessa Ryerson before that. The two of them got into it at school one day. That's when he and I started dating."

"Did he tell you what his argument with Shelby was about?"

She shrugged. "Eventually everyone has a falling-out with Shelby—except for her BFFs." She made a face, then listed off their names like a mantra. "Shelby, Tessa, Ashley, Whitney and Brittany."

Liza noted that Brittany was on the list. "When did Alex and Shelby have the falling-out?"

Crystal frowned. "It was around the time that Tanner committed suicide. After that Alex hadn't wanted anything to do with her. That is until recently."

Liza could tell that Crystal was having second thoughts about accusing her husband of infidelity.

"You said your father was killed in a hunting accident. Did you hunt?"

"No. Alex did and so did his friends," she said distractedly.

"What about Shelby?"

"She actually was a decent shot, I guess, although I suspected the only reason she and her friends hunted was to be where the boys were." Her expression turned to one of horror. "You don't think Shelby killed Alex, do you?"

Chapter Thirteen

Dana stared at the sleeping Ella as her husband updated her on Liza's condition. She'd had a scare, but she was going to be fine. In fact, she'd already checked herself out of the hospital and was working.

"You didn't try to stop her?" Dana demanded of her husband.

He gave her a look she knew too well.

"All right, what did you find out about Stacy?" she asked and braced herself for the worst.

"There is really nothing odd about her having Clay's car," she said when he finished filling her in. "Obviously they've been in contact."

"It wouldn't be odd if Clay had been cashing his checks for the last six months," Hud said. "Why would he be driving an old beater car if he had money?"

"Maybe it was a spare car he let Stacy have," she suggested.

Hud rolled his eyes. "It is the only car registered to your brother. Nice theory." He instantly seemed to regret his words. "I'm sorry. I'm not telling you these things to upset you. On the contrary, I know you'll worry more if I keep them from you."

"Which proves you're smarter than you look," she

said, annoyed that he was treating her as if she was breakable. "The babies are fine. I'm fine. You'd better not keep anything from me."

He smiled. "As I said…"

"So you can't find Clay or Stacy."

"No. But I've put an APB out on Stacy's car. It was the only thing I could do."

"Something's happened to her," Dana said. "She wouldn't leave Ella." When Hud said nothing, she shot him an impatient look. "You saw how she was with that baby. She loves her."

"Dana, we haven't seen your sister in six years. She doesn't write or call when she gets pregnant. She just shows up at the door with a baby, which she then leaves with us. Come on, even you have to admit, something is wrong with this."

She didn't want to admit it. Maybe more than anything, she didn't want to acknowledge that Stacy could have done something unforgivable this time. Something that might land her in prison.

"What do we do now?" she asked her husband.

"I've held off going global with Ella's description, hoping Stacy would show back up. But, Dana, I don't think I have any choice."

"You haven't heard anything on the DNA test you did on Ella and me?"

"I should be hearing at any time. But if the two of you aren't related, then I have to try to find out who this baby belongs to—no matter what happens to Stacy."

LIZA DROVE TO THE APARTMENT address Crystal Winslow had given her. She used the key to get into the studio apartment. As the door swung open, she caught her breath and pulled her weapon.

The apartment had been torn apart. Every conceivable hiding place had been searched, pillows and sofa bed sliced open, their stuffing spread across the room, books tossed to the floor along with clothing from the closet.

Liza listened, then cautiously stepped in. A small box of photographs had been dumped onto the floor and gone through from the looks of them. She checked the tiny kitchen and bath to make sure whoever had done this was gone before she holstered her weapon and squatted down to gingerly pick up one of the photographs.

It was a snapshot of Jordan Cardwell with two other handsome boys. All three were wearing ski clothing and looking cocky. She recognized a young Alex Winslow and assumed the other boy must be Tanner.

A curtain flapped loudly at an open window, making her start. Carefully, she glanced through the other photographs, assuming whatever the intruder had been looking for wasn't among these strewn on the floor.

It took her a moment, though, to realize what was missing from the pile of photos. There were none of Crystal. Nor any of Shelby or the rest of her group. That seemed odd that the women Alex had apparently been close to were missing from the old photographs. Nor were there any wedding pictures. Crystal had said she'd taken the ones of her. But who would have taken ones of Shelby and the rest of the young women he'd gone to school with in the canyon?

Rising, Liza called it in to the Bozeman Police Department, then waited until a uniformed officer arrived.

"I doubt you'll find any fingerprints, but given that Alex Winslow is a murder victim and he hasn't lived here long, I'm hoping whoever did this left us a clue," she told the officer. "I've contacted the crime lab in Missoula. I just want to make sure no one else comes in here until they arrive."

As she was leaving, Liza saw an SUV cruise slowly by. She recognized Crystal Winslow behind the wheel before the woman sped off.

JORDAN HAD JUST REACHED the bottom of the gondola for the ride up the mountain to the reunion picnic, when he spotted Liza.

She wasn't moving with her usual speed, but there was a determined look in her eye that made him smile.

"What?" she said when she joined him.

"You. After what happened, you could have taken one day off."

"I'm going to a picnic," she said. "I'm not even wearing my uniform."

She looked great out of uniform. The turquoise top she wore had slits at the shoulders, the silky fabric exposing tanned, muscled arms as it moved in the breeze. She wore khaki capris and sandals. Her long ebony-dark hair had been pulled up in back with a clip so the ends cascaded down her back. For as banged up as she was, she looked beautiful.

"I'm betting, though, that you're carrying a gun," he said, eyeing the leather shoulder bag hanging off one shoulder.

"You better hope I am." She laughed, but stopped quickly as if she was still light-headed.

"Are you sure you're all right?" he whispered, stepping closer.

"Dandy."

Past her, he saw Whitney and Ashley. Neither looked in a celebratory mood. When they spotted the deputy marshal, they jumped apart as if talking to each other would make them look more guilty.

"This could be a fun picnic," he said under his breath.

A few moments later Brittany arrived with her husband and small brood. Jordan was taken aback again at how happy and content she looked.

I want that, he thought as his gaze shifted to Liza.

As their gondola came around, they climbed in and made room for Whitney and Ashley, who'd come up behind them. Both women, though, motioned that they would take the next one.

"I'd love to know what they're hiding," Jordan said as he sat across from the deputy marshal. The gondola door closed then rocked as it began its ascent up the mountain. He had a view of the resort and the peaks from where he sat. And a view of Liza.

He could also see the gondola below them and the two women inside. They had their heads together. He wondered at the power Shelby still held over these women she'd lorded over in high school. Did anyone ever really get over high school?

"There's something I need to ask you," Liza said, drawing his attention back to her, which was no hardship. "How was it that you were the first person on the scene last night?"

He smiled, knowing that Hud was behind this. "I got worried about you and I wanted to see you. I drove up the canyon thinking I could talk you into having dinner with me. Another car had stopped before I got there.

I was just the first to go into the river." He hated that she was suspicious of him, but then again he couldn't really blame her.

"Did you see the pickup that forced me off the road?"

He nodded. "But it was just an old pickup. I was looking for your patrol SUV so I really didn't pay any attention."

She nodded. "I'd already told you I wasn't having dinner with you."

He grinned. "I thought I could charm you into changing your mind." He hurried on before she could speak. "I know you already told me no, but I thought we could at least pick up something and take it back to my cabin or your condo."

"You just don't give up, do you?"

"Kind of like someone else I know," he said and smiled at her. "I didn't have any ulterior motives. I've given this a lot of thought. Somehow, I think it all goes back to that party Tanner had at the cabin that night and the vandalism."

"And the photographs?" she asked.

He nodded. "I wish I'd stayed around long enough that night to tell you who took them."

They were almost to the top of the gondola ride. Off to his left, he saw where the caterers had set up the food for the picnic.

The gondola rocked as it came to a stop and the door opened. Jordan quickly held the doors open while the deputy marshal climbed out, then he followed, recalling what he could of that night, which wasn't much.

LIZA HOPED THE PICNIC WOULDN'T be quite as bad as the dinner had been. Jordan got them a spot near Shelby and the gang on one of the portable picnic tables that had been brought up the mountain.

"*Whatever* happened to you?" Shelby exclaimed loud enough for everyone to hear when she saw Liza.

While everyone in the canyon would have heard about her accident, Liza smiled and said, "Tripped. Sometimes I am so clumsy."

Shelby laughed. "You really should be more careful." Then she went back to holding court at her table. The usual suspects were in attendance and Tessa had been allowed to join in.

Liza watched out of the corner of her eye. Shelby monopolized the conversation with overly cheerful banter. But it was as if a pall had fallen over her group that not even she could lift.

After they ate, some of the picnickers played games in the open area next to the ski lift. When Liza spotted Tessa heading for the portable toilets set up in the trees, she excused herself and followed.

Music drifted on the breeze. A cloudless blue sky hung over Lone Peak. It really was the perfect day for a picnic and she said as much to Tessa when she caught up with her.

"Deputy," Tessa said.

"Why don't you call me Liza."

The woman smiled. "So I forget that I'm talking to the *law?*"

"I'm here as Jordan Cardwell's date."

Tessa chuckled at that, then sobered. "What happened to you?"

"Someone tried to stop me from looking into Alex's and Tanner's deaths."

The woman let out a groan.

"I was hoping you would have contacted me to talk," Liza said. "I can see you're troubled."

"Troubled?" Tessa laughed as she glanced back toward the group gathered below them on the mountain.

Liza followed her gaze and saw Shelby watching them. "We should step around the other side."

Tessa didn't argue. As they moved out of Shelby's sight, Tessa stopped abruptly and reached into her shoulder bag. "Here," she said, thrusting an envelope at the deputy marshal. "Alex left it with me and told me not to show it to anyone. He said to just keep it and not look inside until I had to."

Liza saw that it was sealed. "You didn't look?"

Tessa shook her head quickly.

"What did he mean, 'until you had to'?"

"I have no idea. I don't know what's in there and I don't care. If anyone even found out I had it…"

"Why did he trust *you* with this?" Liza had to ask.

Tessa looked as if she wasn't going to answer, then seemed to figure there was no reason to lie anymore. "I was in love with him. I have been since high school. Shelby always told me he wasn't good enough for me." She began to cry, but quickly wiped her eyes at the sound of someone moving through the dried grass on the other side of the portable toilets.

Liza hurriedly stuffed the envelope into her own shoulder bag.

An instant later Shelby came around the end of the stalls. "Are they all occupied?" she asked, taking in the two of them, then glancing toward the restrooms.

"I just used that one," Liza improvised. She turned and started back down the hillside.

Behind her she heard Shelby ask Tessa, "What did she want?"

She didn't hear Tessa's answer, but she feared Shelby wouldn't believe anything her friend said anyway. Tessa was running scared and anyone could see it—especially Shelby, who had her own reasons for being afraid.

Liza thought about the manila envelope Alex had left in Tessa's safekeeping. What was inside it? The photographs that Shelby had been trying to get her hands on? Liza couldn't wait to find out.

HUD HAD PUT A RUSH ON ELLA'S relational DNA test. He'd done it for Dana's sake. He saw that by the hour she was getting more attached to that baby. If he was right and Stacy had kidnapped it, then Dana's heart was going to be broken.

He was as anxious as she was to get the results. Meanwhile he needed to search for Stacy as he continued to watch for possible kidnappings on the law enforcement networks.

So far, he'd come up with nothing.

He found himself worrying not only about Stacy's disappearance, but also everything else that was going on. He'd done his best to stay out of Liza's hair. She could handle the murder case without him, he kept telling himself. Still, he'd been glad when Hilde had called and said she could come stay with Dana if he needed her to.

His phone rang as he paced in the living room. He'd never been good at waiting. He saw on caller ID that it was Shelby Durran-Iverson.

"Marshal Savage," he answered and listened while Shelby complained about Liza. It seemed she'd seen the deputy kissing Jordan. Hud swore silently. He had warned Liza about Jordan, but clearly she hadn't listened.

"Deputies get to have private lives," he told Shelby.

"Really? Even with the man who was with Alex

when he was murdered? I would think Jordan Cardwell is a suspect. Or at least should be."

It was taking all his self-control to keep from telling Shelby that she was more of a suspect than Jordan was.

"I'll look into it," he said.

"I should hope you'd do more than that. Isn't fraternizing with a suspect a violation that could call for at least a suspension—if not dismissal?"

"I said I would look into it." He hung up just as a car pulled up in front of the house. With a sigh of relief, he started to open the door to greet Hilde when he saw that it wasn't her car. Nor was it Stacy's.

When he saw who climbed out, he let out a curse. Before he could answer the door, his phone rang again. Figuring to get all the bad news over with quickly, he took the call from the lab as he heard footfalls on the porch and a tentative knock at the door.

"Hud, who is that at the door?" Dana called.

He listened to the lab tech give him the news, then thanked him and, disconnecting, stepped to her bedroom doorway.

"What is it?" she demanded. "Was that the lab on the phone?"

He nodded. "Ella *is* your niece."

Dana began to cry and laugh at the same time as she looked into Ella's beautiful face.

There was another knock at the door.

"Is that Stacy?" she asked, looking up, her eyes full of hope.

He shook his head. "I wish," he said and went to answer the door.

Chapter Fourteen

"Clay?" Dana said as her younger brother appeared in the bedroom doorway, Jordan at his heels.

"Hi," he said shyly. Clay had always been the quiet one, the one who ducked for cover when the rest of them were fighting. "Jordan told me you're pregnant with twins. Congratulations."

"Jordan?" she asked, shooting a look at her older brother. "Clay, what are you doing here?"

"I called Clay at the studio where I knew he was working," Jordan said.

"The studio let me use the company plane, so here I am," Clay said.

"Tell me what is going on. Why haven't you cashed your checks for the past six months and why does Stacy have your car?"

"Easy," Hud said as he stepped into the room. He gave both her brothers a warning look.

She didn't look at her husband. Her gaze was on her younger brother.

"I've been in Europe the past six months, then I changed apartments and forgot to put in a change of address," Clay said. "That's why I haven't cashed my checks. As for the car, I wasn't using it, so I told Stacy she could have it. I'm working for a movie studio in L.A. so I have a studio car that picks me up every morning."

"I'm glad things are going well for you," Dana said. "But you know what's going on with Stacy, don't you?"

"All I know is that she said she needed to get here to the ranch and could she borrow my car," Clay said. "So where is she?"

"That is the question," Hud said next to him. "She seems to have disappeared."

"Well, if you're worried because she has my car, it's no big deal."

"It's not the car that we're worried about," Dana said. "She left her baby here."

"Her *baby?*" Clay said. "Stacy has a baby?"

At the sound of another vehicle, Hud quickly left the room. Dana assumed it would be Hilde, but when he returned, he had Liza with him.

"You've met my brother Clay," Dana said.

Liza nodded. "Looks like you're having a family reunion."

"Doesn't it though," Hud said under his breath.

"Yes, all we need is Stacy," Dana said. "And a larger bedroom." She saw a look pass between the deputy and her husband. "I know that look. What's happened?"

"I just need to talk to the marshal for a few moments," Liza said. "But I'm going to need Jordan." He nodded and stepped out of the room with her and Hud, closing the door behind them.

"I can't stand being in this bed and not knowing what's going on," Dana said.

Clay was looking at the baby lying next to her. "Is that Stacy's?"

"Yes," Dana said with a sigh as Ella stirred awake.

At least Stacy hadn't kidnapped Ella. This little baby was Dana's niece. But where was Stacy? And did whatever Liza needed to talk to Hud and Jordan about have something to do with her sister or the murder?

"I THINK YOU'D BETTER SEE these photographs," Liza said to Hud the moment the bedroom door closed behind him. "Tessa gave them to me. She said Alex had left them in her safekeeping."

"Alex *trusted* Tessa?" Jordan said. "He had to know how close she was to Shelby."

"Obviously Alex trusted her not to give the photos to Shelby," Hud said and gave Jordan a how-did-you-get-involved-in-this-discussion? look.

"Tessa and Alex had a history," Liza said and told them what Crystal Winslow had told her. "She thought Alex was having an affair with Shelby, but I think it might have been Tessa. The two of them were dating in high school when Shelby broke them up so Tessa could spy on Tanner, right, Jordan?" He nodded and she continued. "That's a bond that Alex and Tessa shared against Shelby. With Tessa's marriage over and Alex's apparently not going well, they reconnected."

Hud looked through the photos then reluctantly handed them to Jordan. "You know the people in the photos?" he asked his brother-in-law.

Jordan nodded. "So someone took photos of the party. This can't be enough to get Alex killed over."

She waited until Jordan had finished going through the photos before she took them back, sorted through them until she found the two she wanted, then produced a magnifying glass from her pocket. "Check this out."

They all moved over to the table as Liza put the large

magnifying glass over the first photograph. "You can clearly see Malcolm Iverson's construction equipment in the background. But look here." She pointed at a spot to the left of one of the large dump trucks.

Jordan let out a surprised, "Whoa. It's Shelby."

Liza moved the magnifying glass to the second photo and both men took a look.

"Shelby vandalized the equipment," Jordan said. He let out a low whistle and looked at Liza. "You can clearly see Shelby dressed in black, dumping sugar into one of the two-ton trucks' gas tanks. If these photographs would have come out back then, she could have gone to jail."

Liza nodded. "Shelby has every reason in the world not to want these photographs to ever see daylight. She's married to the man whose father she bankrupted by vandalizing his construction equipment. The rest is like knocking over dominos. She vandalizes the equipment, Malcolm Iverson blames Harris Lancaster and shoots him, Malcolm goes to prison, then gets out and mysteriously dies in a boating accident."

"She didn't pull this off alone," Jordan said.

"No," Liza agreed. "In these two photos you can see Whitney and Ashley are keeping everyone's attention on them at the campfire," she said as she showed them two other photographs of the girls pretending to strip to whatever music was playing.

"Where was Tessa?" Jordan asked.

"With Tanner in the woods," Liza said and sifted through the photos until she found one of Tanner and Tessa coming out of the woods together.

Jordan let out a low whistle. "Shelby thought of everything."

"She just didn't realize that someone was taking photographs of the party," Liza said.

"I wonder where the negatives are. Alex wasn't dumb enough to trust Tessa completely. So who has the negatives?"

"Jordan has a point," Liza said.

Hud looked at his brother-in-law. "You should have gone into law enforcement."

Jordan smiled. "I'm going to take that as a compliment."

"I'm sure Hud meant it as one," Liza said.

"If Alex had the goods on Shelby and was blackmailing her, then why ask around about photos that were already in his possession? Or hint that Tanner's death wasn't a suicide?" Hud asked.

"Maybe he just wanted to shake up those involved. Or shake them down. What I'd like to know is who took the photos," Jordan said.

She looked over at him. "I just assumed Alex did since he isn't in any of them. Was he at the party that night?"

Jordan shrugged. "He was earlier."

"So these could merely be copies of photographs taken at the party," Hud said. "Which means there could be more than one person shopping the photos. That is what you're getting at, right, Deputy? Blackmail? For the past twenty years?"

Liza shook her head. "At least Alex hasn't been blackmailing Shelby for twenty years that I can find. I got his bank records for the past two years faxed to me. He made his first deposits only four months ago. Nine thousand dollars each month. He must have known that anything over ten thousand dollars would be red flagged by the bank."

"Why wait twenty years if he was going to blackmail Shelby?" Hud asked.

"I suspect that when his wife threw him out—along with all his stuff including some old photographs from high school, he hadn't looked at them in years," Liza said. "When he did, he saw what we're seeing and, since he already had reason to hate Shelby over the Tessa deal, decided to blackmail her."

"And she killed him," Jordan said.

Hud sighed. "Can we prove it?"

"Not yet," Liza said as she sorted through the photographs. "But I overheard Shelby on the phone with a creditor saying the check was in the mail. I asked around. Yogamotion has been having trouble paying its bills the past few months, but Hilde says it is packed for every class and it isn't cheap to join."

"So have you talked to Shelby yet?" Hud asked.

She shook her head. "There's something else you need to see." She pointed to a figure in the shadows of the pines at the edge of the campfire in one of the photographs.

"Stacy?" Hud said after taking the photo from her and using the magnifying glass to bring his sister-in-law's face into focus. He groaned and looked at Jordan.

"She wasn't there when I left," he said, holding up his hands. "It never dawned on me that she might have been at the party. We never went to the same parties or hung with the same crowd, so I have no idea what she was doing there."

"This could explain why Stacy came back to the canyon," Hud said with a curse.

"Maybe it is just bad timing on her part." Liza tapped

the photo. "But Stacy knows who was taking the photographs. She's looking right at the person with the camera."

"Which means she also knew there were photographs taken of the party that night."

"HUD?"

"Dana, what is it?" he cried, hearing something in his wife's voice that scared him. He rushed to the bedroom door to find Clay holding Dana's hand. Ella was crying.

"Can you take Ella? She needs a bottle," Dana said.

He tried to calm down. "That's all?" Then he saw his wife grimace. "What was that?" he demanded as Liza volunteered to take the crying baby and get Ella a bottle. Jordan had moved to the side of Dana's bed.

"A twinge. I've been having them all day," Dana admitted.

"Why didn't you tell me?" he demanded.

"Because I didn't want to worry you." She cringed as she had another one, this one definitely stronger from her reaction.

"I'm calling the doctor," he said and started to turn from the crowded room.

Hud hadn't heard a car drive up let alone anyone else enter the house so he was surprised to turn and see Stacy standing in the doorway of Dana's bedroom.

Maybe more shocking was how bad she looked. Both eyes were black and the blood from a cut on her cheek had dried to a dark red. Her hair was matted to her head on one side with what Hud guessed was also blood.

Dana let out a startled cry when she saw her sister.

"I wasn't completely honest with you," Stacy said in a hoarse voice as she stumbled forward.

That's when Hud saw the man behind her, the one holding the gun.

"Just get the baby," the man ordered Stacy, jabbing her in the back with the barrel of the gun. "Then we won't be troubling you people any further."

Stacy moved toward the bassinet that had been brought in next to Dana's bed. She leaned over it, gripping the sides.

Hud saw the bruises on her neck and noticed the way she was favoring her left side as if her ribs hurt her. He looked at the man in the doorway still holding the gun on Stacy.

"What's this about?" he asked the man, trying to keep his tone calm while his heart was pounding. Dana was in labor. He needed to get her to the hospital. He didn't need whatever trouble Stacy was in right now.

"Didn't Stacy tell you? She made off with my kid."

"She's my baby, too, Virgil," Stacy said, still staring down into the bassinet.

Hud remembered that the bassinct was empty because Liza had taken the baby into the kitchen with her to get her a bottle.

"He took Ella away from me," Stacy said, crying.

"Her name isn't *Ella,*" Virgil snapped. "I told you I was naming her after my mother. Her name is Katie, you stupid b—"

"He took her from me right after she was born and has been raising her with his girlfriend," Stacy said through her tears. "He would only let me come see her a few times."

"Because you'd make a crappy mother. Letting you even see her was a mistake," the man spat. "Now get the damned baby and let's go."

Even the thought of this man taking Ella made Hud

sick to his stomach. But he couldn't have any gunplay around Dana, especially since his own gun was locked up like it always was when he was home with the kids.

Dana still kept a shotgun by the kitchen back door, though, high on the wall where the kids couldn't reach it, but handy for adults. He wondered if Liza had heard Stacy and the man come in, if she had any idea what was going on?

Stacy turned her head, her gaze locking with Hud's, as she pleaded for his help.

"Let me get the baby for you," Hud said and stepped to the bassinet.

LIZA HAD BEEN HEATING A BOTTLE of formula for Ella when she heard the door open, then close softly. She listened, drawn by the faint sound of footfalls crossing the living room to Dana's door.

She peered around the corner in time to see the man with the gun. Her heart leaped to her throat. She was out of uniform, her weapon was in the car and she had a baby in one arm. She carefully opened the door of the microwave before it could ding and looked at Ella. The baby grinned at her and flapped her arms.

"I'm going to have to put you down. I need you to be really quiet," Liza whispered. She looked around for a place to put the baby and decided the rug in front of the sink was going to have to do. Carefully, she put down the baby. As she was rising, she saw the shotgun hanging high on the wall over the back door.

Knowing Dana, the shotgun would be loaded. All she could do was pray that it was since she wouldn't have the first idea where to look for shells. She could hear Ella babbling on the rug behind her and trying to snake toward her.

Hurry. She reached up on tiptoes and eased the shotgun off its rack. Trying not to make a sound, she cracked the gun open. Two shells. She dearly loved Dana who knew there was nothing more worthless than an unloaded shotgun.

Ella was watching her expectantly as she crept to the kitchen doorway. She could see the man with the gun, but she could hear voices coming from Dana's bedroom. Normally, she was cool and calm. It was what made her a good cop. But so much was riding on what she did now, she felt the weight of it at heart level.

She had no idea what she would be walking into. No idea who the man was or why he was in this house with a gun. Moving along the edge of the room to keep the old hardwood floor from creaking, she headed for the bedroom doorway.

"Come on, hurry it up. Give me the baby," snapped a male voice she didn't recognize. "We don't have all day."

Liza was next to the doorway. She could see the man holding the gun. He had it pointed at Stacy who was standing next to Hud beside the empty bassinet. Hud had his hands inside the bassinet. He appeared to be rolling up Ella's quilt.

Taking a breath, she let it out slowly, the same way she did at the gun range just before she shot.

Then she moved quickly. She jammed the barrel of the shotgun into the man's side and in a clear, loud voice said, "Drop the gun or I will blow a hole in you the size of Montana."

The man froze for a moment, then slowly turned his

head to look at her. When he saw her, he smiled. "Put down the shotgun before you hurt yourself, little lady."

"There's something I wasn't honest with you about, either," Stacy said, turning from the bassinet. "My brother-in-law is a marshal and that woman holding a shotgun is a deputy. She will kill you if you don't drop your gun."

"But I'll kill you first," he snarled and lifted the gun to take aim.

Liza moved in quickly, slamming the barrel hard into his ribs as Hud threw Stacy to the floor. Her momentum drove the man back and into the wall. She knocked the pistol from his hand, then cold-cocked him with the shotgun. As his eyes rolled back into his head, he slid down the wall to the floor.

Hud already had the man's gun and bent to frisk him, pulling out his wallet. "Dana, are you all right?" he asked over his shoulder. Liza could hear Stacy sobbing.

"I'm fine," Dana said.

The marshal rose. "I'll get my cuffs." He was back an instant later and had the man cuffed. Liza hadn't taken her eyes off their prisoner. She'd seen his hand twitch and knew he was coming around.

"Stacy, Ella is in the kitchen on the floor," Liza said over her shoulder.

"I'm not leaving without my baby," the man screamed at Stacy as she hurried past her and into the kitchen. "I'll kill you next time. I swear, I'm going to kill you."

Hud hauled him to his feet. "You aren't going anywhere but jail. You just threatened to kill my sister-in-law in front of a half dozen witnesses."

"I'll take him in," Liza said. "You take Dana to the hospital. I heard her say her water just broke." As she led him out of the house, Liza began to read him his rights.

Chapter Fifteen

After booking Virgil Browning, Liza was just in time to catch Shelby as she was coming out of Yogamotion. She had a large bag, the handles looped over one shoulder, and seemed to be in a hurry. As Liza had walked past Shelby's SUV, she'd noticed there were suitcases in the back.

"I'm sorry, we're closed, Deputy," Shelby said. "And I'm in a hurry."

"You might want to open back up. Unless you want to discuss why you were being blackmailed at your house with your husband present."

All the color washed from the woman's face. She leaned into the door as if needing it for support. "I don't—"

"Don't bother lying. Alex would have bled you dry since his wife was taking everything in the divorce, right? He needed money and he had you right where he wanted you. *Of course,* you had to kill him."

"I didn't kill Alex." When Liza said nothing, Shelby opened the door to Yogamotion and turned on the light as they both stepped back inside.

Liza saw the sign that had been taped to the door.

Closed Until Further Notice. Shelby was skipping town, sure as the devil.

"I swear I didn't kill him," she said as they went into her office and sat down. "Why would I kill him? I had no idea who was blackmailing me," Shelby cried.

Liza studied her face for a moment, trying to decide if she was telling the truth or lying through her teeth.

"So how was it you made the payment if you didn't know who was blackmailing you?"

"I sent ten thousand dollars in cash to J. Doe, general delivery in Bozeman each month."

"You were that afraid of the truth coming out?" Liza had to ask.

"How can you ask that?" Shelby cried. "It wasn't just the vandalism. Wyatt's father lost his business, went to prison and probably killed himself, all because of what I did." She was crying now, real tears.

"You had to know it would eventually come out."

She shook her head adamantly. "It would destroy my marriage, my reputation, I'd have to leave town. Wyatt has said if he ever found out who did that to his father, he'd kill them."

Liza felt a chill run the length of her spine. "Maybe he's already killed. Didn't he blame Tanner for what happened?"

She quit crying for a moment and wiped at her tears, frowning as she realized what Liza was saying. "Yes, he blamed Tanner, but he wouldn't..." The words died off. "Tanner killed *himself*."

"Did he? Was Wyatt jealous of your relationship with Tanner?" Liza saw the answer in the woman's expression. "Tanner was supposed to be watching the equipment, right?"

"No, Wyatt wouldn't…" She shook her head. "He's had to overcome so much."

"Does he know about the blackmail?"

"No, of course not."

But Liza could see the fear in the woman's eyes. "If he found out that you were being blackmailed and thought it was Alex Winslow behind it, what would your husband do?"

"He couldn't have found out," she said. "If he knew, he would have left me."

Liza thought about that for a moment. "What if you weren't the only one being blackmailed?"

Shelby's head came up. "What?"

"Has your husband been having similar financial problems to yours?" Liza asked.

"It's the economy," Shelby said. "It's not…"

"Because he's been paying a blackmailer just like you have?"

"Why would he do that?" Her eyes widened and Liza saw that, like her, Shelby could think of only one reason her husband might be paying a blackmailer.

"Oh, no, no." She began to wail, a high keening sound. "He wouldn't have hurt Tanner. Not Tanner." She rocked back and forth, hugging her stomach.

"I have to ask you," Liza said. "Were you ever pregnant with Tanner's baby?"

Her wailing didn't stop, but it slowed. She shook her head, before she dropped it into her hands. "I didn't want him to leave Big Sky after graduation. I thought that if he married me I could say I had a miscarriage. Or with luck, I could get pregnant quickly."

"Where is your husband?" Liza asked her.

"He's been out of town, but I expect him back tonight."

"That's why you were leaving. You're afraid your husband has found out."

Shelby didn't have to answer. The terror in her eyes said it all.

"I'd tell you not to leave town," Liza said, "but I'm afraid that advice could get you killed tonight."

Shelby's cell phone rang. She glanced at it. "I need to take this."

As Liza was walking away, she heard Shelby say, "I'm so sorry." She was crying, her last words garbled but still intelligible. "Really? Just give me a few minutes."

AFTER LEAVING THE RANCH, Jordan drove around aimlessly. His mind whirled with everything that had happened since his return to the canyon.

Foremost was Alex and Liza's blackmail theory. Alex had always resented the rich people who came and went at Big Sky—but especially those who built the huge houses they lived in only a few weeks each year.

So had Alex blackmailed Shelby for the money? Or for breaking him and Tessa up all those years ago?

But was that what had gotten him killed? As much as he disliked Shelby, he couldn't imagine her actually shooting Alex. True she used to hunt, maybe still did, and hadn't been a bad shot. And she was cold-blooded, no doubt about that.

It just felt as if there had to be more.

Both Hud and Liza had warned him to leave town and stay out of the investigation. He couldn't, even if he wanted to. Driving past Yogamotion, he saw that the lights were out. There was a note on the door. Getting out, he walked to the door. Closed Until Further Notice.

He pulled out his cell phone and tried Shelby's house. No answer. Then he got Crystal Winslow's number from information and waited for her to pick up.

"Hello?"

"Crystal, you probably don't remember me, I'm Jordan Cardwell."

"I remember you." Her voice sounded laced with ice.

"I need to ask you something about Alex. I heard he majored in engineering at Montana State University. Is that how he made his money?"

"He was a consultant. He worked for large construction projects like bridges and highways and some smaller ones that I am only now finding out about."

He heard something in her voice, a bitterness. "Smaller jobs?"

"Apparently, he was working for Shelby Iverson and had been for years. Her husband signed the checks, but I'm betting she was behind it. He must have thought I was so stupid. What could Iverson Construction need an engineer consultant for? They build houses."

"Crystal, how often did they hire Alex?"

"Every month for years."

"Twenty years?"

"All these years." She was crying. "That bitch has been…playing my husband like a puppet on a string."

More likely it was Alex playing her. So he had been blackmailing not Shelby, but Wyatt since Tanner's death and hiding it as work-related payments. No wonder Liza hadn't found it.

As he told Crystal how sorry he was and hung up, he wondered how Wyatt had been able to hide this from

Shelby all these years. With building going crazy at Big Sky until recently, maybe it hadn't been that much of a strain on Wyatt.

He would ask Wyatt when he saw him. Which would be soon, he thought as he parked in front of the Iverson mansion on the hill. The place looked deserted. As he started to get out a big black SUV came roaring up.

WYATT IVERSON LOOKED HARRIED and dirty as if he'd just been working at one of his construction sites. He had a cut on his cheek that the blood had only recently dried on and bruises as if he'd been in a fistfight. "If you're looking for Shelby, she's not here."

"Actually, I was looking for you," Jordan said, not caring what had happened to Wyatt Iverson or his wife. "Have a minute?"

"No, I just got home. I've been out of town."

"This won't take long," Jordan said, following him up the steps to the front door and pushing past him into the large marble foyer. "I just need to know how you killed Tanner Cole. I already suspect *why* you did it, misguided as it was." Through an open doorway he saw a large bedroom with women's clothing strewn all over the bed and floor. Shelby either had trouble finding something to wear tonight or she had hightailed it out of town.

"I really don't have time for this," Wyatt said behind him.

He got as far as the living room with its white furniture he would bet no one had ever sat on, before he turned to look into the other man's face. Wyatt was magazine-model handsome, a big, muscled man, but Jordan was sure he could take him in a fair fight.

Unfortunately, when he saw the gun in Wyatt Iverson's hand, he knew he wasn't going to get a chance to find out.

"You want to know how your friend died?" Wyatt demanded. "I told him that everything was going to be all right. That he shouldn't blame himself for my father's construction equipment being vandalized. He'd already had a few drinks by the time I got to the cabin." Wyatt stopped just inches from Jordan now.

"Tanner felt horrible about what had happened, blamed himself," he continued, a smirk on his face. "I suggested we have more drinks and bury the hatchet so to speak. By the time we went out by the fire pit, he was feeling no pain. I kept plying him with booze until he could barely stand up, then I bet him he couldn't balance on an upturned log. You should have seen his expression when I put the noose around his neck."

Jordan knew the worst thing he could do was go for the gun. Wyatt had the barrel aimed at his heart and, from the trapped look in the man's eyes, he would use it if provoked. But seeing that Wyatt Iverson felt no remorse for what he'd done and realizing the man was ready to kill again, Jordan lunged at the gun.

Wyatt was stronger than he looked and clearly he'd been expecting—probably hoping—Jordan would try something. The sound of the gunshot ricocheted through the expanse of the large living room, a deafening report that was followed by a piercing pain in Jordan's shoulder.

Wyatt twisted the gun from his fingers and backhanded him with the butt. Jordan saw stars and suddenly the room started spinning. The next thing he knew he was on the floor, looking up at the man. His shoulder hurt like hell, but the bullet appeared to have only grazed his skin.

"You lousy bastard." Jordan struggled to get up, but Wyatt kicked him hard in the stomach, then knelt down beside him, holding the gun to his head.

"Your friend knew he deserved it. I told him how my old man had let his insurance on the equipment lapse, how this would destroy my family and your friend Tanner nodded and closed his eyes and I kicked the log out."

"You *murdered* him," Jordan said between clenched teeth.

"He got what he deserved."

"He didn't deserve to die because of some vandalized equipment even if he had been responsible. Shelby set up Tanner that night—from the party to the vandalism—to get back at him. It was that old story of a woman scorned."

With a start Jordan saw that this wasn't news. Wyatt had known. "How long have you known that you killed the wrong person? Then you killed Alex to keep it your little family secret and end the blackmail?"

"*Alex?* I didn't kill Alex."

Jordan started to call the man a liar. But why would he lie at a time like this when he'd already confessed to one murder? With a jolt, Jordan realized that Wyatt was telling the truth. He didn't kill Alex. *Shelby.* No wonder she'd taken off. Not only would it now come out about her vandalizing the Iverson Construction equipment, but that she'd killed Alex to keep the photographs from going public.

"Where's your wife, Iverson?" Jordan asked through the pain as Wyatt jerked him to his feet and dragged him toward the front door with the gun to his head.

"Have you known all along it was her? No? Then you must be furious. Did you catch her packing to make her getaway?" Jordan had a thought. "Does she know that you killed Tanner?"

Wyatt made a sound that sent a chill up Jordan's spine.

He thought about the cut and bruise on Iverson's cheek, that harried look in his eye—and the dirt on him as if he'd been digging at one of his construction sites. "What did you do to her?" he demanded. "You wouldn't kill your own wife!"

"One more word and I'll kill you right there," the man said as he pulled him outside to the rental car. He reached inside and released the latch on the hatchback.

"You're going to kill me anyway. But you have to know you can't get away with this." He felt the shove toward the open back of the SUV just an instant before the blow to his head. Everything went dark. His last clear thought was of Tanner and what he must have felt the moment Wyatt kicked the log out from under his feet.

LIZA CALLED HUD'S CELL ON HER way to the Iverson house.

"How is Dana?" she asked first.

"In labor. We're at the hospital and they are making her comfortable. They're talking C-section, but you know Dana. She's determined she's going to have these babies the natural way."

"Give her my best. Did you get a chance to ask Stacy about Tanner's party?" she asked as she drove toward the mountain and the Iverson house.

"She was pretty shaken up after what happened and I got busy, but she's standing right here. I'll let you talk to her since I have to get back to Dana." He handed off the phone.

A moment later a shaky-voiced Stacy said, "Hello?"

"I need to know about the party Tanner Cole had at the Iverson Construction site twenty years ago."

"What?"

"You were there. I've seen a photograph of you standing around the campfire. I need to know who shot the photos. Come on, Stacy, it wasn't that long after that that Tanner died. Don't tell me you don't remember."

"I remember," she said, sounding defensive. "I was just trying to understand why you would ask me who took the photos. I did. It was my camera."

"*Your* camera? Why were you taking photographs at the party?"

"Jordan. I wanted to get something on him," she said. "He was always telling on me to Mother."

Blackmail, great. Liza sighed. "If it was your camera, then how is it that there's a photo of you?"

Silence then. "Alex Winslow. He wanted to borrow the camera for a moment. I made him give it back—"

"By promising to get him copies," Liza finished.

"Yes, how did you—"

"Do you still have the negatives?"

"I doubt it. Unless they're stored in my things I left here at the ranch."

"Let me talk to Jordan," Liza said, feeling as if all the pieces of the puzzle were finally coming together.

"Jordan? He's not here. He asked me who took the photos, then he left, saying he'd come by the hospital later."

"Do you know where he went?" Liza asked, suddenly worried.

"He said something about blackmail and the other side of the coin."

Ahead, Liza saw the Iverson house come into view in her headlights. "If you see him, tell him to call my cell." She gave Stacy the number, then disconnected as she pulled into the wide paved drive.

Parking, she tried Jordan's cell phone number. It went straight to voice mail. She left a message for him to call her.

The Iverson house could only be described as a mansion. But then Wyatt Iverson was in the construction business. Of course his home would have to be magnificent.

Liza got out and walked up the steps to the wide veranda. She rang the doorbell, heard classical music play inside and was reminded of Crystal Winslow's house down in Bozeman. It wasn't anywhere as large or as grand.

Liza thought about an old Elvis Presley song about a house without love. Or honesty, she thought as she rang the bell again.

Getting no answer, she checked the five-car garage. There was a large ski boat, a trailer with four snowmobiles and the large black SUV, the same one Liza had seen Wyatt Iverson driving the night of the reunion dinner.

He'd returned home. So where was he? And where was Jordan? She tried his cell phone again. As before, it went straight to voice mail.

Something was wrong. She felt it in her bones. If Wyatt Iverson had returned, where else might he have gone? She recalled overhearing Shelby say what sounded like she was going to meet someone. Was she stupid enough to agree to see her husband? If so, where would they have gone if not their house?

Yogamotion was her first thought. But she'd seen Shelby hightail it out of there. Was it possible Wyatt had taken another vehicle? She thought about Jordan. What if he'd come up here as she suspected?

She didn't want to go down that particular trail of thought. Maybe Wyatt Iverson had gone by his construction office. Unlike his father, Wyatt kept all his equipment under lock and key at a site back up Moonlight Basin.

She hurried to her rental SUV and, climbing behind the wheel, started the engine and headed for Moonlight Basin. All her instincts told her to hurry.

Chapter Sixteen

Jordan came to in darkness. He blinked, instantly aware of the pain. His wrists were bound with duct tape behind him. More duct tape bound his ankles. A strip had been placed over his mouth. He lay in the back of the rented SUV. Outside the vehicle he heard a sound he recognized and sat up, his head swimming. Something warm and sticky ran down into his left eye. Blood.

Through the blood he looked out through an array of construction equipment. He couldn't see the piece of equipment that was making all the noise, but he could see a gravel pit behind the site and catch movement.

Now seemed an odd time to be digging in a gravel pit. Unless, he thought with a start, you wanted to bury something.

Jordan knew he was lucky to be alive. He'd been a damned fool going to Iverson's house unarmed. What had he hoped to accomplish? The answer was simple. He'd wanted to hear Wyatt Iverson admit to Tanner's murder. He'd also wanted to know how he'd done it.

So he'd accomplished what he'd set out to do—a suicidal mission that had been successful if one didn't take his current predicament into consideration.

Hurriedly, he began to work at the tape on his wrists.

There were few sharp edges in the back of the SUV. Nor could he get the door open thanks to child locks. In frustration at modern advances, he threw himself into the backseat and was headed for the front seat to unlock the doors, when he heard it.

The noise of the running equipment had dropped to a low purr.

Jordan felt around quickly for a sharp edge. He found it on the metal runner of the front passenger seat and began to work frantically at the tape. Whatever Wyatt Iverson had been up to, he'd stopped. Jordan had a bad feeling that he'd be coming for him any moment.

The tape gave way. He quickly peeled the strip from his mouth then reached down to free his ankles.

The back door of the SUV swung open and he was instantly blinded by the glaring beam of a heavy-duty flashlight.

"Get out," Iverson barked.

Jordan saw that the gun was in the man's other hand and the barrel was pointed at him. He freed his ankles and did as he was told. As he stepped out, he breathed in the cold night air. It made him shiver. Or it could have been the sudden knowledge of what Iverson planned to do with him.

Standing, he could see where the earth had been dug out in a long trench. There was already one vehicle at the bottom of the trench. He recognized Shelby's expensive SUV.

"Get behind the wheel," Iverson ordered, and holding the gun on him, climbed in behind him in the backseat.

Jordan could feel the cold hard metal of the gun barrel pressed against his neck.

"Start the car." Iverson tossed him the keys.

His hand was shaking as he inserted the key. The engine turned right over even though he was wishing for a dead battery right then.

"Now drive through the gate to the back of the property. Try anything and I'll put a bullet into your brain and jump out."

Jordan drove through the gate and down the path that led to the gravel pit and ultimately the trench Iverson had dug for Shelby—and now him. He realized there was only one thing he could do. Iverson would have him stop at the high end of the trench. He would get out and send Jordan to his death—either before he buried him at the bottom of the trench or after.

He hit the child locks so Iverson couldn't get out and gunned the engine. He would take Iverson with him, one way or the other.

As the Iverson Construction site came into view, Liza noticed that the large metal gate hung open. She cut her headlights and slowly pulled to the side of the road.

It wasn't until she shut off her engine and got out that she heard the sound of a front-end loader running in the distance. Drawing her weapon, she moved through the darkness toward the sound.

She'd just cleared the fence and most of the equipment when she saw an old red pickup parked back between some other old trucks. She could see where the right side of it was all banged up. Some of the paint of the patrol SUV was still on the side. It was definitely the pickup that had run her off the road.

Ahead she heard a car start up. She could make out movement in the faint starlight. She hurried toward it, keeping to the shadows so she wasn't spotted.

But the car didn't come in her direction as she'd thought it would. Instead, it went the other way. In its headlights she saw the gravel pit and finally the trench and the front-end loader idling nearby.

To her amazement the vehicle engine suddenly roared. The driver headed for the trench.

Liza ran through the darkness, her heart hammering, as the vehicle careened down the slope and into the narrow ditch. She reached the fence, rushed through the gate and across the flat area next to the gravel pit in time to see the lights of the vehicle disappear into the trench.

Her mind was racing. What in the—

The sound of metal meeting metal filled the night air. She came to a skidding stop at the edge of the trough and looked down to see two vehicles. Smoke rose from between their crumpled metal, the headlights of the second one dimmed by the dirt and gravel that had fallen down around it.

She waited a moment for the driver to get out, then realizing he must be trapped in there, the trench too narrow for him to open his door, she scrambled down into the deep gully, weapon ready.

As she neared the vehicle, she recognized it. The rental SUV Jordan had been driving. Her pulse began to pound. Jordan did crazy things sometimes, she thought, remembering how he'd swum out into the river to be with her while she waited for the ambulance to arrive.

But he wouldn't purposely drive into this trench, would he? Which begged the question, where was Wyatt Iverson?

"COME ON, BABIES," DANA SAID under her breath and pushed.

"That's it," her doctor said. "Almost there. Just one more push."

Dana closed her eyes. She could feel Hud gripping her hand. Her first twin was about to make his or her way into the world. She felt the contraction, hard and fast, and pushed.

"It's a boy!" A cheer came up at the end of the bed. She opened her eyes and looked into the mirror positioned over the bed as the doctor held up her baby.

A moment later she heard the small, high-pitched cry of her son and tried to relax as Hud whispered that they had a perfect baby boy.

Dr. Burr placed the baby in Dana's arms for a moment. She smiled down at the crinkled adorable face before the doctor handed the baby off to the nurses standing by. "One more now. Let's see how that one's doing."

Dana could hear the baby's strong heartbeat through the monitor. She watched the doctor's face as Dr. Burr felt her abdomen first, then reached inside. Dana knew even before the doctor said the second baby was breech.

"Not to worry. I'll try to turn the little darling," the doctor assured her. "Otherwise, sometimes we can pull him out by his feet. Let's just give it a few minutes. The second baby is generally born about fifteen minutes after the first."

Dana looked over at her son now in the bassinet where a nurse was cleaning him up. "He looks like you," she said to her husband and turned to smile up at him as another contraction hit.

LIZA REACHED THE BACK of the car. She could hear movement inside. "Jordan!" she called. A moment later the back hatch clicked open and began to rise. She stepped to the side, weapon leveled at the darkness inside the SUV, cursing herself for not having her flashlight. "Jordan?"

A moan came from inside, then more movement.

"Liza, he has a gun!" Jordan cried.

The shot buzzed past her ear like a mad hornet. She ducked back, feeling helpless as she heard the struggle in the car and could do little to help. Another shot. A louder moan.

"I'm coming out," Wyatt Iverson called from inside the SUV. "I'm not armed."

"I have him covered," Jordan yelled out. "But you can shoot him if you want to."

Liza leveled her weapon at the gaping dark hole at the back of the SUV. Wyatt Iverson appeared head-first. He fell out onto the ground. She saw that he was bleeding from a head wound and also from what appeared to be a gunshot to his thigh. She quickly read him his rights as she rolled him over and snapped a pair of handcuffs on him.

"Jordan, are you all right?" she called into the vehicle. She heard movement and felt a well of relief swamp her as he stumbled out through the back. "What is going on?"

"He planned to bury me in this trench," Jordan said. "I think Shelby is in the other car. I suspect he killed her before he put her down here."

Wyatt was heaving, his face buried in his shoulder as he cried.

"Can you watch him for a moment?" Liza asked, seeing that Jordan was holding a handgun—Wyatt's, she assumed.

She holstered her own weapon and climbed up over the top of the SUV to the next one. Dirt covered most of the vehicle except the very back. She wiped some of the dirt from the window and was startled to see a face pressed against the glass.

There was duct tape over Shelby's mouth. Her eyes were huge, her face white as a ghost's. Blood stained the front of her velour sweatshirt where she'd been shot in the chest at what appeared to be close range since the fabric was burned around the entry hole.

Liza pulled out her cell and hit 911. "We'll need an ambulance and the coroner." She gave the dispatcher directions, then climbed back over the top of Jordan's rental SUV to join him again.

Wyatt was still crying. Jordan, she noticed, was more banged up than she'd first realized. He was sitting on the SUV's bumper. He looked pale and was bleeding from a shoulder wound.

"Come on, let's get out of this trench before the sides cave in and kill us all," she said. "Are you sure you're all right?"

He grinned up at her. "Just fine, Deputy," he said, getting to his feet. "I sure was glad to see you."

As she pulled Wyatt to his feet and the three of them staggered up out of the hole, she smelled the pine trees, black against the night sky. The air felt colder as if winter wasn't far behind. She looked toward Lone Peak. The snow on the top gleamed in the darkness. Everything seemed so normal.

The rifle shot took them all by surprise. Wyatt suddenly slumped forward and fell face-first into the dirt. Jordan grabbed her and knocked her to the ground behind one of the huge tires of a dump truck as a second shot thudded into Wyatt's broad back.

Liza rolled and came up with her weapon. She scrambled over to Wyatt, checked for a pulse and finding none, swore as she scrambled back over to Jordan out of the line of fire. She could hear the sound of sirens in the distance. It was too dark to tell where the shots had come from.

But over the high-pitched whine of the sirens, she heard a vehicle start up close by. "Stay here," she ordered Jordan and took off running toward her SUV.

A SECOND SON WAS BORN seventeen minutes after the first. Dana began to cry when she saw him.

"Identical twin boys," Dr. Burr told her. "Congratulations."

Hud hugged her. "We really have to quit doing this," he whispered. "I can't take it."

She laughed through her tears. No one was more fearless than her husband, but she knew what he meant. Her heart had been in her throat, afraid something would go wrong. She couldn't bear the thought of losing her babies.

"You did good," the doctor said, squeezing her hand. "Do you have names picked out yet?"

Dana shook her head and looked to Hud. "I have a couple of ideas though."

He laughed. "I'm sure you do. I'd better call everyone."

"You mean Liza," she said. "You haven't heard from her?"

He checked his phone. "No."

She could tell he was worried.

"Jordan left without telling anyone where he was going, but everyone else is out in the hall waiting for the news."

"Go do whatever it is you have to do, Marshal," she said, smiling. "But let me know when you hear from Liza—and my brother."

He grinned at her. "It's going to be so nice to have you back on your feet."

LIZA REACHED HER SUV just moments after seeing a set of headlights coming out of the pines in the distance. Jordan was hot on its heels. He leaped into the passenger seat as she started the engine. She hurriedly turned around and went after the killer.

The other vehicle was moving fast. She saw the headlights come around as the vehicle hit the narrow strip of pavement, the driver almost losing control.

Liza followed the other vehicle headed down the mountain. The road was treacherous with lots of switchbacks. She had to assume whoever had killed Wyatt knew the road. But the driver was also running scared.

She glanced over at Jordan. He needed medical attention. "You should have stayed back there to wait for the ambulance," she said as she managed to keep the vehicle in front of her in sight. "Call and tell the ambulance to wait in Meadow Village. The coroner might as well wait, too."

"See, you would have missed my company if I hadn't come along," he said. "And Wyatt wasn't great company when he was alive, let alone dead."

She shot him another look, worried that he might be hurt worse than she thought. "Did he say anything about why he killed Shelby?"

"We didn't get to talk much. He knew she vandalized his father's equipment. I don't think he took it well. He swore he didn't kill Alex. But he killed Tanner and Alex has been blackmailing Wyatt for years, writing it off as a business expense."

Liza suspected that whoever had killed Alex

Winslow had just killed Wyatt Iverson as well, but why? Shelby was dead. So who had just shot Wyatt?

"All of this started because Shelby was going to force Tanner into marriage, one way or the other," Jordan said. "When he broke up with her, she vandalized the construction equipment he was responsible for to get even with him. She hadn't given a damn whose equipment it was. Ironic it turned out to be her future father-in-law's. And look where the repercussions of that one malicious act have landed us all."

The vehicle ahead swung through a tight curve, fishtailed and for a moment Liza thought the driver would lose control and crash. She could make out a figure behind the wheel, but still couldn't tell who it was. All the SUVs looked similar.

Liza knew who wasn't behind the wheel of the car in front of her. Shelby was dead. So was Malcolm Iverson and his son Wyatt. Alex had found the photographs and gotten himself killed when he'd blackmailed Shelby— her husband. She'd been so sure that Wyatt had killed Alex because of it. Alex had somehow figured out that Wyatt had killed Tanner.

Now she suspected that the last piece of the puzzle was in that SUV ahead of her. Whoever had shot Wyatt Iverson must have shot Alex. But why? Was it possible Alex had been blackmailing someone else?

Ahead she caught a glimpse of the lights of Meadow Village. She was right behind the vehicle in front of her. The driver didn't stand a chance of getting away.

She thought about the photos and tried to remember if there was anything else in them. "That one photograph," she said more to herself than to Jordan. "Wasn't it of Tanner and Tessa coming out of the woods?"

"Like I said, Shelby thought of everything."

"Including making her best friend go into the woods with Tanner?"

Jordan let out a curse. "I never could understand why Tessa did what Shelby told her to. She said Shelby even talked her into marrying Danny Spring, when apparently she has always been in love with Alex."

Liza felt a chill race up her spine. "But Alex had these photographs. He would have seen Tessa coming out of the woods with Tanner."

"What are you saying?" Jordan asked.

"Alex would have known just how far Tessa would go to protect Shelby. So why give her the photographs for safekeeping?"

"That's what I said. Unless he *wanted* her to look at the photos. But once she did, why wouldn't she destroy them to protect Shelby?"

"Because she was through protecting Shelby," Liza said. "Shelby had finally done something that she couldn't forgive. Alex's estranged wife believed Alex was having an affair with *Shelby*. I suspect Tessa thought the same thing."

"That would have been the last straw for Tessa. She would have felt betrayed by all of them."

"You're saying if Tessa found out, it would have been the last straw."

Ahead the SUV fishtailed on one of the turns and Liza had to back off to keep from hitting it.

"Tessa. She's in that car, isn't she?" Jordan said. "She used to go out shooting for target practice before hunting season with Shelby and the rest of us. She always pretended to be a worse shot than Shelby, but I always suspected she was better and just didn't dare show it.

She's been hiding her light under a bushel for years, as my mother used to say."

"Not anymore," Liza said as the vehicle ahead of them went off the road on the last tight turn. It crashed down into the trees. Liza stood on the brakes. "Stay here or I'll arrest you!" she shouted to Jordan and jumped out.

With her weapon drawn she hurried to where the SUV had gone off. She hadn't gone far when she heard the shot.

Liza scrambled down into the trees, keeping out of the driver's sights until she finally reached the back of the vehicle. She saw that just as she'd suspected, Tessa was behind the wheel. There was a rifle next to her, the barrel pointed at her. She was bleeding heavily from the crash and the gunshot wound to her side, but she was still breathing.

Liza quickly called for the ambulance. "Just stay still," she told Tessa. "Help is on the way."

Tessa managed a smile. "There is no help for me. Is Wyatt dead?"

"Yes."

"And Shelby?"

"She's dead, too."

Tessa nodded. "Good. They all ruined my life."

"Why kill Alex, though?" Liza asked. "I thought you loved him?"

Tessa got a faraway look in her eyes. "Alex was the only man I ever really loved. I thought he loved me but he was only using me. He said he forgave me for the past, but he lied. He used me just like Shelby and Wyatt used me." She smiled sadly. "They all used me. But I showed them. I wasn't as good at playing their games, but I was always a better shot than any of them."

Epilogue

The hospital room was packed with well-wishers, flowers, balloons and stuffed animals. Dana looked around her and couldn't help the swell of emotion that bubbled up inside of her.

"It's the hormones," she said as she wiped her eyes.

Clay and Stacy had brought Hank and Mary to the hospital to see their new little brothers.

"Hank wants to name them after his horses," Stacy told her. "Mary wanted to name them after her dolls." Stacy looked stronger. Hud had promised her that Virgil would never bother her again. Apparently, there were numerous warrants out on him, including the fact that he'd broken his probation. So added to the latest charges, Virgil would be going back to prison for a very long time.

Dana watched her elderly ranch manager make his way through the crowd to her. Warren Fitzpatrick was as dried out as a stick of jerky and just as tough, but he knew more about cattle than any man she'd ever known. He'd also been there for her from the beginning. As far as she was concerned he was a permanent fixture on the Cardwell Ranch. She'd already promised him a spot in the family cemetery up on the hill.

He gave her a wink. "That's some cute little ones. I just had a peek at them down the hall. Goin' to make some fine ranch hands," he said with a chuckle. "I've got a couple of fine saddles picked out for them. Never too early for a man to have his own saddle."

She smiled up at him. It was the first time she'd ever seen a tear in his eye.

Her father arrived then with a giant teddy bear. "How's my baby girl?" he asked. She'd always been his baby girl—even now that she was the mother of four and only a few years from forty.

"I'm good," she said as she leaned up to hug him. He put the bear down and hugged her tighter than usual.

"I was worried about you," he whispered.

"I'm fine."

"Yes, you are," he said, smiling at her.

Then Uncle Harlan came in with the second giant teddy bear and her father grinned, knowing that she'd thought he'd forgotten she was having twins.

Her father-in-law called. Brick Savage had been sick for some time, but he promised to make the trip down from his cabin outside West Yellowstone to see his new grandsons soon.

"I think we should all leave and let her get some rest," Hilde said to the crowd of friends and family.

"I agree," Hud said. He looked exhausted and so did Liza, who'd stopped in earlier. It had been a shock to hear about the deaths up on the mountain and Tessa Ryerson Spring's involvement. Tessa had died before the ambulance got to her.

Jordan had stopped by earlier, his shoulder bandaged. Dana had hugged him for a long time after hearing what he'd been through. Both he and Liza were lucky to be alive.

Dana noticed that they had left together. She smiled to herself. There was nothing like seeing two people falling in love.

Now as everyone said their goodbyes with Stacy and Clay taking Hank and Mary home, she finally relaxed. Everything was turning out just fine. Stacy had her baby—and a job working for Hilde at Needles and Pins.

"I want to stay around, if that's all right," her sister had said. "I want Ella to know her cousins."

Dana couldn't have been happier. Clay, though, said he would be returning to Hollywood, but that he would come visit more often.

And Jordan, well, Liza was right. Jordan *had* changed. Love did that to a man, she thought, studying her own husband as he came back into the room pushing two bassinets.

"I thought you'd like to see your sons," he said. "Isn't it time you told me what names you've picked out? I know you, Dana. Or do you want me to guess?"

She merely smiled at him.

Hud laughed and shook his head. "You do realize what you're doing to these two innocent little boys by naming them after our fathers, don't you?"

Dana nodded. "I'm giving them a little bit of family history. It isn't just about the ranch. It's about the lives we've carved out here."

Hud looked into the bassinets. "Angus?" he asked as he picked up one of their sons. "And Brick?" He handed her both infants. "So when is the building going to start on the new house?" he asked as he climbed up in the bed beside her and the babies.

"What new house?"

"Jordan's. You know he's staying."

"Did he tell you that?" she asked, unable to keep the hope out of her voice.

Hud gave her a disbelieving look. "You know darned well he is. I wouldn't be surprised if you haven't already picked out a spot on the ranch for him and Liza to live."

"You're taking this pretty well," Dana noted.

He chuckled at that. "Your mother always said Jordan would be back. Stacy, though, I think even that would have surprised your mother."

Dana nodded. "Mom did know her children. She always knew that one day you and I would be together. Mary Justice Cardwell was one smart woman."

"So is her youngest daughter," he said and kissed her.

LIZA REINED IN HER HORSE and looked out over the canyon. The day was warm and dry, possibly one of the last before winter set in. A light breeze stirred the fallen aspen leaves and sighed through the pine boughs.

Jordan brought his horse up beside hers.

"It's beautiful, isn't it?" she said.

"Yes. Beautiful."

She heard something in his voice and looked over at him. He was grinning at her and not looking at the view at all.

"She is *very* beautiful."

"You know you can't charm me," she said, embarrassed. No one had ever told her she was beautiful before. Cute, maybe. Unusual, often. But not beautiful. It wasn't even the word that warmed her to the toes of her boots, though. It was the way he looked at her. He made her *feel* beautiful.

She thought of the scars she'd carried since high school. This case had brought back those awful years, worse, those awful feelings about herself. It had also brought Jordan back to the canyon, a surprise in so many ways.

"You think I'm trying to charm you?" He chuckled as he swung down from his horse.

Before she knew what was happening, he cupped her waist with his large hands and pulled her off her horse and into his arms.

"No, Miss Turner, quite the opposite," he said, his lips just a breath away from hers. "You're the one who's charmed me. All I think about is you. You're like no one I've ever known. I'm under your spell."

She shook her head and laughed softly.

"I'm serious, Liza. You have me thinking crazy thoughts."

"Is that right?"

"Oh, yeah. I've been thinking that I want to stay here and work the ranch with my sister. How crazy is that? Worse, right now, I'm thinking there is only one thing that could make this day more perfect."

She grinned at him. "I'm afraid to ask."

"I'm the one who is afraid to ask." He dropped to one knee. "Marry me and make an honest man out of me."

"Jordan—"

"I know this seems sudden. We should probably at least go on a real date where I'm not just another one of your suspects."

"Be serious."

"I am. I've fallen hopelessly in love with you. Say you at least like me a little." Jordan looked into her wide green eyes and thought he might drown in them. "Just a little?"

"I like you."

He grinned.

"A lot. But marriage?"

"Yes, marriage because I'm not letting you get away, Deputy, and I can't stand to spend another day away from you. I'd marry you right now, but we both know that my sister Dana isn't going to allow it. She's going to insist on a big wedding at the ranch. But that will give us time to go on a few dates. So what do you say?"

Liza's laugh was a joyous sound. "What can I say but yes."

He laughed and swung her up into his arms, spinning them both around. As he set her down, he kissed her, then he drew back to look into her lovely face. Their gazes locked. Electricity arced between them, hotter than any flame.

"I suppose we should wait until our wedding night," he said ruefully.

"Not a chance," Liza said, putting her arms around him. "I can think of no place more wonderful to make love to you the first time than up here on this mountain."

THE WEDDING OF JORDAN CARDWELL and Liza Turner was a glorious affair. Hud and Clay gave Liza away, and stood up with Jordan. Hilde and Dana were Liza's attendants. Hilde had made Liza's dress, a simple white sheath that made her feel like a princess.

The ceremony was short and sweet and held in the large house on the ranch. Stacy baked the wedding cake and the kids helped decorate it. There were balloons and flowers and music. Jordan's father and uncle came with their band to play old-fashioned Country-Western music for the affair.

Neighbors and friends stopped throughout the day to offer felicitations. Even Brick showed up to congratulate them on their wedding and Liza on solving the Tanner Cole case.

The murders and deaths had rocked the small community. Only a few people knew the story behind them and the twisted motives of those involved.

Fall and winter had come and gone. Jordan had been right about Dana insisting on a big wedding. It was spring now. The canyon was turning green from the tall grass on the ranch to the bright leaves on the aspen trees. Work had begun on a ranch house up in the hills from the main house for the two of them.

Liza had never been so happy. She had loved this family even before she fell in love with Jordan. Now she was a part of it. Raised as an orphan, she'd never known this kind of family. Or this kind of love.

Construction on their house on the ranch wasn't quite done, but would be soon. In the meantime, the two of them had been staying in Liza's condo and dating.

Jordan had insisted on a honeymoon. "Hawaii? Tahiti? Mexico? You name it," he'd said.

But Liza didn't want to leave Montana. "Surprise me," she'd said. "Wherever you take me will be perfect."

"How did I get so lucky?" he asked and kissed her as they left in a hail of birdseed.

She had no idea where they were going. She didn't care. With Jordan she knew it would always be an adventure.

* * * * *

CRIME SCENE AT CARDWELL RANCH

When I think of the Gallatin Canyon, I remember rubber gun fights at our cabin, hikes to Lava Lake and stopping by Bessie and Russell Rehm's place near the current Big Sky. Russell is gone now, but I will always remember Bessie's cooking—and the treat she used to make me at her ranch in Texas: a mixture of peanut butter and molasses. I still make it, and I always think of Bessie.

This book is for you, Bessie. Thanks for all the memories!

Prologue

The fall knocked the air out of her. She'd landed badly, one leg bent under her. On the way down, she'd hit her head and the skin on her arms and legs was scraped raw.

Stunned, she tried to get to her feet in the darkness of the tight, confined space. She'd lost both shoes, her body ached and her left hand was in terrible pain, her fingers definitely broken.

She managed to get herself upright in the pitch-blackness of the hole. Bracing herself on the cold earth around her, she looked up, still dazed.

Above her, she could see a pale circle of starlit sky. She started to open her mouth to call out when she heard him stagger to the edge of the old dry well and fall to his knees. His shadow silhouetted over part of the opening.

She stared up at him in confusion. He hadn't meant to push her. He'd just been angry with her. He wouldn't hurt her. Not on purpose.

The beam of a flashlight suddenly blinded her. "Help me."

He made a sound, an eerie, low-keening wail like a wounded animal. "You're alive?"

His words pierced her heart like a cold blade. He'd thought the fall would kill her? *Hoped* it would?

The flashlight went out. She heard him stumble to his feet and knew he was standing looking down at her. She could see his shadow etched against the night sky. She felt dizzy and sick, still too stunned by what had happened.

His shadow disappeared. She could see the circle of dim light above her again. She listened, knowing he hadn't left. He wouldn't leave her. He was just upset, afraid she would tell.

If she pleaded with him the way she had the other times, he would forgive her. He'd tried to break it off before, but he'd always come back to her. He loved her.

She stared up until, with relief, she saw again his dark shape against the starlit sky. He'd gone to get a rope or something to get her out. "I'm sorry. Please, just help me. I won't cause you any more trouble."

"No, you won't." His voice sounded so strange, so foreign. Not the voice of the man she'd fallen so desperately in love with.

She watched him raise his arm. In the glint of starlight she saw it wasn't a rope in his hand.

Her heart caught in her throat. "No!" The gunshot boomed, a deafening roar in the cramped space.

She must have blacked out. When she woke, she was curled in an awkward position in the bottom of the dry well. Over the blinding pain in her head, she could hear the sound of the pickup's engine. He was driving away!

"No!" she cried as she dragged herself up onto her feet again. "Don't leave me here!" As she looked up to the opening high above her, she felt something wet and sticky run down into her eye. Blood.

He'd shot her. The pain in her skull was excruciating. She dropped to her knees on the cold, hard earth. He'd said he loved her. He'd promised to take care of her. Tonight, she'd even worn the red dress he loved.

"Don't leave! Please!" But she knew he couldn't hear her. As she listened, the sound of the engine grew fainter and fainter, then nothing.

She shivered in the damp, cold blackness, her right hand going to her stomach.

He'd come back.

He couldn't just leave her here to die. How could he live with himself if he did?

He'd come back.

Chapter One

As the pickup bounced along the muddy track to the old homestead, Dana Cardwell stared out at the wind-scoured Montana landscape, haunted by the premonition she'd had the night before.

She had awakened in the darkness to the howl of the unusually warm wind against her bedroom window and the steady drip of melting snow from the eaves. A chinook had blown in.

When she'd looked out, she'd seen the bare old aspens vibrating in the wind, limbs etched black against the clear night sky. It felt as if something had awakened her to warn her.

The feeling had been so strong that she'd had trouble getting back to sleep only to wake this morning to Warren Fitzpatrick banging on the door downstairs.

"There's something you'd better see," the elderly ranch manager had said.

And now, as Warren drove them up the bumpy road from the ranch house to the old homestead, she felt a chill at the thought of what waited for her at the top of the hill. Was this what she'd been warned about?

Warren pulled up next to the crumbling foundation and cut the engine. The wind howled across the open hillside, making the tall yellowed grass keel over and gently rocking the pickup.

It was called the January Thaw. Without the blanket of white snow, the land looked wrung out, all color washed from the hills until everything was a dull brown-gray. The only green was a few lone pines swaying against the wind-rinsed sky.

Little remained of the homestead house. Just part of the rock foundation and the fireplace, the chimney as stark as the pines against the horizon.

Past it, in the soft, wet earth, Dana saw Warren's tracks where he had walked to the old well earlier this morning. All that marked the well was a circle of rock and a few weathered boards that covered part of the opening.

Warren cocked his head as if he already heard the marshal's SUV coming up the ranch road. Dana strained her ears but heard nothing over the pounding of her heart.

She was glad Warren had always been a man of few words. She was already on edge without having to talk about what he'd found.

The ranch manager was as dried out as a stick of jerky and just as tough, but he knew more about cattle than any man Dana had ever known. And he was as loyal as an old dog. Until recently, he and Dana had run the ranch together. She knew Warren wouldn't have gotten her up here unless it was serious.

As Dana caught the whine of the approaching vehicle over the wind, the sound growing louder, her dread grew with it.

Warren had told her last night that he'd noticed the

boards were off the old dry well again. "I think I'll just fill it in. Safer that way. Give me something to do."

Like a lot of Montana homesteads, the well was just a hole in the ground, unmarked except for maybe a few old boards thrown over it, and because of that, dangerous to anyone who didn't know it was there.

"Whatever you think," she'd told him the night before. She'd been distracted and really hadn't cared.

But she cared now. She just hoped Warren was wrong about what he'd seen in the bottom of the well.

They'd know soon enough, she thought as she turned to watch the Gallatin Canyon marshal's black SUV come roaring up the road from the river.

"Scrappy's driving faster than usual," she said, frowning. "You must have lit a fire under him when you called him this morning."

"Scrappy Morgan isn't marshal anymore," Warren said.

"What?" She glanced over at him. He had a strange look on his weathered face.

"Scrappy just up and quit. They had to hire a temporary marshal to fill in for a while."

"How come I never hear about these things?" But she knew the answer to that. She'd always been too busy on the ranch to keep up with canyon gossip. Even now that she worked down in Big Sky, her ties were still more with the ranching community—what little of it was left in the Gallatin Canyon since the town of Big Sky had sprung up at the base of Lone Mountain. A lot of the ranchers had sold out or subdivided to take advantage of having a ski and summer resort so close by.

"So who's the interim marshal?" she asked as the Sheriff's Department SUV bounded up the road, the morning sun glinting off the windshield. She groaned. "Not Scrappy's nephew Franklin? Tell me it's anyone but him."

Warren didn't answer as the new marshal brought the black SUV with the Montana State marshal logo on the side to a stop right next to her side of the pickup.

All the breath rushed from her as she looked over and saw the man behind the wheel.

"Maybe I should have warned you," Warren said, sounding sheepish.

"That would've been nice," she muttered between gritted teeth as she met Hudson Savage's clear blue gaze. His look gave nothing away. The two of them might have been strangers—instead of former lovers— for all the expression that showed in his handsome face.

Her emotions boiled up like one of the Yellowstone geysers just down the road. First shock and right on its heels came fury. When Hud had left town five years ago, she'd convinced herself she'd never have to lay eyes on that sorry son of a bitch again. And here he was. Damn, just when she thought things couldn't get any worse.

OVER THE YEARS as a policeman in L.A., Hudson "Hud" Savage had stared down men who were bigger and stronger. Some had guns, some knives and baseball bats.

But none unnerved him like the look in Dana Cardwell's whiskey-brown glare.

He dragged his gaze away, turning to pick up the heavy-duty flashlight from the seat next to him. *Coward.* If just seeing her had this effect on him, he hated to think what talking would do.

Her reaction to him was pretty much what he'd expected. He'd known she would be far from happy to see him. But he had hoped she wouldn't be as furious as she'd been when he'd left town. But given the look in her eyes, he'd say that was one wasted hope.

And damn if it was no less painful than it had been five years ago seeing her anger, her hurt.

Not that he blamed her. He hadn't just left town, he'd flat-out run, tail tucked between his legs.

But he was back now.

He picked up the flashlight and, bracing himself against the wind and Dana Cardwell, he opened his door and stepped out.

The sun glinted off the truck's windshield so he couldn't see her face as he walked to the front of the SUV. But he could feel her gaze boring into him like a bullet as he snugged his Stetson down to keep it from sailing off in the wind.

When Warren had called the office this morning, Hud had instructed him not to go near the well again. The ranch foreman's original tracks to and from the well were the only ones in the soft dirt. It surprised Hud, though, that Dana hadn't gotten out to take a look before he arrived. She obviously hadn't known the order was from him or she would have defied it sure as the devil.

As he looked out across the ranch, memories of the two of them seemed to blow through on the breeze. He could see them galloping on horseback across that far field of wild grasses, her long, dark hair blowing back, face lit by sunlight, eyes bright, grinning at him as they raced back to the barn.

They'd been so young, so in love. He felt that old ache, desire now coupled with heartbreak and regret.

Behind him, he heard first one pickup door open, then the other. The first one closed with a click, the second slammed hard. He didn't have to guess whose door that had been.

Out of the corner of his eye, he saw Warren hang back, waiting by the side of his pickup, out of the way—and out of earshot as well as the line of fire. Warren was no fool.

"Are we goin' to stand here all day admiring the scenery or are we goin' to take a look in the damned well?" Dana asked as she joined Hud.

He let out a bark of nervous laughter and looked over at her, surprised how little she'd changed and glad of it. She was small, five-four compared to his six-six. She couldn't weigh a hundred and ten pounds soaking wet, but what there was of her was a combination of soft curves and hard-edged stubborn determination. To say he'd never known anyone like her was putting it mildly.

He wanted to tell her why he'd come back, but the glint in her eye warned him she was no more ready to hear it than she'd been when he'd left.

"Best take a look in that well then," he said.

"Good idea." She stood back as he trailed Warren's tracks to the hole in the ground.

A half-dozen boards had once covered the well. Now only a couple remained on the single row of rocks rimming the edge. The other boards appeared to have been knocked off by the wind or fallen into the well.

He flipped on the flashlight and shone the beam down into the hole. The well wasn't deep, about fifteen feet, like looking off the roof of a two-story house. Had it been deeper, Warren would never have seen what lay in the bottom.

Hud leaned over the opening, the wind whistling in his ears, the flashlight beam a pale gold as it skimmed the dirt bottom—and the bones.

Hunting with his father as a boy, Hud had seen his share of remains over the years. The sun-bleached skeletons of deer, elk, moose, cattle and coyotes were strewn all over rural Montana.

But just as Warren had feared, the bones lying at the bottom of the Cardwell Ranch dry well weren't from any wild animal.

DANA STOOD BACK, her hands in the pockets of her coat, as she stared at Hud's broad back.

She wished she didn't know him so well. The moment he'd turned on the flashlight and looked down, she'd read the answer in his shoulders. Her already upset stomach did a slow roll and she thought for a moment she might be sick.

Dear God, what was in the well? *Who* was in the well?

Hud glanced back at her, his blue eyes drilling her to the spot where she stood, all the past burning there like a hot blue flame.

But instead of heat, she shivered as if a cold wind blew up from the bottom of the well. A cold that could chill in ways they hadn't yet imagined as Hud straightened and walked back to her.

"Looks like remains of something, all right," Hud said, giving her that same noncommittal look he had when he'd driven up.

The wind whipped her long dark hair around her face. She took a painful breath and let it go, fighting the wind, fighting a weakness in herself that made her angry and scared. "They're human bones, aren't they?"

Hud dragged his hat off and raked a hand through his hair, making her fingers tingle remembering the feel of that thick sun-streaked mop of his. "Won't be certain until we get the bones to the lab."

She looked away, angry at him on so many levels that it made it hard to be civil. "I *know* there are human remains down there. Warren said he saw a human skull. So stop lying to me."

Hud's eyes locked with hers and she saw anger spark in all that blue. He didn't like being called a liar. But then, she could call him much worse if she got started.

"From what I can see, the skull appears to be human. Satisfied?" he said.

She turned away from the only man who had ever satisfied her. She tried not to panic. If having Hud back—let alone the interim marshal—wasn't bad enough, there was a body in the well on her family ranch. She tried to assure herself that the bones could have been in the well for years. The well had been dug more than a hundred years ago. Who knew how long the bones had been there?

But the big question, the same one she knew Hud had to be asking, was *why* the bones were there.

"I'm going to need to cordon this area off," he said. "I would imagine with it being calving season, you have some cattle moving through here?"

"No cattle in here to worry about," Warren said.

Hud frowned and glanced out across the ranch. "I didn't notice any cattle on the way in, either."

Dana felt his gaze shift to her. She pulled a hand from her pocket to brush a strand of her hair from her face before looking at him. The words stuck in her throat and she was grateful to Warren when he said, "The cattle were all auctioned this fall to get the ranch ready to sell."

Hud looked stunned, his gaze never leaving hers. "You wouldn't sell the ranch."

She turned her face away from him. He was the one person who knew just what this ranch meant to her and yet she didn't want him to see that selling it was breaking her heart just as he had. She could feel his gaze on her as if waiting for her to explain.

When she didn't, he said, "I have to warn you, Dana, this investigation might hold up a sale."

She hadn't thought of that. She hadn't thought of anything but the bones—and her added bad luck in finding out that Hud was acting marshal.

"Word is going to get out, if it hasn't already," he continued. "Once we get the bones up, we'll know more, but this investigation could take some time."

"You do whatever you have to do, Hud." She hadn't said his name out loud in years. It sounded odd and felt even stranger on her tongue. Amazing that such a small word could hurt so much.

She turned and walked back to Warren's pickup, surprised her legs held her up. Her mind was reeling. There was a body in a well on her ranch? And Hud Savage was back after all this time of believing him long gone? She wasn't sure which shocked or terrified her more.

She didn't hear him behind her until he spoke.

"I was sorry to hear about your mother," he said so close she felt his warm breath on her neck and caught a whiff of his aftershave. The same kind he'd used when he was hers.

Without turning, she gave a nod of her head, the wind burning her eyes, and jerked open the pickup door, sending a glance to Warren across the hood that she was more than ready to leave.

As she climbed into the truck and started to pull the door shut behind her, Hud dropped one large palm over the top of the door to keep it from closing. "Dana…"

She shot him a look she thought he might still remember, the same one a rattler gives right before it strikes.

"I just wanted to say…happy birthday."

She tried not to show her surprise—or her pleasure—that he'd remembered. That he had, though, made it all the worse. She swallowed and looked up at him, knifed with that old familiar pain, the kind that just never went away no matter how hard you fought it.

"Dana, listen—"

"I'm engaged." The lie was out before she could call it back.

Hud's eyebrows rose. "To anyone I know?"

She took guilty pleasure from the pain she heard in his voice, saw in his face. "Lanny Rankin."

"Lanny? The *lawyer?*" Hud didn't sound surprised, just contemptuous. He must have heard that she'd been dating Lanny. "He still saving up for the ring?"

"What?"

"An engagement ring. You're not wearing one." He motioned to her ring finger.

Silently she swore at her own stupidity. She'd wanted to hurt him and at the same time keep him at a safe distance. Unfortunately she hadn't given a thought to the consequences.

"I just forgot to put it on this morning," she said.

"Oh, you take it off at night?"

Another mistake. When Hud had put the engagement ring on her finger so many years ago now, she'd sworn she'd never take it off.

"If you must know," she said, "the diamond got caught in my glove, so I took it off to free it and must have laid it down."

His brows went up again.

Why didn't she just shut up? "I was in a hurry this morning. Not that it's any of your business."

"You're right," he agreed. "Must be a big diamond to get stuck in a glove." Not like the small chip he'd been able to afford for her, his tone said.

"Look, as far as I'm concerned, you and I have nothing to say to each other."

"Sorry, didn't mean to pry into your personal life." A muscle bunched in his jaw and he took on that all-business marshal look again. "I'd appreciate it if you and Warren wouldn't mention what you found in the well to anyone. I know it's going to get out, but I'd like to try to keep a lid on it as long as we can."

He had to be joking. The marshal's office dispatcher was the worst gossip in the canyon.

"Anything else?" she asked pointedly as his hand remained on the door.

His gaze softened again and she felt her heart do that pitter-patter thing it hadn't done since Hud.

"It's good seeing you again, Dana," he said.

"I wish I could say the same, Hud."

His lips turned up in a rueful smile as she jerked hard on the door, forcing him to relinquish his hold. If only she could free herself as easily.

The pickup door slammed hard. Warren got in and

started the engine without a word. She knew he'd heard her lie about being engaged, but Warren was too smart to call her on it.

As sun streamed into the cab, Warren swung the pickup around. Dana rolled down her window, flushed with a heat that had nothing to do with the warmth of the sun or the January Thaw. She could see the ranch house down the hillside. Feel the rattle of the tires over the rough road, hear the wind in the pines.

She promised herself she wouldn't do it even as she reached out, her fingers trembling, and adjusted the side mirror to look back.

Hud was still standing where she'd left him, looking after them.

Happy birthday.

Chapter Two

Well, that had gone better than he'd expected, Hud thought with his usual self-deprecating sarcasm.

She was *engaged* to Lanny Rankin?

What did you expect? It's been years. I'm surprised she isn't married by now. But Lanny Rankin?

He watched the pickup disappear over the hill, listening until the sound of the engine died away and all he could hear was the wind again.

Yeah, why *isn't* she married?

Lanny Rankin had gone after Dana before Hud had even driven out past the city limit sign. He'd had five years. So why weren't the two of them married?

He felt a glimmer of hope.

Was it possible Dana was dragging her feet because she was still in love with him—not Lanny Rankin?

And why wasn't she wearing her ring? Maybe she didn't even have one. Maybe she wasn't engaged—at least not officially.

Maybe you're clutching at straws.

Maybe, but his instincts told him that if she was going to marry Lanny, she would have by now.

A half mile down the hillside, he could see Warren's pickup stop in a cloud of dust. Hud watched Dana get out. She was still beautiful. Still prickly as a porcupine. Still strong and determined. Still wishing him dead.

He couldn't blame her for that, though.

He had a terrible thought. What if she married Lanny now just out of spite?

And what was this about selling the ranch? The old Dana Cardwell he knew would never put the ranch up for sale. Was she thinking about leaving after it sold? Worse, after she married Lanny?

She disappeared into the ranch house. This place was her heart. She'd always said she would die here and be buried up on the hill with the rest of her mother's family, the Justices.

He'd loved that about her, her pride in her family's past, her determination to give that lifestyle to her children—to *their* children.

Hud felt that gut-deep ache of regret. God, how he hated what he'd done to her. What he'd done to himself. It didn't help that he'd spent the past five years trying to make sense of it.

Water under the bridge, his old man would have said. But then his old man didn't have a conscience. Made life easier that way, Hud thought, cursing at even the thought of Brick Savage. He thought of all the wasted years he'd spent trying to please his father—and the equally wasted years he'd spent hating him.

Hud turned, disgusted with himself, and tried to lose himself in the one thing that gave him any peace, his work.

He put in a call to Coroner Rupert Milligan. While he waited for Rupert, he shot both digital photographs and video of the site, trying not to speculate on the bones in the well or how they had gotten there.

Rupert drove up not thirty minutes later. He was dressed in a suit and tie, which in Montana meant either a funeral or a wedding. "Toastmasters, if you have to know," he said as he walked past Hud to the well, grabbing the flashlight from Hud's hand on his way.

Rupert Milligan was older than God and more powerful in this county. Tall, white-haired, with a head like a buffalo, he had a gruff voice and little patience for stupidity. He'd retired as a country doctor but still worked as coroner. He'd gotten hooked on murder mysteries—and forensics. Rupert loved nothing better than a good case and while Hud was still hoping the bones weren't human, he knew that Rupert was pitching for the other team.

Rupert shone the flashlight down into the well, leaning one way then the other. He froze, holding the flashlight still as he leaned down even farther. Hud figured he'd seen the skull partially exposed at one edge of the well.

"You got yourself a human body down there, but then I reckon you already knew that," he said, sounding too cheerful as he straightened.

Hud nodded.

"Let's get it out of there." Rupert had already started toward his rig.

Hud would have offered to go down in Rupert's place but he knew the elderly coroner wouldn't have stood for it. All he needed Hud for was to document it if the case ever went to trial—and help winch him and the bones out of the well.

He followed Rupert over to his pickup where the coroner had taken off his suit jacket and was pulling on a pair of overalls.

"Wanna put some money on what we got down there?" Rupert asked with a grin. Among his other eclectic traits, Rupert was a gambler. To his credit, he seldom lost.

"Those bones could have been down there for fifty years or more," Hud said, knowing that if that was the case, there was a really good chance they would never know the identity of the person or how he'd ended up down there.

Rupert shook his head as he walked around to the back of the truck and dropped the tailgate. "Those aren't fifty-year-old bones down there. Not even close."

The coroner had come prepared. There was a pulley system in the back and a large plastic box with a body bag, latex gloves, a variety of different size containers, a video camera and a small shovel.

He handed Hud the pulley then stuffed the needed items into a backpack, which he slung over his shoulder before slipping a headlamp over his white hair and snapping it on.

"True, it's dry down there, probably been covered most of the time since the bones haven't been bleached by the sun," Rupert said as he walked back to the well and Hud followed. "Sides of the well are too steep for most carnivores. Insects would have been working on the bones, though. Maggots." He took another look into the well. "Spot me five years and I'll bet you fifty bucks that those bones have been down there two decades or less," he said with his usual confidence, a confidence based on years of experience.

Twenty years ago Hud would have been thirteen. Rupert would have been maybe forty-five. With a jolt Hud realized that Rupert wasn't that much older than his father. It felt odd to think of Brick Savage as old. In Hud's mind's eye he saw his father at his prime, a large, broad-shouldered man who could have been an actor. Or even a model. He was that good-looking.

"I got a hundred that says whoever's down there didn't fall down there by accident," Rupert said.

"Good thing I'm not a betting man," Hud said, distracted. His mind on the fact that twenty years ago, his father was marshal.

"TELL ME you didn't," Dana said as she walked into Needles and Pins and heard giggling in the back beyond the racks of fabric.

Her best friend and partner in the small sewing shop gave her a grin and a hug. "It's your birthday, kiddo," Hilde whispered. "Gotta celebrate."

"Birthdays after thirty should not be celebrated," Dana whispered back.

"Are you kidding? And miss seeing what thirty-one candles on a cake looks like?"

"You didn't."

Hilde had her arm and was tugging her toward the back. "Smile. I promise this won't kill you, though you do look like you think it will." She slowed. "You're shaking. Seriously, are you all right?"

As much as she hated it, Dana was still a wreck after seeing Hud again. She'd hoped to get to work at the shop and forget about everything that had happened this morning, including not only what might be in the old well—but also who. The last thing she wanted was to even be reminded of her birthday. It only reminded her that Hud had remembered.

"Hud's back," she said, the words coming out in a rush.

Hilde stopped dead so that Dana almost collided with her.

Her best friend's surprise made her feel better. Dana had been worried all morning that everyone had known about Hud's return—and just hadn't told her to protect her. She hated being protected. Especially from news like that. If she'd known he was back, she could have prepared herself for seeing him— Even as she thought it, she knew nothing could have prepared her for that initial shock of seeing Hud after five long years.

"Hud's back in the canyon?" Hilde whispered, sounding shocked. The Gallatin Canyon, a fifty-mile strip of winding highway and blue-ribbon river, had been mostly ranches, the cattle and dude kind, a few summer cabins and homes—that is until Big Sky resort and the small town that followed at the foot of Lone Mountain. But the "canyon" was still its own little community.

"Hud's the new temporary marshal," Dana whispered, her throat suddenly dry.

"Hello?" came the familiar voice of Margo from the back of the store. "We've got candles burning up in here."

"Hud? Back here? Oh, man, what a birthday present," Hilde said, giving her another hug. "I'm so sorry, sweetie. I can imagine what seeing him again did to you."

"I still want to kill him," Dana whispered.

"Not on your birthday." Hilde frowned. "Does Lanny know yet?" she whispered.

"Lanny? Lanny and I are just friends."

"Does Lanny know that?" her friend asked, giving her a sympathetic smile.

"He knows." Dana sighed, remembering the night Lanny had asked her to marry him and she'd had to turn him down. Things hadn't been the same between them since. "I did something really stupid. I told Hud I was engaged to Lanny."

"You didn't."

Dana nodded miserably. "I don't know what I was thinking."

Margo called from the back room. "Major wax guttering back here."

"Let's get this over with," Dana said, and she and Hilde stepped into the back of the shop where a dozen of Dana's friends and store patrons had gathered around a cake that looked like it was on fire.

"Quick! Make a wish!" her friend Margo cried.

Dana closed her eyes for an instant, made a wish, then braving the heat of thirty-one candles flickering on a sheet cake, blew as hard as she could, snuffing out every last one of them to the second chorus of "Happy Birthday."

"Tell me you didn't wish Hud dead," Hilde whispered next to her as the smoke started to dissipate.

"And have my wish not come true? No way."

HUD WATCHED RUPERT, the glow of the coroner's headlamp flickering eerily on the dark dirt walls as he descended into the well. Hud tried not to think about remains down there or the fact that Brick might have investigated the disappearance. Might even have known the victim. Just as Hud and Rupert might have.

Rupert stopped the pulley just feet above the bones

to video the scene on the bottom of the well. The light flickered and Hud looked away as he tried to corral his thoughts. Sure as hell this investigation would force him to deal with his father. The thought turned his stomach. The last time he'd seen his father, more than five years ago now, they'd almost ended up in a brawl, burning every bridge between them—both content with the understanding that the next time Hud saw his father it would be to make sure Brick was buried.

When Hud had decided to come back, he'd thought at least he wouldn't have to see his father. Word was that Brick had moved to a place up on Hebgen Lake near West Yellowstone—a good fifty miles away.

The wind seemed cooler now and in the distance Hud could see dark clouds rolling up over the mountains. He turned his face up to the pale sun knowing it wouldn't be long before it was snowing again. After all, this was January in Montana.

The rope on the pulley groaned and he looked down again into the well as Rupert settled gently on the bottom, the headlamp now focused on the human remains.

Because of the steep sides of the well, the body was contained, none of the bones had been scattered by critters or carried off. The coroner had pulled on a pair of the latex gloves. He opened the body bag and began to carefully fill it with the bones.

"Good thing you didn't bet with me," Rupert said. "I'd say the bones have been here closer to fifteen years." He held up a pelvic bone in his gloved hands. "A woman. White. Late twenties, early thirties."

In the light from the headlamp, Hud watched Rupert pick up the skull and turn it slowly in his hands.

"Well, how about that," he heard Rupert say, then

glance up at him. "You got a murder on your hands, son," the coroner said solemnly. He held up the skull, his headlamp shining through a small round hole in it.

"The bullet entered this side, passed through the brain and lodged in the mastoid bone behind the left ear," Rupert said, still turning the skull in his hands. "The bullet lead is flattened and deformed from impact but there will be enough lands and grooves to match the weapon. Looks like a .38."

"If we could find the weapon after all this time," Hud said. He let out an oath under his breath. Murder. And the body found on the Cardwell Ranch.

"Get one of those containers out of my rig so I can bag the skull separately," Rupert said, his voice echoing up.

Hud ran back to Rupert's truck and returned to lower the container down to him. A few minutes later Rupert sent the filled container up and Hud found himself looking at the dead woman's skull. A patch of hair clung to the top. The hair, although covered with dirt, was still reddish in color. He stared at the hair, at the shape of the skull, and tried to picture the face.

"You think she was young, huh?" he called down.

In the well, Rupert stopped to inspect one of the bones in the light from his headlamp. "Based on growth lines, I'd say twenty-eight to thirty-five years of age." He put down one bone to pick up what appeared to be a leg bone. "Hmm, that's interesting. The bony prominences show muscle development, indicating she spent a lot of time on her feet. Probably made her living as a hairdresser, grocery clerk, nurse, waitress, something like that." He put the bone into the body bag and picked up another shorter one. "Same bony prominences on the arms as if she often carried something heavy. My money's on waitress or nurse."

Few coroners would go out on a limb with such conjecture. Most left this part up to the forensics team at the state crime lab. But then, Rupert Milligan wasn't like most coroners. Add to that the fact that he was seldom wrong.

"What about height and weight?" Hud asked, feeling a chill even in the sun. His father had always liked waitresses. Hell, his father chased skirts no matter who wore them.

Rupert seemed to study the dirt where the bones had been. "I'd say she was between five-four and five-seven. A hundred and twenty to a hundred and forty pounds."

That covered a lot of women, Hud thought as he carried the container with the skull in it over to Rupert's pickup and placed it carefully on the front seat. All the teeth were still intact. With luck, they'd be able to identify her from dental records if she'd been local.

He tried to remember if he'd heard his father talking about a missing person's case about fifteen years ago. Rodrick "Brick" Savage loved to brag about his cases—especially the ones he solved.

But then this one wouldn't have been one he'd solved. And fifteen years ago, Hud had been eighteen and away at college. He wondered if Dana had mentioned a missing woman in one of her letters to him. She'd written him every week, but the letters were more about what was happening on the ranch, I-miss-you letters, love letters.

Leaving the skull at the pickup, he went back to watch Rupert dig through the dirt on the well floor.

The coroner slowed as he hit something, then stooped and shook dirt from what he'd found.

Hud felt his chest heave as Rupert held up a bright red high-heeled shoe.

AFTER THE BIRTHDAY party and in between customers, Dana defied Hud's orders and told Hilde about what Warren had found in the old dry well by the original homestead's foundation.

Dana was sure the news was all over the canyon by now. But still she'd waited, not wanting to say anything to anyone but Hilde, her best friend.

"He really thinks the bones are human?" Hilde asked with a shiver. "Who could it be?"

Dana shook her head. "Probably some ancestor of mine."

Hilde looked skeptical. "You think the bones have been down there that long?" She hugged herself as if she could feel the cold coming up from the well just as Dana had earlier.

"It's horrible to think that someone might have fallen in and been unable to get out, died down there," Dana said.

Hilde nodded. "It's just odd that you found them now." Her eyes lit. "You think the investigation will hold up the sale of the ranch?"

"Maybe, but ultimately the ranch will be sold, trust me," Dana said, and changed the subject. "Thank you for the birthday party. I love the purse you made me."

"You're welcome. I'm sorry you've had such a lousy day. Why don't you go on home? I can handle things here. It's your birthday."

Dana groaned. "I hate to imagine what other horrible things could happen before this day is over."

"Always the optimist, aren't you."

Dana smiled in spite of herself. "I think I will go home." She looked outside. Clouds scudded across the pale sky, taking the earlier warmth with them. The sign over the door pendulumed in the wind and she could almost feel the cold trying to get in.

Across the way from the shop, the top of the mountain had disappeared, shrouded in white clouds. The first snowflakes, blown by the wind, swept across the window. Apparently the weatherman had been right when he'd called for snow before midnight.

Dana would be lucky to get home before the roads iced over.

FROM DOWN IN THE WELL, Rupert signaled for Hud to pull up the body bag. It was heavy, but mostly from the layer of dirt retrieved from the bottom of the well. The dirt would be sifted for evidence later at the state crime lab.

He put down the body bag, noting that the weather had turned. Snowflakes danced around him, pelting him on gusts of wind and momentarily blinding him. He barely felt the cold as he squatted near the edge of the well, pulling up the hood on his marshal's jacket as he watched Rupert finish.

The red high-heeled shoe had triggered something. Not a real memory since he couldn't recall when, where or if he'd even actually seen a woman in a red dress and bright red high-heeled shoes. It could have been a photograph. Even a television show or a movie.

But for just an instant he'd had a flash of a woman in a bright red dress and shoes. She was spinning around in a circle, laughing, her long red hair whirling around her head, her face hidden from view.

That split-second image had left him shaken. Had he known this woman?

The canyon was like a small town except for a few months when the out-of-staters spent time in their vacation homes or condos to take advantage of the skiing or the mild summer weather.

But if the woman had been one of those, Hud knew he'd have heard about her disappearance. More than likely she was someone who'd worked at the resort or one of the local businesses. She might not have even been missed as seasonal workers were pretty transient.

"I'm going to need another container from the truck," Rupert called up.

The wind had a bite to it now. Snowflakes swirled around him as Hud lowered the container down and watched the coroner place what appeared to be a dirt-caked piece of once-red fabric inside. Just as in his memory, the woman had worn a red dress. Rupert continued to sift through the dirt, stooped over in the small area, intent on his work.

Hud pulled his coat around him. The mountains across the canyon were no longer visible through the falling snow. And to think he'd actually missed winters while working for the police department in Los Angeles.

From down in the well, Rupert let out a curse, calling Hud's attention back to the dark hole in the ground.

"What is it?" Hud called down.

Rupert had the video camera out and seemed to be trying to steady his hands as he photographed the well wall.

"You aren't going to believe this." The older man's voice sounded strained as if he'd just found something that had shaken him—a man who'd bragged that he'd seen the worst of everything. "She was still alive."

"What?" Hud asked, his blood running cold.

"Neither the gunshot wound nor being thrown down the well killed her right away," Rupert said. "There are deep gouges in the earth where she tried to climb out."

Chapter Three

Long after Rupert came up out of the well, neither he nor Hud said anything. Snow whirled on the wind, the bank of clouds dropping over them, the sun only a memory.

Hud sat behind the wheel of the SUV, motor running, heater cranked up, drinking coffee from the thermos Rupert had brought. Next to him, Rupert turned the SUV's heater vent so it blew into his face.

The older man looked pale, his eyes hollow. Hud imagined that, like him, Rupert had been picturing what it must have been like being left in the bottom of that well to die a slow death.

The yellow crime scene tape Hud had strung up now bowed in the wind and snow. The hillside was a blur of white, the snow falling diagonally.

"I suppose the murder weapon could still be up here," Hud said to Rupert, more to break the silence than anything else. Even with the wind and the motor and heater going, the day felt too quiet, the hillside too desolate. Anything was better than thinking about the woman in the well—even remembering Dana's reaction to seeing him again.

"Doubt you'll ever find that gun," Rupert said without looking at him. The old coroner had been unusually quiet since coming up out of the well.

Hud had called the sheriff's department in Bozeman and asked for help searching the area. It was procedure, but Hud agreed with Rupert. He doubted the weapon would ever turn up.

Except they had to search for it. Unfortunately this was Montana. A lot of men drove trucks with at least one firearm hanging on the back window gun rack and another in the glove box or under the seat.

"So did he shoot her before or after she went into the well?" Hud asked.

"After, based on the angle the bullet entered her skull." Rupert took a sip of his coffee.

"He must have thought he killed her."

Rupert said nothing as he stared in the direction of the well.

"Had to have known about the well," Hud said. Which meant he had knowledge of the Cardwell Ranch. Hud groaned to himself as he saw where he was headed with this. The old homestead was a good mile off Highway 191 that ran through the Gallatin Canyon. The killer could have accessed the old homestead by two ways. One was the Cardwells' private bridge, which would mean driving right by the ranch house.

Or…he could have taken the Piney Creek Bridge, following a twisted route of old logging roads. The same way he and Dana used when he was late getting her home.

Either way, the killer had to be local to know about the well, let alone the back way. Unless, of course, the killer was a member of the Cardwell family and had just driven in past the ranch house bold as brass.

Why bring the woman here, though? Why the Cardwell Ranch well?

"You know what bothers me?" Hud said, taking a sip of his coffee. "The red high heel. Just one in the well. What happened to the other one? And what was she doing up here dressed like that?" He couldn't shake that flash of memory of a woman in a red dress any more than he could nail down its source.

He felt his stomach tighten when Rupert didn't jump in. It wasn't like Rupert. Did his silence have something to do with realizing the woman in the well hadn't been dead and tried to save herself? Or was it possible Rupert suspected who she was and for some reason was keeping it to himself?

"The heels, the dress, it's almost like she was on a date," Hud said. "Or out for a special occasion."

Rupert glanced over at him. "You might make as good a marshal as your father some day." High praise to Rupert's way of thinking, so Hud tried hard not to take offense.

"Odd place to bring your date, though," Hud commented. But then maybe not. The spot was isolated. Not like a trailhead where anyone could come along. No one would be on this section of the ranch at night and you could see the ranch house and part of the road up the hillside. You would know if anyone was headed in your direction in plenty of time to get away.

And yet it wasn't close enough that anyone could hear a woman's cries for help.

"Still, someone had to have reported her missing," Hud persisted. "A roommate. A boss. A friend. A husband."

Rupert finished his coffee and started to screw the cup back on the thermos. "Want any more?"

Hud shook his head. "You worked with my father for a lot of years."

Rupert looked over at him, eyes narrowing. "Brick Savage was the best damned marshal I've ever known." He said it as if he knew only too well that there were others who would have argued that, Hud among them, and Rupert wasn't going to have it.

Brick Savage was a lot of things. A colorful marshal, loved and respected by supporters, feared and detested by his adversaries. Hud knew him as a stubborn, rigid father who he'd feared as a boy and despised as a man. Hud hated to think of the years he'd tried to prove himself to his father—only to fail.

He could feel Rupert's gaze on him, daring him to say anything against Brick. "If you're right about how long she's been down there…"

Rupert made a rude sound under his breath, making it clear he was right.

"…then Brick would have been marshal and you would have been assistant coroner."

"Your point?" Rupert asked.

Hud eyed him, wondering why Rupert was getting his back up. Because Hud had brought up Brick? "I just thought you might remember a missing person's case during that time."

"You'd have to ask your father. Since no body was found, I might not even have heard about it." Rupert zipped up his coroner jacket he'd pulled from behind the seat of his truck. "I need to get to the crime lab."

Hud handed Rupert the coffee cup he'd lent him. "Just seems odd, doesn't it? Someone had to have missed her. You would think the whole area would have been talking about it."

The coroner smiled ruefully. "Some women come and go more often than a Greyhound bus."

Hud remembered hearing that Rupert's first wife had run off on numerous occasions before she'd finally cleared out with a long-haul truck driver.

"You think this woman was like that?" Hud asked, his suspicion growing that Rupert knew more than he was saying.

"If she was, then your suspect list could be as long as your arm." Rupert opened his door.

"You almost sound as if you have an idea who she was," Hud said over the wind.

Rupert climbed out of the truck. "I'll call you when I know something definite."

Hud watched the older man move through the falling snow and wondered why Rupert, who was ready to bet on the bones earlier, seemed to be backpedaling now. It wasn't like the old coroner. Unless Rupert suspected who the bones belonged to—and it hit a little too close to home.

THE PHONE was ringing as Dana walked through the ranch house door. She dropped the stack of mail she'd picked up at the large metal box down by the highway and rushed to answer the phone, not bothering to check caller ID, something she regretted the moment she heard her older brother's voice.

"Dana, what the hell's going on?" Jordan demanded without even a hello let alone a "happy birthday." Clearly he had been calling for some time, not thinking to try her at her new job.

"Where are you?"

"Where do you think I am?" he shot back. "In case you forgot, I live in New York. What the hell is going on out there?"

She slumped into a chair, weak with relief. For a moment she'd thought he was in Montana, that he'd somehow heard about the bones in the well and had caught a flight out. The last thing she needed today was her brother Jordan to deal with in the flesh. Unfortunately it seemed she would have to deal with him on the phone, though.

Her relief was quickly replaced by irritation with him. "I'm fine, Jordan. Thanks for asking, considering it's my birthday and it's been a rough day." She'd seen the sheriff's department cars go up the road toward the old homestead, making her even more aware of what was happening not a mile from the ranch house.

Jordan let out a weary sigh. "Dana, if this is about the ranch—"

"Jordan, let's not. Not today. Is there a reason you called?"

"Hell yes! I want to know why the marshal thinks there's a body in a well on our ranch."

Our ranch? She gritted her teeth. Jordan had hated everything about the ranch and ranching, distancing himself as far as he could from both.

How had he heard about the bones already? She sighed, thinking of Franklin Morgan's sister, Shirley, who worked as dispatcher. Shirley had dated Jordan in high school and still drooled over him whenever Jordan returned to the canyon. Well, at least Dana didn't have to wonder anymore how long it would take for the word to get out.

She didn't dare tell him that it had been Warren who'd found the bones. Jordan would never understand why Warren hadn't just filled in the well and kept his mouth shut. "I found some bones in the old dry well at the homestead."

"So?"

"I called the marshal's office to report them."

"For God's sake, why?"

"Because it's both legally and morally the thing to do." She really wasn't in the mood for Jordan today.

"This is going to hold up the sale of the ranch."

"Jordan, some poor soul is in the bottom of our well. Whoever it is deserves to be buried properly."

"It's probably just animal bones. I'm flying out there to see what the hell is really going on."

"No!" The word was out before she could call it back. Telling Jordan no was like waving a red blanket in front of a rodeo bull.

"You're up to something. This is just another ploy on your part."

She closed her eyes and groaned inwardly. "I just think it would be better if you didn't come out. I can handle this. You'll only make matters worse."

"I have another call coming in. I'll call you back." He hung up.

Dana gritted her teeth as she put down the phone and picked up her mail and began sorting through it. All she needed was Jordan coming out here now. She thought about leaving so she didn't have to talk to him when he called back.

Or she could just not answer the phone. But she knew that wouldn't accomplish anything other than making him more angry. And Jordan wasn't someone you wanted to deal with when he was angry.

She opened a letter from Kitty Randolph asking her to help chair another fundraiser. Kitty and Dana's mother had been friends and since Mary's death, Kitty had seemed to think that Dana would take her mother's place. Dana put the letter aside. She knew she would probably call Kitty in a day or so and agree to do it. She always did.

She picked up the rest of the mail and froze at the sight of the pale yellow envelope. No return address, but she knew who it was from the moment she saw the handwriting.

Throw it away. Don't even open it.

The last thing she needed was to get something from her sister, Stacy, today.

The envelope was card-shaped. Probably just a birthday card. But considering that she and Stacy hadn't spoken to each other in five years…

She started to toss the envelope in the trash but stopped. Why would her sister decide to contact her now? Certainly not because it was her birthday. No, Stacy was trying to butter her up. Kind of like good cop, bad cop with Jordan opting of course for the bad cop role. Her other brother Clay was more of the duck-for-cover type when there was conflict in the family.

Dana couldn't help herself. She ripped open the envelope, not surprised to find she'd been right. A birthday card.

On the front was a garden full of flowers and the words, *For My Sister.* Dana opened the card.

"Wishing you happiness on your birthday and always."

"Right. Your big concern has always been my happiness," Dana muttered.

The card was signed, Stacy. Then in small print under it were the words, *I am so sorry.*

Dana balled up the card and hurled it across the room, remembering a time when she'd idolized her older sister. Stacy was everything Dana had once wanted to be. Beautiful, popular, the perfect older sister to emulate. She'd envied the way Stacy made everything look easy. On the other hand, Dana had been a tomboy, scuffed knees, unruly hair and not a clue when it came to boys.

What Dana hadn't realized once she grew up was how much Stacy had envied *her.* Or what lengths she would go to to hurt her.

The phone rang. She let it ring twice more before she forced herself to pick up the receiver, not bothering to check caller ID for the second time. "Yes?"

"Dana?"

"Lanny. I thought it…was someone else," she said lamely.

"Is everything all right?" he asked.

She could picture him sitting in his office in his three-piece, pin-striped suit, leaning back in his leather chair, with that slight frown he got when he was in lawyer mode.

"Fine. Just…busy." She rolled her eyes at how stupid she sounded. But she could feel what wasn't being said between them like a speech barrier. Lanny had to have heard that Hud was back in town. Wasn't that why he'd called?

"Well, then I won't keep you. I just wanted to make sure we were still on for tonight," he said.

"Of course." She'd completely forgotten about their

date. The last thing she wanted to do was to go out tonight. But she'd made this birthday dinner date weeks ago.

"Great, then I'll see you at eight." He seemed to hesitate, as if waiting for her to say something, then hung up.

Why hadn't she told him the truth? That she was exhausted, that there was a dead body in her well, that she just wanted to stay home and lick her wounds? Lanny would have understood.

But she knew why she hadn't. Because Lanny would think her canceling their date had something to do with Hud.

ONCE THE TEAM OF DEPUTIES on loan from the sheriff's department in Bozeman arrived and began searching the old homestead, Hud drove back to his office at Big Sky.

Big Sky didn't really resemble a town. Condos had sprung up after construction on the famous resort began on the West Fork of the Gallatin River in the early 1970s. A few businesses had followed, along with other resort amenities such as a golf course in the lower meadow and ski area on the spectacular Lone Mountain peak.

The marshal's office was in the lower meadow in a nondescript small wooden building, manned with a marshal, two deputies and a dispatcher. After hours, all calls were routed to the sheriff's office in Bozeman.

Hud had inherited two green deputies and a dispatcher who was the cousin of the former sheriff and the worst gossip in the state. Not much to work with, especially now that he had a murder on his hands.

He parked in the back and entered the rear door,

so lost in thought that he didn't hear them at first. He stopped just inside the door at the sound of his name being brandished about.

"Well, you know darned well that he had some kind of pull to get this job, even temporarily." Hud recognized Franklin Morgan's voice. Franklin was the nephew of former marshal Scott "Scrappy" Morgan. Franklin was a sheriff's deputy in Bozeman, some forty miles away.

Hud had been warned that Franklin wasn't happy about not getting the interim marshal job after his uncle left and that there might be some hard feelings. Hud smiled at that understatement as he heard Franklin continue.

"At first I thought he must have bought the job, but hell, the Savages haven't ever had any money." This from Shirley Morgan, the dispatcher, and Franklin's sister. Nepotism was alive and well in the canyon.

"Didn't his mother's family have money?" Franklin asked.

"Well, if they did, they didn't leave it to their daughter after she married Brick Savage," Shirley said. "But then, can you blame them?"

"Hud seems like he knows what he's doing," countered Deputy Norm Turner. Norm was a tall, skinny, shy kid with little to no experience at life or law enforcement from what Hud could tell.

"Maybe Brick pulled some strings to get Hud the job," Franklin said.

Hud scoffed. Brick wouldn't pull on the end of a rope if his son was hanging off it from a cliff on the other end.

"Not a chance," Shirley said with a scornful laugh. "It was that damned Dana Cardwell."

Hud felt a jolt. Dana?

"Everyone in the canyon does what she wants just like they did when her mother was alive. Hell, those Cardwell women have been running things in this canyon for years. Them and Kitty Randolph. You can bet Dana Cardwell got him the job."

Hud couldn't help but smile just thinking how Dana would love to hear that she was responsible for getting him back to town.

Franklin took a drink of his coffee and happened to look up and see Hud standing just inside the doorway. The deputy's eyes went wide, coffee spewing from his mouth. Hud could see the wheels turning. Franklin was wondering how long Hud had been there and just what he'd overheard.

Norm swung around and about choked on the doughnut he'd just shoved into his mouth.

Shirley, who'd been caught before, didn't even bother to look innocent. She just scooted her chair through the open doorway to the room that housed the switchboard, closing the door behind her.

Hud watched with no small amount of amusement as the two deputies tried to regain their composure. "Any word from the crime lab?" Hud asked as he proceeded to his office.

Both men answered at the same time.

"Haven't heard a word."

"Nothing from our end." Franklin tossed his foam coffee cup in the trash as if he suddenly remembered something urgent he needed to do. He hightailed it out of the office.

Deputy Turner didn't have that luxury. "Marshal, about what was being said…"

Hud could have bailed him out, could have pretended he hadn't heard a word, but he didn't. He'd been young once himself. He liked to think he'd learned from his mistakes, but coming back here might prove him wrong.

"It's just that I—I…wanted to say…" The young deputy looked as if he might break down.

"Deputy Turner, don't you think I know that everyone in the canyon is wondering how I got this job, even temporarily, after what happened five years ago? I'm as surprised as anyone that I'm the marshal for the time being. All I can do is prove that I deserve it. How about you?"

"Yes, sir, that's exactly how I feel," he said, his face turning scarlet.

"That's what I thought," Hud said, and continued on to his office.

He was anxious to go through the missing person's file from around fifteen years back. But he quickly saw that all but the past ten years of files had been moved to the Bozeman office.

"We don't have any records back that far," the clerk told him when he called. "We had a fire. All the records were destroyed."

Twelve years ago. He'd completely forgotten about the fire. He hung up. All he could hope was that Rupert was wrong. That the woman hadn't been in the well more than twelve years. Otherwise… He swore.

Otherwise, he would be forced to talk to the former marshal. After all this time, the last thing Hud wanted was to see his father.

"I'M TAKING THE FIRST flight out," Jordan said without preamble when he called Dana back. "I'll let you know what time I arrive so you can pick me up at the airport."

Dana bit down on her tongue, determined not to let him get to her. He seemed to just assume she wouldn't have anything else to do but pick him up at Gallatin Field, a good fifty miles away. "Jordan, you must have forgotten. I have a job."

"You're half owner of a…fabric shop. Don't tell me you can't get away."

She wasn't going to chauffeur him around the whole time he was here, or worse, let him commandeer her vehicle. She took a breath. She would have loved to have lost her temper and told him just what she thought of him. He was in no position to be asking anything of her.

She let out the breath. "You'll have to rent a car, Jordan. I'll be working." A thought struck her like the back of a hand. "Where will you be staying in case I need to reach you?" Not with her. Please not with her at the ranch.

She heard the knife edge in his voice. "Don't worry, I'm not going to stay at that old run-down ranch house with you."

She almost slumped with relief. She'd suspected for some time that he was in financial trouble. Ever since two years ago when he'd married Jill, an out-of-work model, Jordan had seemed desperate for money.

"I assume Jill is coming with you?" Dana said, assuming just the opposite.

"Jill can't make it this time."

"Oh?" Dana bit her tongue again, just not quick enough. Jill had set foot in Montana only once and found it too backwoodsy.

"You have something to say, Dana? We all know what an authority you are on romantic relationships."

The jab felt all the more painful given that Hud was back in town. "At least I had the sense not to marry him." Instantly she wished she could snatch back the words. "Jordan, I don't want to fight with you." It was true. She hated how quickly this had escalated into something ugly. "Let's not do this."

"No, Dana, you brought it up," Jordan said. "If you have something to say, let's hear it."

"Jordan, you know this isn't what Mom wanted, us fighting like this."

He let out a cruel laugh. "You think I care what she wanted? The only thing she ever loved was that damned ranch. And just like her, you chose it over a man."

"Mom didn't choose the ranch over Dad," Dana said. "She tried to make their marriage work. It was Dad who—"

"Don't be naive, Dana. She drove him away. The same way you did Hud."

She wasn't going to discuss this with him. Especially today. Especially with Hud back. "I have to go, Jordan."

He didn't seem to hear her. "At least I have someone to warm my bed at night. Can your precious ranch do that?"

"Enjoy it while it lasts," Dana snapped. "Jill will be long gone once you don't have anything else you can pillage to appease her."

She knew at once that she'd gone too far. Jordan had never liked to hear the truth.

Dana smacked herself on the forehead, wishing she could take back the angry words. He'd always known how to push her buttons. Isn't that what siblings were especially adept at because they knew each other's weaknesses so well?

"Jordan, I'm sorry," she said, meaning it.

"I'll have Dad pick me up. But, dear sister, I will deal with you when I see you. And at least buy a damned answering machine." He ended the call abruptly.

She felt dirty, as if she'd been wrestling in the mud, as she hung up. She hadn't wanted the conversation to end like that. It would only make matters worse once he hit town.

She told herself that with luck maybe she wouldn't have to see him. She wouldn't have to see any of her siblings. The only one she'd been even a little close to was Clay, the youngest, but she wasn't even talking to *him* lately.

And she didn't want an answering machine. Anyone who needed to reach her, would. Eventually. She could just imagine the kind of messages Jordan would leave her.

She shuddered at the thought. As bad as she felt about the argument and her angry words, she was relieved. At least Jordan wasn't staying at the ranch, she thought with a rueful smile as she went into the kitchen and poured herself a glass of wine.

As she did, she heard the sound of a vehicle coming up the road to the house and groaned. Now what?

Glancing out the window she saw the marshal's black SUV barreling toward her.

This day just kept getting better.

Chapter Four

Across the river and a half mile back up a wide valley, the Cardwell ranch house sat against a backdrop of granite cliffs and towering dark pines. The house was a big, two-story rambling affair with a wide front porch and a new brick-red metal roof.

Behind it stood a huge weathered barn and some outbuildings and corrals. The dark shapes loomed out of the falling snow and darkness as Hud swung the SUV into the ranch yard.

He shut off the engine. Out of habit, he looked up at Dana's bedroom window. There was nothing but darkness behind the glass but in his mind he could see her waving to him as she'd done so many times years before.

As he got out of the patrol car, ducking deep into his coat against the falling snow, he ran to the porch, half expecting Dana's mother, Mary Justice Cardwell, to answer the door. Mary had been a ranch woman through and through. No one had ever understood why she'd married Angus Cardwell. He'd been too handsome and charming for his own good, with little ambition and even less regard for ranch work. But he'd also been heir to the C-Bar Ranch adjacent to the Justice Ranch.

When the two had married, so had the ranches. The combined spread became the Cardwell Ranch.

No one had been surprised when the two divorced. Or when Angus gave up the ranch to Mary.

People were just surprised that the two stayed together long enough to have four children.

And Angus and Mary had certainly produced beautiful children.

Jordan, the oldest, was almost too good-looking and had definitely taken after his father. Clay was the youngest, a slim, quiet young man who worked in local theater groups.

Then there was Stacy, two years older than Dana, cheerleader cute. Stacy had cashed in on her looks her whole life, trading up in three marriages so far. He didn't like to think about Stacy.

There was no comparison between the two sisters. While Dana also had the Justice-Cardwell good looks, she had something more going for her. She'd been the good student, the hard worker, the one who wanted to carry on the family tradition at the ranch, while the others had cut and run the first chance they got.

Dana, like her mother, loved everything about ranching. It and breathing were one and the same to her. That's why he couldn't understand why Dana would be selling the place. It scared him.

He couldn't stand the thought that he'd come back too late. Or worse that he'd been carrying a torch for a woman who no longer existed.

As he started to knock, he heard a dog growl and looked over to see a gray-muzzled, white-and-liver springer spaniel.

"Joe?" He couldn't believe his eyes. He knelt as the

dog lumbered over to him, tail wagging with recognition. "Joe, hey, old boy. I didn't think you'd still be around." He petted the dog, happy to see a friendly face from the past.

"Was there something you wanted?"

He hadn't heard the front door open. Dana stood leaning against the frame, a glass of wine in her hand and a look that said she was in no mood for whatever he was selling.

He wished like hell that he wasn't going to add to her troubles. "Evening," he said, tipping his hat as he gave Joe a pat and straightened. "Mind if I come in for a few minutes? I need to talk to you."

"If this has something to do with you and me…"

"No." He gave her a rueful smile. There was no "you and me"—not anymore. Not ever again from the look in her brown eyes. "It's about what we found in the well."

All the starch seemed to go out of her. She stepped back, motioning him in.

He took off his hat and stepped in to slip off his boots and his jacket before following her through the very Western living area with its stone and wood to the bright, big airy kitchen. Joe followed at his heels.

"Have a seat."

Hud pulled out a chair at the large worn oak table, put his Stetson on an adjacent chair and sat.

Dana frowned as Joe curled up at his feet. "Traitor," she mouthed at the dog.

Hud looked around, memories of all the times he'd sat in this kitchen threatening to drown him. Mary Justice Cardwell at the stove making dinner, Dana helping, all of them chatting about the goings-on at the ranch, a new foal, a broken-down tractor, cows to be moved.

He could almost smell the roast and homemade rolls baking and hear Dana's laughter, see the secret, knowing looks she'd sent him, feel the warmth of being a part of this family.

And Dana would have made her mother's double chocolate brownies for dessert—especially for him.

Dana set a bottle of wine and a glass in front of him, putting it down a little too hard and snapping him back to the present. "Unless you think we're both going to need something stronger?" she asked.

"Wine will do." He poured himself some and topped off her glass as she took a chair across from him. She curled her bare feet under her but not before he noticed that her toenails were painted coral. She wore jeans and an autumn gold sweater that hugged her curves and lit her eyes.

He lifted his glass, but words failed him as he looked at her. The faint scent of her wafted over to him as she took a drink of her wine. She'd always smelled of summer to him, an indefinable scent that filled his heart like helium.

Feeling awkward, he took another drink, his throat tight. He'd known being in this house again would bring it all back. It did. But just being here alone with Dana, not being able to touch her or to say all the things he wanted to say to her, was killing him. She didn't want to hear his excuses. Hell, clearly she'd hoped to never lay eyes on him again.

But a part of him, he knew, was still hoping she'd been the one who'd sent him the anonymous note that had brought him back.

"So what did you find in the well?" she asked as if she wanted this over with as quickly as possible. She took another sip of wine, watching him over the rim of her glass, her eyes growing dark with a rage born of pain that he recognized only too well.

Dana hadn't sent the note. He'd only been fooling himself. She still believed he'd betrayed her.

"The bones are human but you already knew that," he said, finding his voice.

She nodded, waiting.

"We won't know for certain until Rupert calls from the crime lab, but his opinion is that the body belonged to a Caucasian woman between the ages of twenty-eight and thirty-five and that she's been down there about fifteen years." He met her gaze and saw the shock register.

"Only fifteen years?"

Hud nodded. It seemed that, like him, she'd hoped the bones were very old and had no recent connection to their lives.

Dana let out a breath. "How did she get there?"

"She was murdered. Rupert thinks she was thrown down the well and then shot."

Dana sat up, her feet dropping to the floor with a slap. "No." She set the wineglass down on the table, the wine almost spilling.

Without thinking, Hud reached over to steady the glass, steady her. His fingers brushed hers. She jerked her hand back as if he'd sliced her fingers with a knife.

He pulled back his hand and picked up his wineglass, wishing now that he'd asked for something stronger.

Dana was sitting back in the chair, her arms crossed, feet on the floor. She looked shaken. He wondered how much of it was from what he'd told her about the bones in the well and how much from his touch. Did she ever wonder what their lives might have been like if she hadn't broken off the engagement? They would be husband and wife now. Something he always thought about. It never failed to bring a wave of regret with it.

He didn't tell Dana that the woman had still been alive, maybe even calling to her attacker for help as he left her down there.

"I'm going to have to question your family and anyone else who had access to the property or who might have known about the dry well," he said.

She didn't seem to hear him. Her gaze went to the large window. Outside, the snow fell in huge feathery flakes, obscuring the mountains. "What was she shot with?"

He hesitated, then said, "Rupert thinks it was a .38." He waited a beat before he added, "Does your father still have that .38 of his?"

She seemed startled by the question, her gaze flying back to him. "I have no idea. Why—" Her look turned to stone. "You can't really believe—"

"Do you have any guns in the house?" he asked in his official tone.

Her eyes narrowed in reaction. "Just the double-barreled shotgun by the door. But you're welcome to search the house if you don't believe me."

He remembered the shotgun. Mary Justice Cardwell had kept it by the door, loaded with buckshot, to chase away bears from her chicken coop.

"You have any idea who this woman in the well might have been?" he asked.

"Fifteen years ago I was sixteen." She met his gaze. Something hot flashed there as if she, too, remembered her sixteenth birthday and their first kiss.

"You recall a woman going missing about that time?" he asked, his voice sounding strange to his ears.

She shook her head, her gaze never leaving his face. "Won't there be a missing person's report?"

"The law and justice center fire in Bozeman destroyed all the records twelve years ago," he said.

"So we might never know who she was?" Dana asked.

"Maybe not. But if she was local, someone might remember her." He pulled his notebook and pen from his pocket. "I'm going to need Jordan's phone number so I can contact him."

"He's flying in tomorrow. He'll probably stay with Angus, but I'm sure he'll be contacting you."

He thought it strange she referred to her father as Angus. He wondered what had been going on in the years he'd been gone.

"You know where to find them," she continued. "Angus on the nearest bar stool. Clay at his studio in the old Emerson in Bozeman. And Stacy—" Her voice broke. "Well, she's where you left her."

Hud surprised himself by taking the jab without flinching.

"I was really sorry to hear about your mom's accident." He'd heard that Mary had been bucked off a horse and suffered severe brain damage. She'd lived for a short while, but never regained consciousness.

Dana locked eyes with him. "She always liked you." She said it as if it was the one mistake her mother ever made.

"Is that why you're selling the ranch?"

She got up from the table. "Is there anything else?"

He could see that he shouldn't have mentioned the

sale. Not only was it none of his business, but he also got the feeling today really wasn't the day to ask.

He finished his wine and pushed himself up from the chair. Picking up his Stetson, he settled it on his head. "I see you forgot your ring again."

DANA CURSED HERSELF for ever lying about the engagement let alone the ring. "The stone was loose," she said, compounding the lies. She'd spent thirty-one years telling the truth and Hud came back to town and she became an instant liar.

"You're not engaged to Lanny Rankin," he said softly. "Are you?"

She lifted her chin ready to defend her lie to the death. "Not that it's any of your business—"

"Why did you lie to me, Dana?"

Something in his tone stopped her cold. Obviously he thought she'd done it to make him jealous because she still cared. This was turning out to be the worst day of her life.

"I didn't want you thinking there was any chance for you and me."

He smiled. "Oh, your attitude toward me made that pretty clear. You didn't have to come up with a fiancé." His eyes suddenly narrowed. "Why *hasn't* the guy asked you to marry him? Something wrong with him?"

"No," she snapped. "My relationship with Lanny is none of your business." She could see the wheels turning in his stubborn head. He thought more than ever that she was still carrying a torch for him.

"You're the most annoying man I've ever known," she said as she headed for the door to show him out.

His soft chuckle chased after her, piercing her heart

with memory. So many memories of the two of them together.

"At least I still have that distinction," he said as she snatched open the front door and he stepped through it.

Joe, she noticed, had followed them and now stood by her feet. The old dog might be deaf and barely getting around anymore, but he was no fool. When push came to shove, he knew where his loyalties lay.

Hud turned in the doorway to look at her, all humor gone from his expression. "At some point, I'll need to talk to you about this investigation. I can come here or you can come down to the Big Sky office—"

"The office would be fine," she said. "Just let me know when."

"Dana, I really am sorry about—" he waved a hand "—everything."

Her smile felt as sharp as a blade. "Good night, Hud." She closed the door in his face but not before she heard him say, "Good night, Dana," the way he used to say it after they'd kissed.

She leaned against the door, her knees as weak as water. Damn it, she wasn't going to cry. She'd shed too many tears for Hud Savage. He wasn't getting even one more out of her.

But she felt hot tears course down her cheeks. She wiped at the sudden wetness, biting her lip to keep from breaking down and bawling. What a lousy day this had been. This birthday was destined to go down as the worst.

Joe let out a bark, his old eyes on her, tail wagging.

"I'm not mad at you," she said, and squatted to wrap her arms around him. "I know you always liked Hud. Didn't we all?"

Dana had never been one to wallow in self-pity. At least not for long. She'd gone on with her life after Hud left. His coming back now wasn't going to send her into another tailspin.

She rose and walked to the kitchen window, drawn to it by what she now knew had been in the old well all these years. The horror of it sent a shudder through her. Was it possible she had known the woman? Or worse, she thought, with a jolt, that Angus had? Hud had reminded her that her father had owned a .38.

With a groan, she recalled the time her father had let her and Hud shoot tin cans off the ranch fence with the gun.

Through the falling snow, she looked toward the hillside and hugged herself against the chill of her thoughts before glancing at the kitchen clock.

There was time if she hurried. She'd heard that her dad and uncle were playing with their band at the Corral Bar tonight. If she left now she might be able to talk to both of them and still get back in time for her date with Lanny.

She was anxious to talk to her father—before he and her uncle had time to come up with a convincing story. The thought surprised her. Why had she just assumed he had something to hide? Because, she thought with a rueful grin, he was her father and she knew him.

By now the canyon grapevine would be humming with the news about the body in the well. After all, Jordan had heard all the way back in New York City.

She'd just have to weather the blizzard—the storm outside as well as the arrival of her brother tomorrow from New York.

She groaned at the thought as she took her coat from

a hook by the door. It was a good ten miles down the road to the bar and the roads would be slick, the visibility poor. But she knew she wouldn't be able to get any sleep until she talked to her father.

She just hoped it was early enough for him to be halfway sober, but she wasn't counting on it.

As HUD DROVE AWAY FROM the ranch, he kept saying the words over and over in her head.

She isn't engaged. She isn't engaged.

He smiled to himself. Admittedly, it was a small victory. But he'd been right. She wasn't engaged to Lanny.

Maybe even after all this time, he knew Dana better than she'd thought.

As snow continued to fall, he drove across the narrow bridge that spanned the Gallatin River and turned onto Highway 191 headed south down the Gallatin Canyon, feeling better than he had in years.

The "canyon," as it was known, ran from the mouth just south of Gallatin Gateway almost to West Yellowstone, ninety miles of winding road that trailed the river in a deep cut through the steep mountains on each side.

It had changed a lot since Hud was a boy. Luxury houses had sprouted up all around the resort. Fortunately some of the original cabins still remained and the majority of the canyon was national forest so it would always remain undeveloped.

The drive along the river had always been breathtaking, a winding strip of highway that followed the river up over the Continental Divide and down the other side to West Yellowstone.

Hud had rented a cabin a few miles up the canyon from Big Sky. But as he started up the highway, his headlights doing little to cut through the thick falling snow, his radio squawked.

He pulled over into one of the wide spots along the river. "Savage here."

The dispatcher in Bozeman, an elderly woman named Lorraine, announced she was patching through a call.

"Marshal Savage?" asked a voice he didn't recognize. "This is Dr. Gerald Cross with the crime lab in Missoula."

"Yes." Hud wondered why it wasn't Rupert calling.

"I have information on the evidence you sent us that I thought you'd want to hear about right away." There was the fluttering sound of papers, then the doctor's voice again. "We got lucky. Normally something like this takes weeks if not months, but your coroner was so insistent that we run the tests ASAP… The bullet lodged in the skull of the victim matches a bullet used in a shooting in your area."

Hud blinked in confusion. "What shooting?"

Another shuffle of papers. "A Judge Raymond Randolph. He was murdered in his home. An apparent robbery?"

Hud felt the air rush from his lungs. Judge Randolph. And the night Hud had been trying to forget for the past five years.

He cleared his throat. "You're saying the same gun that killed the Jane Doe from the well was used in the Randolph case?"

"The striations match. No doubt about it. Same gun used for both murders," the doctor said.

"The Randolph case was only five years ago. Hasn't

this body been down in the well longer than that? The coroner estimated about fifteen years."

"Our preliminary findings support that time period," Dr. Cross said.

Hud tried to take it in: two murders, years apart, but the same gun was used for both?

"We found further evidence in the dirt that was recovered around the body," the doctor was saying. "An emerald ring. The good news is that it was custom-made by a jeweler in your area. Should be easy to track."

Hud felt hopeful. "Can you fax me the information on the ring along with digital photos?"

"I'll have that done right away," the doctor said. "Also, three fingers on her left hand were broken, the ring finger in two places. Broken in the fall, I would assume, unless she tried to fight off her assailant.

"But what also might be helpful in identifying the woman is the prior break in the Jane Doe's radius, right wrist," the doctor continued. "It appears it was broken and healed shortly before her death. The break had been set, indicating she sought medical attention. She would have been wearing a cast in the weeks prior to her death."

A woman with a broken wrist in a cast.

"I've sent the information to both the dentists and doctors in your area," Dr. Cross said. "All her teeth were intact and she'd had dental work done on several molars not long before her death, as well. You got lucky on this one."

Lucky? Hud didn't feel lucky. Again he wondered why Rupert hadn't made the call. "Is Dr. Milligan still there? I wanted to ask him something."

"Sorry, but Rupert left some time ago. He said he had an appointment."

Hud thanked him and hung up the radio, wondering what was going on with Rupert. Why hadn't he been the one to call? It wasn't like him. Especially since he'd been right about everything. He would have called if for nothing else than to say, "Good thing you didn't bet me."

Because, Hud thought, Rupert wanted to get the information to someone else first? For instance, his friend the former marshal, Brick Savage?

Hud stared out at the falling snow. The night was bright, the scene past the windshield a tableau of varying shades of white and gray. Next to him the Gallatin River ran under a thick layer of ice. He couldn't remember ever feeling this cold.

He reached over and kicked up the heat, letting the vent blow into his face.

The same gun used to murder the woman in a red dress was used during what had appeared to be a robbery of Judge Randolph's residence. The judge had been shot and killed—the two incidents years apart.

Hud rubbed his hand over his face. No, he didn't feel lucky in the least. Judge Randolph had been one of Brick Savage's most outspoken opponents. Hud had never known what had spurred the judge's hatred of Marshal Brick Savage. The two had butted heads on more than one occasion, but then his father butted heads with a lot of people, Hud thought.

The difference was the judge had been in a position to make his threats come true. There had been talk that Judge Randolph was determined to see Marshal Brick Savage fired.

If the judge hadn't met such an untimely demise, who knows what would have happened, Hud thought as he pulled back onto the highway, the snow falling now in a dizzying white blur.

He hadn't been looking forward to going back to the cabin he'd rented near Big Sky. The cabin was small with just the bare essentials—exactly what he'd thought he wanted.

Except tonight he had too much on his mind to go back there yet. He turned around and headed for Bozeman. He wouldn't be able to sleep until he looked at the case file on Judge Raymond Randolph's robbery-murder.

He thought again about the anonymous note he'd received. Someone had wanted him back here. Someone with an agenda of their own?

As he drove down the canyon, the snow falling in a blinding wall of white, he feared he was being manipulated—just as he'd been five years ago.

Chapter Five

Dana brushed snow from her coat as she pushed open the door to the Corral Bar. The scent of beer and smoke hit her as she stepped in, pulled off her hat and, shaking the snow from it, looked around the bar for her father.

It was early. The place was relatively empty, only a few locals at the bar and a half-dozen others in booths eating the burgers the Corral was famous for.

A Country-Western song played on the jukebox, competing with the hum of conversation. The bartender was busy talking with a couple at her end of the bar.

Dana spotted her father and uncle at the far end on adjacent stools. They each had two beers in front of them and hadn't seemed to notice her come in. That was because they had their heads together in deep conversation.

As she approached, she saw her father look up and catch her reflection in the mirror. He sat up straighter, pulling back but mouthing something to Harlan as if warning him of her approach. Uncle Harlan turned on his stool to flash her a smile, both men appearing nervous. Clearly she had interrupted something.

"Dana," Harlan said, sounding surprised. "Haven't

seen you for a while." Like his brother, he was a big man with a head of dark hair peppered with gray.

"Uncle Harlan." She patted his arm as she passed, her gaze on her father.

While Angus Cardwell resembled his brother, he'd definitely gotten the looks in the family. He'd been a devastatingly handsome young man and Dana could see why her mother had fallen for him.

Angus was still handsome and would have been quite the catch in the canyon if it wasn't for his love of alcohol. Thanks to the healthy settlement he'd received from Dana's mother in the divorce, he didn't have to work.

"How's my baby girl?" Angus asked, and leaned over to kiss her cheek. She smelled the familiar scent of beer on his breath. "Happy birthday."

Dana had always been his baby girl and still was— even at thirty-one. "Fine. Thank you.

"Is there someplace we could talk for a minute?" she asked. Angus shot a look at Harlan.

"We could probably step into the back room," her father said. "I'm sure Bob wouldn't mind." Bob owned the place and since Angus was likely the most regular of the regulars who frequented the bar, Bob probably wouldn't mind.

"Guess I'll tag along," Uncle Harlan said, already sliding off his stool.

The back room was part office, part spare room. It had a small desk and an office chair along with a threadbare overstuffed chair and a sofa that looked like it might pull out into a bed. The room smelled of stale cigarette smoke and beer.

"So what's up?" Angus asked. Both he and Harlan had brought along their beers.

She studied them for a moment, then said, "I'm sure you've heard about what happened at the ranch today." She could see by their expressions that they had.

"Hell of a thing," Angus said.

Harlan nodded in agreement and tipped his beer bottle to his lips.

"Any idea how the bones got into our well?" she asked, wondering how much they'd heard on the canyon grapevine.

"Us?" Harlan said, looking puzzled. "Why would we know anything about her?"

Her. So they'd heard it was a woman. She couldn't believe how quickly word spread.

She hadn't meant to sound so accusing. "I just thought you might have some idea since you were both on the ranch during that time." Her parents were still together then, kind of, and her uncle had been working on the ranch and living in one of the spare bedrooms.

A look passed between them.

"What?" she asked.

"We were just talking about this," her father said.

"And?" she prodded.

"And nothing," Angus said.

"Anyone could have come onto the ranch and done it," Harlan said. "Could have driven right by the house or come in the back on one of the old loggin' roads. Could have been anyone." He looked embarrassed, as if he'd spoken out of turn. Or maybe said too much. He took a drink of his beer.

"So you two have it all figured out," she said, studying them. "That mean you've figured out who she was? Seems she went into the well about fifteen years ago."

"Fifteen years?" Clearly, Angus was surprised by that.

"Bunch of cowhands on the ranch back then," Harlan said. "Anyone could have known about the well. There's old wells and mine shafts all over Montana. Usually an old foundation nearby. Not that hard to find if you're looking for one."

Dana thought about the homestead chimney still standing and part of the foundation visible from the ranch house. Stood to reason, she supposed, there would be an old well nearby.

"All this seasonal help around here, the woman didn't have to be a local," Harlan said. "She could have been working in the canyon for the summer or even at the ski hill for the winter."

"Wouldn't someone have missed her, though?" Dana said, noticing her father was nursing his beer and saying little.

Harlan shrugged. "If she had family. If her family knew where she'd gone to in the first place. You know how these kids are who show up for the seasonal employment. Most move on within a few weeks. Could have been a runaway even. Wasn't there some bones found in the canyon a few years ago and they never did find out who that guy was?"

She nodded. The other remains that had been found were male and no identification had ever been made. Was the same thing going to happen with the woman's bones from the well?

She started to ask her father about his .38, but changed her mind. "You all right?" she asked her father.

Angus smiled and tossed his now empty beer bottle into the trash. "Fine, baby girl. I just hate to see you upset over this. How about I buy you a drink to celebrate your birthday and we talk about something else?"

he asked as he opened the door to the bar. The blare of the jukebox swept in along with a blue haze of smoke and the smell of burgers and beer.

Dana met his gaze. His eyes were shiny with alcohol and something else. Whatever he was hiding, he was keeping it to himself whether she liked it or not.

"Maybe some other time," she said. "I have a date tonight."

"I heard Hud was back," he said, and grinned at her.

"I'm not with Hud, Dad." How many times did she have to tell him that she was never getting back together with Hud? "Lanny's taking me out to dinner for my birthday."

"Oh," Angus said. He'd never been fond of Lanny Rankin and she'd never understood why. All her father had ever said was, "I just don't think he's the right man for you."

AT THE LAW AND JUSTICE CENTER, Hud sat with the file on the Judge Raymond Randolph killing, still haunted by that night. Most of the night was nothing but a black hole in his memory. He couldn't account for too many hours and had spent years trying to remember what he'd done that night.

He shook his head. It was one of the questions he was bound and determined to get answered now that he was back in Montana.

How strange that his first case as acting Gallatin Canyon marshal was tied to that night. Coincidence? He had to wonder.

He opened the file. Since he'd left town right after the judge's death, he knew little about the case.

The first thing that hit him was the sight of his father's notes neatly printed on sheets of eight-and-a-half-by-eleven, lined white paper. Brick Savage had never learned to type.

Hud felt a chill at just the sight of his father's neat printing, the writing short and to the point.

The judge had been at his annual Toastmasters dinner; his wife, Katherine "Kitty" Randolph, was away visiting her sister in Butte. The judge had returned home early, reason unknown, and was believed to have interrupted an alleged robbery in progress. He was shot twice, point-blank in the heart with a .38-caliber pistol.

A neighbor heard the shots and called the sheriff's department. A young new deputy by the name of Hudson Savage was on duty that night. But when he couldn't be reached, Marshal Brick Savage took the call.

Hud felt his hands begin to shake. He'd known he was going to have to face that night again when he'd come back, but seeing it in black-and-white rattled him more than he wanted to admit.

Brick reported that as he neared the Randolph house, he spotted two suspects fleeing the residence. He gave chase. The high-speed chase ended near what was known as the 35-mile-an-hour curve, one of the worst sections in the winding canyon road because it ended in a bridge and another curve in the opposite direction.

The suspect driving the car lost control after which the car rolled several times before coming to a stop upside down in the middle of the Gallatin River.

Both the driver and the passenger were killed.

Marshal Brick Savage called for an ambulance, wrecker and the coroner before returning to the Randolph house where he discovered signs of a break-in and the judge lying dead in the foyer.

According to Brick's account, evidence was later found in the suspects' car that connected the two to the robbery-murder. The suspects were Ty and Mason Kirk, two local brothers who had been in trouble pretty much all of their lives.

The case seemed cut-and-dried. Except now the murder weapon appeared to have been used in the murder of a woman in a well a good decade before.

Tired and discouraged, he photocopied the file and drove back up the canyon. Still, he couldn't face the small cabin he'd rented. Not yet.

He drove to his office in the deepening snow. His headlights shone on the evergreens along each side of the road, their branches bent under the weight of the snowfall. A white silence had filled the night. The streets were so quiet, he felt as if there wasn't another soul within miles as he neared his office.

Had he made a terrible mistake coming back here, taking the job as marshal even temporarily? It had been instantaneous. When he'd gotten the offer, he'd said yes without a moment's hesitation, thinking it was fate. After the note he'd received, he was coming back anyway. But to have a job. Not just a job, but the job he'd always said he wanted....

He pulled up to the office, turned off the engine and lights, and sat for a moment in the snowy darkness, trying to put his finger on what was bothering him.

Something about the Judge Raymond Randolph murder case. Something was wrong. He could feel it deep in his bones, like a sliver buried under the skin.

As he picked up the copied file from the seat next to him, he had that same sick feeling he'd had when he'd looked down into the dry well and seen human bones.

IT WASN'T UNTIL DANA returned home from the bar that she noticed the tracks on the porch. She stopped and turned to look back out through the falling snow.

Someone had been here. The tire tracks had filled with snow and were barely visible. That's why she hadn't noticed them on her way in. Plus she'd had other things on her mind.

But now, standing on the porch, she saw the boot tracks where someone had come to the door. She checked her watch. Too early for it to have been Lanny.

Her breath caught in her throat as she realized the tracks went right into the house. She'd never locked the front door in her life. Just as she hadn't tonight. This was rural Montana. No one locked their doors.

Carefully she touched the knob. It was cold even through her gloves. The door swung open.

The living room looked just as she'd left it. Except for a few puddles of melted snow where someone had gone inside. Her heart rate tripled as she trailed the wet footprints across the floor to the kitchen.

That's when she saw it. A small wrapped package on the kitchen table.

A birthday present. Her relief was quickly replaced by anger. She had a pretty good idea who'd left it. Hud. He'd returned and, knowing the door would be unlocked, had come in and left it.

Damn him. Why did he have to come back? Tears burned her eyes. She wouldn't cry. She…would…not…cry.

Her heart was still pounding too hard, the tears too close after the day she'd had. She turned on the lights, shrugged out of her coat to hang it on the hook by the door and wiped angrily at her eyes. *Damn you, Hud.*

She had to get ready for her date. Stumbling up the

stairs, she went to the bathroom, stripped down and stepped into the shower. She turned her face up to the water for a moment. The memory of the Hud she'd loved filled her with a pain that almost doubled her over. A sob broke loose, opening the dam. Leaning against the shower stall she couldn't hold back the pain any longer. It came in a flood. She was helpless to stop it.

After a while she got control again, finished showering and got out. She'd have to take care of the package on the kitchen table. She quickly dressed. Her eyes were red from crying, her face flushed. She dug in the drawer looking for makeup she seldom if ever wore, but it did little to hide her swollen eyes.

The doorbell rang. Lanny was early. She'd hoped to get back downstairs and throw away Hud's birthday present before Lanny arrived.

She ran downstairs without glancing toward the kitchen and Hud's present, unhooking her coat from the hook as she opened the door and flipped on the porch light.

Lanny looked up from where he stood about to ring the doorbell again. He was tall and slim with sandy-colored hair and thick-lashed brown eyes. Any woman with good eyesight would agree he was handsome. Even Dana.

But she'd never felt that thumpity-thump in her pulse when she saw him. She didn't go weak in the knees when they kissed, hardly thought about him when they were apart.

She enjoyed his company when they were together, which over the past five years hadn't been very often. Her fault. She'd put Lanny off for a long time after Hud left because she hadn't been ready to date. And then she'd been busy much of the time.

She'd thought that in time she would feel about him the way he felt about her. She'd wished she could feel more for him, especially after he'd confessed that he'd had a crush on her since first grade.

"So it's true," he said, now looking into her face.

She knew her eyes were still red, her face puffy from crying and she'd done enough lying for one day. "It's been a rough birthday."

"It's all over town," Lanny said. "According to the rumor mill, you and I've been upgraded."

She groaned. Hud must have asked someone about the engagement. That's all it would take to get the rumor going. "Sorry. I got a little carried away."

He nodded ruefully. "Then it's not true?"

She shook her head and saw the hurt in his expression. For the first time she had to admit to herself that no matter how long she dated Lanny, she was never going to fall in love with him. She'd only been kidding herself. And giving Lanny false hope. She couldn't keep doing that.

"I figured I'd probably have heard if it was true," he said. "But you never know."

Yeah, she did know. "I'm sorry," she said again, unable to think of anything else to say. She hated to break it off tonight. He would think she was going back to Hud and that's the last rumor she wanted circulating. But she had to get it over with. She didn't think it would come as too big of a surprise to Lanny.

"You still want to go out tonight?" he asked, as if he sensed what was coming.

"Nothing's changed," she said too quickly.

"Yeah, that's kind of the problem, huh?" He glanced into the house.

She didn't want to have this discussion here, on her doorstep, and she didn't want to invite him inside. She didn't want him to see the present Hud had left her. It would only hurt him worse and that was something she didn't want to do.

"Ready?" she asked.

Lanny hesitated for only a moment, then walked her through the falling snow to his large SUV.

She chattered on about the weather, then the sewing shop and Hilde, finally running out of safe conversation as he pulled into the restaurant.

Once inside, Dana found herself watching the door. She couldn't help it. Now that she knew Hud was back in the canyon, she expected to run into him at every turn, which kept him on her mind. Damn him.

"Hud's working late tonight," Lanny said.

She jerked her head around. "I wasn't—" The beginning of a lie died on her lips. "I just hate running into him," she said sheepishly.

Lanny nodded, his smile indulgent. "After all this time, it must be a shock, him coming back." He wiped a line of sweat off his water glass, not looking at her. "He say what brought him back?"

"No." That was one of the things that bothered her. Why after so long?

"He must think he has a chance with you." He met her gaze.

"Well, he doesn't." She picked up her menu, the words swimming in front of her. "What did Sally say was the special tonight?"

Lanny reached over and pulled down the menu so

he could see her face. "I need you to be honest with me," he said, his voice low even though because of the weather there were only a couple of people in the restaurant and they weren't close by.

She nodded, her throat a desert.

"Dana, I thought you'd gotten over Hud. I thought after he hurt you the way he did, you'd never want to see him again. Am I wrong about that or—" He looked past her, his expression telling her before she turned that Hud had come into the restaurant.

Her heart took off at a gallop at just the sight of him. She looked to see if he was alone, afraid he wouldn't be. He was. He stepped up to the counter and started to sit down, instantly changing his mind when he saw her and Lanny.

"You need a table, Hud?" Sally asked him from behind the counter.

"Nah, just wanted to get a burger," he said, turning his back to Dana and Lanny. "Working late tonight."

Dana recalled now that Lanny had said Hud was working tonight. How had he known that?

"Working, huh," Sally said, glancing toward Dana's table. "You want fries with that?" She chuckled. "Daddy always said if I didn't pay more attention in school I'd be saying that. He was right."

"No fries. Just the burger." He sat at the counter, his shoulders hunched, head down. Dana felt her traitorous heart weaken at the sight. She'd thought she wanted to hurt him, hurt him badly, the way he'd hurt her. Seeing her on a date with Lanny was killing him. She should have taken pleasure in that.

Sally must have seen his discomfort. "You know I can have that sent over to you since you have work to do."

"I'd appreciate that," he said, getting up quickly, his relief so apparent it made Dana hurt. He laid some money on the counter and, without looking in her direction, pulled his coat collar up around his neck as he stepped out into the snowstorm.

A gust of winter washed through the restaurant and he was gone. Just like that. Just like five years ago. Dana felt that same emptiness, that same terrible loss.

"We don't have to do this," Lanny said as she turned back to the table and him.

Her heart ached and her eyes burned. "I'm sorry."

"Please, stop apologizing," Lanny snapped, then softened his expression. "You and I have spent too long apologizing for how we feel."

"Can we just have dinner as friends?" she asked.

His smile never reached his eyes. "Sure. Friends. Why not? Two friends having dinner." The words hit her like thrown stones. Anger burned in his gaze as he picked up his menu.

"Lanny—"

"It's your birthday, Dana. Let's not say anything to spoil it."

She almost laughed. Her birthday had been spoiled from the moment she'd opened her eyes this morning.

They ordered, then sat in silence until Sally arrived with their salads.

Dana felt terrible on so many levels. She just wanted to get through this dinner. She asked him about his work and got him talking a little.

But by the time they left, they'd exhausted all topics of conversation. Lanny said nothing on the drive back to the ranch. He didn't offer to walk her to her door.

"Goodbye, Dana," he said, and waited for her to get

out of the car. He met her gaze for an instant in the yard light and she saw rage burning in his eyes.

There was nothing she could say. She opened her door. "Thank you for dinner."

He nodded without looking at her and she got out, hurrying through the falling snow to the porch before she turned to watch him drive away.

It wasn't until she entered the house that she remembered the present on her kitchen table.

The box, the size of a thick paperback book, was wrapped in red foil. There was a red bow on top with a tag that read Happy Birthday!

She knew exactly what was inside—which gave her every reason not to touch it. But still she picked up the box, disappointed in herself.

She felt the weight of the chocolates inside, felt the weight of their lost love. She'd tried to get over Hud. Tried so hard. Why did he have to come back and remind her of everything—including how much she had loved him?

Still loved him.

All the old feelings rained down on her like a summer downpour, drowning her in regret.

Damn Hud.

She set the box down, heard the chocolates rattle inside. Not just any chocolate. Only the richest, most wonderful, hard-to-find chocolates in the world. These chocolates were dark and creamy and melted the instant they touched your tongue. These chocolates made you close your eyes and moan and were right up there with sex. Well, not sex with Hud. Nothing could beat that.

Making love with Hud was a whole other experience—and she hated him even more now for reminding her of it.

Knowing her weakness, Hud had found these amazing chocolates and had given them to her on her twenty-fifth birthday—the night he'd asked her to marry him.

She glared down at the box and, like niggling at a sore tooth with her tongue, she reminded herself of how Hud had betrayed her five years ago. That did the trick.

Grabbing up the box of chocolates, she stormed over to the trash. The container was empty except for the balled up card from her sister that she'd retrieved from the floor and thrown away. She dropped the box of chocolates into the clean, white plastic trash bag, struck by how appropriate it was that the card from Stacy and the chocolates from Hud ended up together in the trash.

The chocolates rattled again when they hit the bottom of the bag and for just a moment she was tempted. What would it hurt to eat one? Or even two? Hud would never have to know.

No, that's exactly what he was counting on. That she wouldn't be able to resist the chocolates—just as there was a time when she couldn't resist him.

Angrily she slammed the cupboard door. He'd broken her heart in the worst possible way and if he thought he could worm his way back in, he was sadly mistaken.

She stormed over to the phone and called his office.

"Hello?"

"It didn't work," she said, her voice cracking. Tears burned her eyes. She made a swipe at them.

"Dana?"

"Your…present… The one you left me after sneaking into my house like a thief. It didn't work. I threw the chocolates away."

"Dana." His voice sounded strange. "I didn't give you a present."

Her breath caught. Suddenly the kitchen went as cold as if she'd left the front door wide-open. "Then who…?"

"Dana, you haven't eaten any of them, have you?"

"No." Who had left them if not Hud? She walked back over to the sink and was about to open the cabinet door to retrieve the box, when her eye was caught by something out the window.

Through the snow she saw a light flickering up on the hillside near the old homestead. Near the well.

She stepped over and shut off the kitchen light, plunging the kitchen into darkness. Back at the window she saw the light again. There was someone up there with a flashlight.

"Dana? Did you hear what I said? Don't eat any of the chocolates."

"Do you still have men up on the mountain at the well?" she asked.

"No, why?"

"There's someone up there with a flashlight."

She heard the rattle of keys on Hud's end of the line. "Stay where you are. I'll be right there."

Chapter Six

Dana hung up the phone and sneaked into the living room to turn out that light, as well. She stood for a moment in total darkness, waiting for her eyes to adjust.

Through the front window, the sky outside was light with falling snow. She listened for any sound and heard nothing but the tick of the mantel clock over the fireplace. After locking the front door, she crept back into the kitchen to the window again.

No light. Had she only imagined it? And now Hud was on his way over—

There it was. A faint golden flicker through the falling snow. The light disappeared again and she realized that the person must have stepped behind the old chimney.

She stared, waiting for the light to reappear and feeling foolish even with her pulse still hammering in her ears. If she hadn't been on the phone with Hud when she'd seen the light, she wouldn't have called for help.

She'd had trespassers on the ranch before. Usually they just moved along with a warning. A few needed to see the shotgun she kept by the door.

Obviously this was just some morbid person who'd heard about the body in the well and had sneaked in the back way to the ranch hoping to find…what? A souvenir?

She really wished she hadn't told Hud about the light. She could handle this herself. The light appeared again. The person moved back and forth, flashing the light around. Didn't the fool realize he could be seen from the house?

A thought struck her. What if it was a member of her family? She could just imagine her father or uncle up there looking around. Hud wasn't one to shoot first and ask questions later, but if he startled whoever was up there— Even if he didn't kill them, he'd at least think them guilty of something.

Or…what if it was the killer returning to the scene of the crime? What if he was looking for evidence he believed the marshal hadn't found?

The thought sent a chill running up her spine. She stepped away from the window and moved carefully to the front door again in the darkness. The roads were icy; she didn't know how long it would take Hud to get here.

She found the shotgun by the door, then moved to the locked cabinet, found the hidden key and opened the drawer to take out four shells. Cracking the double-barreled shotgun open, she slipped two shells in and snapped it closed again, clicking on the safety. Pocketing the other two shells, she returned to the kitchen.

No light again. She waited, thinking whoever it was had gone behind the chimney again. Or left. Or…

Her heart began to pound. Had he seen the lights go out in the ranch house and realized he'd been spotted? He could be headed for the house right now.

She'd never been afraid on the ranch. But then, she

hadn't known there was a murdered woman's remains in the well.

The shotgun felt heavy in her hands as she started to move toward the back door, realizing too late that she'd failed to lock it. She heard the creak of a footfall on the back porch steps. Another creak. The knob on the back door started to turn.

She raised the shotgun.

"Dana?"

The shotgun sagged in her arms as the back door opened and she saw Hud's familiar outline in the doorway.

He froze at the sight of the shotgun.

"I didn't hear you drive up," she whispered, even though there wasn't any need to.

"I walked the last way so your visitor wouldn't hear my vehicle coming and run. When I didn't see any lights on, I circled the house and found the back door unlocked…" His voice broke as he stepped to her and she saw how afraid he'd been for her.

He took the shotgun from her and set it aside before cupping her shoulders in his large palms. She could feel his heat even through the thick gloves he wore and smell his scent mixed with the cold night air. It felt so natural, she almost stepped into his arms.

Instead he dropped his hands, leaving her aching for the feel of him against her, yearning for his warmth, his strength, even for the few seconds she would have allowed herself to enjoy it before she pushed him away.

She stepped past him to the window and stared up the hillside. There was only falling snow and darkness now. "I don't see the light now."

"I want you to stay here," Hud said. "Lock the door behind me."

"You aren't going up there alone?"

He smiled at her. "Does that mean you're not wishing me dead anymore?"

She flushed, realizing she *had* wished that. And fairly recently, too. But she hadn't meant it and now she was afraid that foolish wish might come true if he went up that hillside alone. "I'm serious. I don't want you going up there. I have a bad feeling about this."

He touched her cheek. Just a brush of his gloved fingertips across her skin. "I'll be all right. Is that thing loaded?" he asked, tilting his head toward the shotgun where he'd left it.

"It would be pretty useless if it weren't."

He grinned. "Good. Try not to shoot me when I come back." And with that, he was gone.

HUD MOVED STEALTHILY through the snowy night, keeping to the shadows of the house, then the barn and outbuildings as he made his way toward the pines along the mountainside.

Earlier, he'd caught glimpses of the light flickering through the falling snow as he'd run up the road toward the ranch house, his heart in his throat.

Now, the falling snow illuminated the night with an eerie cold glow. No light showed by the well, but he didn't think whoever it was had left. He hadn't heard a vehicle. More to the point, he didn't think whoever it was had finished what he'd come here to do.

His breath puffed out in a cloud around his face as he half ran through the fallen snow in the darkness of the pines.

He stopped at the edge of the trees in view of the old homestead. Snow fell silently around him in the freezing night air. He watched the play of shadows over the new snow. A quiet settled into his bones as he stilled his breathing to listen.

From this position, the dark shape of the chimney blocked his view of the well. He could see no light. No movement through the blur of snow.

The night felt colder up here, the sky darker. No breeze stirred the flakes as they tumbled down. He moved as soundlessly as possible, edging his way toward the dark chimney.

He hadn't gone far when he saw the impression of tracks in the new snow. He stopped, surprised to find that the footprints had formed a path back and forth along the edge of the old homestead's foundation as if the person had paced here. Making sure Dana saw the light and went to investigate? he thought with a start.

Again Hud listened and heard nothing but the occasional semi on the highway as it sped by into the night. The snow was falling harder, visibility only a few feet in front of him now.

If any place could be haunted, this would be the place, he thought. A gust of sudden wind whirled the snow around him and he felt a chill as if the woman from the well reached out to him, demanding justice.

He pulled his weapon and made his way toward the chimney, staying in the shadow it cast.

That's when he saw it. Something lying in the snow. A rope. As he moved closer, he saw that it was tied to the base of the old chimney and ran across the snow in the direction of the well.

Hud stared into the falling snow, but he couldn't see

the top of the well at this distance. He took the flashlight from his coat pocket but didn't turn it on yet. Holding his gun in one hand and the flashlight in the other, he moved soundlessly along the length of rope toward the well opening.

DANA COULDN'T STAND STILL. She'd lost sight of Hud as well as the old homestead chimney as the storm worsened. Nor had she seen the light again.

She couldn't stand it any longer. She couldn't wait here for Hud.

She knew he'd be furious with her and had even tried to talk herself out of going up there as she pulled on her boots, hat, coat and gloves.

But ever since last night, she hadn't been able to shake the feeling that something horrible was going to happen. This morning when she'd found out about the bones in the well and that Hud was back in town, she'd thought that was the something horrible the premonition had tried to warn her about.

But as she picked up the shotgun and stepped out the back door into the darkness and snow, she was still plagued with the feeling that the worst was yet to come. And then there was her stupid birthday wish!

She took the road, feeling fairly safe that she couldn't be seen since she couldn't see her hand in front of her face through the snowfall. Sometimes she would catch a glimpse of the mountainside as a gust of wind whirled the snow away. But they were fleeting sightings and she was still too far away to be seen, so she kept moving.

The air was cold. It burned her throat, the snow getting in her eyes. She stared upward, straining to see the chimney, reminded of ranchers' stories about stringing clotheslines from the house to the barn so they didn't get lost in a blizzard.

She'd always prided herself on her sense of direction but she didn't chance it tonight. She could feel the rut of the road on the edge of her boot as she walked, the shotgun heavy in her hands, but at the same time reassuring.

As she neared the homestead, the wind swirled the snow around her and for an instant she saw the chimney dark against the white background. It quickly disappeared but not before she'd seen a figure crouched at the edge of the old homestead foundation.

HUD FOLLOWED THE ROPE to the well, stopping just short of the edge to listen. He edged closer to the hole. The rope dropped over the side into blackness. Still hearing nothing, he pointed the flashlight down into the well, snapped on the light and jerked back, startled.

He wasn't sure what he'd expected to see dangling from the rope. Possibly a person climbing down. Or trying to climb out.

He holstered his weapon, then kneeling, he shone the flashlight to get a better look. It was a doll, the rope looped like a noose around its neck.

What the hell?

He picked up the rope and pulled it until the doll was within a few feet of the top. Its face caught in the beam of his flashlight and he let out a gasp, all his breath rushing from him.

The doll had Dana's face.

He lost his grasp on the rope. The doll dropped back into the well. As he reached for the rope to stop its fall, he sensed rather than heard someone behind him.

Half turning, he caught movement as a large dark figure, the face in shadow, lunged at him, swinging one of the boards from the well.

A shotgun discharged close by as he tried to pull his weapon but wasn't quick enough. The board slammed into his shoulder, pitching him forward toward the gaping hole in the earth.

Hud dropped the flashlight and grabbed for the rope with both hands, hoping to break his fall if not stop it.

His gloved hands wrapped around the rope, but the weight of his falling body propelled him over the side and partway down into the cold darkness of the well. He banged against the well wall with his left shoulder and felt pain shoot up his arm. But he'd managed to catch himself.

He dangled from the rope, the doll hanging below him. He was breathing hard, his mind racing. Where the hell had the shotgun blast come from? He had a bad feeling he knew.

Bracing his feet against the wall, he managed to pull the gun from his holster, telling himself it couldn't have been Dana. He'd told her to stay in the ranch house.

He looked up, pointing the gun toward the well opening. He could wait for his attacker or climb out. Snowflakes spiraled down from a sky that seemed to shimmer above him iridescent white. He squinted, listening.

Another shotgun blast, this one closer.

Hud climbed as best he could without relinquishing his weapon. Only seconds had passed since the attack. But now time seemed to stand still.

Then in the distance he heard the growl of an engine

turning over and, a moment later, another shadow fell over the top of the well above him.

He looked up through the falling snow and saw the most beautiful woman in the world lay down her shotgun and reach for him.

DANA'S HEART WAS IN HER THROAT as she looked down into the well and saw Hud hanging there.

He was alive, not broken at the bottom, but partway down a rope. That's all that registered at first. Then she saw him wince as he tried to use his left arm to holster his gun and pull himself up.

"You're hurt," she said, as if the pain were her own. "Here, let me help you."

She managed to get him up to the edge and drag him out into the snow. They lay sprawled for a few moments, both breathing hard from the exertion.

"Thanks," Hud said, turning his head to look over at her.

She nodded, more shaken now than she'd been when she'd looked over the edge of the well and had seen him hanging down there. Aftershock, she supposed. The time when you think about what could have happened. Realized how close it had been. She breathed in the night air as the sound of a vehicle engine died off until there was nothing but the sound of their labored breaths.

They were alone. Entirely alone, as if the rest of the world didn't exist.

Hud sat up and looked at her. He was favoring his left arm and she saw now that his jacket was ripped and dark with blood.

"Your arm... It's bleeding!"

He shook his head. "I'm fine. What about you?"

"Fine." She pushed herself up, her arms trembling with the effort.

His gaze met hers and he shook his head. Couldn't fool him.

She started to get to her feet, but he caught her sleeve, pulling her back to the ground beside him.

"Dana."

Her face crumpled as he encircled her with his good arm and pulled her tightly against him. His hug was fierce.

She buried her face into his chest, the snow falling around them.

When she pulled back, the kiss was as natural as sunrise. Soft, salty, sweet and tentative. And for a moment nothing mattered. Not the past, the pain, the betrayal. In that moment, she only recalled the love.

The snow stopped. Just like that. And the moment passed.

Dana pulled back, drowning in all the reasons she shouldn't love this man—wouldn't love this man. Not again.

HUD SAW THE CHANGE in her eyes. A quick cooling, as if her gaze had filmed over with ice. Just as her heart had five years ago.

She pulled away to pick up the shotgun from where she'd dropped it earlier. He watched her rise, keeping her back to him.

He got to his feet, searching the snow for his flashlight. His left arm ached from where he'd smacked it against one of the rocks embedded in the side of the well and split it open. The pain was nothing compared to what he'd seen in Dana's eyes.

Maybe he couldn't make up for what he'd done to her five years ago, but he sure as hell would find whoever had put the doll down the well. Whoever had tried to kill him tonight.

He heard a sound from Dana, part cry, part gasp, and realized that she'd found his flashlight and was now shining it down into the well.

Stepping to her side, he took the light from her, seeing the shock on her face as well as the recognition. "It's your doll?"

She nodded. "My father gave it to me for my sixth birthday. He thought it looked like me. How…" She met his gaze. "It was on a shelf in my old playroom along with the rest of the toys Mom saved for her—" Dana's voice broke "—grandchildren."

Mary Cardwell hadn't lived long enough to see any grandchildren be born. He could see what a huge hole losing her mother had left in Dana. Desperately he wanted to take her in his arms again. The need to protect her was so strong he felt sick with it.

He wanted to believe the doll had been put in the well as just a cruel prank meant to frighten her, but he feared it had been a trap. If Dana had come up here alone to investigate after seeing the light on the hillside, she would have been the one knocked into the well and there wouldn't have been anyone here with a shotgun to scare the would-be killer away. The thought was like a knife to his heart but as he stepped past her, pulled the doll the rest of the way up and removed the noose from its neck, he told himself that Dana needed a marshal now more than she needed a former lover.

"When was the last time you saw the doll?" he asked. The doll's hair was flattened with snow. Careful not to disturb any fingerprints that might be on it, he brushed the snow away, shocked again how much the face resembled Dana's.

"I don't know. The toys have been on the shelves in the playroom for so long I hardly notice. I don't go into that room much." Another catch in her voice. The playroom would only remind her of her mother, he thought. "I'd forgotten about the doll."

Well, someone else hadn't.

She shivered as if she'd had the same thought.

"Let's get back to the house and out of this weather," he said.

The sky over their heads was a deep, cold midnight-blue as they walked back toward the ranch house. A few stars glittered like ice crystals as a sliver of moon peeked out from behind a cloud.

He made her wait on the porch, leaving her still armed with the reloaded shotgun while he searched the house. There was no sign that anyone had been there—not to drop off a box of chocolates or to steal a doll from a shelf in her old playroom.

"All clear," he said, opening the front door.

She stepped in, breaking down the shotgun and removing the shells. He watched her put the shotgun by the door, pocket the shells and turn toward him again. "Let me see your arm," she ordered.

He started to protest, but she was already helping him off with his jacket. His uniform shirt was also torn and bloodied, though the cut in his upper arm didn't look deep from what he could see.

"Come in here," she said, and he followed her to the kitchen where she motioned to a chair.

He sat, watching her as she brought out a first aid kit.

He rolled his shirtsleeve up as she sat next to him, all her attention on the three-inch gash in his arm.

"You shouldn't have come up there, but I appreciate what you did," he said, his voice hoarse with emotion. "You quite possibly saved my life tonight."

"You should get stitches," she said as if she hadn't heard him. "Otherwise it will leave a scar."

"It won't be my first," he said.

She mugged a disapproving face and said, "This is going to sting." Her fingers gripped his upper arm.

He winced, the disinfectant burning into the cut.

"I warned you," she said, glancing up into his face. "Sure you don't want a ride to the emergency room?"

"Positive. A few butterfly bandages and I'll be as good as new."

She looked doubtful but went to work. He'd seen her doctor horses and cows before. He doubted doctoring him was any different for her. Except she liked the horses and cows better.

He couldn't help but think about the kiss. Man, how he had missed her.

"There, that should at least keep it from getting infected," she said, slamming the lid on her first aid kit and rising from the chair.

He touched her wrist and she met his gaze again. "Thanks."

She nodded and went to put the kit away.

He rose from the chair. "Mind if I take a look where that doll was kept?"

"I don't see how—" She stopped, then shrugged as if she didn't have the energy to argue.

He reminded himself that it was her birthday for a few more hours. What a lousy birthday.

He followed her up the stairs to what had once been her playroom. Mary had left it just as it had been when the kids were little.

The room was large with a table at its center surrounded by small chairs. There were books everywhere in the room and several huge toy boxes. The Cardwell kids had been blessed. One wall was filled with shelves and toys. There was a small tea set, stuffed animals, dolls and large trucks.

In the center, high on the wall, was a gaping hole where something had been removed. "That's where she has always been," Dana said, hugging herself as she stared at the empty spot on the shelf as if the realization that someone had to have come into the house and taken the doll had finally hit home.

"Who knew about the doll?" he asked.

She shook her head. "Only everyone who knew me. Angus probably showed it off at the bar for days before my sixth birthday. You know how he is."

Hud nodded. Anyone in the canyon could have known about the doll. "But how many people knew where you kept it?"

"Anyone who ever visited when we were kids knew about the playroom," she said.

"Or anyone in the family," he said, not liking what he was thinking.

"No one in my family would do this." Her face fell the instant the denial was out. It was a blood instinct to take up for your brothers and sister. But clearly, Dana wasn't entirely convinced her siblings were innocent of this.

She reached out for the doll he hadn't even realized he'd carried up the stairs.

He held it back. "Sorry, it's evidence. But I'll make sure you get it back. I want to take the chocolates you received, too."

She nodded, then turned and headed for the playroom doorway, moving like a sleepwalker. The day had obviously taken its toll on her. He looked around the room, then down at the doll in his gloved hand, thinking about Dana's siblings before following her to the kitchen.

She opened the cabinet doors under the sink and pulled out the trash can. Their gazes met. She'd thrown the candy away believing it had come from him. He never thought he'd be thankful for that.

"Mind if I take the plastic bag and all?" he asked.

"Be my guest."

"I could use another bag for the doll."

She got him one. He lowered the doll inside and tightened the drawstring, then pulled the other trash bag with the present in it from the container.

"I'll have the gift box dusted for prints and the candy tested," he said.

Her eyes widened. "You think the chocolates might have been...poisoned?"

He shrugged, the gesture hurting his arm.

The phone rang. She picked it up. He watched her face pale, her gaze darting to him, eyes suddenly huge.

He reached for the phone and she let him take it. But when he put the receiver to his ear, he heard only the dial tone. "Who was it?"

She shook her head. "Just a voice. A hoarse whisper. I didn't recognize it." She grabbed the back of the chair, her knuckles white.

"What did the caller say to you?" he asked, his stomach a hard knot.

"'It should have been you in the bottom of that well.'"

Hud checked caller ID and jotted down the number. He hit star 69. The phone rang and rang and finally was answered.

"Yeah?" said a young male voice.

"What number have I reached?" Hud asked.

What sounded like a kid read the number on the phone back to him. Hud could hear traffic on the street and what sounded like skateboarders nearby. A pay phone near the covered skate park in Bozeman?

"Did you see someone just make a call from that phone?" he asked the boy.

"Nope. No one was around when I heard it ringing. Gotta go." He hung up.

"I'm not leaving you alone in this house tonight," Hud said to Dana as he replaced the receiver. "Either you're coming with me or I'm staying here. What's it going to be?"

Chapter Seven

"You look like you've seen better days," Hilde said the next morning when Dana walked into the shop. "I heard you were at the Corral. So you decided to celebrate your birthday, after all."

"Who told you I was at the Corral?" Dana hadn't meant her tone to sound so accusing.

Hilde lifted a brow. "Lanny. I ran into him this morning at the convenience store." She tilted her head toward the two coffee cups on the counter. "I brought you a latte. I thought you might need it."

How had Lanny known that she was at the Corral last night? she wondered as she placed her purse behind the counter. "Thanks for the coffee. I really could use it."

Hilde handed her one of the lattes. She held it in both hands, trying to soak up some of the heat. Lanny had also known that Hud was working late. With a shiver, she realized he'd been checking up on her. And Hud.

"Are you all right?" Hilde asked, looking concerned.

Dana shook her head. "I went by the Corral last night to talk to Dad, then Lanny took me to dinner for my birthday."

"Oh, you didn't mention you were going out with Lanny."

"I'd forgotten we had a date."

Hilde gave her a look she recognized only too well. "It was our *last* date. I'd hoped we could be friends...."

"I hate to say this, but it's just as well," Hilde said.

Dana couldn't believe her ears.

Hilde raised her hands in surrender. "Hey, you were never going to fall in love with Lanny and we both know it."

Dana started to protest, but saved her breath. It was true.

"Maybe Hud coming back was a good thing."

Dana eyed her friend. "I beg your pardon?"

"I mean it. You need to resolve your issues with him."

"Resolve my issues? He slept with my sister when we were engaged!"

"Maybe."

"Maybe? There is no maybe about it. I caught them in bed together."

"Going at it?"

"No." Dana stepped back as if afraid she would ring her friend's neck.

"That's my point. You caught him in her bed, but you don't know what happened. If anything. Stacy has always been jealous of you. I wouldn't put anything past her."

"And what ready excuse do you have for Hud?" She held up her hands. "No, that's right, he was drunk and didn't know what he was doing."

"I know it sounds clichéd—"

"It sounds like what it is, a lie. Even if Stacy threw herself at him. Even if he was falling-down drunk—"

"Which would mean nothing happened."

Dana shook her head. "Hud wouldn't have left town the way he did if he'd been innocent."

"Did you ever give him a chance to explain?" Hilde asked.

"There was nothing that needed explaining. End of story." She turned and walked to the back of the store, surprised how close she was to tears. Again.

A few moments later she heard Hilde come up behind her. "Sorry."

Dana shook her head. "It's just seeing him again. It brings it all back."

"I know. I just hate to see you like this."

Dana turned, biting her lip and nodding as tears spilled out.

Hilde pulled her into a hug. "Maybe you're right. Maybe you should just kill the bastard. Maybe that's the only way you'll ever be free of him."

Hilde was joking but Dana knew that even in death she would still be haunted by Hud Savage. And after last night, she knew she didn't want him dead. Far from it.

She dried her tears and said, "Hud spent the night at my place last night."

Her friend's eyebrows shot up. "No way."

"He slept on the couch." She practically groaned at the memory of Hud's bare chest when she'd gone downstairs earlier. The quilt she'd given him down around his waist. His bare skin tanned from living in southern California. Muscled from working out.

"Dana, what's going on?"

She shook off the image and took a sip of the latte. It was wonderful. Just like her friend. "It's a long story." She filled Hilde in on what had happened last night.

"That's why I look like I didn't get any sleep. I didn't." She shook her head. "Hilde, I can't understand why anyone would do those things."

"This voice on the phone, was it a man or a woman?"

"I don't know. It was obviously disguised." She shivered and took another drink of the coffee. It warmed her from her throat to her toes and she began to relax a little. In the daylight, she wasn't quite so scared. "You know what bothers me the most is that whoever put that doll in the well had to have taken it from the house. Just like whoever left the chocolates."

"Everyone knows you never lock your doors," Hilde said.

"I do now. I just can't understand why I'm being threatened. It has to have something to do with the woman whose remains were found in the well."

There was a soft knock on the door and both women turned to see their first customer—Kitty Randolph—looking at her watch.

"She's early but we're going to have to let her in, huh," Hilde said with a laugh. "You sure you're up to this today?"

"I would go crazy if I stayed home, believe me," Dana said as she started toward the door to unlock it and put up the open sign. "Good morning, Mrs. Randolph."

"Dana," the older woman said, then added, "Hilde," by way of greeting. Kitty Randolph was a petite gray-haired woman with a round cheery face and bright blue eyes.

"I was going to get back to you about the fundraiser," Dana said, instantly feeling guilty for not doing so.

Kitty patted her hand with a cool wrinkled one of her own. "Now, dear, don't you worry about that. I know something dreadful happened out at the ranch. You must tell me all about it while you match this color thread." She pulled the leg of a pair of blue slacks from a bag hooked on her arm. "I need to raise the hem. I hate it, but I'm shrinking and getting shorter every day." She chuckled. "Now what's this about a body being in the well?" she asked conspiratorially as she took Dana's arm and steered her toward the thread rack.

Dana picked up several spools of thread and held them to the pants in Kitty Randolph's bag.

She gave the elderly woman a short version of the discovery in the well.

"Any idea who she was?" Kitty asked.

Dana shook her head. "We might never know."

Kitty purchased her thread and left, promising to bring some of her wonderful chocolate chip cookies the next time she stopped by.

ARMED WITH PHOTOGRAPHS and information about the emerald ring found in the well, Hud drove to Bozeman first thing.

The jewelry store was one of those small, exclusive shops on Main Street. Hud tapped at the door just over the closed sign and a fit-looking, gray-haired man unlocked the door.

"Marshal Savage," the jeweler said, extending his hand. "You made good time."

Hud handed him the photographs and information taken from the ring.

"Oh, yes," Brad Andrews said as he examined the photos. "I remember this ring very well. A one-carat emerald set in a pear-shape with two half-carat diamonds on each side. A beautiful ring. Something you would notice a woman wearing." He looked up, still nodding.

"You can tell me who purchased the ring?" Hud asked.

"Of course. I remember this ring well. It was a twenty-fifth anniversary present. Judge Randolph purchased it for his wife, Kitty."

As KITTY RANDOLPH LEFT Needles and Pins, several other ladies from the canyon entered the shop, also using the excuse of needing fabric or patterns or thread when they were really just interested in the latest goings-on at the Cardwell Ranch.

Dana could see how her day was going to go, but better here than being at the ranch. Especially alone.

At least that's what she thought until the bell over the door at Needles and Pins jangled and the last person she wanted to see came through the door.

Dana looked up from the fabric she was pricing and swore under her breath. Hilde had gone to the post office to mail a special fabric order so Dana was alone with no place to run as her sister, Stacy, stepped into the shop.

Stacy glanced around, looking almost afraid as she moved slowly to the counter and Dana.

Dana waited, wondering what her sister was doing here. Stacy didn't sew and, as far as Dana knew, had never been in the store before.

Stacy was two years her senior, with the same dark hair, the same dark eyes, and that was where the similarities ended. Stacy was willowy-thin, a true beauty and all girl. She'd never been a tomboy like Dana, just the opposite. Stacy had hated growing up on the ranch, wanting even from a very young age to live on a street in town that had sidewalks. "I never want to smell cow manure again," she'd said when she'd left home at eighteen. "And I will *never* marry a cowboy."

Dana always thought Stacy should have been more specific about the type of man she would marry. She'd married at nineteen, divorced at twenty-two, married again at twenty-four, divorced at twenty-nine, married again at thirty-two and divorced. None of them were cowboys.

"Hi, Dana," Stacy said quietly.

"Is there something I can help you with?" Dana asked in her store-owner tone.

Stacy flushed. "I…no…that is I don't want to buy anything." She clutched her purse, her fingers working the expensive leather. "I just wanted to talk to you."

Dana hadn't seen Stacy since their mother's funeral and they hadn't spoken then. Nor did she want to speak to her now. "I don't think we have anything to talk about."

"Jordan asked me to stop by," Stacy said, looking very uncomfortable.

Jordan. Perfect. "He didn't have the guts to do it himself?"

Stacy sighed. *"Dana."*

"What is it Jordan couldn't ask me?" She hated to think what it would be since her brother hadn't seemed to have any trouble making demands of her yesterday on the phone.

"He would like us all to get together and talk at the ranch this evening," Stacy said.

"About what?" As if she didn't know, but she wanted to hear Stacy say it. So far Jordan had been the one who'd spoken for both Clay and Stacy. Not that Dana doubted the three were in agreement. Especially when it came to money.

But Stacy ignored the question. "We're all going to be there at seven, even Clay," Stacy continued as if she'd memorized her spiel and just had to get the words out.

That was so like Jordan to not ask if it was convenient for Dana. She wanted to tell her sister that she was busy and that Jordan would have to have his family meeting somewhere else—and without her.

Stacy looked down at her purse. Her fingers were still working the leather nervously. As she slowly lifted her gaze, she said, "I was hoping you and I could talk sometime. I know now isn't good." Her eyes filled with tears and for a moment Dana thought her sister might cry.

The tears would have been wasted on Dana. "Now definitely isn't good." She'd gotten by for five years without talking to Stacy. Recently, she'd added her brothers to that list. Most of the time, she felt she could go the rest of her life without even seeing or hearing from them.

Stacy seemed to be searching her face. Of course, her sister would have heard Hud was back in town. For all Dana knew, Hud might even have tried to see Stacy. The thought curdled her stomach. She felt her skin heat.

"Mother came by to see me before she died," Stacy said abruptly.

It was the last thing Dana expected her sister to say. A lump instantly formed in her throat. "I don't want to hear this." But she didn't move.

"I promised her I would try to make things right between us," Stacy said, her voice breaking.

"And how would you do that?"

The bell over the door of the shop jangled. Kitty Randolph again. "This blue still isn't quite right," the older woman said, eyeing Stacy then Dana, her nose for news practically twitching.

"Let me see what else we have," Dana said, coming out from behind the counter.

"I hope I didn't interrupt anything," Mrs. Randolph said, stealing a look at Stacy who was still standing at the counter.

"No, Mrs. Randolph, your timing was perfect," Dana said, turning her back on her sister as she went to the thread display and began to look through the blues. She'd already picked the perfect shade for the slacks, but pretended to look again.

She suspected that Kitty had seen Stacy come into the shop and was only using the thread color as an excuse to see what was going on.

"How about this one, Mrs. Randolph?" Dana asked, holding up the thread the woman had already purchased.

"That looks more like it. But, please, call me Kitty. You remind me so much of your mother, dear."

Dana caught a glimpse of Stacy. Her face seemed even paler than before. She stumbled to the door and practically ran to her car. Unfortunately, Mrs. Randolph witnessed Stacy's hasty exit.

"Is your sister all right? She seems upset," Kitty said.

"Who wouldn't be upset after a body's been found in the family well," Dana said.

"Yes, who isn't upset about that," Kitty Randolph said, watching Stacy drive away.

Dana sighed, feeling guilty and then angry with herself for only upsetting her sister worse. But damn it, she had every reason to hate her sister.

She could practically hear her mother's voice filled with disapproval. "Families stick together. It isn't always easy. Everyone makes mistakes. Dana, you have to find forgiveness in your heart. If not for them, for yourself."

Well, Mom, now all three of them have banned together against me. So much for family.

And there was no getting out of the family meeting—or probably having to listen to her sister say she was sorry again. She just hoped Stacy didn't think that saying she was sorry over and over was going to fix things between them. Not even when hell froze over.

Sorry, Mom.

WHEN HUD RETURNED to his office, he had a message to call Coroner Rupert Milligan.

"Got an ID on your woman from the well," Rupert said, then cleared his throat. "It's Ginger Adams."

Hud had to sit down. He moved the files stacked on his chair and dropped into it.

"The doctor and dental records the crime lab sent down came back with a match on both dental and emergency room records," Rupert said.

Good God. Ginger Adams. In a flash, Hud saw her. A pretty redhead with a stunning body and the morals of an alley cat.

Hud closed his eyes as he kneaded his forehead. "You're sure it's Ginger?"

"It's a ringer," Rupert said, not sounding any happier about it than Hud. "I told you your suspect list could be as long as your arm, didn't I?"

"You were right about her being a waitress, too," Hud noted. Was that why Rupert had been acting strangely after coming out of the well yesterday? Because he'd suspected it was Ginger?

Ginger had waited tables at the Roadside Café, the place where locals hung out every morning, gossiping over coffee. Both of his deputies had been there just this morning. It was an old hangout for sheriff's department deputies, the local coroner—and the marshal.

Hud swore softly under his breath. "I thought she left town with some guy."

"Guess that's what we were supposed to think," Rupert said. "I gotta go. Calving season."

"I didn't realize you were still running cattle on your place."

"Helping a friend."

Hud had that feeling again that Rupert knew more about this case than he was saying. "Thanks for letting me know."

"Good luck with your investigation."

"Yeah." Hud didn't mention that he'd found the owner of the ring. He was still trying to figure out how it ended up in the same well as Ginger Adams— years later.

Holy hell. The woman had been rumored to have broken up more marriages in the canyon than Hud could shake a stick at. But there was at least one marriage that had definitely bit the dust because of Ginger—the marriage of Mary and Angus Cardwell.

Damn. As he hung up, he wondered how Dana was going to take the news. He started to dial her number. But he realized he couldn't tell her this over the phone. Everyone knew the Cardwell marriage had been on the rocks, but Ginger, it seemed, had been the last straw. And now her body had turned up on the ranch. Add to that, someone was targeting Dana.

He picked up his hat, grabbing his new marshal jacket on the way out the door. His left arm still ached, the skin around the cut bruised, but Dana had done a good job of patching him up.

It was only a few blocks to Needles and Pins. He knew he had more than one reason for wanting to tell Dana the news in person. He wanted to see how she was doing. She'd left the ranch house so quickly this morning he hadn't even had a chance to talk to her.

Clearly she'd been avoiding him. Last night after he'd announced he wasn't leaving her alone, she'd started to argue, but then got him some bedding from the closet and pointed at the couch.

She'd gone to bed and he hadn't seen her again until this morning—and only for the length of time it had taken her to grab her coat and leave.

He was her least favorite person in the world, true enough. Except maybe for whoever had put that doll in the well—and called and threatened her afterward.

But he also wanted to see her reaction to the news that the body had been Ginger's. He was the marshal and he needed to find Ginger's killer as fast as possible so he could put a stop to whoever was threatening Dana. He couldn't help but believe the two incidents were connected somehow.

As he started to cross the street to Needles and Pins, Lanny Rankin stepped into his path.

Hud hadn't seen Lanny since he'd returned, but he'd known eventually he'd run into him. The canyon wasn't wide or long enough for their paths not to cross.

"Lanny," he said, seeing the set of the man's broad shoulders, the fire in his eyes. There'd been bad blood between the two of them as far back as Hud could remember. Lanny seemed to have a chip on his shoulder and it didn't help when Hud had started dating Dana.

Hud had known that Lanny would move in on Dana as soon as he was out of the picture. He'd seen the way Lanny had looked at Dana back in high school. In fact, Hud had wondered over the past five years if Lanny hadn't just been waiting for Hud to screw up so he would have his chance with Dana.

"Stay away from Dana," Lanny said. "I don't want her hurt again."

"Lanny, I don't want to get into this with you but my relationship with Dana is none of your business."

"Like hell," Lanny said, advancing on him. "I know you're the marshal now and you think you can hide behind that badge…"

"Go ahead. Take your best shot," Hud said, removing the marshal star from his coat and pocketing it.

Lanny's eyes narrowed as if he thought it was a trick. "You think you can get her back after everything you did to her?" He took a wide roundhouse swing.

The punch caught Hud on the left side of his jaw, a staggering blow that about took his feet out from under him.

He rubbed his jaw, nodding at Lanny who was breathing hard. "That's the end of it, Lanny." He reached into his pocket, took out the silver star and reattached it to his coat. "Dana's a grown woman with a mind of her own. She'll do whatever it is she wants to do no matter what either of us has to say about it."

Lanny rubbed his bruised knuckles.

Hud waited. He wanted this over with right here, right now.

"What the hell are you doing back here anyway?" Lanny asked, cradling his hand, which looked broken the way it was swelling up. "I would have thought you wouldn't have the nerve to show your face around here after what you did to her."

Hud ignored him. "Might want to have Doc Grady take a look at that hand, Lanny," he said, gingerly touching his jaw. Fortunately it wasn't broken but it hurt like hell. Lanny packed quite a wallop for a lawyer.

"She wasn't worth it," Lanny snarled, evening his gaze at him.

Hud knew Lanny was talking about Stacy now. And he couldn't have agreed more.

"She used you. She wanted a divorce in the worst way, but Emery didn't want to lose her. The old fool loved her for some crazy reason. But then she found a way to force his hand. After what happened between the two of you while he was out of town, he couldn't wait to get rid of her. Better than being the laughing-stock of the canyon."

This was news to Hud. For years he'd tried to remember that night. He'd been told he got stinking drunk. He remembered wanting to. But after that, there was nothing in his memory banks until he woke up the next morning—in Dana's sister's bed.

After getting the anonymous note, Hud had come back to Montana convinced Stacy had somehow manipulated the incident just to get back at Dana. It was no secret that Stacy was jealous of her younger sister. He'd just never considered there might be more to it.

The thought gave him hope that he really had been

set up. Maybe nothing had happened that night, just as he'd always wanted to believe. More to the point, maybe there was a way to prove it.

"You played right into Stacy's hands," Lanny said.

Hud nodded, saying nothing because he had no defense.

Lanny seemed to consider hitting him again, but must have changed his mind. "You hurt Dana again and that badge isn't going to stop me." With that, he turned and stormed off.

Hud watched Lanny go, hoping this really would be the end of it. But he couldn't get what Lanny had said about Stacy out of his head.

He needed to know what had happened that night. Nothing could have gotten him into Stacy's bed. At least nothing he remembered.

With a curse, he turned and saw Dana standing in the doorway of the sewing shop. From the expression on her face, she'd not only witnessed the ugly display between him and Lanny, she'd overheard it, as well.

DANA QUICKLY TURNED AND WENT back inside the shop, not wanting Hud to see her shock.

It was bad enough that everyone in the canyon knew about Hud and Stacy, but to hear Lanny talking about it… And could it be true that Stacy had done it—not to spite her—but to force Emery to give her a divorce?

She had to remind herself that whatever her sister's reasoning, Hud had gone along with it. So why was it getting harder and harder to call on that old anger?

She heard Hud come into the shop and tried to quit shaking. She was the one who should have left here and never come back, she thought. Instead it had been

Hud who'd taken off, a sure sign of his guilt, everyone had said. While she'd stayed and faced all the wagging tongues.

"Dana?"

She turned to Hud, just as she'd faced the gossip that had swept through the canyon like wildfire.

"I'm sorry you heard that," he said.

"I'm sure you are. You'd much rather pretend it never happened."

"As far as I'm concerned, it didn't," he said.

"Let me guess," she said with a humorless laugh. "Your story is you don't remember anything."

"No, I don't."

All the anger of his betrayal burned fire-hot as if she'd just found out about it. "I really don't want to talk about this."

"We're going to have to at some point," he said.

She gave him a look that she hoped seared his skin. "I don't think so."

He shifted on his feet, then held up his hands in surrender. "That isn't why I came by." He glanced around the shop as if trying to lasso his emotions. In an instant, his expression had transformed. He was the marshal again. And she was... She saw something in his gaze. Something that warned her.

"We got an ID on the remains found in the well," he said. "Is there someplace we could sit down?"

She gripped the edge of the counter. If he thought she needed to sit, the news must be bad. But what could be worse than having a murdered woman's body found on your property?

Meeting Hud's gaze, she knew the answer at once—*having the marshal suspect that someone in your family killed her.*

Chapter Eight

Hud had expected more resistance but Dana led him to the back of the shop where there was a small kitchen with a table and chairs. The room smelled of chocolate.

"Hilde made some brownies," she said, then seemed to remember brownies were his favorite and something *she* used to make for him using a special recipe of her mother's.

"I'll pass on the brownies, but take some coffee," he said, spotting the coffeemaker and the full pot.

She poured them both some, her fingers trembling as she put down the mugs, and took a chair across from him. He watched her cup her mug in both hands, huddling over it as if it were a fire.

"So who is she?" Dana asked.

"Ginger Adams."

Dana paled as the name registered. She took a sip of the coffee, her hands shaking. "Ginger," she said on a breath, and closed her eyes.

He got up to get some sugar and cream for his coffee. He'd never really liked coffee. How could something that smelled so good taste so awful?

He took his time adding the cream and sugar before taking a sip. Her eyes were open again and she was watching him intently, almost as if she was trying to read his mind. If she could have, she'd know that all he could think about was how she used to feel in his arms.

"Have you talked to my father?" she asked.

"Not yet."

Her spine seemed to take on a core of steel. "It was over between them almost before it began. Ginger wasn't the reason my mother divorced Angus."

He said nothing, but wondered if she was defending her father. Or her mother. He'd known Mary Justice Cardwell. He couldn't imagine her killing anyone. But he knew everyone had the capability if pushed far enough.

And Mary was a crack shot. He doubted she would have only wounded Ginger Adams.

"I know it sounds like I'm defending him, but Ginger dumped him months before she supposedly left town with some other woman's husband," Dana said.

"Ginger dumped *him?*"

Dana seemed to realize her mistake. She'd just given her father a motive for murder. No man liked being dumped. Especially if he felt the woman had cost him his marriage. And then there was her father's old .38.

"Did Angus tell you Ginger was involved with a married man?" he asked.

She shrugged. "I can't remember where I heard that."

He studied her. Was there a grain of truth to Ginger being involved with another woman's husband? Maybe, given Ginger's propensity for married men. But he got the feeling Dana might be covering for someone.

"Any idea who the man was?" Hud asked.

Dana shook her head and looked down into her coffee mug. Whatever she was hiding would come out. Sooner or later, he thought.

In the meantime, he needed to talk to Kitty Randolph about her emerald ring.

"I NEED TO RUN AN ERRAND," Dana said the moment Hilde returned. "Can you watch the shop?"

"Are you all right? I saw Hud leaving as I was pulling in," her friend said.

"The woman in the well was Ginger Adams. That's what he came by to tell me."

Hilde frowned. "Ginger Adams? Not the Ginger who your dad…"

"Exactly," Dana said, pulling on her coat. "I'll be back."

Her father had a small place along the river on the way to Bozeman.

Dana took the narrow dirt road back into his cabin. His truck was parked out back. She pulled up next to it and got out. A squirrel chirped at her from a nearby towering evergreen; the air smelled of river and pine.

When she got no answer to her knock, she tried the door. Of course it opened. No one locked their doors around here. She stepped inside, struck by a wash of cool air, and saw that the door leading to the river was open. He must have gone fishing.

She walked out onto the deck, looked down the river and didn't see him. Turning, she spotted her father's gun cabinet and moved to it.

There were numerous rifles, several shotguns and a half-dozen different boxes of cartridges and shells. No .38 pistol, though.

"What are you looking for?"

Dana jumped at the sound of her father's voice behind her. She turned, surprised by his tone. "You startled me." She saw his expression just before it changed. Fear?

"You need to borrow a gun?" he asked, stepping past her to close the gun cabinet.

"I was looking for your .38."

He stared at her as if she'd spoken in a foreign language.

"The one you always kept locked in the cabinet."

He glanced at the gun cabinet. "I see you found the key."

"You've hidden it in the same place since I was nine." She waited. He seemed to be stalling. "The .38?"

"Why do you want the .38?"

"Are you going to tell me where it is or not?" she said, fear making a hard knot in her stomach.

"I don't know where it is. Wasn't it in the cabinet?"

Her father had never been a good liar. "Dad, are you telling me you don't have it?" She could well imagine what Hud was going to think about that.

"Why do you care? It wasn't like it was worth anything."

She shook her head. "Do I have to remind you that Ginger Adams was killed with a .38 and her remains were found on our property?"

All the color drained from his face in an instant. "Ginger?" He fumbled behind him, feeling for a chair and finding one, dropped into it. "Ginger?"

His shock was real. Also his surprise. He hadn't known it was Ginger in the well. "They're sure it's Ginger?" he asked, looking up at her.

She nodded. Had her father really cared about the

woman? "Dad, you know Hud will want to see a .38 owned by someone with a connection to Ginger."

"Well, I don't know where it is. I guess I lost it."

"That's it?" Dana said, aghast, thinking what Hud would think.

Angus frowned and shrugged, but this time she saw something in his expression that made her wonder again what he was hiding from her. Was he protecting someone?

When she didn't say anything, he said, "I don't know what you want from me."

Her heart caught in her throat. She wanted him to tell her he was sorry for what he'd done. Splitting up their family. What she didn't want was for him to have killed Ginger Adams. Or be covering for someone else.

"I know that you and Jordan were both interested in Ginger," Dana said, the words coming hard.

His head jerked up in shock. "You knew?"

She'd found out quite by accident when she'd seen Jordan kissing a woman in the alley behind the building that would one day be Needles and Pins. Who could have missed Ginger Adams in that outfit she was wearing? The dress and shoes were bright red—just like her hair.

"It isn't what you think," her father said defensively. "I was never…" He waved a hand through the air. "You know. I can't speak for Jordan."

Like father like son. She shook her head in disgust as she sat in a chair next to him.

"Ginger was a nice young woman."

"You were *married*," she pointed out. "And Jordan was just a kid."

"Your mother and I were separated. I only lived at

the ranch so you kids wouldn't know. Jordan was eighteen. I wouldn't say he was a kid."

"And you were forty."

He must have heard the accusation in her tone.

"And you're wondering what she could have seen in a forty-year-old man?" He laughed. "Sometimes you are too naive, sweetheart." He patted her head as he'd done when she was a child. "Dana," he said patiently, his eyes taking on a faraway look. "We can't change the past even if we'd like to." He got up from his chair, glancing at his watch. "I'm going to have a beer. I'm sure you won't join me but can I get you a cola?"

She stared at his back as he headed into the kitchen and after a moment she followed him. Sometimes he amazed her. Talk about naive.

"I don't think the past is going to stay buried, Dad, now that Ginger has turned up murdered and at the family ranch well. You and Jordan *are* suspects."

He glanced around the fridge door at her, a beer can in one hand, a cola in the other. He raised the cola can. She shook her head.

"If I were you I'd come up with a better story than you lost the .38," she continued, angry at him for thinking this would just pass. But that had been his attitude for as long as she'd known him. Just ignore the problem and it will fix itself—one way or another. That was her father.

Only this time, the problem wasn't going to go away, she feared. "Hud knows you had the gun. You used to let the two of us shoot it, remember?"

Her father nodded as he popped the top on his beer and took a drink. "Ahh-hh," he said, then smiled. "Of course I remember. I remember everything about those days, baby girl. Truthfully, honey? I don't know what happened to the gun. Or how long it's been gone. One day it just wasn't in the cabinet."

She was thankful that Hud didn't know about Ginger and Jordan. She'd never told Hud about the kiss in the alley she'd witnessed. And she doubted Jordan would be forthcoming about it.

She watched her father take a long drink and lick the foam from his lips. His gaze settled on her and a strange look came into his eyes. It was gentle and sad and almost regretful. "Sometimes you look so much like your mother."

Hud called the judge's number, a little surprised to learn that Kitty Randolph still lived in the same house she had shared with her husband. The same house where he'd been murdered five years before.

The maid answered. Mrs. Randolph had gone out to run a few errands and wasn't expected back until after lunch.

Lunch. Hud felt his stomach growl as he hung up. He hadn't eaten all day, but he knew a good place to get a blue plate special—and information at the same time.

Leroy Perkins had been a cook at the Roadside Café back when Ginger had been a waitress there. Now he owned the place, but hung out there most days keeping an eye on his investment.

Leroy was tall and thin and as stooped as a dogwood twig. His hair, what was left of it, was gray and buzz-cut short. He was drinking coffee at the end stool and apparently visiting with whoever stopped by and was willing to talk to him.

Hud slid onto the stool next to him.

"Get you a menu?" a young, blonde, ponytailed waitress asked him. She looked all of eighteen.

"I'll take the lunch special and a cola, thanks," Hud said.

She was back in a jiffy with a cola and a glass of ice along with the pot of coffee. She refilled Leroy's cup then went back into the kitchen to flirt with the young cook.

Leroy was shaking his head as he watched the cook. "Hard to find anyone who knows anything about the grill. There's a knack to cooking on a grill."

Hud was sure there was. "Leroy, I was wondering if you remember a waitress who used to work here back about twenty years ago."

"Twenty years? You must be kidding. I can barely remember what I had for breakfast."

"Her name was Ginger Adams."

Leroy let out a laugh. "Ginger? Well, hell yes. That cute little redhead? Who could forget *her?*" He frowned. "Why would you be asking about her? It's been…how many years? It was the year we got the new grill. Hell, that was seventeen years ago, the last time I saw her."

There was no avoiding it. Everyone in the canyon knew about the bones. Once he started asking about Ginger, any fool would put two and two together. "It was her bones that were found in the Cardwell Ranch well."

"No kiddin'." Leroy seemed genuinely surprised.

"You ever date her?" Hud asked.

The old cook let out a cackle. "She wasn't interested in some cook. Not that girl. She was looking for a husband—and one who could take care of her."

"Someone with money."

"Money. Position. Power. And it didn't matter how old he was, either," Leroy said grudgingly.

"Like Angus Cardwell."

Leroy nodded. "He was old enough to be her daddy, too. Guess she thought the Cardwell Ranch was his. Dropped him like a hot potato once she found out Mary Cardwell wasn't going to let loose of that land, though."

"Know who she dated after Angus?" Hud asked.

Leroy chuckled and took a sip of his coffee before he said, "Sure do. Went after the eldest son."

Hud couldn't hide his surprise. "Jordan?"

"Oh, yeah," Leroy said.

He wondered why he'd never heard about this. "You're sure? You said you could barely remember what you had for breakfast this morning...."

"I was here the night Jordan came by and the two had quite the row," Leroy said. "They didn't see me. I was just getting ready to bust the two of them up when he shoved her and she fell and broke her arm."

Hud felt a start. The broken wrist bone. "Jordan broke her arm?" he asked in surprise. "How, in this canyon, did something like that happen and not be public knowledge within hours?"

Leroy flushed. "Well, that could be because she was ready to file an assault charge against Jordan—until he promised to pay for all her expenses, including medical costs and lost wages."

"He paid you off, too," Hud guessed.

Leroy shrugged. "Cooking is the most underpaid profession there is."

So that's how Leroy started his nest egg to buy the café. "So what were Jordan and Ginger arguing about?"

"Seems he thought they had something going on,"

Leroy said. "She, however, had moved on to higher ground, so to speak."

The waitress returned and slid a huge plate covered with thick-sliced roast beef and a pile of real mashed potatoes covered with brown gravy and a side of green beans and a roll.

"So they didn't patch things up?" Hud asked in between bites.

Leroy laughed again. "Not a chance. Jordan tried to make it up to her, but she wasn't having any of it. Nope, Jordan was history after that."

"And this higher ground you spoke of?" Hud asked.

Leroy wrinkled his brow. "I just knew Ginger. She'd found herself someone else, probably someone with more potential than Jordan. Ginger didn't go five minutes without a man."

"But you don't know who he was?"

Leroy shook his head. "She took off time from the café while her arm healed. Didn't see much of her and then…she was just gone. I assumed she'd taken off with the guy. Her roommate said she packed up what she wanted of her things, even gave away her car, and left."

"Her roommate?"

"A bunch of girls bunked in one of those cheap cabins near the café but you know how it is, some last a day on the job, some a week. Very few last a summer. I barely remember the one roommate that Ginger used to hang with. A kind of plain girl, not a bad waitress, though."

"This friend never heard from her again?" Hud asked as he ate. The food was excellent.

Leroy shrugged. "None of us did, but we didn't think

anything of it. Girls like Ginger come and go. The only thing they leave behind is broken hearts."

"Ginger have any family?" Hud asked.

"Doubt it or wouldn't someone have come looking for her? I got the feeling she might not have left home under the most congenial circumstances."

Hud had the same feeling. "Try to remember something more about this girl who befriended Ginger."

"She didn't work at the café long." He slapped his forehead. "I can almost think of her name. It was something odd."

"If you remember it, call me," Hud said, throwing down enough money to cover his meal and cola. "I wish you wouldn't mention this to anyone."

Leroy shook his head, but Hud could tell that the moment he left, Leroy would be spreading the word.

"Wait a minute," Leroy said. "There might be someone you could ask about Ginger." He seemed to hesitate. "Ginger used to flirt with him all the time when he came in." The cook's eyes narrowed. "You're probably not going to want to hear this…"

Hud let out a snort. "Let me guess. Marshal Brick Savage."

"Yeah, how'd you know?" Leroy asked, sounding surprised.

Hud smiled. "Because I know my father." He had another flash of memory of a woman in red. Only this time, he heard her laughter dying off down the street.

As Hud climbed into his patrol SUV, he turned south onto the highway and headed toward West Yellowstone and the lake house his father had bought on Hebgen Lake.

He couldn't put off talking to his father any longer.

Chapter Nine

"I wondered when I'd be seeing you," Brick Savage said when he answered the door. The former marshal shoved the door open wider and without another word, turned and walked back into the house.

Hud stepped in, closed the door, then followed his father to the back part of the house to the kitchen and small dining nook in front of a bank of windows.

He studied his father under the unkind glare of the fluorescent lights, surprised how much the elder Savage had aged. Hud remembered him as being much more imposing. Brick seemed shrunken, half the man he'd once been. Age hadn't been kind to him.

Brick opened the refrigerator door and took out two root beers. Hud watched him take down two tall glasses and fill each with ice cubes.

"You still drink root beer," Brick said. Not really a question. Root beer was about the only thing Hud had in common with his father, he thought as he took the filled glass.

"Sit down," Brick said.

Hud pulled up one of the chairs at the table, his gaze going to the window. Beyond it was a huge, flat, white expanse that Hud knew was the frozen snow-covered surface of Hebgen Lake. Not far to the southeast was Yellowstone Park.

He wondered why Brick had moved up here. For the solitude? For the fishing? Or had his father just wanted out of the canyon for some reason? Bad memories maybe.

"So what can I do for you?" Brick asked and took a long swig of his root beer.

Hud doubted his father was so out of touch that he hadn't heard about the woman's body that was found in the Cardwell Ranch well. In fact, Hud suspected the coroner had filled him in on every facet of the case.

"I'm investigating the murder of Ginger Adams," Hud said, watching his father's expression.

Nothing. Brick seemed to be waiting for more.

"Ginger Adams, a pretty redheaded waitress who worked at the Roadside Café seventeen years ago?" Hud said.

"What does that have to do with me?" Brick asked, sounding baffled.

"You knew her."

Brick shrugged. "I'm sorry, but I don't remember her. I don't remember most of them."

Hud cursed under his breath. "Well, I remember. I keep seeing Ginger in a slinky red dress and red high heels. And for some reason, I keep seeing you with her."

"Could have been me," he admitted congenially. "That was how many years ago?"

"Seventeen according to Leroy at the café."

Brick nodded. "The year your mother died. Oh, yeah, it could have been me." Brick looked down at his half-empty glass of root beer.

Hud rubbed a hand over his face, feeling the old

anger toward his father. "You broke her heart, you know."

"I broke your mother's heart long before she got sick," his father said. "I was your mother's number one disappointment." He looked up at Hud. "Isn't that what she always told you?"

"She loved you."

Brick laughed. "Maybe. At one time. You won't believe this, but your mother was the only woman I ever loved."

"You had an odd way of showing it."

"You disappoint a woman enough times and you quit trying not to. But you didn't drive all this way to talk about this, did you?"

Hud cleared his throat. There was no point getting into the past. He couldn't change it. He couldn't change his father and his mother was dead. He dropped the case file on the table between them. "I need to ask you some questions about Judge Raymond Randolph's killing."

Something showed in Brick's face. "Is there something new in that case?"

Hud thought he heard a slight waver in his father's voice, but then he might have imagined it.

"If you read my report, you know as much as I do about the case," Brick said, glancing down at the file but not reaching for it.

"I've read the file," Hud said.

"Then you know what happened that night," Brick said. "I took the call from a neighbor who heard gunshots at the judge's house. I tried to reach you and couldn't, so I went instead."

Hud knew Brick would remind him of that.

"According to your report, you saw the Kirk brothers coming out of the judge's house and gave chase."

His father eyed him, no doubt bristling at the use of his exact words. "That's exactly what happened."

"The vehicle, an older model car, was being driven by one of the Kirk brothers, Ty. Mason was with him in the passenger seat."

"That's right," Brick said. "I chased them down the canyon almost to Gallatin Gateway."

"Almost. According to your report, Ty lost control of the car at the 35-mile-an-hour curve just before the bridge. Both men were killed. Later you reported that several items from the judge's house were found in the car. The conclusion was that the judge had come home early, caught the Kirk brothers in the act of burglarizing the house and was fatally injured when one of the brothers panicked and shot him with a .38-caliber pistol. The judge's wife, Kitty, was out of town. The boys ran, you chased them, they both died in the car wreck."

"You have a problem with my report?"

Hud rubbed his bruised jaw, never taking his eyes off his father. "It's just a little too cut-and-dried, because now, something stolen from the judge's house that night has turned up in the Cardwell Ranch well—along with the remains of Ginger Adams."

The older man's shock was real. Rupert couldn't have told him about the owner of the ring because the coroner hadn't known.

"If Ginger was killed the night she allegedly left town seventeen years ago and the robbery was only five years ago, then how did Kitty Randolph's ring end up in the well?"

Brick shook his head. "I'm supposed to know?"

"You know what bothers me about this case?" Hud said. "Nowhere in the original report does it say that there was any item found on the brothers that connected them to the robbery and murder of the judge."

"Doesn't it say that a pair of gold cuff links and a pocket watch were found in the glove box of the car?" Brick said.

Hud nodded. "That information was added later." Both items were small and could easily have been put in the car—after the accident. "You know what else is missing? The .38. What happened to the gun? And where did they get a gun that had been used in a murder years before—back when both brothers were barely out of diapers?"

"They could have found the gun. Then after using it, threw it in the river during the chase," Brick said with a shrug.

"Maybe…" Hud agreed "…but I'm sure you had deputies looking for the gun, right?" His father nodded, a muscle bunching in his jaw. "Never found, right?" Again his father nodded. "Leaves a lot of questions since both Kirk boys are dead and the gun is missing."

"Life is like that sometimes," Brick said. "You don't always find the answers."

"Weren't drugs found in their car after the accident?"

His father nodded slowly and picked up his glass to take a drink.

"If the Kirks had gotten caught with drugs again wouldn't they both have been sent to Deer Lodge? It would have been the third offense for both of them. They would have been looking at some hard time."

"Rather a moot point since they were both killed," Brick said.

"My point exactly. Isn't it possible that the drugs were the reason they ran that night and not that they'd just burglarized Judge Randolph's house and murdered him?"

Brick put down his glass a little too hard. "Son, what exactly are you accusing me of?"

What was he accusing his father of? "I'm not sure justice was done that night."

"Justice?" His father let out a laugh. "For years I chased down the bad guys and did my best to get them taken off the street. The Kirk brothers are just one example. Those boys should have been locked up. Instead, because of overcrowding in corrections, they got probation for the first offense and saw very little jail time for the second. The law put them back on the street and they ended up killing Judge Randolph. I saw them come running out of his house, no matter what you believe."

"You sure you didn't see a chance to get Ty and Mason Kirk off the streets for good?"

Brick shook his head sadly. "You're wrong, but let me ask you this. This murder you got on your hands, what if you find out who killed her but you can't prove it? You think you'll be able to pass that killer on the street every day knowing he did it and him thinking he got away with it?"

"We aren't talking about the Kirk brothers now, are we."

Brick took a drink of his root beer. "Just hypothetical, son."

"Right before he was killed five years ago, Judge Randolph was threatening to have you fired from your job," Hud said. "He seemed to think you'd been playing fast and loose with your position of power."

"Five years ago, I was getting ready to retire, you know that. What would I care if the judge got me fired?"

"If you'd gotten fired, you would have lost your pension," Hud said.

Brick laughed. "And you think I'd kill someone for that measly amount of money?" He shook his head still smiling as if he thought this was a joke.

"Maybe the judge had something on you that would have sent you to jail."

He laughed again. "Hell, you would have gotten the marshal job if I had gone to jail."

Hud knew now that he'd only taken the deputy job to show his father. Brick had been dead set against it and done everything he could to keep Hud out of the department. But his father was right about one thing, Hud would have been up for marshal in the canyon.

"Tell me something," Hud said. "Why were you so dead set against me being a deputy?"

"I knew what kind of life it was. I didn't want that for you. Maybe I especially didn't want it for Dana. I know how much your mama hated me being in law enforcement. Isn't it possible that I was trying to protect you?"

It was Hud's turn to laugh. "I think you were protecting yourself. You knew I'd be watching you like a hawk. I think you were worried I'd find out what the judge had on you."

"I hate to burst your bubble, but the judge had nothing on me. In fact, he was about to be removed from the bench," Brick said. "He had Alzheimer's. He was losing his mind. His allegations against me were just part of his irrational behavior."

Hud stared at his father. Could that possibly be true?

Brick picked up their empty glasses and took them to

the sink. "I'll admit I've made my share of mistakes," he said, his back to Hud. "I thought you only took the deputy job to prove something to me. I didn't want you following in my footsteps for the wrong reasons."

Hud *had* taken the job for all the wrong reasons. But law enforcement must have been in his blood. It had turned out to be the right career for him.

His father turned to look back at him. "Did you know your mother wanted me to go into business with her father? She married beneath her. We both knew it. Everyone told her she could do better than me. She just wouldn't listen. She thought I'd change my mind once you were born." He turned back to the sink.

Hud stared at his father's back, thinking about the things his mother used to say about Brick. She'd been angry at her husband as far back as Hud could remember. Now he wondered if a lot of that anger and resentment hadn't stemmed from Brick not going to work for her father. Had she been embarrassed being married to a small-town marshal?

Brick shut off the water and dried his hands. "I know you think I killed your mother, not cancer. Maybe I did. Maybe her disappointment in me caused the cancer." He stood against the sink, looking small and insubstantial. "I was sorry to hear about you and Dana. I always thought you made a nice couple."

Hud picked up the Judge Randolph case file from the kitchen table. He'd thought coming up here to see his father would be an end to all his questions. Now he had even more questions. "I'm going to solve these murders."

"I don't doubt you will," Brick said. "You were always a damned good deputy. I thought after what happened five years ago, you'd be soured on the profession. You know I had to suspend you the night the judge was killed just like I would have had to any deputy who blew his shift. I couldn't protect you because you were my son."

He studied his father. "It must have been a shock to you then to hear that I'm the temporary marshal until they can advertise the job."

Brick smiled but said nothing.

Hud started toward the door, stopped and turned. "You didn't seem surprised."

"About what?"

"About the ring that was found in the well with Ginger's remains." He studied his father. "Because you already knew, didn't you?"

"Good luck with your investigation, son."

DANA RETURNED TO THE SHOP to find it packed with customers. She met Hilde's eye as she came in the door and saw her friend wink mischievously. They hadn't even had this much business during the rush before Christmas—and January was when most businesses felt a slump.

But here it was January and the shop was full of women. It didn't take a genius to figure out what was up.

Hilde cut fabric while Dana rang up purchases and answered questions relating to the bones found in the ranch well and a rumor that was circulating that the bones belonged to Ginger Adams.

Dana fudged a little. "Ginger Adams? *Really?*"

The afternoon whizzed by. Dana tried not to watch the door, afraid Hud would pay her another visit. But by closing, he hadn't shown and she breathed a sigh of relief when Hilde offered to take the deposit to the bank and let Dana finish closing up.

"Can you believe this?" Hilde said, hefting the deposit bag. She grimaced. "Sorry. I do feel bad making money at your expense. And Ginger's."

"S'all right," Dana said, laughing. "It's a windfall for the store. At least something good is coming out of it."

Hilde left and Dana straightened the counter before going to lock up. As she put the closed sign up on the front door, she was surprised how dark it was outside. It got dark early this time of year. Plus it had snowed off and on most of the day, the clouds low, the day gloomy. There was no traffic on the street and only a few lights glowed at some of the businesses still open this time of the afternoon.

As she looked out, a movement caught her eye. She stared across the street into the shadowy darkness at the edge of the building. Had she only imagined it or was someone standing there looking in her direction?

She stepped to the side to make sure the light in the back wasn't silhouetting her and waited, unable to shake the feeling that someone had been watching her as intently as she had been staring across the street at them.

Lanny? He'd spied on her last night and on Hud, as well. But surely he wasn't still doing it.

Or Hud? That would be just like him to keep an eye on her.

Another thought struck her. Could it be the person who had left the chocolates for her? The same person who'd taken her doll and put it in the well last night? She shivered, remembering the voice on the phone. Just a prank call, she kept telling herself.

A sick, morbid cruel prank. Was it possible that's all the chocolates and the doll in the well were meant to be? The prankster had just been having fun at Dana's expense but then she'd had to go and call the marshal and things got out of hand?

That's what she wanted to believe as she stepped to the window again and looked out. Nothing moved. The lights of a car came down the winding street, blinding her for a moment as it swept past.

In that instant as the car passed, the headlights illuminated the building across the street.

No one was there.

She'd been so sure she'd seen a person watching her.

On impulse, she reopened the front door and ran across the street without her coat, leaving the shop door wide-open.

It would only take a second to find out if she was losing her mind or not.

THE MOMENT HUD HIT the highway, he called Judge Raymond Randolph's widow to see if Kitty had returned home. It would have been better to stop by and see her, but she lived at the other end of the canyon. He'd spent longer at his father's than he'd meant to. Now he was running late. He wouldn't be able to drive down to see her and still get back to Needles and Pins before Dana left for the night, and he was worried about Dana.

But he needed to know if anything his father had told him was the truth.

"Hello?" Kitty's voice was small but strong.

"Mrs. Randolph?" He remembered Katherine "Kitty" Randolph as being tiny and gray with smooth pink skin and twinkling blue eyes. She baked the best chocolate chip cookies and always brought them to the church bake sales.

"Yes?"

"My name is Hudson Savage. You probably don't remember me."

"Hud," she said, her tone more cheerful. "Of course I remember you. You and your mother used to sit near me in church. Your mother baked the most wonderful pies. I think her apple pie was my favorite. I couldn't help myself. I always purchased a slice at every sale. For a good cause, I'd tell myself." She let out a soft chuckle, then seemed to sober. "I remember your mother fondly. You must miss her terribly."

He'd forgotten about his mother's pies. Her crust would melt in your mouth. Pies were her one pride.

He cleared his throat. "Yes. I hate to bother you this evening but I'm the new interim marshal in Gallatin Canyon and I'm involved in an investigation." He hesitated, unsure how to proceed.

"That woman's bones that were found in the well on the Cardwell Ranch," Kitty Randolph said. "Yes, I heard about it. How horrible. But I don't see what I—"

"The woman is believed to have been killed with the same gun that killed your husband."

Kitty let out a small gasp and Hud wished he'd been more tactful. He should have done this in person. He should have waited. But since he hadn't, he dove right in.

"I need some information about the last few months the judge was alive." He took a breath. "Did he have Alzheimer's and was he about to be asked to step down from the bench?"

Silence, then a shaky croak. "Yes, I'm afraid so."

Hud let out a breath. "I'm sorry. That must have been very difficult for you. I understand his behavior was sometimes irrational."

"Yes," she repeated. "This is about your father, isn't it?"

Behind the twinkling blue eyes, Kitty had always shown a sharp intelligence.

"Yes. Mrs. Randolph, do you know what the judge had against my father?"

"No, I never understood his animosity toward Marshal Savage," she said, sounding sad. "But the judge was a hard man. Much like your father. And who knows how much of it was just my husband's illness."

"Were there any papers missing after the judge's death?" Hud asked.

"You mean, some evidence my husband might have had on your father?"

That was exactly what he meant.

"No. I doubt any existed." She sounded tired suddenly.

"I know it's late. I just have one more question. In the burglary report, you didn't mention a ring."

"No," she said, sounding tentative.

"Well, Mrs. Randolph, an emerald ring was found." Another gasp. "You found my ring?"

"Yes, I'm afraid it's being held as evidence."

"I don't understand."

He cleared his throat again. "The ring was found in the well with the remains of Ginger Adams."

Another gasp, this one more audible than the first. For a moment he thought she might have dropped the phone. Or even fainted. "Mrs. Randolph?"

"I had to sit down," she said. "I don't understand. How is that possible?"

"I was hoping you might have some idea," Hud said.

"This is very upsetting."

"I'm sorry to have to give you the news on the telephone," he said as he drove. "Do you have any idea how long the ring has been missing?"

"No, I didn't look for it for months after the judge's death and when I did, I realized it was missing. I thought about calling the marshal and letting him know, but your father had retired by then and I just assumed it had been lost when those young men wrecked their vehicle in the river. I never thought I'd see it again." She sounded like she might be crying. "The judge had it made for me in honor of our twenty-fifth wedding anniversary."

"I understand it's an expensive piece of jewelry," Hud said.

"The only piece of real jewelry the judge ever bought me. When we married, he couldn't afford a diamond." Her voice broke.

Hud frowned. "Wouldn't you have kept a piece of expensive jewelry like that in a safe or a safe-deposit box at the bank?"

Ahead he could see the lights of Big Sky. The Kirk brothers hadn't found the safe. Nor would they have known how to open it if they had.

"I thought it was in the safe," Kitty said. "Obviously, I had taken it out to wear it and forgot to put it back. The judge probably saw it and put it in the jewelry box with his cuff links and his father's old pocket watch."

But it didn't explain how the ring ended up in the

well. "I'll see what I can do about getting the ring returned to you as soon as possible," Hud told her.

"Thank you. I can't tell you what your call has meant to me. Good night, Hud."

He disconnected as he turned off and drove up to Big Sky's lower meadow. As he started to turn down the street to Needles and Pins, a car whipped out of the marshal's office parking lot, tossing up gravel.

The driver spotted him and threw on his brakes. The vehicle's door flew open and Jordan Cardwell jumped out.

"I want to talk to you, Savage," he said, storming over to the SUV.

"How about that," Hud said. "I want to talk to you, too, Jordan. Now just isn't a great time."

"Too bad," Jordan said. "I want to know what the hell is going on out at the ranch."

DANA STOPPED AT THE EDGE of the building across the street from the fabric shop, waiting for her eyes to adjust to the darkness. The air was cold, the shadows dark and deep along the side of the building.

She saw that the sidewalk across the front had been shoveled but there was new snow along the side of the closed office building. She stepped into the dark shadows, almost convinced she'd only imagined a figure standing here. What fool would stand in all that snow just to—

She saw the fresh tracks. Her heart lodged in her throat. The snow was tramped where someone had stood. Waiting. She glanced behind her and saw that from this spot, the person had a clear view of the shop.

Behind the spot where the snow was trampled was a

set of tracks that came up the narrow passage alongside the building. Another set returned to the alley.

For one wild moment she thought about following them. She even placed her boot into one track. The shoe size was larger than her own, but the edges caved in after each step the person had taken so it was impossible to gauge a true size of the print.

She shivered as she looked toward the dark alley, seeing nothing but the tracks. Only a fool would follow them. Whoever had been standing here watching the shop only minutes ago might not be gone, she told herself. He'd seen her look out the window. Maybe that's what he'd been waiting for. For her to see him. And follow him?

But why? It made no sense. It was as if someone was just trying to scare her. Unless the chocolates were filled with poison. And she was the one who was supposed to have been knocked down into the well last night.

Just like Ginger Adams had been?

Just like her caller had said.

She hugged herself against the bone-deep cold of her thoughts as she turned and ran back across the street. Halfway across she noticed the shop door. She'd left it wide-open, but now it was closed. The wind must have blown it shut.

But as she opened it and stepped tentatively inside, she tried to remember feeling even the slightest breeze while she was across the street—and couldn't.

As she stood in the darkened shop, she realized someone could have slipped in while she was gone. It had been stupid to run out like that and leave the door wide-open. Worse, she realized, she hadn't locked the back door of the shop because she was planning to go out that way.

She held her breath, listening for a sound. The shop was deathly quiet. The small light still burned in the back room, casting a swath of pale gold over the pine floor.

Her teeth began to chatter. Glancing out into the street, she saw only darkness. Again she looked toward the back of the shop where she'd left her purse, her cell phone, her car keys.

There's no one in here. No one hiding behind the rows of fabric.

Even if the person who'd been across the street *had* been watching her, what were the chances he had circled around and come into the shop when she wasn't watching and was now waiting for her?

She started to take a step toward the back of the shop.

Silent and huge, a shadow loomed up from the darkness and came out of the stacks of fabric. A large silhouette against the light in the back.

She screamed as he reached for her. She shot an elbow out, stumbling backward into one of the fabric rows.

"Dana. It's me."

But it was too late. She'd already driven her elbow into his ribs and sent a kick to his more private parts. Fortunately for Hud, the kick missed its mark.

She heard him let out a curse followed by her name again. "It's me. Hud."

As if she hadn't already recognized his voice.

A flashlight beam illuminated a spot on the floor at their feet.

"What are you doing?" she demanded. "You scared the life out of me."

He rubbed his thigh where her boot had made contact and eyed her suspiciously.

"What are you doing here anyway?" she asked.

"I came in through the back. The door was unlocked. When I saw the front door standing open, I was afraid something had happened to you." He turned on the light and she saw how worried he looked.

She swallowed back a retort. "That wasn't you watching from across the street then?"

"There was someone watching you from across the street?" He was already headed for the door.

"Whoever it was is gone," she called after him.

"Stay in the shop. Lock the doors," he called over his shoulder without looking back as he crossed the street.

Hurriedly, she locked the back door, then the front, and from the window watched the flicker of his flashlight beam moving across the snow.

She saw him stop at the spot she'd discovered between the buildings, no doubt following the footprints she'd seen in the snow.

She waited, hating that Hud had acted so quickly on something that was probably innocent. Maybe it had been someone waiting for a friend who didn't show. Maybe the whole thing had nothing to do with her. Hud taking it seriously only made her more anxious.

Was she really in danger?

What scared her was that he seemed to think so.

He came back across the street and she unlocked the door to let him in. He closed the door behind him, locking it.

"Nothing, right?" she asked hopefully.

"I don't want you going back to the ranch by yourself."

She'd let him stay last night because she'd been as scared for him as for herself. But she hadn't been able to sleep knowing he was downstairs, so close.

She shook her head. "I won't be driven out of my home."

"Then I'm staying with you."

"No. That is, I won't be alone tonight. We're having a family meeting. I'll get Clay or Jordan to stay with me. I'll be fine. Anyway, no one has any reason to harm me," she said, trying to convince herself as well as him. "I didn't put Ginger Adams in that well."

"But someone in your family might have. And quite frankly, having one of the suspects staying in the house with you might not be the best plan." His gaze softened. "Dana, why didn't you tell me that Jordan is forcing you to sell the ranch?"

Dana stared at Hud. "Jordan told you that?"

"In so many words, yes. Is there really a will?"

"I don't know." She sighed. His gaze filled with such tenderness it was like a physical pain for her. "I thought so at first. Mom told me she wrote up a draft and signed and dated it. Unfortunately, I can't find it and since she never got a copy to her lawyer before her death… Jordan is convinced I made up the whole story about Mother's new will."

"So, the ranch goes to all her heirs," Hud said, sympathy in his voice.

"Yes, and they have decided they want the money, which means I have no choice but to sell," Dana said. "I'm fighting to hang on to the house and a little land. That is what has been holding things up."

"Dana, I am so sorry."

She turned away. "Please, I hate talking about this." She remembered something he'd said and frowned as she turned to face him again. "You don't really think someone in my family had anything to do with Ginger's death, do you?"

He had on his cop face again, giving nothing away. "Anyone who had contact with Ginger or access to the ranch is a suspect."

She let out a surprised breath. "So I'm a suspect, too."

He sighed. "Dana, I've been thinking about what happened at the ranch last night. Is there anyone who might want to hurt you?"

She laughed. "What were we just talking about? I'm holding up the sale of the ranch and my three siblings are all chomping at the bit to get their hands on the money from the property."

"You seriously believe one of them would try to hurt you?" he asked.

"You know them." Her gaze locked with his. "There is little they wouldn't do to hurt me. Have done to hurt me."

"I have to ask you this," he said. "Last night, did you see the person who attacked me?"

"Why are you asking me this now?"

"I need to know if the reason you fired that shotgun in the air last night was to help someone in your family get away."

She stared at him, anger rising in her. "How can you ask me that?"

"Dana—" He reached for her, but she stepped back.

"You broke my heart." The words were out, surprising her as much as they did him. They had nothing to do with what he'd accused her of. They were also words she never thought she would admit to him of all people.

"I'll never forgive myself for letting it happen."

"Good." She started to step past him, but he grabbed her wrist.

"I made the worst mistake of my life that night," he said quickly.

Wouldn't Stacy love to hear that?

"You were everything to me."

"Apparently not," she snapped, trying to pull free. But his grip was firm, his fingers warm and strong.

"I truly don't remember that night," he said, his voice low and filled with emotion. "The last thing I remember is having a drink at the bar—"

"I told you I don't want to talk about this," she said.

"You have never let me tell you what happened. At least what I remember."

"Finding you in my sister's bed was sufficient enough."

"Dana, I've thought about this for five years, thought of little else. One drink and then nothing. I remember *nothing.*"

"Well, that's your story, isn't it? That lets you off the hook."

"Damn it, why do you think I came back? Because of you and to prove that nothing happened that night."

"I thought you don't remember."

"I don't. I couldn't be sure before but I got a note from someone in the canyon that said I was set up that night."

"Who?"

"It was anonymous, but, Dana, I believe I *was* set

up. Otherwise, why can't I remember that night? What I've never been able to understand is why? All I knew for sure is that your sister had to be in on it. But after what Lanny said earlier... Your sister couldn't have acted alone. Someone helped her."

Dana didn't move. Didn't breathe. All she could do was stare at him, remembering what she'd overheard Lanny tell him. That Stacy had used Hud to force Emery into giving her a divorce. Emery had been thirty years Stacy's senior, an older man with money. That was until he hooked up with Stacy. Stacy got her divorce five years ago—and took half of Emery's assets and his home.

What if Stacy had done it not to hurt Dana but for her own selfish reasons?

"Dana, if I was as drunk as everyone at the bar said I was, then believe me, I didn't sleep with your sister," Hud said. "I swear to you. I had one drink at the bar, then the rest of the night is a total blank. What does that sound like to you?"

That he'd been drugged.

"How was it that you showed up at Stacy's house so early the next morning?" he asked.

She swallowed, remembering the strange phone call, the strange voice. *Do you know where your fiancé is? I do. In your sister's bed.* She'd just thought it was some canyon busybody and told Hud about the call.

"I figured it had to be something like that. Which only makes me more convinced Stacy was behind it—and she wasn't working alone. My guess is that Stacy got some man to help her. I don't know why or how they did it, but I'm going to find out." He let go of her wrist, the look in his eyes a painful reminder of the love they'd once shared. "I've never wanted anyone but you. And I'm going to prove it to you."

She stood just looking at him, afraid of what she might say at that moment. Even more afraid of what she might do. They were so close that she could smell the faint hint of his aftershave and the raw maleness of him. She wanted desperately to believe him.

Her gaze went to his lips. The memory of his mouth on hers was like a stabbing pain. All she wanted was for him to take her in his arms, to kiss her again, to make her forget everything that had happened.

He reached for her, his large palm cupping her cheek, as he pulled her to him. She felt her body start to lean toward him like metal to magnet and the next thing she knew their lips brushed then locked.

She clutched the front of his jacket, balling up the fabric in her fists as his arms came around her. His tongue touched hers and desire shot through her. She moaned as he deepened the kiss, so lost in his mouth that she didn't even hear the first ring.

His cell phone rang again, shattering the silence, shattering the moment. She pulled back. He looked at her as if the last thing he wanted to be at that moment was marshal. The phone rang again. Slowly, he withdrew his arms and checked caller ID.

"I have to take this," he said, sounding as disappointed as she felt.

She stepped away from him, taking a deep breath and letting it out slowly. What had she done? She shook her head at how easily she had weakened. What was wrong with her? How could she forget the pain Hud had caused her?

Did she really believe he'd been set up? That nothing had happened that night except someone trying to drive them apart?

"Sheriff's department business. Sorry," he said behind her.

She touched her tongue to her upper lip, then turned to face him and nodded. "I need to get home, too. Wouldn't want to miss the family meeting Jordan's scheduled at the ranch tonight."

Hud swore. "Be careful. I'll call you later. I don't want you staying at the ranch house, especially with Jordan there. He told me just a while ago that he doesn't remember Ginger Adams nor did he have any contact with her." Hud seemed to hesitate. "I have a witness who saw him fighting with her. It was clear they'd had some type of intimate relationship before that and that Ginger was trying to end it. Jordan broke her wrist. This was soon before her death."

Dana couldn't hide her shock.

"It was apparently an accident. Jordan shoved her, she fell and broke her wrist. The thing is, he lied about his relationship with her and my witness says he paid her to keep quiet about the incident." Hud cursed under his breath as he must have seen something in her expression. "You knew about Ginger and Jordan?"

"Dad told me, but years ago I'd seen Ginger and Jordan in the alley kissing."

Hud swore. "I know Jordan is your brother and even with you being on the outs with him right now, you'd still take up for him when push comes to shove. But, Dana, I'm afraid of what Jordan might be capable of when he doesn't get his way. Right now from what I can gather, what he wants more than anything is the

Cardwell Ranch. And you're the only thing standing between him and the money from the sale. Watch your back."

Chapter Ten

Dana had stopped off to see Hilde on the way home, putting off the family meeting as long as possible—and trying to keep her mind off Hud and the kiss and everything he'd told her, as well as the person she'd spotted across the street watching the shop. Watching her.

"Someone is trying to scare me," she told Hilde. "Or worse." She filled her in.

"I'm with Hud. You shouldn't be alone out there. Maybe especially with your family. Come stay with me."

"Thanks, but Hud is coming out later," Dana said. "I really think it's just one of my siblings trying to get me out of the house so they can do a thorough search for Mom's new will."

"Didn't you say you looked for it and couldn't find it?"

Dana nodded. "They would be wasting their time and I could tell them that, but they wouldn't believe me."

"You're sure one of them hasn't already found it?"

"I hope not, because then it is long gone," Dana said. "But then how do I explain these threats?"

"That is too creepy about the doll in the well last night. It sounds like something Jordan would do."

She shook her head. "He wasn't in town." She thought about the doll her father had given her. Why that doll? "I just have a feeling that the person at the well wanted me to see the light and come up and investigate. And I would have, if I hadn't been on the phone with Hud."

"Did he find out who left you the chocolates?"

Dana shook her head. "He's having them checked to see if they might have been poisoned."

Hilde shivered. "Dana, someone came into your house to take that doll and leave the chocolates. That person had to know the house. Not just the house. He knows *you*."

"That's why it's probably one of my siblings." She pulled on her coat. "I kissed Hud."

Hilde's eyebrow shot up. "And?"

"And it was…" She groaned. "Wonderful. Oh, Hilde, I want to believe him. He thinks he was set up five years ago. That someone other than just Stacy wanted to see us broken up and that nothing happened."

"Didn't I tell you that was a possibility?"

Dana nodded.

"You're the only woman he's ever loved," Hilde said. "You know that. Why can't you forgive him?"

"Could you if you caught him in your sister's bed?"

Hilde looked uncertain. "It would be hard. But imagine how he must be feeling? If he really believes nothing happened. Have you ever asked Stacy about it?" Hilde asked.

Dana shook her head. "What was there to ask? You should have seen the expression on her face that morning when I caught them. I can't bear to be in the same room with her, let alone talk to her. And anyway, what was there to ask? 'How was my fiancé?'"

"Given everything that's been going on, maybe this family meeting isn't such a bad idea," Hilde said. "If it was me, I'd corner that sister of yours and demand some answers."

On the way to the ranch, Dana thought about what Hilde had said. How many people knew about the chocolates that Hud had always bought for her birthday? Her family, not that any of them seemed to pay much attention or care. All three of her siblings knew about the doll upstairs and that the ranch house was never locked. But so did a lot of other people.

Stacy, Clay and Jordan seemed the most likely suspects. She couldn't imagine any of them hanging out in a blizzard with a flashlight just to scare her away from the house, though.

But if this wasn't about her siblings trying to speed up the sale of the ranch, then what?

Ginger Adams's murder?

Jordan had always had a terrible temper when he didn't get his way, just as Hud had said.

On top of that, Jordan had lied about his relationship with Ginger Adams—and apparently been so angry when she'd dumped him that he'd knocked her down and broken her wrist. And all this right before she'd ended up in the well.

With a shudder, Dana realized that Jordan also had access to their father's .38. And now the gun was missing.

But that didn't explain the incident last night at the well. Unless Jordan hadn't been in New York when he'd called her yesterday.

As she turned into the ranch house yard, she saw a car parked out front with a rental sticker in the back window. Jordan. Apparently he'd arrived early. She could see lights on in the house and a shadow moving around on the second floor—in what had been their mother's bedroom.

HUD FOUND DEPUTY LIZA TURNER waiting for him in his office. "What was so important that you had to see me right away?" he demanded and instantly regretted it. "Sorry."

"Oh, I caught you in the middle of something," she said, stepping tentatively to him to wipe a smudge of lipstick from the corner of his mouth with her thumb. She grinned and he knew he looked sheepish. "But I thought you'd want to see this right away," Liza said, unfazed.

He noticed that her eyes shone with excitement. Then he looked at what she held up. A .38 pistol in a plastic evidence bag. "Where—"

"I was going through the list of names you had me put together, checking to see if I recognized any names on the list of people who owned registered .38 firearms, when Angus Cardwell drove up." She grinned. "I thought it wouldn't hurt to ask him if he had a .38. He told me he did, but he'd lost it. I asked if he'd mind if I took a look in his truck." Her grin broadened. "Don't worry, I got him to sign a release. And lo and behold, the .38 was right under the seat behind some old rags."

"Nice work, Deputy."

"Tomorrow's my day off," she said quickly. "I was wondering if you'd like me to take the gun up to the crime lab."

"You'd drive all the way to Missoula on your day off?" he asked, amused. She reminded him of the way he'd been when he'd first started working for the sheriff's department.

"Truthfully? I can't stand the suspense," she said. "You should have seen Angus's face when I pulled out the gun— Don't worry, I was careful not to get any of my prints on it. He looked like he might faint. No kidding. He grabbed the side of his pickup. You would have sworn he'd just seen a ghost."

"It might take a while before the lab can run a ballistics test on the pistol," Hud said distractedly, thinking of Angus's reaction.

"I can be pretty persuasive when I need to," Liza said with a grin. "It's about the only advantage of being a woman deputy."

He smiled. Liza was cute, with dark hair, green eyes and freckles. "Call me as soon as you get the results."

"I left the list on your desk," she said as she locked the .38 in the evidence room. "I'll pick it up first thing in the morning."

"One more thing," he said, thinking about what she'd said about being persuasive. "Think you could get the fingerprints of our main suspects before you go off duty?"

She grinned. "Just give me a list."

He jotted down the names: Jordan Cardwell, Clay Cardwell, Angus Cardwell, Stacy Cardwell, Harlan Cardwell. He left off Dana's name. He could get those himself.

She took the list, read down it, then looked at him. "Just about all of the Cardwells, huh?"

He nodded, wishing now that he'd put Dana's name on it.

Liza started for the door. "Oh, I almost forgot. I found a card in that plastic garbage bag with the box of chocolates when I sent it and the doll to the lab for you this morning. I left the card on your desk. And I just took a phone message for you from the airlines regarding the passenger you'd inquired about." Hud could see curiosity burning in her gaze. "Also on your desk."

"Thanks." Hud stepped into his office and picked up the note Liza had left. His heart began to race.

Jordan Cardwell flew in yesterday—not today. He had taken a morning flight. When Dana said he'd called her to let her know he was flying out—he was probably already in the canyon. Maybe even on the ranch.

He picked up the other item Liza had left him. A wadded-up birthday card. He stared at the front. This had been in Dana's wastebasket? He opened the card and saw Stacy's name. His heart stopped dead in his chest.

He recognized this handwriting. Hurriedly, he pulled out the anonymous note he'd received in California. The handwriting matched.

It had been Stacy who'd gotten him back here?

JORDAN MUST HAVE HEARD Dana's pickup approaching because as she parked, the lights upstairs went off. A moment later she saw her brother rush past one of the living room windows.

When she entered the house, he was sitting in one of the overstuffed chairs, one shiny new cowboy boot resting on his opposite leg, a drink in his hand.

"Finally," he said. "I thought you got off at six?"

"Not that it's any of your business, but I had a stop to make. Anyway, Stacy told me the family meeting was at seven," she said, taking off her coat. "Aren't you a little early?"

"I wanted us to visit before the others got here."

She turned to look at him. He was trying to give her the impression he'd been sitting there waiting patiently for her—not upstairs snooping around. Her brother really was a liar. She'd always known that Jordan was a lot of things, but she was starting to worry that he could be a lot more than just a liar. He could be a murderer.

"Visit?" she said, unable to keep the sarcasm out of her voice. "Let me guess what you want to visit about."

"Isn't it possible I might just want to see you before the others arrive?" he demanded. Another lie.

"No. Not unless you want to tell me the truth about what you were doing up in Mother's old room."

He made an ugly face in answer to being found out.

"Or I can tell you," she said against the advice of the little voice in her head warning her to be careful. "You were looking for Mom's will. The one you said didn't exist. In fact, you accused me of making up the story to hold up the sale of the ranch."

"I still believe that."

She felt her anger rise. "If I didn't know better I'd swear you staged that scene last night at the well."

Jordan stared at her. "What are you talking about?"

"Last night," Dana said, biting off each word. "Someone tried to trick me into coming up to the well. To kill me. Or just get me away from the house so you could search for the will. Hud was almost killed."

"I have no idea what you're talking about," Jordan snapped. "Remember? I didn't even fly in until today."

"How do I know you aren't lying again."

Jordan downed the rest of his drink and slammed the glass down on the end table as he launched himself to his feet. "I'm sick of this." He stormed across the room until he stood towering over her. "The ranch is going on the market," he snapped, grabbing both of her shoulders in his hands. "You are going to quit using every legal maneuver possible to hold up the sale."

She tried to pull free, his fingers biting into her flesh.

He gave her a shake. "There is no will. Or if there is, you can't produce it." His words were like the hiss of a snake, his face within inches of hers. "You have no choice, Dana, so stop fighting me or you'll be sorry you were ever born, you stubborn damned—"

The sound of the front door opening killed the rest of his words. He let go of Dana at once and stepped back as Stacy asked, "What's going on?"

"Nothing," Jordan said sullenly. "We were just waiting for you and Clay. Where the hell is Clay, anyway? And what is that?"

Dana never thought she'd be relieved to see her sister. She was also surprised by Stacy's attitude. Her sister never stood up to Jordan but clearly she was angry with him now. Because of what she'd just witnessed?

Her hands trembling, Dana reached for the container in Stacy's hand and instantly regretted taking it.

Through the clear plastic lid she could see the crudely printed words: *Happy Birthday, Dana!* on what was obviously a homemade cake. Stacy had baked?

Dana didn't want to feel touched by the gesture, but she did as she heard the sound of another car coming in from the highway. She realized she and Jordan would have heard Stacy arrive if they hadn't been hollering at each other. Her shoulders still hurt from where he'd grabbed her.

"That must be Clay now," Stacy said, still glaring at Jordan.

He shoved past Stacy and out the front door.

Stacy shrugged out of her coat as she looked around the living room as if she hadn't seen it in a very long time. She hadn't and Dana wondered if her sister might be starting to have doubts about selling the place.

"I wish you hadn't done this," Dana said to her sister, holding up the cake.

"It was nothing," Stacy said, dropping her head.

Dana studied her for a moment wondering if the cake wasn't just a ploy to get back into her good graces so Dana would quit fighting the sale of the ranch. Now that Dana thought about it, she wouldn't have been surprised if the cake was Jordan's idea.

Jordan came back in the house, stomping his feet loudly, Clay at his heels.

"Hi, sis," Clay said quietly. He looked as if he might hug her, but changed his mind. He didn't seem to know what to do with his big hands. They fluttered in the air for a moment before he stuffed them into the pockets of his pants. "Happy birthday."

Had he been in on this? He sounded as if he'd only remembered her birthday when he'd seen the cake in her hands, though.

"Hello, Clay." Clay was what was called lanky. He was tall and thin, his bones seeming too large for his body. His hair was shorter than Dana had ever seen it, a buzz cut, and he wore chinos and a T-shirt. He wasn't so much handsome as he was beautiful.

She saw Jordan give him a disgusted look. He'd always thought Clay weak.

Stacy had taken down plates from their mother's good china. Dana watched her stop for a moment as if admiring the pattern. Or maybe she was just speculating on how much the china might be worth on the market.

Their mother should have been here, Dana thought as she watched everyone take a seat around the large table. Jordan pulled out a chair and sat at the spot their mother used to sit. Obviously he now considered himself the head of the family.

Clay sat where he always had, near the other end of the table. Stacy put plates and forks on the table, then took the cake Dana realized she was still holding.

As Dana slumped into her chair, Stacy carefully cut the cake. Dana noticed that her sister's hands were trembling. She served everyone a piece, then started to ask, "Should we sing—"

"No," Dana interrupted. "The cake is more than enough."

Stacy looked disheartened but sat and picked up her fork. "I hope it tastes all right. I don't do much baking."

Jordan snorted at the understatement.

Dana studied her older brother as she took a bite of the cake. What would Jordan have done if Stacy hadn't arrived when she had?

"It's good," Dana said, touched by her sister's kind gesture even though she didn't want to be.

Jordan downed his and shoved his plate and fork aside. "Could we please get this settled now?"

Stacy looked angrily at their brother. "You are such a jerk," she snapped, and got up to take everyone's dishes to the sink.

"Leave the dishes. I'll do them," Dana said, getting up from the table. The kitchen felt too small for this discussion, the smell of chocolate cake too strong. "Let's go in the living room."

They all filed into the adjacent room. Clay sat in the corner, Stacy teetered on the edge of the fireplace hearth, Jordan went straight to the bar and poured himself a drink.

"Dana, you're killing us," Jordan said after gulping down half a glass of her bourbon. "All these attorney fees to fight you. You know we're going to win eventually. So why put us through this?"

Dana looked around the room at each of her siblings. "I can't believe any of you are related to me or Mother. If she knew what you were doing—"

"Don't bring her into this," Jordan snapped. "If she wanted you alone to have the ranch then she should have made the proper arrangements."

"She tried to and you know it," Dana said, fighting not to lose her temper. "I know Mother talked to each of you before she drafted her new will and explained how you would be paid over the long term."

"Produce the document," Jordan demanded.

"You know I can't."

He made an angry swipe through the air. "Then stop fighting us. You can't win and you know it. Dragging your feet has only made things worse. Now we have a dead body on the ranch."

"The body's been there for seventeen years," Dana said. "It would have turned up sooner or later."

"Not if Warren had filled in the well like he was supposed to," Jordan snapped.

Dana narrowed her gaze at him. "You told him to fill in the well?"

Jordan glared at her. "I told him to get the ranch ready to sell. Filling in the well was his idea. How did I know he was going to find human bones in it?"

How indeed?

"We just need to stop fighting among ourselves," Clay said from the corner.

Jordan rolled his eyes. "No, what we need is to get this ranch on the market and hope to hell this investigation is over as quickly as possible. In the meantime, Dana, you could stop being so antagonistic toward the marshal."

Dana felt all the air rush from her lungs as if he'd hit her. "You aren't seriously suggesting that I—"

"Your attitude is making us all look guilty," Jordan said.

"And you think if I'm nice to Hud, it will make you look any less guilty?" she snapped.

"Please, can't we all just quit arguing?" Stacy said, sounding close to tears.

"After the ranch sells, I'm leaving," Clay said out of the blue, making everyone turn to look at him. He seemed embarrassed by the attention. "I have a chance to buy a small theater in Los Angeles."

"You'd leave Montana?" Dana asked, and realized she didn't know her younger brother at all.

Clay gave her a lopsided smile. "You're the one who loves Montana, Dana. I would have left years ago if I could have. And now, with everyone in town talking about our family as if we're murderers... Did you know that a deputy made me stop on the way here to have my fingerprints taken?"

"Stop whining, Clay, I got a call from the deputy, too," Jordan said, and looked at Stacy. She nodded that she had, too.

"What do you expect?" Dana said, tired of her siblings acting so put-upon. "A woman's body was found in our well. We all knew her. She broke up Mom and Dad's marriage. And, Jordan—"

"Maybe Mom killed her and threw her down the well," Jordan interrupted.

The room went deathly quiet.

"Don't give me that look, Dana," he said. "You know Mom was capable of about anything she set her mind to."

"I've heard enough of this," Dana said, and headed for the kitchen.

"Well, that's a surprise," Jordan said to her retreating back. "We knew we couldn't count on you to be reasonable."

Seething with anger, she turned to face him. "I have another month here before the court rules on whether the ranch has to be sold to humor the three of you and I'm taking it. If you don't like it, too bad. I'm fighting to save the ranch my mother loved. All the three of you want is money—any way you can get it. Even by destroying something that has been in our family for generations."

Jordan started to argue but she cut him off. "And as for the murder investigation, you're all on your own. Frankly, I think you're all capable of murder."

Clay and Stacy both denied that they had anything to hide. Jordan just glared at her and said, "You're making a very big mistake, Dana. I hope you don't live to regret it."

She turned and stalked off into the kitchen. Going to the sink, she grabbed the cool porcelain edge and gripped it, Jordan's threat ringing in her ears.

HUD GOT THE CALL FROM the crime lab just as he was starting to leave his office.

"We've found some latent prints on both the box of chocolates and the doll," Dr. Cross said. "I decided to do the tests myself since it tied in with your ongoing case. Interesting case."

"Did you come up with a match?" Hud asked.

"No prints on file that matched any of the prints on the doll or the package. We found multiple prints on the doll, all different. As for the gift, only one set."

Hud felt his heart rate quicken. "My deputy is bringing you up some fingerprints to compare those to. What about the chocolates themselves?"

"No prints on them. Also no sign of a drug or poison. As far as I can tell, they were nothing but chocolate."

Relieved, Hud sighed. "Thanks for doing this so quickly." He hung up. There was one set of prints he hadn't asked Liza to get for him. Lanny Rankin's.

Hud planned to get those himself tonight.

He picked up the phone and started calling the local bars on a hunch. The bartender at the second one Hud called said that Lanny was there.

"Try to keep him there. I'm buying," Hud said. "I'll be right down."

DANA WASN'T SURPRISED to hear tentative footfalls behind her and smell her sister's expensive perfume. Standing at the sink with her back to her sister, she closed her eyes, waiting for the next onslaught. Obviously, Jordan and Clay had sent Stacy in to convince her to change her mind.

"Dana," her sister said quietly. "I have to tell you something."

Dana kept her back turned to her sister. She'd planned on asking her sister point-blank what had happened that night five years ago with Hud. But quite frankly, she just wasn't up to the answer tonight.

"You can't just keep ignoring me. I'm your sister."

"Don't remind me," Dana said, finally giving up and turning to look at her.

Tears welled in Stacy's eyes, but she bit her lip to stem them, no doubt realizing that tears would only anger Dana more. Likewise another apology.

"I have to tell you the truth," Stacy said.

"Don't," Dana said. "I told you, I don't want to hear anything you have to say. I know they sent you in here to try to get me to change my mind."

"I didn't come in here to talk about the ranch," she said, and sounded surprised that Dana would think that. "I need to tell you about Hud."

Dana felt her face flush. "I'd rather talk about selling the ranch." She started to step past Stacy, but her sister touched her arm and whispered, "I lied."

Dana froze, her gaze leaping to Stacy's face.

Her sister nodded slowly, the tears in her eyes spilling over. "I didn't sleep with him," she whispered, and looked behind her as if afraid their brothers might be listening.

"What is this? Some ploy to get me to sell the ranch?" Dana couldn't believe how low her sister would stoop.

"This doesn't have anything to do with the ranch." Stacy shook her head, tears now spilling down her cheeks. "I have to tell you the truth, no matter what happens to me. I didn't want to do it."

Dana felt her pulse jump. "What are you talking about?" she asked, remembering what Hud had said about Stacy not acting alone that night.

Stacy gripped her arm. "I didn't have a choice."

"You always have a choice," Dana said, keeping her voice down. "What happened that night?"

Stacy looked scared as she let go of Dana and glanced over her shoulder again.

"Don't move," Dana ordered, and walked to the doorway to the living room. "Leave," she said to Jordan and Clay. Clay got up at once but Jordan didn't move.

"We're not finished here," Jordan said angrily. "And I'm not leaving until this is settled. One way or the other."

"Stacy and I need to talk," Dana said, letting him believe she had to iron things out with her sister before she would give in on selling the ranch.

Clay was already heading for the door as Jordan reluctantly rose. Clay opened the front door then stopped. Dana saw why. Their father's pickup had just pulled into the yard.

"I'll be outside talking to Dad," Jordan said, and practically shoved Clay out the door.

What was their father doing here? Dana wondered as she hurried back to the kitchen. No doubt her siblings had commandeered his help to convince her to sell the ranch. Bastards.

Stacy had sat at the table, her head in her hands. Dana closed the kitchen door as she heard her brothers and their father talking out on the porch. It almost sounded as if Jordan and Angus were arguing.

What was that about? She'd find out soon enough, she feared. But right now she wanted some answers out of her sister.

Stacy looked up when Dana closed the kitchen door. "I'm so sorry."

"Don't start that again. Just tell me." Dana didn't sit. She stood, her arms folded across her chest to keep her hands from shaking, to keep from strangling Stacy. "Tell me *everything* and whatever you do, don't lie to me."

Stacy started to cry. "I'm telling you I didn't sleep with Hud, isn't that enough?"

"No. I need to know how he got there. Did he pick you up at the bar? Or did you pick him up?"

Stacy was crying harder. "I picked him up."

"How?" Hud swore he'd had only one drink. But she recalled hearing from people at the bar that night that he'd been falling-down drunk when he'd left with Stacy.

"I drugged him."

Dana stared at her sister in disbelief. "You drugged him!"

"I had to do it!" she cried. "Then before the drug could completely knock him out, I got him outside and into my car."

Dana could hear raised voices now coming from the living room. The three had brought their argument in out of the cold. But the fact barely registered. Stacy had admitted that she'd drugged Hud and taken him out to her car.

"I was to take him to my place," Stacy said, the words tumbling out with the tears. "I thought that was all I had to do. I didn't want to do it. I swear. But if I didn't..." She began to sob. Angus and Jordan were yelling at each other in the living room, the words incomprehensible.

"What did you do?" Dana demanded, moving to stand over her.

"I didn't know part of the plan was to make it look like we'd slept together until when you got there the next morning," Stacy cried. "I didn't want to hurt you."

Dana remembered the look of shock on Hud's and Stacy's faces when they'd seen her that morning. She'd thought it was from being caught. But now she recalled it was bewilderment, as well.

"Why tell me now?" Dana demanded. "Why not tell me five years ago before you ruined everything?"

"I couldn't. I was scared. I'm still scared, but I can't live like this anymore." Stacy looked up, her gaze meeting her sister's. The fear was as real as the anguish, Dana thought. "I've hated myself for what I did. No matter what happens to me now, I had to tell you. I couldn't live with what I did."

"What do you mean, no matter what happens to you now?"

Stacy shook her head. "I used to be afraid of going to jail, but even that is better than the hell I've been in these past years. I'm not strong like you. I couldn't stand up to them."

Them? "Jail?" Dana repeated. For just an instant she flashed again on the memory of Stacy's face that morning five years ago. Stacy had looked scared. Or was it trapped? "Are you telling me someone was threatening jail if you didn't go along with setting Hud up?"

The kitchen door banged open and Clay appeared, panicked and breathless. "It's Dad. I think he's having a heart attack!"

Chapter Eleven

Lanny Rankin was anything but happy to see Hud take the stool next to him at the bar.

The lawyer had two drinks in front of him and was clearly on his way to getting drunk.

"What do you want?" Lanny slurred.

"Just thought I'd have a drink." Hud signaled the bartender who brought him a draft beer from the tap. He took a drink and watched Lanny pick up his glass and down half of what appeared to be a vodka tonic.

"Bring Lanny another drink," Hud told the bartender.

Lanny shoved his glass away and picked up the second drink and downed it, as well, before stumbling to his feet. "Save your money, Marshal. I'm not drinking with you."

"I hope you're not driving," Hud said.

Lanny narrowed his gaze. "You'd love to arrest me, wouldn't you? She tell you about us? Is that what you're doing here? Tell you we're engaged? Well, it's all a lie. All a lie." His face turned mean. "She's all yours. But then again, she always has been, hasn't she?"

He turned and stumbled out the back door.

Hud quickly pulled an evidence bag from his jacket pocket and slipped both of the glasses with Lanny's prints on them inside. He paid his bill and went outside to make sure Lanny wasn't driving anywhere.

Lanny was walking down the street toward his condo.

Hud watched him for a moment, then headed for his office. If he hurried, he could get both glasses ready for Liza to take to the crime lab in the morning.

He wondered if Liza had any trouble getting the Cardwell clan's fingerprints.

Just the thought of the family meeting going on at the ranch made him uneasy. Maybe he would swing by there later.

Back at his office, Hud got the drink glasses with Lanny's prints ready and locked the box in the evidence room with the .38 Liza had taken from Angus's pickup.

As he started to leave, he remembered the list of registered owners of .38 pistols in the county Liza had left on his desk. The list was long. He thumbed through it, his mind more on the family meeting going on at the Cardwell Ranch than the blur of names.

This list had probably been a waste of time. There was a very good chance that Liza had already found the murder weapon and it was now locked in the evidence room. By tomorrow, Hud worried that he would be arresting Angus Cardwell. He didn't even want to think what that would do to Dana.

He folded the list and stuck it in his pocket. As he started to leave, planning to go out and check on Dana, no matter how angry it made her, he heard the call come in on the scanner. An ambulance was needed at the Cardwell Ranch.

"How's Dad?" Dana asked when she found Jordan and Clay in the waiting room at Bozeman Deaconess Hospital. She hadn't been able to get any information at the desk on her way in and the roads down the canyon had been icy, traffic slow.

Clay shrugged, looking miserable and nervous in a corner chair.

"The doctor's in with him," Jordan said, pacing the small room, clearly agitated.

"Where's Stacy?" she asked. Earlier Dana had glanced through the open living room doorway and seen her father on the floor, Jordan leaning over him. She'd let out a cry and run into the living room. Behind her she'd heard Clay on the phone calling for an ambulance on the kitchen phone.

It wasn't until later, after the ambulance had rushed Angus to the hospital and Dana began looking for her keys to follow in her pickup, that she'd realized Stacy was gone.

"When did Stacy leave?" Dana asked, glancing around.

Both brothers shrugged. "After I called 911 I turned around and I noticed your back door was open, and when I went out to follow the ambulance, I saw that her car was already gone."

"Stacy just left?" Dana asked in disbelief. Why would her sister do that without a word? Especially with their father in the next room on the floor unconscious?

Stacy's words echoed in Dana's ears. "No matter what happens to me now." Was it possible her sister was in danger because she'd told Dana the truth?

Dana couldn't worry about that now. "What were you and Dad fighting about?" she asked Jordan.

"This is not my fault," Jordan snapped.

"I'll get us some coffee," Clay said, and practically bolted from the room.

Jordan and Angus couldn't have been arguing about the sale of the ranch. Her father had said he wasn't going to take sides, but he did add that he felt the ranch was too much for Dana to handle on her own.

"Sell it, baby girl," he'd said to Dana. "It's an albatross around your neck. Your mother would understand."

"That's how you felt about the ranch, Dad, not me," she'd told him.

But he'd only shook his head and said, "Sell it. Some day you'll be glad you did. And it will keep peace in the family." He'd always been big on keeping peace in the family. Except when it came to his wandering ways.

"I heard the two of you yelling at each other in the other room," Dana said. "What was going on?"

Jordan stopped pacing to look at her. "The stupid fool thinks I killed Ginger."

Ginger Adams, the woman whose wrist he'd broken in an argument. The woman who'd ended up in the Cardwell Ranch well. The floor under her seemed to give way. "Why would Dad think that?"

"Who the hell knows? He's always been a crazy old fool."

Dana bristled. "Dad is a lot of things. Crazy isn't one of them."

Jordan's look was lethal. "Don't play games with me. Dad told me you knew about me and Ginger. What's crazy is that he thinks I took his gun."

She stared at him. "The missing .38?"

"Turns out it wasn't missing," Jordan said. "It was under the seat of his pickup and now the cops have it.

He thinks I took the gun and then when Ginger's body was found, I put it under the pickup seat to frame him for her murder."

Dana felt her heart drop to her feet. Hadn't Hud told her that the gun was used in both Ginger's murder and Judge Randolph's? What motive could Jordan have to kill the judge, though? "Jordan, you didn't—"

Jordan let out a curse. "You think I'm a murderer, too?" His angry gaze bore into her. "Not only a murderer, but I framed my own father, as well?" He let out a scornful laugh and shook his head at her. "I guess I didn't realize how little you and Dad thought of me until now." He turned and stormed out of the waiting room, almost colliding with Clay who was carrying a cardboard tray with three cups of coffee on it.

What bothered Dana was the guilty look in Jordan's eyes before he left.

"Thanks," she said as she took one of the foam cups of hot coffee Clay offered her and stepped out in the hallway, fighting the terrible fear that had settled in the pit of her stomach.

At the sound of footfalls, she turned to see her father's doctor coming toward her. She froze. All she could think about was the day of her mother's accident and the doctor coming down the hall to give her the news. She couldn't lose another parent.

Hud spotted Dana the moment he walked into the Bozeman hospital emergency room waiting area. Relief washed through him, making his legs feel boneless. She was all right.

She was talking to the doctor and he could see the

concern in her face. He waited, studying her body language, fear closing his throat.

Her shoulders seemed to slump, and he saw her hand go to her mouth then brush at her tears. She was smiling and nodding, and Hud knew that whatever had happened, there had been good news.

She saw him then. He tried not to read anything into her expression. For a moment there she'd actually looked glad to see him.

She said something to the doctor and walked toward him. He caught his breath. Sometimes he forgot how beautiful she was. Her eyes were bright, cheeks flushed from crying, her face glowing with the good news the doctor had given her.

"Dana?" he said as she closed the distance. "What's happened?"

"Dad. He had a heart attack." Her voice broke. "But the doctor says he's stable now." She looked up at him, tears in her eyes. "I have to talk to you."

"Okay." He couldn't help but sound tentative. She hadn't wanted to lay eyes on him—let alone talk to him. "Did you want to talk at the office or—"

She glanced around, making him wonder where her brothers were. And Stacy. "Could we go back to your place?"

His place? "Sure." Whatever she wanted to talk to him about was serious. "You want to follow me?"

She shook her head. "I need to stop by Stacy's. You go on. I'll meet you there."

Whatever that was about he didn't want to know. But at the same time, he didn't like the idea of her going alone.

"I could go with you," he said.

She shook her head again. "I'll meet you at the cabin you're renting." She knew where he lived?

"I'll see you soon," he said.

She nodded distractedly. "Soon."

As he got into his patrol car, he tried not to even guess what this was about. But he had a bad feeling it could have something to do with her father's gun now locked in his evidence cabinet at the office.

The night was clear, stars bright dots in the crystalline cold blue of the sky overhead. Snow covered everything. It sat in puffy white clumps in the branches of the trees and gleamed in the starlight like zillions of diamonds on the open field across the road.

The drive home was interminable. He kept looking in his rearview mirror, hoping to see the headlights of Dana's pickup. She'd said she needed to make a stop by Stacy's. He wished he'd asked how long she might be.

He parked in front of the cabin, the night darker than the inside of a gunny sack. In the cabin, he straightened up, built a fire and put on some coffee.

A wind had come up. It whirled the light fresh snow in a blizzard of white outside the window. He should have insisted she ride with him as upset as she was. But he'd had no desire to go to Stacy's, and Dana hadn't wanted him along.

The sky over the tops of the pines darkened as another storm moved in. He'd forgotten how dark it could be in the dead of winter.

He watched the road—what little of it he could see through the swirling snow. Surprisingly he really had missed winters while in Los Angeles. Missed the seasons that were so dramatic in Montana. Especially winter. Two feet of snow could fall overnight. It wasn't unusual to wake up to the silence and the cold and know that something had changed during the night.

Dana should be here by now. He began to worry, thinking about what he'd heard in her voice. She'd been upset about her father. But that hadn't been all of it. Something had happened. Something she needed to talk to him about. But first she had to see Stacy.

Hud was to the point where he was ready to go looking for her when he spotted headlights through the drifting snow.

She pulled in beside his patrol car and got out, seeming to hesitate. She was wearing a red fleece jacket, her dark hair tucked up under a navy stocking cap. A few strands whipped around her face as she stared at the cabin.

He opened the front door and stood looking at her. A small drift had formed just outside the door and now ran across the porch. The steps down had disappeared, the snow smooth and deep.

He met her gaze through dancing snowflakes, then reached for the shovel. But before he could clean off the steps, she was coming up them, all hesitation gone.

To his utter shock, she rushed to him. He took her in his arms, now truly afraid.

"I'm sorry." Her words were barely audible over the howl of the wind across the roof. "I'm so sorry."

He held her, his heart in his throat. He hugged her to him, breathing in the smell of her. God, how he'd missed that scent. But what could she possibly be sorry about?

Holding her felt so good, he hated it when she stepped from his arms and went inside the cabin. He followed, closing the door to the wind and snow.

She had walked to the fireplace. When she turned,

he saw the tears. Dana crying. He could count on one hand the times he'd seen that. His fear escalated.

"Whatever it is, I'll help you," he said, wanting to hold her again but afraid to step toward her.

She let out a laugh at his words and shook her head. Her face was flushed, her eyes bright. "I haven't killed anyone. Although it did cross my mind." She sobered, her gaze locked on his. "I talked to my sister."

His heart dislodged from his throat and dropped to his stomach.

She jerked her cap from her head, shaking off the snow as her hair fell around her shoulders. "She told me everything."

He didn't move—didn't breathe. He'd told himself that he'd come back here to learn everything that had happened that night but now he wasn't so sure he wanted to know.

"You were right. She lied. She was sent to the bar to drug you, get you out of there before the drug completely knocked you out and take you to her place. It was just as you suspected—" her voice broke, eyes shimmering with tears "—nothing happened. You *were* set up." A tear trailed down her cheek. "*We* were set up."

It took him a moment. So it had been just as he'd believed in his heart. No matter how drunk he might have been, he wouldn't have bedded Dana's sister or any other woman for that matter. He'd known it. And yet he'd feared that for that night, he'd lost his mind and his way.

"I'm so sorry I didn't believe you. That I didn't even give you a chance to explain."

He found himself shaking with relief and anger as he stepped to Dana and pulled her into his arms again. "I couldn't have explained it. That's why I left. I thought it would be easier on you if you never had to see me again."

"But you came back."

"Thanks to your sister."

Dana raised her head to look into his face. "Stacy sent you the note?"

He nodded. "I found the birthday card she mailed you, the one you'd thrown away. It was under the box of chocolates. I recognized the handwriting."

"So she was responsible for you coming back." She leaned into him again.

He rested his chin on the top of her head. Her hair felt like silk. Her body softened against his. He could feel his heart pounding. Nothing had happened that night. He closed his eyes and pulled Dana even closer, wishing he could turn back the clock. These wasted years apart felt like a chasm between them.

"I SHOULD HAVE TRUSTED YOU." Dana hadn't believed that he'd been set up, that nothing had happened. She hadn't loved him enough. If she'd trusted him, if she'd even let him tell her his side of the story...

"Hey, there were times I didn't believe in my innocence myself," he said, holding her at arm's length to look into her face. "I thought maybe I'd lost my mind. Or worse, that I was about to become my father."

The blaze in the fireplace popped and cracked, the flames throwing shadows on the walls. She could hear the wind howling outside. Snow hit the windows, sticking, then melting down. Inside, the fire burned. Outside, the storm raged, the snow piling deeper and deeper.

She looked up into Hud's eyes and saw nothing but

love. All her anger at herself and her sister melted like the snow at the windows.

She covered one of his hands with her own, turning the palm up to kiss the warm center. She heard him let out a breath. Their eyes locked, the heat of his look warming her to her core.

"Oh, Hud," she breathed. She heard his breath catch, saw the spark of desire catch fire in his eyes. "I've never stopped wanting you."

He groaned and took her with a kiss, his mouth capturing hers as he tugged her even closer to him. She could feel the pounding of his heart, felt her body melt into his.

"I didn't want to live without you," he said as he pulled back. "The only way I was able to get through the past five years was to believe that you still loved me."

She touched his cheek, then cupped his face in her hands and kissed him, teasing the tip of his tongue with her own.

He moaned against her lips, then swept her up into his arms, carrying her to the rug in front of the fire.

She pulled him down to her. His kiss was gentle and slow, as if they had all night to make love. They did.

"You are so beautiful," he whispered, his hand trailing down the length of her neck. He leaned in to kiss her, his hand cupping her breast, and she groaned with the exquisite pleasure of his touch.

The fire warmed her skin as he slowly unbuttoned her blouse and pressed his lips to the hard nipple of one breast, then the other. She arched against him, her fingers working at the buttons of his shirt.

Their clothes began to pile up in the corner as the fire popped and crackled, the heat shimmering over their naked bodies, damp with perspiration and wet warm kisses.

Their lovemaking was all heat and fire, a frenzied rush of passion that left them both breathless.

Hud held her, smoothing her hair under his hand, his eyes locked with hers as their bodies cooled.

Dana looked into his eyes, still stunned by the powerful chemistry that arced between them. Nothing had killed it. Not the pain, not the years.

She curled into his strong arms and slept. On this night, no wind woke her with a premonition. She had no warning what the day would bring. If only for one night, she felt safe. She felt loved.

Chapter Twelve

Dana drove to Bozeman to the hospital before daylight the next morning. Her father was still in stable condition, sedated and sleeping. She peeked in on him and then drove back to Big Sky and the shop.

She spent the quiet early morning before the shop opened unloading the latest shipment of fabric and pricing it. Unfortunately the task wasn't difficult enough that it kept her from thinking about last night with Hud.

She wasn't surprised when she heard a knock at the back door and saw him.

"Good morning," he said, but his look said there was nothing good about it.

"Good morning." She couldn't believe how glad she was to see him. She'd never stopped being in love with him and even when she hadn't known the truth, he'd been much harder to hate in the flesh than he'd been in her memory.

He pulled off his hat to rake his fingers through his thick sandy-blond hair. It was a nervous habit. She felt a jolt, wondering what he had to be nervous about.

"You left before I woke up this morning," he said.

She nodded sheepishly. "I needed to think about some things and go see my father."

"Think about some things?"

She sighed, picking up a bolt of fabric and carrying it over to its spot on the wall. "About last night."

"You're afraid I'm going to hurt you again?" he asked behind her.

She turned and looked up into his wonderful face. "Do you blame me? You left me for five years."

"But if you believe that Stacy was finally telling the truth—"

"I do, but…"

"You still can't forget," he said softly.

She reached up to cup his rough jaw. He hadn't taken the time to shave. Instead he'd rushed right over here. "Last night made me feel all those old wonderful feelings again that we shared."

"You know I came back here because of you. Because I still love you. I'm sorry I didn't come back sooner. I should never have left."

"You thought you'd lost everything, your career—"

"Losing you is what devastated my life, Dana. It took a while to get my head on straight."

She nodded. "I just need to take it slow." She dropped her hand and turned her back to him. Otherwise, she would be in his arms and Hilde would find them between racks of fabric making love on the hardwood floor when she came in.

"We can take it as slow as you need," he said. "Just don't push me away again." He pulled her around to face him and into his arms, kissing her until she was breathless.

She leaned into his strong, hard body and rested her cheek against his chest, his jacket open, his cotton shirt warm and soft. She could hear his heart beating fast and realized she'd scared him with her disappearing act this morning.

"I'm sorry I took off this morning," she said against his chest.

He hugged her tighter. "I know you're worried about your dad. And Stacy." He sighed. "Dana, I found out that your brother Jordan got into town the day of your birthday."

She pulled back a little to look at him. "He lied about that, too?"

Hud nodded. "I'm sorry, but I think he's responsible for what happened at the well the night before last, and if he is, I'm going to have to arrest him."

She made a sound deep down in her throat as she realized that most of her family could end up in jail the way things were going. "Hud, you and I both know that if Jordan had found those bones in the well he'd have covered them with fifteen feet of dirt and never given them another thought."

Blood was thicker than water. But this was Hud and the truth was the truth.

"And don't try to make me sound so noble," she said. "I didn't tell you everything." She told him about going to see her father about his .38, then about finding Jordan searching the ranch house and finally that Jordan and her father had been arguing just before Angus Cardwell's collapse. "Is Dad's .38 the murder weapon?" she asked, her heart in her throat.

"We don't know yet. But I'm worried. I'd like you to drive out with me to talk to Stacy."

"When I stopped by her place last night on the way to your cabin," Dana said, "she wasn't there."

"Maybe she's come back. Or maybe she left something behind that will give us an idea of where she's gone. If what she told you is true, then someone was behind setting me up. I need to know who it was. And why. If she was being threatened with jail, then, Dana, I have a pretty good idea who was behind it. I just have to prove it. I need your help. Your sister might open up if we're there together."

As if on cue, Hilde came in the back door on a gust of wind. She looked surprised to see Dana at work so early and even more surprised to see Hud. She looked from one to the other, her gaze finally settling on Dana. She smiled, obviously seeing what Dana had hoped to keep a secret.

"Hello, Hud," Hilde said.

"Nice to see you again, Hilde," he said. "I just came by to steal your partner for a little while."

"Be my guest," Hilde said, giving Dana a meaningful look.

"We're just going to look for Stacy," Dana said. "It's a long story."

"I'm sure it is," Hilde said, still smiling.

Dana groaned inwardly. Her friend knew her too well. Hilde had seen the glow in her cheeks this morning, the sparkle in her eye. Hud had always been able to put it there. "Let me get my coat."

SNOW WAS PILED HIGH on each side of the highway. Beside it, the river gurgled blue-green under a thick skin of transparent ice.

"You're sure she said 'jail'?"

Dana nodded. "She looked scared, Hud. I guess that's why I believed her. She seemed to think she was in danger."

"I think she set me up to keep me away from Judge Randolph's house that night," Hud said. "It's the only thing that makes any sense."

"You think Stacy had something to do with the judge's murder?"

"Look at the evidence, Dana. The judge was murdered the same night Stacy drugged me at the bar and made sure I wasn't the one who responded to the call about shots fired at the Randolph house. Instead, my father took the call. Or at least that's the story."

"What are you saying, Hud? You can't seriously think your own father was behind it."

"Stacy was being threatened with jail, isn't that what she said? Now she seems to be running scared." Hud glanced over at Dana. "I think she's afraid because she knows the truth about that night."

"You can't believe your father killed the judge."

He sighed. "I don't know what I believe. The judge had Alzheimer's. He was about to be asked to step down from the bench. Unless he had hard evidence against Brick, then the judge wasn't really a threat."

"So then your father had no motive."

"So it would seem," Hud said as he turned off Jackrabbit Road onto Cameron Bridge Road.

"Maybe the fact that the judge was killed that night was just a coincidence," Dana said.

He wished he could believe that.

Stacy was in between husbands right now and living in the house she was awarded in the divorce settlement from Emery Chambers. The divorce that, according to Lanny, Hud had helped her get.

"It has to be about more than just splitting us up.

Who would care enough to go to all that trouble?" Hud said.

"Stacy for one."

"What about Lanny?" He saw Dana shiver. "What?"

"When he heard you were back in town he was very angry."

Hud rubbed his still sore jaw. "I noticed."

He drove a few miles down the river before turning into a graveled yard in front of a large older house. There were no fresh tracks in the snow. No one had been in or out since Dana had stopped by last night.

Through the windows in the garage, Dana could see that Stacy's car was still gone.

"Let's give it a try anyway," Hud said, and opened his door.

Dana followed him up the unshoveled walk and waited while he knocked. Through the trees, he could see an open hole in the ice on the Gallatin River, the water a deep, clear green. The air smelled of fresh snow and cottonwoods.

He knocked again, then turned to see Dana bend to pick up something from the snow beside the front step. A black glove.

"It's one of the cashmere gloves my sister was wearing yesterday when she came to the house."

His mouth went dry. Stacy had come back here after the family meeting, then left again?

He reached for the doorknob. It turned in his hand, the door swinging into the empty living room. He signaled Dana to wait as he moved quickly through the house, weapon drawn. Something about the empty feel of the house made him fear he wasn't going to find Stacy. At least not alive.

Upstairs, the bedroom looked as if a bomb had gone off in it.

"It's clear," he called down to Dana.

"My God," Dana said as she saw the room, the drawers hanging open and empty, clothes hangers on the floor or cocked at an odd angle as if the clothing had been ripped from them.

She moved to the closet and touched one of the dresses that had been left behind. "She's either running scared or someone wants us to believe she is."

He nodded, having already come to the same conclusion. If Stacy was as scared as Dana had said and decided to blow town, she would have grabbed just what she needed. Or left without anything. She wouldn't have tried to take everything. Or would she? Maybe she wasn't planning to ever come back.

"Who are you calling?" Dana asked, sounding worried.

"I'm going to have some deputies search the wooded area behind the house," he said. "Just as a precaution."

Dana nodded, but he saw that she feared the same thing he did. That Stacy had been telling the truth. Her life had been in danger.

While they waited for the deputies to arrive and search the woods around the house, they searched the house again, looking for anything that would give them a clue.

They found nothing.

"Do you want me to take you home?" Hud offered.

Dana shook her head. "Please just take me back to the shop."

"Hilde's working with you all day, right?" Hud asked.

"Yes, I'll be fine. We both have work to do. And maybe Stacy will contact me."

He nodded. "I just don't want you alone. Especially now with your sister missing." His cell phone rang.

It was Roadside Café owner and former cook Leroy Perkins. "You were asking about Ginger's old roommate the other day," Leroy said. "I finally remembered her name. Zoey Skinner. I asked around. You'd be surprised how much cooks know about what's going on. The good ones anyway can cook *and* listen." He laughed. "Zoey's working at a café in West Yellowstone. The Lonesome Pine Café."

"Thanks." Hud broke the connection and looked over at Dana. "I need to go up to West Yellowstone. I'll be back before you get off work." He hesitated. "I was hoping we could have dinner together."

"Is that what you were hoping?" she asked with a smile.

"Actually, I was hoping you would come back to the cabin tonight. I could pick up some steaks… But maybe that's moving too fast for you." He gave her an innocent grin. "I can't stand having you out of my sight."

"I told you I'll be safe at the shop," she said.

"I wasn't thinking of your safety."

She met his gaze and felt that slow burn in her belly. "Dinner at your cabin sounds wonderful. I just need to go home and feed Joe."

"I'll stop off and feed Joe and then pick you up at the shop," he suggested.

She knew he just didn't want her going back to the ranch house. The thought of it did make her uncomfortable, but it was still her home—a home she was fighting to keep. "I at least need to go out to the ranch and pick up some clothes. Why don't you meet me there?"

She could see he didn't like that idea.

"I'll be waiting for you at your house," he said.

She didn't argue. She felt safe believing that no one would attack either her or Hud in broad daylight. But once it got dark, she would think again of the doll in the well and remember that she was more than likely the target. It chilled her to the bone to think of what could have happened if she hadn't gone up there with the shotgun.

"Just be careful, okay?" Hud said.

"You, too." She touched his cheek and ached to be in his arms again. Whose fool idea was it to take things slow?

As Hud pulled into the lake house, he found his father shoveling snow.

"I don't see you for years then I see you twice in two days?" Brick said with a shake of his head as Hud got out of the patrol car.

Brick set aside the snow shovel he'd been using on the walk. "I suppose you want to talk. It's warmer inside."

Without a word, Hud followed.

"I could make some coffee," Brick said, shrugging out of his coat at the door.

"No need." Hud stood just inside, not bothering to take off his boots or his coat. He wouldn't be staying long.

Brick slumped down onto the bench by the door and worked off his boots. He seemed even smaller today in spite of all the winter clothing he wore. He also seemed stoved-up as if just getting his boots off hurt him but that he was trying hard not to let Hud see it.

"So what's on your mind?" Brick said. "If it's about the robbery again—"

"It's about Stacy Cardwell."

Brick looked up from unlacing his boots, cocking his head as if he hadn't heard right. "What about her?"

"She admitted that she helped set me up the night the judge was killed five years ago."

Brick lifted a brow. "And you believe her?" He let his boot drop to the floor with a thud as he rose and walked stocking-footed toward the kitchen.

"She said she did it so she wouldn't have to go to jail," he said, raising his voice as he spoke to his father's retreating back.

Brick didn't turn, didn't even acknowledge that he'd heard. Hud could hear him in the kitchen running water. He stood for a moment, the snow on his boots melting onto the stone entryway. "Did you hear me?"

"I heard you." Brick appeared in the kitchen doorway, an old-fashioned percolator coffeepot in his hand. "I'm going to make coffee. You might as well come on in. You can't hurt the floor." He turned his back, disappearing into the kitchen again.

"Well?" Hud said after he joined him. The kitchen was neater than it had been yesterday. He wondered if his father had cleaned it because of Hud's visit.

"Sit down," Brick said, but Hud remained standing.

"Were you the one behind coercing Stacy to set me up?" Hud demanded.

Brick turned to look at him. "Why would I do that?"

"To keep me from marrying Dana."

"Falling for Dana Cardwell was the only smart thing you ever did. Why wouldn't I want you to marry her?"

"Then you did it to get to the judge. You just wanted me out of the way so you used me, not caring what it would do to my life."

His father frowned and turned back to the stove. The coffee began to perk, filling the small house with a rich, warm aroma that reminded Hud of all the mornings his father had gotten up to make coffee over the years, especially when Hud's mother was sick.

"Why would Stacy make up something like that?" Hud asked.

"Why does Stacy do half the things she does?" Brick turned, still frowning. "She said she did it to keep herself out of jail?" He shook his head. "I never picked her up for anything. Maybe she did something she thought she would be arrested for and someone found out about it."

"You mean, blackmail?" Hud asked. Clearly he hadn't considered that.

Brick nodded. "Hadn't thought of that, huh? Something else you probably haven't considered is who else had the power to make a threat like that stick." Brick smiled and nodded. "That's right. Judge Raymond Randolph."

Hud felt the air rush out of him. "That doesn't make any sense. Why would the judge get her to keep me out of the picture?" A thought struck him. "Unless the judge wanted to make sure you responded to the call."

His father raised a brow. "You think he staged it so I'd show up and then what? He'd kill me?" Brick shook his head. "I wouldn't put it past him. Especially since he was losing his mind. But that would mean it backfired on him if that were the case and, no matter what you think, I didn't kill the judge."

"It seems more likely that I was set up so someone could use it as a way to get to the judge," Hud said.

"I agree. But you're just barking up the wrong tree if you think it was me. No matter how strongly I felt about you not staying in law enforcement, I would never set you up to get rid of you. I'm sorry you believe I would."

"I hope that's true," Hud said, and realized he meant it. He started for the door.

"Sure you don't want some coffee? It's almost ready."

"No thanks."

"Son."

Hud stopped at the door and turned to look back at his father.

Brick stood silhouetted against the frozen lake through this front window. "Be careful. It sounds like you've got at least one killer out there. Someone who thought they'd gotten away with murder. It's easier to kill after the first time, they say." His father turned back to his coffee.

IN BETWEEN CUSTOMERS, Dana told Hilde about everything else that had happened, including Stacy's confession—and disappearance.

"I can't believe this," Hilde said. "I mean, I do believe it. I never thought Hud would ever betray you. He just isn't that kind of man."

"Why didn't I see that?" Dana said, still feeling guilty and ashamed she hadn't given the man she loved a chance to even explain.

"Because you were too close to it," her friend said. "Any woman would have reacted the same way. If I would have found my man in bed with another woman, I would have shot first and asked questions later."

Dana smiled, knowing that Hilde was just trying to make her feel better.

"Oh, darn," Hilde said.

"What is it?"

"Mrs. Randolph. She left her fabric package."

Dana laughed. "She came back to the shop again? Don't tell me. She was still looking for the perfect blue thread to match those slacks of hers."

"No," Hilde said on a sigh. "This time she bought fabric for some aprons she was making for some charity event. She said you were going to help her with it?"

Dana groaned. Had she volunteered to make aprons? "Let me run it over to her. I need to find out what I've gotten myself into this time."

"Are you sure? Didn't Hud say that you weren't to leave here alone?"

Dana shook her head at her friend. "I'm just going up the canyon as far as the Randolph house. I will be back in twenty minutes tops. And, anyway, you have bookkeeping to do. It makes more sense for me to go since you're the one with the head for figures."

Hilde laughed. "You just don't want to do this. Can't fool me." She handed her the package. "Good luck. Who knows what Kitty Randolph will talk you into before you get back."

"She always tells me how close she and my mother were and how much I look like my mother and how my mother would love that I'm working on fundraisers with her now."

"You're just a girl who can't say no," Hilde joked.

"That's probably why I agreed to have dinner at

Hud's cabin tonight." She grinned at her friend on her way out.

The highway had been plowed and sanded in the worst areas so the drive to Kitty Randolph's was no problem. It felt good to get out for a while.

Dana hadn't been completely honest, though, with her friend. There was another reason she wanted to see Mrs. Randolph. She wanted to ask her about something she'd heard that morning from one of the customers.

Nancy Harper had come in to buy drapery fabric and had mentioned seeing Stacy last night.

"What time was this?" Dana had asked, trying not to sound too interested and get the gossip mill going.

"Must have been about nine," Nancy said. "She drove past. I saw her brake in front of Kitty Randolph's house." Nancy smiled. "Is your sister helping with the clinic fundraiser? I knew you were, but I was a little surprised Stacy had volunteered. She's never shown much interest in that sort of thing, not after that one she helped with. And this fundraiser is going to involve cooking and sewing."

Dana had joined Nancy in a chuckle while cringing inside at everyone's perception of her sister. "You're right, that doesn't sound much like my sister."

"Well, you know Kitty. She can be very persuasive."

"You're sure it was Stacy?" Dana had asked, convinced Nancy had to be mistaken. Stacy had helped with one fundraiser years ago while she was between husbands. By the end of the event, Stacy wasn't speaking to Kitty. The two had stayed clear of each other ever since from what Dana could tell.

"Oh, it was Stacy, all right," Nancy said. "I didn't see her get out of her car because my view was blocked by the trees. But I saw her behind the wheel and I recognized the way she drives. She really does drive too fast for road conditions." Her smile said it was too bad Stacy wasn't more like Dana.

As Dana drove past Nancy Harper's house and parked in front of the Randolph house, the only other house on the dead-end road, she wondered again why Stacy would have come here last night. If indeed she did.

The double garage doors to Kitty's house were closed and there were no visible windows so she could see if Kitty was home or not. Getting out, she walked up the freshly shoveled steps and rang the doorbell.

No answer. She rang the bell again and thought she heard a thud from inside the house. Her first thought was that the elderly woman had been hurrying to the door and fallen.

"Mrs. Randolph?" she called, and knocked on the door. She tried the knob. The door opened.

Dana had expected to see the poor woman lying on the floor writhing in pain. But she saw no one. "Hello?" she called.

Another thud. This one coming from upstairs.

"Mrs. Randolph?" she called as she climbed the stairs. "Kitty?"

Still no answer.

At the top of the stairs she heard a sound coming from down the hall. A series of small thumps. One of the doors was partially open, the sound coming from inside.

She hurried down the hall, her mind racing as she shoved the door all the way open and stepped inside.

At once, she saw that the room was the master bedroom, large and plush, done in reds and golds.

At first she didn't see Kitty Randolph on the floor in front of the closet.

Dana realized why the woman hadn't heard her calling for her. Kitty Randolph was on her hands and knees, muttering to herself as she dug in the back of the huge closet. One shoe after another came flying out to land behind the woman.

Dana stumbled back, bumping into the door as one shoe almost hit her.

Kitty Randolph froze. Her frightened expression was chilling as she turned and saw Dana.

"I'm sorry if I frightened you," Dana said, afraid she would give the elderly woman a heart attack. "I rang the bell, then tried the door when I heard a sound…" She noticed the bruise on Kitty's cheek.

The older woman's hand went to it. "I am so clumsy." She looked from Dana to the floor covered with shoes.

Dana followed her gaze. The bedroom carpet was littered with every color and kind of shoe imaginable from shoes the judge had worn sole-bare to out-of-date sandals and pumps covered with dust.

"I was just cleaning out the closet," Kitty said awkwardly, trying to get to her feet. She had a shoe box clutched under one arm. "My husband was a pack rat. Saved everything. And I'm just as bad."

Dana reached a hand out to help her, but the older woman waved it away.

As Kitty rose, Dana saw the woman pick up a high-heeled shoe from the floor, looking at it as if surprised to see it.

She tossed it back into the closet and turned her attention to Dana. "I see you brought my fabric."

Dana had forgotten all about it. Embarrassed by frightening the woman, she thrust the bag at her.

Kitty took it, studying Dana as she put the shoe box she held onto the clean surface of the vanity. "How foolish of me to leave my package at your shop. You really shouldn't have gone out of your way to bring it to me."

"It was no trouble. I wanted to see you anyway to ask you if my sister stopped by to see you last night."

The older woman frowned. "What would give you that idea?"

"Nancy Harper said she saw Stacy drive down the road toward your house."

"That woman must have no time to do anything but look out the window," Kitty Randolph said irritably. "If your sister drove down here, I didn't see her." She turned to place the fabric package next to the shoe box on the vanity. She fiddled with the lid of the shoe box for a moment. "Why would Stacy come to see me?"

"I have no idea. I'd hoped you might." A lot of people drove cars like her sister's and it had been dark out. "Nancy Harper must have been mistaken," Dana said, glancing again at the shoes on the floor. "Can I help you with these?"

"No, you have better things to do, I'm sure," Kitty said as she stepped over the shoes and took Dana's arm, turning her toward the door. "Thank you again for bringing my fabric. You really shouldn't have."

It wasn't until Dana was driving away that she remembered the high heel Kitty Randolph had thrown back into the closet. She couldn't imagine the woman wearing anything with a heel that high. Or that color, either.

But then, who knew what Kitty Randolph had been like when she was young.

At the turn back onto Highway 191, Dana dialed her friend. "Hilde?"

"Is everything all right?"

"Fine. Listen, I was just thinking. I'm so close to Bozeman I thought I'd drive down and see my dad. I called and he's doing better. They said I could see him. Unless it's so busy there that you need me?"

"Go see your dad," Hilde said without hesitation. "I can handle things here. Anyway, it's slowed down this afternoon. I was thinking that if it doesn't pick up, I might close early."

"Do," Dana said. "We've made more than our quota for the month in the past few days."

"Tell your dad hello for me."

Dana hung up. She did want to see her father, but she also hoped that Stacy had been by to see him.

But when she reached the hospital, her father was still groggy, just as he'd been that morning. She didn't bring up anything that might upset him and only stayed for a few minutes as per the nurse's instructions.

As Dana was leaving, she stopped at the nurses' station to inquire about her father's visitors.

"Your brother was here," the nurse said. "That's the only visitor he's had today."

"My brother?"

"The skinny one."

Clay. That meant that neither Jordan nor Stacy had been here.

"But there have been a lot of calls checking on his condition," the nurse added.

Dana thanked her and headed back toward the ranch. She wanted to get a change of clothing if she was going to be staying at Hud's again tonight.

She knew she was being silly, wanting to slow things down. She loved Hud. He loved her. They'd spent too much time apart as it was. So why was she so afraid?

Because she didn't believe they could just pick up where they'd left off. They'd both changed. Didn't they need to get to know each other again—everything else that was going on aside?

And yet even as she thought it, she knew that the chemistry they shared was still there as well as the love. She knew what was holding her back. This investigation. Until Ginger Adams's killer was caught, Dana didn't feel safe. And she had no idea why.

As she drove down the road to the ranch house, she saw the tracks in the snow. Hud would have driven in to feed Joe. But there was at least another set of tire tracks. Someone else had been to the house today.

ZOEY SKINNER WAS FILLING salt and pepper shakers during the slow time between lunch and dinner in the large West Yellowstone café.

Hud couldn't say he remembered her. But she wasn't the kind of woman who stood out. Quite the opposite, she tended to blend into her surroundings.

The café was empty this time of the day, with it being a little too early yet for dinner.

He took a chair at a table in a far corner and glanced out the window at the walls of snow.

The town had changed over the years since the advent of snowmobiles. Where once winters were off season and most of the businesses closed and lay dormant under deep snowbanks, now the town literally buzzed with activity.

A large group of snowmobilers in their one-piece suits, heavy boots and dark-shielded helmets roared past in a cloud of blue smoke and noise.

"Coffee?"

He turned to find Zoey Skinner standing over his table, a menu tucked under her arm, a coffeepot in one hand and a cup in the other.

"Please. Cream and sugar."

Zoey was bone-thin, her arms corded from years of waiting tables, her legs webbed with blue veins although she was no more than in her early forties.

She filled the cup, produced both sugar and cream packages from her apron pocket. "Menu?"

He shook his head. "Just coffee, thanks. And if you have a moment—" he said, flashing his badge "—I'm Marshal Hudson Savage. I'd like to ask you a few questions."

She stared down at the badge, then slowly lifted her gaze to his. "This is about Ginger, isn't it?"

He nodded.

She dropped into the chair opposite his, her body suddenly limp as a rag doll's. She put the coffeepot on the table and cradled her head in her hands as she looked at him.

"I always wondered what happened to her," she said. "I heard that she'd been found in that well and I couldn't believe it."

"When was the last time you saw her?" he asked, taking out his notebook and pen.

"The night she left to get married."

"She was getting *married*?"

"Well, not right away." Zoey's face softened. "Ginger was so happy and excited."

"Who was she marrying?"

He saw her face close. "She said it was better I didn't know. Better that no one knew until they were married."

He studied the small, mousy-haired waitress. "Why was it so important to keep it a secret?"

"Ginger was afraid of jinxing it, you know? She'd been disappointed so many times before."

He didn't believe that for a minute. "Was it possible this man was married?" He saw the answer in Zoey's face. Bull's-eye. "So maybe that's why she didn't want anyone to know. Maybe he hadn't told his wife he was leaving her yet."

Zoey frowned and chewed at her lower lip. "Ginger just wanted to be loved. That's all. You know, have someone love her and take care of her." He got the feeling that Zoey not only knew who the man was but she also knew something else, something she wanted to tell him and for some reason was afraid to.

He took a shot in the dark. "This man, did he have money? He must have been older. Powerful?" The kind of man a woman like Ginger would have been attracted to.

Zoey looked away but not before he'd seen the answer in her eyes along with the fear. He felt his heart rate quicken. He was getting close. Was it possible the man was still around?

"Zoey, someone threw your best friend down a well, but when that didn't kill her, he shot her and left her there to die."

All the color drained from her face.

"Before she died, she tried to crawl out," he said.

A cry escaped Zoey's lips. She covered her mouth, her eyes wide and filled with tears.

"Ginger wanted desperately to live. Whoever threw her down that well was trying to get rid of her for good. If this man she was going to marry really loved her, then he would want you to tell me everything you know."

Zoey pulled a napkin from the container on the table and wiped at her eyes. "What about the baby?"

"Baby?"

Zoey nodded. "She was pregnant. Just a few weeks along."

That explained why there hadn't been another skeleton in the well.

Ginger hadn't been far enough along for there to be any evidence of a baby in a pile of bones at the bottom of a well.

But Hud realized it did give the father of the baby a motive for murder. "Did Ginger tell the father about the baby?" Zoey looked down. "Let me guess, he didn't want the baby."

"He *did,*" Zoey protested, head coming up. "Ginger said he promised to take care of her and the baby."

"Maybe he did," Hud said solemnly. "Didn't you suspect something was wrong when you didn't hear from her again or she didn't come back for her things?"

"She took everything she wanted with her."

"Didn't she have a car?"

"She sold that."

"But didn't you think it was strange when you didn't hear from her?" he persisted.

"I just thought when things didn't work out that she was embarrassed, you know?"

He stared at Zoey, all his suspicions confirmed. "What made you think things didn't work out?"

She saw her mistake and tried to cover. "I never heard that she got married so..."

"You know things didn't work out because you knew who the man was. He's still in town, isn't he, Zoey? He never left his wife. He killed your friend and her baby and he got away with it."

Her face filled with alarm. "He wouldn't hurt her. He *loved* her." Her expression changed ever so slightly. She'd remembered something, something that made her doubt what she'd just said.

"They fought?" he guessed. "He ever hit her?" Hud was pretty sure he had, given what he suspected the man had done to Ginger at the end.

"Once. But that was just because he didn't want her wearing the engagement ring until...you know...until he was ready for them to announce it," she said. "Ginger forgot to take it off and was wearing the ring around town."

"Engagement ring?"

She nodded. "They fought about it. He wanted her to give it back so she didn't forget and wear it in public again. She refused. He hit her and tried to take it back."

Hud thought of the crime lab's report on the broken fingers of Ginger's left hand.

"What did this ring look like?" he asked, trying to keep the fear out of his voice.

"It was shaped like a diamond only it was green," she said. "He told Ginger it was an emerald, a really expensive one. It looked like it really was. And there were two diamonds, too. So don't you see? He wouldn't have given her an expensive ring like that unless he loved her, right?"

Chapter Thirteen

Dana pulled into the yard in front of the ranch house and parked, relieved to see no other vehicles. She'd worried she would come home to find Jordan searching the house again.

She wondered what he'd been up to all day since apparently he hadn't visited their father in the hospital. Why had Jordan lied about when he'd gotten into town if he hadn't been the one who'd put the doll in the well, who'd left the chocolates, who'd been trying to drive her from the ranch?

Getting out of the pickup, she walked to the porch. Someone had shoveled the steps. Hud no doubt.

Joe came around the side of the porch from his doghouse wagging his tail. He was pretty much deaf but he still seemed to know when she came home.

She rubbed his graying head and climbed the porch, digging for her keys she'd tossed in her purse after forgetting she was locking up the house now.

But as she shoved open the door and looked inside, she wondered why she'd bothered. Someone had ransacked the place.

She cursed and looked down at Joe. He seemed as perplexed as she was. Had he even barked at the intruder? She doubted it. She watched him as he followed her into the torn-up living room. He wasn't even sniffing around or acting as if a stranger had been here.

Because the person who'd torn up the house wasn't a stranger, she thought angrily. It was someone in her family, sure as hell. Jordan.

The house was a mess but nothing looked broken. It appeared he had done a frantic search not taking the time to put anything back where it had been.

She thought about calling Hud, but if she was right and Jordan had done this, his prints were already all over the house so it would prove nothing to find more of them.

Cursing under her breath, she took off her coat and went to work, putting the living room back in order. She had to pull out the vacuum since one of the plants had been turned over and there was dirt everywhere.

She promised she would fix whoever had done this as she turned on the vacuum. Over the roar of the vacuum, she didn't hear the car drive up, didn't hear someone come up the steps and tap at the door. Nor did she see her visitor peer inside to see if she was alone.

HUD DIALED NEEDLES AND PINS the minute he left the Lonesome Pine Café and Zoey.

"Hilde, I need to speak to Dana."

"Hud? Is everything all right?"

"No," he said. "Tell me she's still there."

He heard Hilde sigh and his heart dropped like a stone.

"Hud, she left earlier. She ran an errand and then went to visit her dad. But she should be at the ranch by now."

Hud groaned. Of course she would want to visit her dad again. He should have put a deputy on her. Right. Wouldn't Dana have loved having Norm Turner following her around all day? But Hud would have gladly put up with her wrath just to know she was safe right now.

"Hud, what is it?" Hilde cried. "Do you want me to try to find her?"

"No, I'm not that far away. I can get there quicker." He disconnected, his mind racing with everything he'd learned. The highway was slick with ice. He drove as fast as he could, dialing the ranch house as he did.

The phone rang and rang. Either Dana wasn't home yet or— The woman didn't even have an answering machine?

His radio squawked. He closed the cell phone and grabbed the radio. "Marshal Savage."

"It's Deputy Turner," Liza said, all business. "Angus Cardwell's .38. It doesn't match. Not even close. It wasn't the murder weapon." She sounded disappointed since she'd been so sure it was—based on Angus Cardwell's reaction to her finding the gun in his pickup.

He took in the information, his heart racing a little faster. He'd been sure it would be the gun. And after what Dana had told him about Angus's argument and heart attack, Hud had suspected Jordan Cardwell would turn out to be the person who'd used the gun. Could he be wrong about Jordan's involvement?

"But we do have a match on the prints found on both the doll and the box of chocolates," she said. "They were Jordan Cardwell's."

Jordan. He'd suspected Jordan of a lot more. What bothered Hud was the incident with the doll in the well and the box of undoctored chocolates didn't go together. One was so innocuous. The other was possibly attempted murder on Dana. At the very least, assault on an officer of the law.

"I'm on my way back from Missoula," Liza said. "Anything else you want me to do?"

"No, it's supposed to be your day off. Drive carefully." He disconnected and radioed his other deputy.

"Deputy Turner," Norm said.

"Pick up Jordan Cardwell ASAP," Hud ordered. He heard the deputy's feet hit the floor.

"On what charge, sir?"

"Let's start with assault on a marshal," Hud said. Jordan's mother and Kitty Randolph had been friends. Jordan could have had access to Kitty's ring. "Just find him and get him locked up. Let me know the minute he's behind bars."

As he disconnected, Hud thought about Kitty Randolph's emerald ring. He now knew how it had ended up with Ginger Adams in the well. He just hoped to hell he was wrong about who had killed her.

As DANA SHUT OFF THE VACUUM, she sensed someone watching her and turned, startled to see a shadow cross the porch.

The doorbell rang. She opened the door and blinked in surprise. "Mrs. Randolph?" The bruise on the older woman's face was darker than it had been earlier in the day. She had what appeared to be that same shoe box under one arm and her hat was askew.

Kitty Randolph smiled. "Hello, dear. I'm sorry to drop by unannounced like this." She looked past Dana. "Did I catch you at a bad time? I was hoping to talk to you. Alone, if possible?"

"Of course, come in."

"You're sure it's not a bad time?" Kitty asked, her gaze going again past Dana into the house.

"Not at all. I was just doing some cleaning myself."

The older woman turned and stuck out one leg to show off her blue slacks. "That thread you sold me was the perfect color blue, don't you think?"

Dana admired the recently hemmed slacks, telling herself this couldn't possibly be the reason Kitty had driven all the way out here. It was probably the upcoming fundraiser. Dana groaned at the thought. The fundraiser was weeks away. Was she going to find Kitty on her doorstep every day until it was over?

"Can I take your coat?" Dana asked, wondering what was in the worn-looking shoe box. Probably old apron patterns. Or recipes.

"The judge always liked me in blue," Kitty said as if she hadn't heard Dana. "That was until his tastes changed to red."

Dana smiled, remembering the red-and-gold master bedroom—and the bright red high-heeled shoe Kitty had tossed back into the closet earlier at her house.

"Would you like something to drink?" Dana asked. "I could put on some coffee. Or would you prefer tea?" She hoped Hud showed up soon, as he'd promised earlier. He might be the only way she could get rid of the woman.

"Neither, thank you. I couldn't help thinking about your visit to my house today," she said, glancing toward the kitchen again. "Sometimes I am so forgetful. You did say you're alone, didn't you?"

"Yes." Was it possible Kitty Randolph had forgotten

that Stacy had visited her last night? "Did you remember something about Stacy?"

"Stacy, interesting woman." Her twinkling blue eyes settled on Dana's face. "How could two sisters be so different? You're so much like your mother and your sister is…" She raised a disapproving brow. "She's an alley cat like your father. But then some women are born to it."

Dana frowned and almost found herself defending her sister. Instead she studied the older woman, noticing that Kitty seemed…different somehow. Oddly animated. She'd always been a soft-spoken, refined woman who'd obviously come from old wealth. She'd never heard Kitty talk like this.

"This must all be very upsetting for you," Dana said. Ginger Adams's body being found in the well had dredged up the judge's murder. Of course Kitty would be distraught.

"Yes, dear, I can't tell you how upsetting it's been." Kitty stepped over to one of the old photographs on the wall and Dana noticed with a start that it was of the old homestead up on the hillside.

"Did I ever tell you that the judge's family were well drillers?" Kitty asked.

"I didn't know that."

Kitty turned and smiled. "The judge's father drilled most every well around here. Including the one up at your family's old homestead."

THE RADIO SQUAWKED AS HUD neared Big Sky—and the Cardwell Ranch.

"I've got Jordan Cardwell here, sir," Deputy Norm Turner said. "He insists on talking to you for his one phone call."

Hud breathed a sigh of relief that Jordan was behind bars. Now at least Dana should be safe. "Put him on."

"Is this about the other night, that thing with the doll and the well?" Jordan demanded.

"You mean, where you tried to kill me?" Hud said.

"I'm telling you the same thing I told Dana, I had nothing to do with it."

"You lied about when you flew in, you lied about your relationship with Ginger Adams, and you expect me to believe you? Save your breath, your fingerprints were found on both the doll—and the box of chocolates."

"I did fly in the day before, the instant I heard about the bones in the well, and I knew Ginger," Jordan said. "I probably touched the stupid doll when I was searching for the will. And I also gave Dana the chocolates. I wanted her to think they were from you. I thought it might make her treat you a little nicer and that it would speed up the investigation so we could get on with selling the ranch."

"You are so thoughtful."

"Listen to me, I do care about my sister," Jordan said. "If I didn't put some stupid doll down in the well to scare Dana, then who did? That person doesn't seem to be behind bars in your quaint little jail."

Hud was silent for a moment, thinking this might be the first time he'd ever believed anything that had come out of Jordan Cardwell's mouth. "Did you steal a ring and give it to Ginger Adams?"

"What? Look, Ginger and I didn't last a month. As soon as she found out I didn't have any money…"

Hud pulled the list of registered .38-caliber gun owners out of his pocket as he drove. It was starting to get dark in the canyon. He had to turn on the overhead light in the SUV, taking his attention off the road in short glances as he scanned the list again.

He found the name he'd feared would be on the sheet. He hadn't even thought to look for it before. Probably because it never dawned on him to look for Judge Raymond Randolph's name. What were the chances he would have been killed with his own gun? The same gun that had killed Ginger Adams?

Hud threw down the sheet, snapped off the light and said, "Let me talk to the deputy." He told Norm to keep Jordan locked up and to get over to Kitty Randolph's and make sure she didn't go anywhere.

Then Hud tried Dana's number again, driving as fast as possible. He had to get to Dana. Every instinct told him she was in trouble.

DANA FELT A SENSE OF DISQUIET settle over her as she stared at Kitty Randolph. "The judge's father drilled the homestead well?"

The phone rang.

"The judge knew every well his father had drilled," Kitty said proudly. "He took me to most of them when we were dating. Most women wouldn't think that very romantic nowadays. But the judge never wanted to forget where he came from. Common well drillers. But that was one reason he was so cheap. The judge was the only one in his family to go to college, you know."

The phone rang again. Mind racing, Dana barely heard it as she watched Kitty move around the room, picking up knickknacks, touching old photographs, admiring antiques that had belonged to Dana's mother's family. The older woman still had the shoe box tucked under her arm.

"Your mother, now there was a woman," Kitty said

as she circled the room. "I admired her so much. Your father put her through so much and yet she never complained. She proved she could make it without him just fine. I wish I had been more like her."

Another ring. "I need to get that," Dana said, but for some reason didn't want to leave Kitty alone.

"Have I told you how much you look like your mother?"

"Yes, you've mentioned it," Dana said, thinking again about what Kitty had said about the judge's family drilling the old homestead well.

"It's funny, for a moment earlier today when I saw you standing behind me at my house, I thought you were your mother," Kitty said, then gave her head a light shake. "Sometimes I am so foolish. Your mother was such a strong woman. I admired the way she took care of *her* problems."

Dana felt a chill crawl up her spine as she recalled a comment Jordan had made about how their mother had been capable of killing Ginger Adams and dumping her down the old well.

"Is there something you wanted to tell me about my mother?" Dana asked, frightened of the answer and suddenly afraid of what was in that shoe box under the older woman's arm.

"Oh, Dana, don't be coy with me," Kitty said, her smile shifting ever so slightly. "I know you saw the shoe."

The shoe? The phone rang again. She realized it might be Hud. He'd be worried if she didn't answer it.

"I don't know what shoe you're talking about." Dana had seen a lot of shoes on the floor of Kitty's bedroom and the older woman digging in the closet as if looking for more. She wondered if the older woman wasn't getting senile as she glanced at the shoe box still curled in the crook of the woman's arm.

"The red high heel, dear, you know the one," Kitty said. "Oh, didn't your boyfriend tell you? Only one was found in the well. The other one was in the judge's closet. I'd forgotten all about it until my dear friend Rupert Milligan happened to mention that one red high heel had been found in the well. Rupert has a little crush on me." She actually blushed.

Dana felt her heart stop cold at the realization of what Kitty was saying.

The phone, she really needed to answer the phone. She started to move toward the kitchen.

"Let it ring, dear," Kitty said, and opened the shoe box.

Dana stared in shock as Kitty brought out a .38 and pointed it at her. Dana glanced toward the front door where her shotgun was leaning against the wall as the phone continued to ring.

"I wouldn't if I were you, dear," Kitty said, leveling the gun at Dana's heart. "Let's take a walk."

The phone stopped ringing. "A walk?" Dana said into the deathly silence that followed. What if Hud had been calling to say he was running late? "Mrs. Randolph—"

"Kitty. Call me Kitty, dear." The hand holding the gun was steady, the glint in the twinkling blue eyes steely. "Get your coat. It's cold out."

"I don't understand," Dana said as she carefully took her coat from the hook, afraid she understood only too well. The shotgun was within reach but it wasn't loaded. Even if it had been, she suspected she would never be able to fire it before Kitty Randolph pulled the trigger.

"I'll explain it to you on our walk," Kitty said agreeably as she jabbed the gun into Dana's back. "We really need to get moving, though. It gets darks so early in the canyon, especially this time of year. We wouldn't want to step in a hole, now would we?" She laughed as Dana opened the door and they descended the porch steps.

Dana suspected she knew where they were headed long before Kitty motioned her up the road toward the old homestead—and the well.

"Oh, and in case you're wondering, the judge taught me how to use a gun," Kitty said. "I'm sure he regretted it since I was a much better shot than he was."

As they walked up the road, Dana saw that a vehicle had been up the hill recently. The same person who'd ransacked the house? Her mind raced. Was it possible Jordan was up here planning to pull another stunt to scare her into selling the ranch?

She couldn't believe it had been Jordan—didn't want to believe it. But right now, she would love to see any member of her family.

"Ginger was a tramp, you know," Kitty said as they walked up the road. The older woman was surprisingly spry for her age. "Your mother wasn't the least bit fazed by her. She knew your father would never have left her for a woman like Ginger Adams. For all your father's flaws, he had better taste than that."

Dana wouldn't have bet on that, she thought as she looked up at the homestead chimney. Had she seen movement up there? Twilight had turned the sky gray.

From the highway she could hear the hum of tires. Hud was on his way. He'd said he would meet her at the ranch house before she got off work. Except she'd come home early. Still he should be here soon. Unless he really had been calling to say he was running late.

"The judge, the old fool, thought he was in love with Ginger," Kitty was saying. "He thought I would give him a divorce so he could marry her. He forgot that the money was all mine. But even then, he would have left me for her and lived on nothing, he was that besotted with her. After thirty years of marriage. Can you imagine? She was just a *child*."

Dana heard the pain in the older woman's voice and looked up, surprised they had reached the old homestead in record time. No wonder, with Kitty nudging her along with the gun.

"He begged me to let him go, the stupid old fool. But I had insurance, something I knew he'd done that could get him disbarred, disgraced and leave him penniless so he wouldn't be able to support his precious Ginger and their baby." Kitty sounded as if she was crying. "We couldn't have a child, you know. But this tramp... I remember the night he brought me that red high-heeled shoe. He was sobbing like a baby. 'Look what you made me do,' he kept saying. 'Oh, God, look what you've made me do.' As if he didn't have a choice."

Dana stumbled and turned to look at Kitty, shocked by the revelation. The judge had killed Ginger Adams on his wife's orders?

"Oh, don't look so shocked," Kitty Randolph said. "Imagine what I would have done that night if I'd known he'd given her my ring? It was the only decent piece of jewelry he'd ever bought me. It never meant that much to me because I'd had to force him to buy it for our anniversary. But even if I never wore it, it was mine and he gave it to that woman. And then to hear it turned up in your well—with *her*."

Dana was too stunned to speak for a moment.

"Let's get this over with," Kitty said and jabbed Dana with the gun, prodding her toward the well opening. Kitty's voice changed, sounding almost childlike. "You don't want to get too close to the edge of the well, dear. You might fall in. It's only natural that you would be curious. Or perhaps you're distraught over the news about your mother. Sorry, dear, but after you're gone it's going to come out that your mother killed Ginger. Mary wouldn't mind, after all she's dead."

Dana balked. "You wouldn't blame my mother."

"I've given it a lot of thought," Kitty said matter-of-factly. "Your mother was afraid, living out here alone, and I lent her the judge's .38. I'd completely forgotten the gun was in the closet until the marshal called to say that Ginger had been killed with the same gun the judge was."

"No one will believe my mother killed Ginger Adams—*and* your husband."

"You are so right, dear. Your sister, the common thief, took the gun while it was in your mother's possession and killed the judge. I'll work out the details later. But when it comes out about your sister stealing fundraiser money and me having it all on video…"

"*You're* the one who forced Stacy to make it look like she and Hud had slept together."

"Oh, dear, you are so smart," Kitty said as she backed Dana toward the well. "I was quite the mastermind if I say so myself. First I hired the Kirk brothers to mow my lawn and then I planted the judge's cuff links and pocket watch in their car. I said I'd be at my sister's that night. With cell phones, no one can tell where you are. Aren't they amazing devices?"

As Kitty backed her into the darkness, Dana could feel the well coming up behind her.

"The judge was at his stupid Toastmasters. I called and told him I thought I'd left the stove on, then I waited until he was on his way home before I called those awful

Kirk brothers and told them I'd left them a bonus and to stop by the house and pick it up. The door was open. It was all too easy. You should have seen the judge's face when I shot him twice in the chest."

Dana grimaced. If she'd had any doubt that Kitty would shoot her, she didn't now.

"The Kirk brothers arrived right after that," she continued. "They reacted just as I knew they would when they heard the sirens. Hud's father had been trying to get the goods on them for years. I knew he'd chase them to the ends of the earth. And he literally did. All I had to do was make it look as if the Kirks had broken into my house and then go to my sister's and wait for the terrible news."

Dana stopped moving. She could feel the well directly behind her. One more step and she would fall into it. "Why set up Hud with my sister?"

"Stacy had to do whatever I told her and I knew how badly Hud's father wanted to put those awful Kirk brothers away. He was more apt to believe they had robbed my house and killed my husband than your boyfriend." Kitty smiled, pleased with herself. "Anyway, by doing that I freed you up for my nephew."

"Your *nephew?*"

Something moved by the chimney and Dana watched as a large dark figure came out of the shadows behind Kitty. Jordan. Let it be Jordan.

"Step back, dear," Kitty said. "Let's not make this any more painful than we have to."

As the figure grew closer, Dana saw the man's face. Not Jordan. "Lanny, be careful, she has a gun!"

Kitty began to laugh, but didn't turn as if she thought Dana was kidding. Then Dana watched in horror as Lanny made no attempt to disarm Kitty.

He leaned down to plant a kiss on the older woman's cheek. "Why would I hurt my dear auntie? Really, Dana, I can attest to how irrational you've been the last few days."

"Kitty is your aunt?"

"By marriage twice removed, but Dana you know that half the people in the canyon are related in some way, you shouldn't be surprised," Lanny said.

"Say your goodbyes, Lanny," Kitty said.

"You aren't going to let her do this," Dana said. "You and I were friends."

Lanny laughed. "Friends? But you are right about one thing, I'm not going to let her do it. I'm going to take care of you, Dana, because quite frankly I'd rather see you dead than with Hudson Savage."

He reached for her and in the twilight she saw the hard glint of anger in his eyes—the same look she'd seen at the restaurant the night of her birthday.

She dodged his grasp and felt one of the stones around the well bump against her ankle as she was forced back. She looked over her shoulder, estimating whether or not she could jump the opening. Maybe if she had a run at it, but the hole was too wide, the snow too slick around it.

She put out her hands, bracing her feet, ready to take Lanny down into the well with her if he grabbed for her again.

"You can make this easy on yourself, Dana. Or fight right up until the end." Lanny smiled. "Makes no difference to me."

"But it does to me," Hud said from out of the darkness.

Both Lanny and his aunt turned in surprise. Dana saw her chance. She dove at Lanny, slamming her palms into his chest with all her strength. He stumbled backward, colliding with his aunt Kitty, but managed to grasp Dana's sleeve and pull her down, as well.

The air exploded with a gunshot and Dana couldn't be sure who'd fired it as she fell to the ground next to Lanny.

She scrambled away from him but he grabbed her ankle and crawled, dragging her, toward the well opening. She noticed that his side bloomed dark red and she realized he'd been shot. But his grip on her ankle was strong.

She tried to latch on to anything she could reach but there was nothing to hang on to and the snow was slick and she slid across it with little effort on Lanny's part.

More gunshots and Dana saw now that Kitty was firing wildly into the darkness. Dana couldn't see Hud, wasn't even sure now that she'd heard his voice. Lanny had a death grip on her leg.

The black gaping hole of the well was so close now that she felt the cold coming up from the bottom.

This time the gunshots were louder, echoing across the hillside. Dana saw Kitty stumble, heard her cry. Out of the corner of her eye, Dana watched Kitty start to fall.

Dana kicked out at Lanny with her free leg. His grip on her ankle loosened as his aunt tripped over him, but managed to remain standing.

He let go of Dana's ankle and for an instant they were all frozen in time. Kitty was looking down at her blue slacks. One leg appeared black in the darkening light. Dana scooted out of Lanny's grasp and was getting to her feet when she heard Hud order, "Put down the gun, Mrs. Randolph."

Kitty looked up, her spine straightening, her chin going up. "I had a bad feeling when you came back to town, Hudson Savage." She smiled and Dana watched the rest play out in slow, sick motion.

Kitty dropped the gun, but Lanny grabbed it up and started to turn it on Dana. She saw the crazed look in his eyes as he gripped the gun and frantically felt for the trigger.

Hud's weapon made a huge booming sound in the deafening silence. The shot caught Lanny in the chest but he was still trying to pull the trigger as another shot exploded and he fell back, his head lolling to one side on the edge of the well.

Dana wrenched the gun from his hands and crawled back away from him and the well.

Kitty was still standing there, head up. The one leg of her slacks looked black with blood. She didn't seem to notice Lanny lying on the ground next to her.

Dana turned as Hud came out of the shadows, his weapon still pointed at Kitty. Out of the corner of her eye, she caught the movement and heard Hud yell, "No!"

Dana turned in time to see Kitty Randolph smile as she stepped back and dropped into the well.

A few seconds later Dana heard the sickening thud as Kitty hit the bottom. But by then, Hud was pulling Dana into his arms and telling her he loved her, over and over again. In the distance she could hear the wail of sirens.

Chapter Fourteen

Hud parked by the Hebgen Lake house and got out, noting that his father's vehicle was in the garage and there were no fresh tracks.

But when he knocked at the door, he got no answer. He tried the knob, not surprised when the door opened in. "Dad?" he called. The word sounded funny and he tried to remember the last time he'd said it.

As he moved through the house, it became more apparent that Brick wasn't there. Hud felt his pulse start as he reminded himself how old his father had seemed the other day, then recalled with shame and embarrassment what he'd said to Brick.

But Hud knew the panicky feeling in the pit of his stomach had more to do with what he hadn't yet said to his father.

"Dad?" he called again.

No answer. He glanced into the bedrooms. Both empty, beds made. Hud had never expected his father to keep such a neat house. Hud's mother had hated housework.

The kitchen was also empty, still smelling faintly of bacon and coffee. But as he looked out the window across the frozen white expanse of the lake, he spotted a lone figure squatting on the ice.

Hud opened the back door and followed the well-worn footprints across patches of glistening wind-crusted ice and drifted snow, his boot soles making a crunching sound as he walked toward his father.

Dressed in a heavy coat and hat, Brick Savage sat on a log stump, a short ice-fishing pole in his gloved hands. The fishing line disappeared down into the perfect hole cut in the ice at his feet.

His father looked up and smiled. "Heard the news. You solved both murders. Figured you would."

Just then the rod jerked. Brick set the hook and hauled a large rainbow trout out of the slushy water and up onto the ice. He picked up the flopping trout, unhooked it and dropped it back into the water.

Hud stood, trying to put into words everything he wanted—needed—to say to his father. Hud had been so sure that his father had set him up so he could kill Judge Raymond Randolph and frame the Kirk brothers. "Dad, I—"

"There's an extra rod," Brick said, cutting him off. He motioned to the rod resting against an adjacent stump.

"You knew I'd be showing up?" Hud asked in surprise.

His dad smiled. "I'd hoped you would."

"There's some things I need to say to you."

Brick shook his head. "Your coming here today says everything I need to hear." He reached over and picked up the short rod and handed it to his son. "If you want, we could keep a few fish and cook them up for lunch. Or if you're in a hurry—"

"No hurry. I haven't had trout in a long time," Hud said, taking a seat across from his father. "I could stay to eat trout for lunch."

His dad nodded and Hud thought he glimpsed something he'd never seen, tears in his father's eyes. Brick dropped his head to bait his hook and when he looked up again, the tears were gone. If they were ever there.

He watched his father, thinking he might call Dana after lunch to see if she'd like trout for dinner tonight. "I've been offered the marshal job," he said as he baited his line and dropped it into the hole.

"I'm not surprised."

"I heard you put in a good word for me," Hud said, feeling his throat tighten.

"Rupert's got a big mouth," Brick said but smiled. "The canyon's lucky to get you. Dana pleased about it?"

He nodded and hooked into a fish. "You know about Rupert and Kitty Randolph?"

"I knew he liked her. He's taking it all pretty hard. He likes to think he's smarter than most people when it comes to figuring out criminals," Brick said.

"Kitty fooled a lot of people."

"Yes, she did," Brick said.

They spent the rest of the morning fishing, talking little. Later while Brick was frying up the trout for lunch, Hud called Dana and told her he was bringing trout for dinner.

"You ask her to marry you yet?" Brick asked after he hung up and they were sitting down to eat lunch.

"I'm going to tonight," Hud said.

Without a word, his dad got up from the table and returned a few minutes later with a small velvet box. He set it beside Hud's plate and sat. "I know you bought her an engagement ring before. I couldn't afford an engagement ring for your mother so she never had one. But I was wondering if you'd like to have your grandmother's?"

Hud frowned. He'd never known either of his grandparents. His father's parents were dead before he was born and from what he'd heard, his mother's family had disowned his mother when she'd married Brick. "My grandmother...?"

"Christensen. Your grandmother on your mother's side," he said, and handed the small velvet box to Hud. "She left it to me in her will. I guess it was her way of saying she was sorry for making it so hard on your mother for marrying me." He shrugged. "Anyway, I know your mother would want you to have it."

Hud opened the small velvet box and pulled back in surprise. "It's beautiful."

Brick helped himself to the trout. "Just like Dana."

Hud studied his father. "Thank you."

"There's some money, too," Brick said. "Probably not near enough to pay off Dana's brothers and sister and keep the ranch, though."

"I doubt there is enough money in the world for that," Hud said. "Jordan won't be happy until the ranch is sold, but I'm sure he'll be disappointed when he realizes how small his share is. He would have been much better off if his mother's new will had been found. He would have gotten money for years from the ranch instead of a lump sum, and in the end come out way ahead."

"But he wants it all now," Brick said. "You think he found the new will and destroyed it?"

"Probably."

Brick handed him the plate of trout.

"I got a call from Stacy Cardwell this morning. She's in Las Vegas. She said Kitty threatened to kill her when she stopped by the woman's place the night before she left. I guess Stacy thought she could get some traveling money out of Kitty as if blackmail went both ways," Hud said, shaking his head.

"It's a wonder Kitty didn't shoot her on the spot."

Hud remembered Dana's story about finding Kitty on her hands and knees digging in the closet. "Probably would have but she'd forgotten she still had the .38. There was a struggle, though. Dana said Kitty had a bruise on her cheek."

Brick nodded. "You could bring Stacy back to face charges."

Hud shook his head. Both Lanny and Kitty were dead. It was over.

He and Brick ate in silence for a while, and then Hud said, "I saw you with Ginger that night."

His father paused, then took a bite of fish. "I remembered after you were gone. I pulled her over that night. She'd been drinking. I thought about taking her in, made her get out of the car and go through the sobriety tests."

Hud recalled the sound of Ginger's laughter. As Hud had driven past, she'd been flirting with Brick, spinning around in that red dress and those bright red high-heeled shoes.

"I saw all her stuff in the back of her car," Brick said.

Hud wondered if the judge or Kitty had gotten rid of Ginger's belongings and her car. No one would have ever known about her death, if Warren hadn't seen her skull at the bottom of the Cardwell Ranch well.

"She told me she was leaving town," Brick was saying. "I told her to be careful. If I'd locked her up that night, she might still be alive."

DANA STOOD IN THE KITCHEN after Hud's call, looking up the hillside. There was no old chimney or foundation anymore. It was as if there'd never been an old homestead up there. Or an old well. A backhoe operator had filled in the well. Soon after the land was cleared, it had begun to snow again, covering up the scarred earth.

Dana thought she could get used to the new view, but it would take time. She frowned at the thought, realizing she didn't have time. After everything that had happened, she had given up her fight to save the ranch. Jordan was right. All she was doing was costing them all attorneys' fees and eventually, she would lose and have to sell anyway. She'd told Jordan he could list the property with a Realtor.

She turned away from the window, turning her thoughts, as well, to more pleasant things. Hud. She smiled, just thinking about him. They'd been inseparable, making love, talking about the future. Even now she missed him and couldn't wait for him to get back.

He was bringing trout for dinner. She was glad he'd gone up to see his father. Her mother had been right about one thing. Family. It *did* matter. Her own father was out of the hospital and planning to be back playing with Uncle Harlan in the band. They'd both offered to play at the wedding. Her father had promised to cut back on his drinking but Dana wasn't holding her breath. She was just glad to still have him.

She smiled, thinking of the wedding she and Hud would have. That is, if he asked her to marry him again.

Since Kitty Randolph's death, a lot of things had

come out about the judge. Some of the things Hud had blamed on his father had been the judge's doing.

Hud had even realized that his mother's bitterness toward Brick was fueled by her family and that it had made Brick into the hard man he was when Hud was growing up.

The past few days had changed them all. At least Dana had decided she was ready to let go of all the old hurts and move on, whatever the future held.

She stopped in the middle of the kitchen as if she'd just felt a warm hand on her shoulder and it was as if she could feel her mother's presence. Wasn't this what her mother had wanted? For her to forgive and forget?

Dana smiled, the feeling warming her as she moved to the cupboard that held all her mother's cookbooks. Like her mother, she loved cookbooks, especially the old ones.

She pulled out her mother's favorite and ran her fingers over the worn cover. Maybe she would make Hud's favorite double-chocolate brownies from her mother's old recipe. She hadn't made them since Hud had left five years before.

As she opened the book, several sheets of lined paper fluttered to the floor. Stooping to pick them up, she caught sight of her mother's handwriting. Her heart leaped to her throat. Hurriedly, she unfolded the pages.

Her heart began to pound harder as she stared down at her mother's missing will.

* * * * *

YOU HAVE
JUST READ A
HARLEQUIN
INTRIGUE®
BOOK

If you were **captivated** by the **gripping, page-turning romantic suspense,** be sure to look for all six Harlequin Intrigue® books every month.

HARLEQUIN
INTRIGUE